VENTURE'S STORY

LIFE & TIMES OF A GUIDE DOG

by

Diana Dawne

About the cover:
Venture has 12 Ph.D.s, and even though he didn't earn them academically, he confers honor on the diploma mill that gave them to him every time his words of wisdom as The Right Reverend Dr. Butz help some poor lost soul find truth and happiness.

Copyright © 1997 by Diana Dawne
Library of Congress Catalog Card Number 96-60832
First Edition

Photos by Gina Luck, copyright © 1997
Design and Typography by Words & Pictures Press, 18002 Irvine Blvd., Suite 200, Tustin, CA 92680, 714-544-7282

Publisher's Cataloging-in-Publication Data
(Prepared by Quality Books Inc.)

Dawne, Diana.
     Venture's story : life & times of a guide dog / by Diana Dawne.
     p. cm.
     ISBN 0-9644857-3-7

     1. Guide dogs. 2. Venture (Dog) I. Title.
HV1780.D38 1996   636.7'0886
                                   QB196-20454

Dedication

To Venture and Little Haze and to all the unknown Ventures and Little Hazes out there who, through their loving faithfulness, bring untold joy and blessings to our lives, this book is dedicated with deep affection and great respect.

Acknowledgments

Writing *Venture's Story* has been an interesting experience and many people have helped to make it possible. I would need to publish a book by itself to list everyone, but I would like to express my gratitude to a number of people.

Probably the first place to start is the publisher. Without their efforts we wouldn't have a book. I believe that my contact with Words & Pictures Press was probably their first real close contact with a guide dog. Not only have they put together a wonderful book, they also became quite involved in the actual happenings of Venture's day-to-day life. Although the story is very much the way I wrote it, there were some very key word changes that helped to make this story more vivid and which I think help the reader to really become more personally involved. Many thanks to them for a great job.

Another key part of the book are the wonderful photographs done by Gina Luck. She has spent many hours trying to make these images just perfect for all of us and I am sure you will delight in that work as I delight in a wonderful friendship with her.

I would want to say a special thanks to Doctor Bruce Levine, DVM, Venture's real life veterinarian, who is pictured in this book and who has long ago won the golden seal of approval from Venture. He is a very good friend to me, and he keeps things running in tip top condition in Venture's life.

Venture and I would like to express many thanks to Eugene S. Louis, M.D., the human vet. This kind and gentle man has always been there when he was needed. Also many thanks go to Peg Sapico, the lady vet who keeps things in order for me and whose loving attention has seen me through many a difficult day.

After the book was written, Linda Mann, Billyum, Jim Adams, Dennis Cole, Robert Behrens, Barbara Rogus and Volt acted as peer readers and their input is most appreciated. Also Lenny Barentine was actually the inspiration behind the title of this book.

Finally, a warm thanks goes to the nice folks at BNCI who have made Venture's own personal Internet web presence a reality. Although Robert R. Behrens is the visible site manager for yumston.com, Jeff Hoeksema and his co-workers are in the background keeping things running smoothly. If you would like to establish a presence on the WWW just write to venture@yumston.com and we will put you in touch with the right people. Venture and I personally don't market web sites but we will gladly send you to someone to get you started. Of course if you have questions about anything in this book and if you have e-mail ability, you can direct any questions to Venture@yumston.com.

Actually it is Volt who has made this book possible. It was his love and support that made it possible for me to undertake this project in the first place. Thanks Volt. Venture and I both love you.

Last but not least, I owe much to Venture because without his warmth and charm, there would be no story. You just have no idea what a positive thing it is to have the "V boys" in my life. Also I would like to say thank you to all the unknown people out there who made it possible for me to have Venture. I don't know who you are, but you have my heartfelt thanks.

Enjoy,

Diana Dawne

Introduction

Last week, I was in a store with the lovely Venture at my side and accompanied by the elegant Volt. As I reached out to touch something near me, a lady introduced herself to me as Irene. She, of course, admired Venture, and he responded with a happy wag and his usual charm. Irene asked me about him for it was obvious that she was losing her heart to my beautiful wagging companion.

It is for people like Irene that I wrote this book. My life with Venture is portrayed, so of course it is my story. But in lots of ways it is typical of many, many good guide dogs' experiences.

There are some important things to remember. All the things I have related in these pages are based on incidents that have actually happened. Venture's ability to speak is something I gave him for the purpose of the story line. The things I have related about the Guide Dog Foundation are to the best of my knowledge correct. It is possible that a well-trained guide dog was not so close to pups or dogs in training, but it fit the purpose of my story to place Banner and Venture together. Auntie Em is a real person and those dogs would about give up their food for love of her.

Billyum is a real person. However, although he loved Little Haze dearly, Billyum has never chosen to have a guide dog. I have created important dialogue with Venture through Little Haze. There was a Little Haze. She was my guide dog before I got Venture. When I describe her, I, in fact, am describing the wonderful Little Haze. She was even more charming than I can express. Volt, an important character, is also very real and is very much as I have told you.

For your convenience, should you wish to contact other persons involved in Venture's life story, their addresses follow:

Diana Dawne's regular mail: P. O. Box 1775, Hawaiian Gardens, CA 90716

Diana Dawne's e-mail: ddawne@crl.com

Venture's (Dr. V. A. Butz) regular mail: same address

Billyum's e-mail: billw@crl.com

Venture's e-mail: venture@yumston.com

Volt's e-mail: volt@concentric.net

Words & Pictures Press's e-mail: publisher@earthlink.net

Venture's web site: http://www.yumston.com

All letters are welcome. We promise to read all of them but it may not be possible to answer everyone.

I invite you to journey through our life as I think Venture probably sees it. I invite you to share with me the joy that is Venture and most of all — as you laugh and cry and ponder — enjoy!

Prologue

Spring had always been his favorite time of year. Many a happy day he had spent here in this park with his precious daughter Lillian. After her mother had left, he had taken Lillian to this very park. It was spring then, too, and he had explained to the shattered little girl that just as her life seemed ugly and dull the way the park looked in winter, soon the wonderful powers of creation would touch her life and it, too, would blossom as the flowers were now doing in the park.

The girl had blossomed as he knew she would. What wonderful friends they became! What wonderful times they had had together exploring the park, looking for buried treasures, fishing and hiking. He had enjoyed every moment of their life together, to the full.

Alas, childhood does not go on forever and all too soon it was time for Lillian to start a life of her own. And what a terrible mess that turned out to be!

She met Brad in college, and her father hadn't liked the smart aleck one little bit. When Lillian said she loved Brad and wanted to marry him, it was more than the old man could take.

Unwilling to stand by and let Lillian ruin her life, he had forbidden her to see Brad. Maybe in a few months, she could forget the fool and then things would go back to the way they used to be.

But it wasn't to be. After a year, Lillian told him she still wanted to marry Brad.

"I forbid you to do it!" he raged.

"You can't forbid me," she replied. "I'm grown up now." With that, she disappeared from his life. They now lived in the northern part of the state and the old man had never seen his little grandson.

True, Lillian had invited him to visit many times. He longed to see them, but not with Brad in the way. That was asking too much.

His life had become very lonely. Now all he had was his Social Security and what little money he could make on the side. He had been lucky enough to find an inexpensive boarding house, though he didn't care for the old witch that ran it. His wants were few and his days melancholy.

He slumped down on a bench. In the distance he could see children playing, just like his little grandson would be doing up north before long. But he, the child's own grandfather, wouldn't even recognize him, and that was Lillian's fault. Leaving him behind for that no-account Brad!

His gaze wandered over to the street. Down the sidewalk came a lady with a dog. He could tell by the dog's harness that this was one of those dogs specially trained to guide a blind person.

The lady appeared very self-assured. She was well dressed and well groomed. But what attracted the old man's attention was the magnificent animal at her side.

"That woman would be OK if she wasn't blind. It's a pity the poor thing cain't amount to nothin'. But that dog is real nice—wonder what he does, and how he learned it all?"

He watched as the lovely dog settled himself under the bus bench. The lady took a small device out of her purse which she seemed to be working with intently. He was on the verge of approaching her, but thought better of it. After all, he was an old man with nothing to offer and probably his questions would not be appreciated. Besides that, he already felt badly enough about himself without being rejected by a blind person.

He turned his attention to the happy children. Their gleeful play only made his isolation worse.

A breeze blew softly, bringing the sweet perfume of nearby flowering shrubs. The soft warm breeze caressed his face. Birds sang a song of joy and fleecy white clouds like big puffs of cotton littered the sky. It was such a perfect day. So fresh with promise and so....

"Excuse me, sir, but what is it you would like to know?"

The old man looked up. The voice that had spoken was so warm and rich and full of melody, but no one was there! Looking down, he saw the beautiful dog. "How strange," he thought.

"Sir — " Again that wonderful voice, but no human was nearby. The old man felt a surge of anger.

"Whoever you are, you're nasty! I know a dog cain't talk and its downright mean of you to try to make a fool out of an old man," he snapped. "I'm just takin' in some sun, not doin' nobody any harm."

"You are no fool and I mean no insult," said the lovely voice. "But you have some questions about me, so here I am to answer them."

"How did you know that?"

"Life is a wonderful gift," came the soft reply, "and yet life in itself can be very bleak. That is why He allows good things to come to us. I am a tool provided to assist my blind master. I am given the resources I require to fulfill her needs. Right now I am here with you because of your needs."

The old man looked at the graceful creature in astonishment. The sweet face turned toward him made his heart melt. The expression was one of such love, peace, and tranquility, that all feelings of anger evaporated.

"I don't understand this," said the old man, "but I know you are very beautiful."

"Yes," replied the dog. "My beauty is one of the tools He gave me which enable me to meet my master's needs. Now about those questions."

"I jess was wondering where you come from, what you do, how you learned to do it? What do you eat, where do ya..."

A soft chuckle interrupted the old man.

"I'll be glad to tell you all of those things and more, but to do that, we will need to start at the beginning."

"All right," said the old man, "so why haven't you started already?"

One

The Beginning

Even though it was warm, I was happy as I rolled over and over in the grass with the other puppies.

I was very interested in everything happening around me. Just that morning, a lady had said that soon I would be sent to a home if I passed all my tests.

What did this mean, *going to a home*? I liked it fine right here. My mother seemed less interested in me than before, but that was all right. She didn't play the fun games the other puppies and I played, and to be honest, I was eating puppy food now, and so didn't really need her.

One of my playfellows, Banner, a black male Labrador who was older than me, came running into the play area, barking excitedly.

"I know why those of us who are chosen will go to special homes," he yapped. "I know what we will be when we grow up if we're good enough. I know, I know, I know!"

"What do you think you know?" asked Harmony, a rather sedate female golden retriever.

"I know it all I know it all," squealed Banner.

"Oh yeah? Out with it. Let's hear it. What is it?" we all yapped at the same time.

"Quiet down so I can tell you," said Banner importantly. "I was taken over to see the vet today and after he checked me over, they put me in a pen next to an adult dog. She told me that she had been 'placed' and that she was just staying for a little while because her master was ill. She explained to me that we are here at Smithtown, New York, at the Training Center of the Guide Dog Foundation. She said that we were born in a special breeding program that the Foundation has. This means that our parents were selected for very special reasons. Good health, willingness to work, being patient and pliable, are characteristics that come from our parents. We will be tested to make sure there is nothing wrong with our sight or hearing, and that in other ways we are normal. After that, we will go to special homes to 'puppy walkers.' These people will be closely supervised by someone from the Foundation. They will take us all kinds of places and we will get to do all kinds of things other dogs can't do. When we're adults, we will be returned to the training center where we will enter a training program and learn to be guide dogs. After we are trained, we will be 'placed.' That means we will be given to some blind person. The blind person and the dog will live here for a month, being together constantly and being taught by a trainer how to work together as though they were one."

"That is stupid," I barked. "You're lying! You're just a—"

"Be quiet, Venture," said Harmony. "Whatever makes you think something like that?"

"Banner's dumb!" I squeaked. "Just yesterday they dropped Buffy from the program because she couldn't see anything. So there you go! If a person is blind, obviously it would have to drop out of life, since it couldn't possibly be any good to anybody!"

"Shut up, you yellow-bellied idiot," snarled Banner. "I was told they watch our attitudes real carefully. So you better watch out, Venture, or you'll be all washed up—which I don't think would be much of a loss."

I headed for Banner, my hackles up. I yelled at him: "You nasty nerd, you nasty tease, may all your life be full of fleas!" And I grabbed his ear and bit down hard.

"All right, you pups, break it up! It's time to go inside."

The voice was full of authority, so I gave it up for the moment.

"Inside" meant chow. Once my tummy was full, I lay down with the others, and soon was fast asleep.

The next day we were again playing in the yard. Janna, a female golden retriever, reported the same things Banner had said. I wondered about this. Why were humans valued above puppies? After all, a blind puppy wasn't much use to anyone; what made a blind human different?

Already I was aware that there were big differences between dogs and humans. We were dependent upon these humans for food, so if they wanted me to grow up and lead some blind person around— well, we would see about that later. Right now there were so many fun things to do with the other puppies.

Something else concerned me. Banner had been taken away several times and he had been bragging that some children had played ball with him. What about me? I was an adorable, cuddly, fluffy Golden Lab, and I resented the attention Banner was getting. Fortunately, the problem resolved itself; Banner was taken away one day and didn't come back.

We older puppies had quite a burden of responsibility. It was up to us to educate the young whelps and make sure they didn't go out into the world with any crazy ideas. I generously shared my knowledge about how we were going to be guide dogs when we grew up. What I kept to myself were my concerns about being with someone who was blind. It sounded pretty dismal, but I kept my muzzle on about it. I wanted to leave all my options open. If I kept my nose clean, the sky was the limit.

I was really involved in a rousing game with the other puppies one morning when three of us were taken inside and put on a table.

"Um," said a man as he picked me up off the table, "so this is Venture. Looks like he's doing just great. He's how old now?

"Eight weeks tomorrow," came the reply. "According to our observations he's doing just fine. He's a ringleader. If something's going on with the other puppies, you can just bet he's at the heart of it."

"How much did he weigh when he was born?" asked the man holding me, whom I recognized as a vet.

"About twelve ounces."

"He's going to be a big fellow," said the man as he gave me a stinging shot. I gritted my teeth and kept smiling. "Maybe seventy-five pounds. You know, I can't help but be amazed although I've seen it hundreds of times—how is it that these selfish, fractious little pups can grow up and become such selfless, dedicated guide dogs?"

"Well," replied the lady I had come to know as Auntie Em, "the program wouldn't be nearly so successful without those people who take the pups into their homes and teach them to love and have some manners. That doesn't just happen. The Puppywalkers are essential to this program. With our special breeding program plus the Puppywalkers, we have a very high success rate. Probably eight out of ten dogs will make it through the program. Before we had a system, we didn't have anywhere near this kind of success rate.

"Puppies are like kids," she went on. "It's hard to imagine that quarrelling little children can grow up to be responsible adults, leading nations, making decisions that may affect millions that are now living and sometimes generations to come. Life is amazing."

"Venture is one of the lines the Guide Dog Foundation developed, isn't he?" asked the vet.

"Yes," said Auntie Em. "As you've noticed, all dogs here are beautiful as well as smart. A guide dog is in the public eye. Things go more smoothly for a good-looking dog. An ugly guide dog would attract the wrong kind of attention, undermining the confidence we work so hard to establish between dog and master.

"Beauty and brains are a great combination, but it doesn't end there. The dog must also be stable, resourceful, adaptable, and many other things. That is why we have a breeding program. We have discovered that by crossing certain breeds, we get very desirable results. Believe me, these dogs aren't mutts."

When I was returned to the play area, I told the others everything I had seen and heard. I still didn't mention my qualms about being so close to a blind human. I would wait and see.

That afternoon, the three of us were taken to the "dormitory." There were blind students waiting to get their guide dogs, and I had mixed feelings about seeing them. When Auntie Em picked me up, however, my feelings changed to pure joy. If this would mean spending some time with her, the unpleasantness (if any) wouldn't matter. It was worth just about anything to make Auntie Em happy.

Meeting the students wasn't at all like I thought it would be. They took turns petting me and telling me how pretty and good I was, but the best part was meeting one of the students. This young man took me in his arms and held me against his cheek. "What a special Puppins," he murmured. "You're such a good boy, I wish I could take you home with me." As he held me close, I felt his love and his desperate need to be accepted. My heart went out to this stranger. I felt myself answering his need with an overpowering feeling of love and compassion. I longed to tell him that I loved him, but his fingers were stroking my fluffy coat so I laid my head on his shoulder and went to sleep.

"Time for this sleepyhead to go," said someone.

I snuggled closer to the young man holding me. "I have to give you back, Puppins," said the young man. We parted reluctantly.

Auntie Em took me back to the office where I was allowed to play for a few minutes. I had heard them say I was going that afternoon to my Puppywalker.

It had been a big day, and as I rested I couldn't help but think about that young man who held me. I didn't realize it then, but I had taken a big step that day. This young man had shown me that blind people were just like everybody else. They had dreams and desires just like me. The difference was that they couldn't see. If there was a way I could help such a person...

I made a solemn promise to myself that whatever life held, I would be the very best that a dog could be.

Two

William

The cold air brought me suddenly out of a deep sleep. I had been in my new home for two weeks now, and it was as though I had always been there. There was a mother and father, but the one I spent the most time with was their young teenage son William. I was William's special project. He and I were inseparable—we went to the store, to Boy Scout meetings, to the bank, and even to church. He kept me in a big tote bag when we went places. However, I was getting bigger, and the bag was getting cramped. We had been in church, and now William was pulling me from the warm blanket and putting me on the cold ground.

I had never seen snow before, and I was interested, but William snapped on my leash and began to walk me about. "Get busy, Venture," he said. "Be a good boy and go to the bathroom because Reverend Stone wants to meet you and good puppies do their business outside." I sniffed around, and did what he asked.

William was very nice. I knew that he loved me a lot, just as I loved him. Some of his friends came over to us and as they talked to one another, they played with me. I couldn't ask for more than what was happening to me. It was wonderful to have so many friends who admired me and looked up to William and me for the great thing he was doing—raising a puppy so that when it grew up, it could become a guide dog.

A little girl came up to us. "Oh William, what a cute puppy you have there. My folks told me you are raising her for the Guide Dog Foundation and I wanted to know how I could get one. Can I pet her?"

"*Him*," William corrected her. "You have to fill out an application and be approved, but it's simple. I have some applications at home. Go ahead and pet him."

"What's his name?" asked the girl, picking me up and hugging me close.

"His name is Venture," said William. "If you're coming to the youth meeting this afternoon, I can bring you an application. I have to go now. Rev. Stone is back and he wants to meet Venture."

"I'll be at the social," said the girl. "I don't live in this town, I'm just visiting my Aunt Mary. Do you think there's a chance I could get a cute puppy like Venture?"

"I think you can get a puppy, but none of them are as cute as Venture. Anyway, you need to know more about it. Raising a puppy is a lot of work, and Mom keeps reminding me I'll have to give him back someday because he is going to be one of those very special dogs who take care of blind people."

I walked alongside William as together we went into a house and into Reverend Stone's study.

"Hi, William. So this is the puppy I've heard so much about," boomed a deep bass voice. "What a little heartbreaker he's going to be. Would you look at those eyes now? He really is beautiful too. Better keep a careful eye on him or somebody is going to take him. What exactly is it you have to do with him?"

"For the next year, Venture will be mine," explained William. "My job is to help him get used to being around all kinds of people and to feel comfortable in all kinds of places. Someday, he will be somebody's eyes, and people don't leave their eyes at home. Also, it's my job to help him learn to be well-mannered and acceptable wherever he goes. He's a real pill. Last night he got hold of one of Mom's slippers and completely destroyed it. When one of us can't watch him, we have to tie him up or put him in the crate they gave us so he'd feel at home. We teach him simple obedience, but mostly we just love him and make him feel that he's an important part of the family. Sometimes he thinks he's the most important part! Raising him is work, but it's great to be given the responsibility."

"Yes," said Rev. Stone. "When your mom told me you were going to be involved in this project, I wholeheartedly endorsed the idea. It's by helping others that we help ourselves. It seems to me that as Christians, doing something like this really demonstrates our faith. By the way, where does Venture sleep?"

"At night I tie him by my bedside," answered William. "The first few nights were really hard. He missed his mother, I guess, and cried and cried. But now he's pretty good—he sleeps all night. He needs to get outside in a hurry in the morning, but he's doing good."

"You make him sleep on the floor?" asked Rev. Stone. "I couldn't leave that precious little ball of fur tied up."

"They told us it is very important to begin making the dogs behave the way they will be expected to behave right from the beginning," answered William. "When he weighs 75 pounds, it won't be so cute to have him jumping on the furniture, especially at somebody else's house. Mom said that when Venture is a guide dog, he won't need permission to come to church, but because he is a pup, it was a good idea for us to ask. Thanks for letting us bring him."

"Sure thing, William. He's always welcome—just don't let him run up and down in the church. I think we would get a lot of complaints. By the way, are you coming to the youth social this afternoon?"

"Yeah," said William. "One of the kids wants an application to raise a puppy."

"Good," said Rev. Stone. "Bring Venture along and I'll give you some time to tell the others about him and explain the program."

"Oh, no!" exclaimed William. "I'd be nervous and embarrassed."

"Nonsense," laughed Rev. Stone. "Venture isn't the only one who needs experiences to help him grow into a responsible adult. Anyway, who cares more and knows more about Venture and his exciting future? This action of yours is like dropping a stone in water. Who knows who may be blessed because of what you are doing."

At the youth meeting, William was nervous. His palms were sweaty as he rubbed them against my coat. As he began to speak, he was very worried. But as we looked at each other, William forgot the group around us and he began earnestly describing our life together and our plans for the future. He was surprised at the applause when he sat down. To his credit, William did do well, but how could he miss when he had me?

After that, William and I were in demand wherever we went. At school meetings, at parties, at social gatherings, even at a Lions Club meeting, we were the rage. William and I did all kinds of things together. I accompanied him on field trips, to museums, to a graveyard, to parties—just about anywhere my blind master might go, I went with William.

When Christmas came, I was included in the celebrations. In spring, I went to picnics, barbecues, vacation Bible school, just about anything you can imagine.

Time flew by, and suddenly it was the day before my scheduled return to the Guide Dog Foundation training center at Smithtown.

It was a disturbed William that took me for one last visit with Rev. Stone.

"My," said the reverend, "hasn't Venture grown to be a handsome dog? You should be very proud, William, as I'm sure you are. Why, that dog is downright noble. I can't get over how he has changed from the little fur ball you brought in here to see me. I remember being impressed by his beautiful eyes. They're still beautiful. In fact, now that he's grown, they have taken on a more serene look. The creature which looks out at you is a confident, self-possessed, intelligent being that knows he's of value, and most of this has happened because of you, William. What happens next?"

"He goes back to the training center tomorrow," said William glumly. "They'll train him to be a guide dog, and then they'll give him to some blind person. If he doesn't work out, then I can have him back."

"William," said Rev. Stone quietly, "you mustn't desire for him to fail. You've invested so much of yourself in his success. You have worked very hard to make Venture what he is, and because of your work, some blind person is going to have a gift he could gain in no other way—a chance to be independent and live life much like the rest of us. It's a pretty terrific gift to be given a pair of eyes even if they are on a leash. Although I'm sure the people who train those dogs really put a lot into it, he's got his basics now and that is all thanks to you and your wonderful family."

"I know," said William huskily, "but it still hurts. I just wonder what kind of person will get him. Where will he live? What kind of home will he have? Will the blind person remember that he is a dog and that he loves to go to the beach and swim and play Frisbee? How he adores a ball! I just hope that person will love him like we do."

"Everything is going to turn out right, William," said Rev. Stone as he put an arm around the young boy's shoulders. "I've always believed in Providence," he continued. "I don't believe in accidents. I think Venture was sent to you so that he would be prepared for someone special. When will you hear something?"

"Well, he'll be in training for at least three months, maybe more. Then he will be issued to a blind person who will come to the school and live there and learn to work with him for a month. When student and dog graduate I will be sent a picture of the guide dog and his blind master and I will be told where they make their home. It could be here in New York, or anywhere in the world."

"That is quite exciting," said Rev. Stone. "Will you be able to keep in touch with the blind person?"

"Only if the person chooses," said William. "It is completely up to them. If they don't want to bother with us, no one will make them."

"Everything is going to work out," Rev. Stone repeated. "You will find the faith to believe as I do."

That night, after carefully brushing my shining coat as usual, William gathered me into his arms like he did when I was little.

"Venture," he said, swallowing hard like he had a big lump in his throat. "Tomorrow you are going away to school, just as I will in a couple of years. I have always loved you, even when you chewed up Mom's new kidskin shoes. Wherever your new life takes you, no matter who else becomes important to you, I will always love you. There will be times when it will be hard, and I hope you remember me then and know how proud I am of what you're doing."

I wagged my tail and washed his ears and William pressed his face against my side. When he let me go my coat was very wet where his face had been. Somehow both of us had changed. Now a young man stood where there had been a gawky awkward teenage boy.

Three

The Guide Dog Foundation Training Center

I had been sleeping soundly when William called to me.

"It's time to go, Venture," he said snapping on my leash.

Usually someone from the Guide Dog Foundation picked up the puppies, but William and his mother wanted to take me and see the school. A picnic basket was being stowed away in the trunk.

"This is a celebration," said William's mother as she started the car. "After all the time we've spent with Venture, it will be more interesting to see the training center again."

"If Venture makes it, can we get another dog?" asked William.

"Well," said his mother, "I have enjoyed having Venture around even though he was a terror sometimes. Remember when he dug up the new vegetable garden? And no matter how hard we all watched him, he was certain death to shoes. It sure wasn't funny at the time, but you know, I'm really going to miss the little devil. Despite the hard work, it has been a joy to have the little fellow around, and to know that we've laid the groundwork for his career as a guide dog. I guess I'd have to say, sure—let's take another one."

"Do you think another one will be as much fun as Venture has been?" wondered William.

"Well, every person is different, so I guess we should expect that each puppy will be different," answered William's mother.

"Do you think there is a chance that we'll ever hear from the person who gets Venture?" asked William.

"We might," said his mother, "but it is quite important that you remember, William, we are going to be Venture's past. Though in our pictures he will be our puppy forever, his life with his blind master is his future. He won't be the shoe monster anymore—at least, I sure hope not!"

I slept. In my dream William had thrown the ball over a fence. I tried and tried to jump over the fence and get the ball, but I just couldn't reach it. Then with a mighty leap I grabbed it and came running back to William. This was living. This was what was important.

I was brought wide awake by William's picking me up and handing me to the puppy supervisor.

"What will happen to him now?" asked William's mother.

"I have been monitoring his progress," answered the puppy supervisor. "It seems very good, but we will run further tests on him. We will X-ray his hips to be certain he doesn't have hip dysplasia. This is a problem for most big dogs, but is probably most common among German Shepherds. If a dog has this problem, he might appear to be all right now, but later on, it could be a real source of pain for the dog when he moves about. That of course would be a terrible problem for a guide dog.

"Once we are as sure as possible that the dog is in perfect physical condition, he will then join a 'string'. This is a group of young dogs who will be given to a trainer who will work with them exclusively. Within about three months of the time he joins a string, he will be ready to be given to a blind person. Of course, each dog is different, and the needs of blind people vary too. For example, we may have a sweet lady in her sixties who isn't real active and who walks slowly. This person will need a placid gentle dog that will be easily controlled. Then we might have a young man who is going to college, who is involved in a lot of activities, constantly on the go. A quiet placid unexcitable dog is not what this young man needs.

"There are always more dogs in a string than there are students so that the trainer can pick and choose what he thinks is best. This means that there will be some leftover dogs. They are assigned to a new trainer and become part of his string. Once a dog has been trained, it is quite necessary that he be worked regularly and those needs are met by being a part of a string."

"What are some of the reasons a dog doesn't make it?" asked William.

"If a dog has a health problem, he will be taken out of the program, but other things can happen. Some dogs just can't handle the stress of being guide dogs. Although they may pass all of our tests, they may develop problems after they join a string. I have seen them develop extreme skin problems which make working impossible. If such a dog is retired from the program and put back in a home, he usually returns to normal. It's like us. Everyone isn't cut out to do everything. We had to reject one dog because it wagged its tail so much. What happened was that somehow a bad sore developed on the dog's tail. We treated it of course, even bandaging it. The dog would continue to wag and break the healing sore open. Since the tail would not heal, we rejected the dog. You can't have a guide dog with an open running sore on its tail that cannot be healed."

"Are there blind people who can't work with a guide dog?" asked William.

"Yes, that happens," replied the puppy supervisor.

"Why?" asked William

"Many things can go wrong," said the puppy supervisor. "Some people just don't want to discipline themselves to taking care of a guide dog. Sometimes someone will come to the school and discover that it just takes too much out of them physically. Then, once in a while, we just don't have the right dog for the right person."

"Could I come see Venture after he's been given to his blind master?" asked William. "That way, I could see him and find out what kind of person has him."

"Of course you would be welcome to visit the school and meet Venture's master when he or she is here," answered the puppy supervisor. "However, you would not be allowed to see Venture."

"Why not?" demanded William. "Venture has been my dog for the last year. When he wanted to play, it was Mom and me who took care of him, fed him, housebroke him, sat up with him when he was a baby. What do you mean, I wouldn't be allowed to see him?"

The puppy supervisor patted William's shoulder. "I think I know how you must feel, William," she said. "Once Venture is given to his blind master he will have completed his training. He will be a well-mannered, effective guide dog. However, we have found that if our young prodigies see their puppyhood playmates, their behavior reverts to that of a puppy. This isn't fair to their new master, who may have trouble controlling his grown puppy. I know that it is hard, but we are here to serve blind people. The Puppywalker program is very important to that program. I think it is the core of it because without you, we wouldn't have nearly so high a success ratio. The hard fact is that you have done your part. Now you must step back and let us do ours."

"Will I ever get to see Venture again?" asked a quiet William.

"Could be," said the puppy supervisor. "Once Venture has graduated with his master, they may choose to keep in touch with you. After graduation, we feel that the graduate should be able to handle the dog all right, so if he lives in your area, it is quite possible."

"You have referred to Venture's blind master," said William's mother. "Does this mean that Venture will be given to a man?"

"No," said the puppy supervisor. "Master is a generic term. I have no idea for whom or for what he may be suited. All I know is that he is a very beautiful dog. You have lavished a lot of time and attention on him. More than many do. I can tell you this. He's an exceptional dog. He'll have a very special master, and that master should be thanking his or her lucky stars he had you in his life. Now why don't you come with me to the dorm and meet some of the students who are in class training with their guide dogs? I think it will give you an interesting perspective on the program, and maybe you can imagine Venture's future."

I looked up as William called goodbye to me, but I was very involved in a game of tag with a Lab. These are the things that are truly important.

Four

The String

My time was taken up from morning till night. The girls who took care of us were so nice. Every day, they took me out and brushed and combed my shining coat. There were always lots of hugs, and lots of telling me what a good boy I was and how very beautiful and special I was. I had known since I was very young that I was to be a guide dog and take care of some blind person, but life in the kennel was wonderful. There were those nice girls, and some of the other dogs were truly magnificent—though of course none could compare with me. They were a lot of fun. I decided that if it worked out that I lived here at the Guide Dog Foundation Training Center, I would be glad to do so for the rest of my life. After all, I was always fed, groomed, played with, admired. What more could anyone possibly want?

One day, several of us were taken to the vet. It was a truly wonderful experience. The vet acted as though he had never seen such a wonderful creature as myself. He went over me with a fine-toothed comb. He looked in my mouth and down my throat. He listened to my heart. He thoroughly examined my body for any defects at all. He spent a lot of time looking at my eyes. He shone a light in them, then turned the light in the room off and shone the light in again.

I was delighted beyond words. It was very obvious to me that this man had never seen such wonderful eyes or such a fine beautiful strong body. I responded by vigorously wagging my tail. I was a little disappointed when he said to another man, "Looks like another fine dog. Put him with the others we're going to X-ray."

I couldn't help but feel glum as I was pushed into a cage. Here I was, a pampered darling, very beautiful, and I had been very warm to this man. All he could say was that here was another healthy dog. How utterly disgusting the whole thing was. Then someone was opening my cage, calling to me, and telling me what a good boy I was. Life did have its little ups and downs, but why worry about it? What counts is what's going on right now.

A lot of things happened over the next few days. I was X-rayed, exposed to loud sounds (which didn't matter to me at all), and lots of other things. The decision was finally made. "Venture is a very sound and healthy dog. He is now ready to be assigned to a string." I wasn't certain just what that meant, but life was so pleasant and if they wanted me to be part of a string, that would be just fine with me.

The next morning, I met the Trainer. He told me how pretty I was and what a good boy he believed me to be. What was important and different in this relationship was that the Trainer really respected me and I loved and respected him. This turned out to be the most important relationship I had ever had with a person. This respect was the gateway to the most important things in my life. Respect isn't something you can turn on like flipping a light switch; it developed from our working relationship.

I was taken from the kennel and while he petted and admired me, he took a piece of lightweight chain about twenty-one inches long with a ring at each end, made a loop, and slipped it over my head. I learned that this was called a "choke chain collar." When I was in the kennel with the other dogs, the collar would be taken off.

Now the Trainer attached a leash to the collar and we did obedience exercises. I sat when I was asked, I lay down when asked, and I sat and stayed as directed. Every time I did what I was told, the Trainer praised me and made me feel I was the most special creature ever. I understood when he said "heel" and the two of us went for a nice long walk. The Trainer took me down a long straight sidewalk, and we pretty much stayed to the center of it. It seemed so very pleasant, like going for walks with William.

There were sixteen other dogs in the string, and one morning, the Trainer put my choke collar on, then put me in a large truck. There were rings along the sides of the truck with short cables called "tie-downs" attached to them. They had snaps on the ends like the snaps on a leash. The Trainer snapped a tie-down on my collar. This prevented me from moving around a lot, but it was not uncomfortable. When all sixteen of us were on board, the arrangement made a lot of sense. I guess it would have been difficult if all sixteen of us had played some of our delightful games. They just could never have sorted us out. The fact that we had to be quiet had another advantage. Since we couldn't romp and play, we generally remained serious. I, for one, was usually in a learning mood, although I'll confess that when a dog near me tried to play a little, I joined in the fun. In fact, I started a few games myself, but they were necessarily quiet games, not the grand free-for-alls that we had in the runs back at the training center.

After the Trainer had taken me on many walks, and he knew I knew what he wanted me to do, he introduced me to the harness. This is a leather device which really is made up of two pieces. The body part went over my head and around my chest and had a strap that buckled behind my front legs. The other piece, the handle, was a kind of U-shaped thing that curved away from my right side. When I went for walks wearing this thing, I continued to wear the choke chain collar and the leash. This was so the person walking with me would always have a means of control. Control seemed to be an important key to success. I thought the harness a little weird but the Trainer acted as if it were important to him that I wear it, so I obliged him willingly. This really seemed to make the Trainer delighted, and he gave me a lot of pats and told me again and again what a good boy I was. I decided wearing the harness was a lot of fun, and whenever I saw the Trainer come toward me with the harness in his hand, my tail would wag just as hard as it could.

The Trainer taught me lots of things. He taught me left and right. He taught me that "inside" meant to find a door that would go in, and outside meant to find a door that would take me out. I soon understood that if I went inside, and the Trainer wanted to go outside, often I could use the same door we came in. The Trainer always seemed pleased with me—until one day he did something really strange.

We were walking along, and there was a pole in the middle of the sidewalk. I'm not a fool, so I walked around it—but the Trainer bumped into it.

"Bad boy," yelled the Trainer. "Venture, you are a very bad boy." And with that he began to beat on the pole.

The man was obviously unhappy with me. "Look at that, Venture, you bad dog," he said. "You see that? Look at that. You ran me into that, you bad dog you," and with that he gave my collar a hard snap.

The jerk on my neck did not feel so good, but what really upset me was how disgusted with me the Trainer was. He dropped the handle of the harness, turned me around, and walked me back a ways. Then we turned around and soon the pole was looming up ahead. I wasn't sure what to do so I stopped but the Trainer urged me in a gentle voice to go on. Slowly, I went around the pole so that the Trainer didn't touch it. He seemed thrilled that I had done this. He praised me and petted me and I just know he thought I was the most wonderful dog that had ever lived. As we worked together, a silly idea formed in my mind. If I pretended that the Trainer were a part of me, and that his height and width belonged to me, and if I were to play like all this extra bulk were me, then if I allowed for my bigger size, the Trainer wouldn't run into anything. The trick worked and everyone began to talk about how remarkable I was. Then I began to wonder. Maybe this wasn't a trick at all. Maybe this was what was wanted all along. When I started thinking of all our work in that way, I was praised so much you wouldn't believe it and I heard others commenting on just how very special I really was.

Other things upset him, though. One time when we were walking along he got mad at me because when we passed by some dogs that barked at us, I wanted to stop and bark back. It was a perfectly natural thing to do, but he would have none of it. If he wasn't the main thing, he got his feelings hurt. Sometimes when this happened he got very sad. Other times when he didn't get his way, he got mad and gave hard jerks or snaps on the leash. I didn't much like that and since this man seemed to need to feel that he was running the show, I let him. After all, it was really worth the affection and praise he was so generous with when I did what he wanted.

Some of the other dogs weren't as smart as me. They told stories about how they were going to show him but in time everybody did what he wanted. Everybody, that is, except a yellow Lab called Ginger. She disliked everything. She didn't do her obedience very well; she really didn't care to go for walks. She positively hated the harness, and she told us she wasn't going to do anything special for a stupid trainer. In fact, she used to throw up when she was made to do something she didn't want to. One day she was taken away. I heard someone say that she was rejected from the program.

We had just come in from a hot and hard day in a very busy place. It had been especially dumb because we had gone down some stairs in the middle of the street and ridden on a train that ran under the ground. The train had been really filthy. As I was savoring the fresh air at the training center, someone called out: "Well, how are you mutts getting along—what with those yucky subways and all?"

I looked over to where the voice came from. There, lounging idly, stood a dog whose dark good looks rivaled my golden ones.

"Well?" he said as he waved his glossy black tail.

I stood open-mouthed. Somewhere a memory stirred. That arrogant figure seemed familiar. Could it be? Then I noticed that he was staring open-mouthed with admiration at me.

"Venture," he said, "you are like a fairy tale. What a beautiful creature you have grown into and what a regal manner you bear. Don't you remember me from when you were just a grubby, scrappy puppy?"

"Banner?" I asked timidly.

"Goodness gracious, his brain has developed too," laughed Banner. "You really do look marvelous. All over the kennel they are singing your praises. It's 'Venture this' and 'Venture that.' I have been dying to get a look at you."

The sunlight cascaded over Banner's glossy blue-black coat and I heard myself wondering aloud about this magnificent and breathtakingly beautiful creature. He was pushed into the run with me and he glided over to where I stood gaping at him.

"Where have you been, Banner?" I asked. "What are you doing here—and how did you know those trains are called subbers?"

"Subways, Venture. I know about them because I am a fully

trained guide dog! My Master had to go to the hospital for a few days. I think he had emergency surgery. I have been with him when he has gone to the vet who sees humans, but since this came up suddenly, he had no one to leave me with so he sent me back here for a couple of weeks."

I looked at the gorgeous dog with interest. "Is it fun to be a guide dog?" I asked.

"It is the most wonderful thing you could ever imagine," answered Banner, "if you are lucky and get issued to someone who is really interesting. When I was in training I daily gave thanks that I hadn't been given to some of the people who were in my class. Like dogs, some people are more interesting than others. Thank goodness I was given to someone very interesting. Getting used to your person is a bit difficult—learning what his special wants and needs are, and the person learning about you. It is not a piece of cake, but once you understand each other, there is nothing that can compare with it.

"I remember when I was in training, I thought that living here in the kennel was the most wonderful thing in the world and I was sure nothing could top it. How wrong I was! When I was in class, the pressure was awful, and I wanted to go back to the kennel and the string more than you can possibly imagine. But once I came to understand my person and we developed a working relationship, I sort of became a part of him. Now, I would much rather be working for him than being here."

"Well, thanks a bunch, Banner," I sniffed. "I find your dark silky charm makes me really ill. I don't know whether to—."

"Come off it, Venture," chortled Banner. "I really didn't mean that I wasn't glad to see you. What I did mean is that it is wonderful being a guide dog. When you work with the Trainer, you do what he says or else. When you work with your person it is different. I don't know if I can properly explain this, but I will try. When you are with your person, he is calling the shots too, but somehow it is different. He tells you what he wants, but then he depends on you to find out if that is possible. For example, he may want to walk down a street but halfway down it, he may discover that the city is tearing up the street. This really puts you in control because although he may tell you how to get out of the difficulty, it is still up to the guide dog to make the final decision. It is interesting. As your master learns that he can trust you, more and more responsibility seems to come your way, and if someone is as beautiful as you, the public will be at your feet and you will find that the world is your oyster."

"It sounds a little frightening to me," I said. "Will I be expected to know where things are and how to get there? For example, will my master say 'Go to the store' and expect me to do all the work?"

"Oh, no, it won't be that bad," wagged Banner. "It is much simpler than that. Let's say your master wants to go to school like mine does. He will harness you and direct you outside. Once you get him outside your job is done until he tells you to do something else."

"Like what?" I asked interestedly.

"Well," replied Banner, "when my master wants to go to school, he will tell me, 'To the elevator.' You see, we live in an apartment house in the city; before we can do anything, we have to get to the sidewalk. Once I take him to the elevator, we ride down to the lobby. He then tells me 'outside.' I take him outside of the elevator and we proceed to the steps, where I halt. He directs me forward and we descend the steps together. Once I get him to the sidewalk, he's the boss and I wait to see what he wants. He is a very active person and goes many places. While I may have an idea where we are going, I wait for instructions from him.

"He always has a plan. To go to school, he has me take him to the corner. From there he directs me to cross the street, turn left, walk three blocks, and then turn right and go into the subway.

"I take him to the train and he directs me to take him 'inside.' After that, it is his responsibility to tell me when to get off. If he doesn't say anything, then we will ride the subway all day. I heard that he knows when he wants to get off by counting the stops. I guess you have already learned that when you go on the subway, you always sit and your master will place his hand under your collar so that he knows exactly where you are at all times."

"Well, you have given me a lot to think about," I said as we lay contentedly together. "It all sounds kind of frightening and awesome and so very exciting."

"Even more so for you," said Banner.

"How's that?"

"I was in the office this morning and I heard them talking about you," he admitted. "It seems that your training is almost completed and that you are considered to be a dream of a guide dog. When Auntie Em makes her trip in behalf of the school, she will take a guide dog with her. You will be that guide dog. She took me around when I was a puppy, so I know firsthand that you are in for a special treat. Most of the dogs here would give their tails to be you."

"That sounds exciting," I said, no longer feeling sleepy. "I remember her. Just before I left to go to the puppy walker, she took me and a couple other puppies over to meet some of the blind students. There was a young man there who was very, very special. Until I met him, I was afraid of what being a guide dog meant; but after seeing him, I have been looking forward to it. Banner, do you think there is any chance that young man will be my person?"

"I doubt it," said Banner. "The students you met were waiting to get their dogs. I'm sure the young man you met has already been given a dog. But don't you worry about a thing, Venture. You are a beautiful, kind and compassionate dog. In another year or so, you will have reached full maturity. Somewhere out there, someone very, very special is waiting for you and he ought to be thanking his lucky stars you are coming to him. I don't quite know what your future holds, but I do know that it will be spectacular. Now why don't you go to sleep and dream about the future? Remember, whatever wonderful things you dream, real life will top it. I am really tired. Sweet dreams, Venture."

I lay quietly beside Banner, but sleep would not come. I thought about the exciting things I had heard. From the time I had accepted the fact that I was to be a guide dog, my life had been awhirl with excitement. I could hardly wait until the next part.

Five

King For a Day

The next few weeks flew by. We were all entertained by Banner's many stories. Although he was now a professional, that didn't stop him from heartily joining in some of the most rousing games ever played in the runs. Neither did his professionalism interfere with his lusty appetite. Not only did he eat his own food; several times he tried to get at mine.

True, he was just about the best looking dog I had ever seen, but he had no idea at all what it meant to be modest and unassuming. It certainly wasn't necessary for the girls in the kennel to make so much over him. He admired himself so much, no one else needed to. Since he had such a high opinion of himself, I didn't see any need at all for anyone to fuss over him. After all, he had a master, and it seemed to me that attention should be lavished on those of us who didn't have anyone.

His stories were spellbinding, though. He told about being taken into houses with plush deep carpeting, and being allowed to roll about on that carpet at will. He told about going to fine restaurants, swimming in the lake, even swimming in the ocean. I began to wonder if maybe he wasn't pulling our tails a little—but his stories were so wonderful, what did it matter?

Then something happened that really confused me.

I had just been groomed and put into the run with the others, when the Trainer came with a leash calling for Banner. I watched as Banner executed a perfect heel and then glided along beside the Trainer. Suddenly, his tail began wagging furiously and he began to quiver.

In the yard stood an ordinary-looking young man who was holding out his arms to Banner. I gawked as I saw the self-possessed Banner whine and bounce up and down then roll as though in ecstasy at the man's feet.

"Oh Banner! I've missed you too," he crooned as he knelt beside the moaning dog. "The last couple weeks I've felt like a part of me was taken away, but we're going to make up for lost time. I am not so strong, so you and I are going to Aunt Elsie's at the Cape. She has a lovely beach house, and you and I can lie on the sand, enjoy sunning ourselves, and of course you can go swimming. When I'm feeling a little stronger, there are some wonderful places we will go and we can just enjoy each other for the next month. How does that sound to you, old man?"

Banner wriggled with joy. I just couldn't believe it. One moment, there was this regal, arrogant dog, and the next minute there was this besotted creature and by the look in his eyes, there was nothing Banner wouldn't go without for love of this man. Such selfless devotion was totally awesome.

Something happened to me, though, that showed me that Banner wasn't making up anything. Instead of being taken to where I was always brushed and combed, I was put into a tub of warm water and given a bath. After I was dried, I was brushed and combed, and then taken to the office where I saw Auntie Em.

I was happy to see her and I wagged my tail with joy. Auntie Em just has to be one of the very nicest people you could ever want to meet, but I remembered how foolishly Banner had behaved, and I wanted to impress her with what a fine gentleman I was. So although I was beyond delighted at seeing her, I took care not to appear a novice.

She was overwhelmed by me. She said that I was a good boy and that she was pleased to meet such a handsome fellow. She said that she thought I must be one of their most beautiful dogs, and that she had heard about what a dream of a guide dog I had become. She said it would be a real treat for her to have such an elegant escort on her trip and she was looking forward to my company.

Then she turned her attention to another woman in the office.

"Don't you think Venture's grand?" she said. "I think we have another Banner here. You weren't here when Scott and Banner were in training, were you?"

"No," said the woman, "but I got all of Scott's calls about Banner while he was in the hospital and after he got home. Don't you think he should have waited a little until he was stronger before he came and got Banner? I told him Banner was enjoying himself and he should look after his own health, but he said Banner was a part of his health and I guess he came for him just as soon as he could get a ride here. I was afraid he would try to take the bus so he could get to his Banner and I don't think he was strong enough for that."

"Certainly not," answered Auntie Em, "but if we had found out he was going to take the bus, he doesn't live that far from here and one of the staff would have taken Banner to him."

"He certainly seems like an ambitious and outgoing young man," observed the woman.

"That he is," said Auntie Em, "but he wasn't always that way."

"What do you mean?" asked the woman.

"Well," said Auntie Em, "Scott has diabetes. He has had it since he was a child. When a child contracts diabetes, it is called juvenile diabetes, and they have to take insulin. The pills just will not work for them. Insulin saves a person's life, but it often has serious side effects. When he was twenty-one, Scott developed a problem called ocular retinopathy. This is a problem that many diabetics have. What happens is that little blood vessels break in the eye, causing a hemorrhage. This leads to serious problems with the retina, and although we have better treatment for it today, it is still a leading cause of blindness in the United States. I have just barely described the problem to you. If you would like more details, there are books in the library that will describe the problem much more clearly.

"Anyway, Scott was twenty-one when he lost his sight. He was captain of his football team. He was a straight-A student. He was involved with many other college activities, and the loss of his sight was a terrible shock to him. He wasn't exactly a quitter, he just stalled. He took mobility (the ability to travel with a cane) and took advantage of one of the centers for the blind to learn practical ways of living with his blindness, but it was as though a part of his personality had died.

"He applied for a dog, and we were in a bit of a quandary. I knew that deep within himself, Scott had a wonderful capacity to live a very meaningful life and have very positive effects on those around him, but at this time, they were not at all in evidence. At that time Banner was ready to be placed. We wavered between Banner and another dog. The other dog we were considering for him was much calmer than Banner. If we gave him Banner, those two personalities would certainly present a challenge to one another. We took the chance."

"A couple weeks passed, and I feared that maybe we had made a mistake. Then something happened between Scott and Banner. I am unsure exactly what it was, but it was as if they decided to become a part of one another's worlds. Gradually, Scott again became the lively young man he had been before he lost his sight. It was as though with Banner at his side, he could do anything he thought about doing and being able to see wasn't always the deciding factor. Scott and Banner hurled themselves into life. The guide dog had helped to restore Scott's belief in himself. Once he believed in himself, he could accomplish the things he set out to do.

"Scott and Banner are a very unusual team. However, there are many situations that are just as remarkable. If a graduate lives far from the school, we may not know how extensively the guide dog has changed someone's life, but usually receiving a guide dog has a major impact."

"Do some guide dogs never have that kind of impact?" asked the woman.

"It can vary," said Auntie Em. "Sometimes the effect of a guide dog is just to give independence to a person. Usually, as I said, feeling independence encourages the person to aspire to other things.

But now and then we come across someone who really would rather be dependent on others. For that person, the guide dog often isn't an important part of his life, and often we get such dogs back."

"What about Venture?" asked the woman. "What kind of a person will he go to and what kind of a guide dog do you think he is going to make?"

"Everything that I have seen and heard about this fellow makes me think he is going to be very special. Banner is wonderful, but Venture is unusually sweet and compassionate. Like Banner, he is very smart, so he will be a challenge to whomever we give him to, but he has a depth of kindness and tranquility that is very unique."

"Oh dear!" said the woman who was talking to Auntie Em. "Since I'm new here at the Foundation, I find the chance to talk with you and hear about the students and their dogs enthralling. While we have been talking, time has been running away from us—we'd better hurry if we're going to get you to the airport so you can make the shuttle to Washington, D.C."

"I've been watching the time," said Auntie Em, "and we're doing fine. We had better get going, though. Venture, come!"

I hurried to do Auntie Em's bidding. As she told me what a good boy I was, she was slipping the harness over my head.

"We'll see how you do on an airplane," she said as we got in the car.

We boarded the airplane like everyone else, and I lay peacefully at Auntie Em's feet. Suddenly the sounds of the engines changed, and soon I felt us tilt as though we were going to go up in the air. I looked about alertly, knowing I must watch out for Auntie Em. No one seemed concerned, so I guessed there was no reason why I should be. Auntie Em scratched my ears, and I settled back contentedly. Whatever these folks wanted was fine with me.

When we arrived in Washington, D.C., the airport was very crowded. People jostled against one another as they went different directions. I listened carefully and acted the perfect guide dog, doing what was asked and guiding Auntie Em around the crowds and posts and piles of suitcases. We were both glad when we got to our hotel and could enjoy a little privacy in our room. Auntie Em had brought a tie-down which she secured to the bed, and I lay quietly while she was busy with things she needed to do. Later, she took me to a meeting where there were other trainers with their guide dogs from other schools.

"That is a magnificent creature you have there," said a very dignified man. "What is his name?"

"His name is Venture," answered Auntie Em. "He has completed his training, and I decided to bring him on this trip with me."

"Well," said the man, "I've been watching him all evening, and to say he is beautiful certainly is an understatement. His behavior is flawless, and it really complements his extraordinary looks. Did you say he has just finished his training?"

"That's correct," answered Auntie Em.

"Well," said the man, "You have something very special there. Many dogs have gone through our program, dogs we are proud of, but I can't say as we've had one as striking as that one. You will keep him for this kind of thing, won't you? It seems a shame to just place him."

"Venture is very special," answered Auntie Em. "At the Guide Dog Foundation, we take a lot of pride in our dogs. We have good ones in every string. You are right. Venture's looks are very striking, and his behavior is, as you say, perfect, but I think that is why we must place him. There is a caring and a tranquility within him that will make him the perfect addition to someone's life. You remember Banner, the black Lab puppy? He's been through the program and now belongs to a young man who lives in the city. That team is a credit to our school and a shining example to everybody involved with a guide dog program. That team demonstrates very graphically what benefits a guide dog can bring to the life of a blind person— opportunities that might not be available if it weren't for the hard work of those who make this program possible."

"Save it for a group you're trying to get money out of," laughed the man. "But didn't you tell me that dog has just completed his training? He must have been raised in the city—or have you taken him with you before?"

"No, answered Auntie Em. "This is the first time I have had him with me. Venture grew up in upstate New York."

"Well," remarked another woman at our table. "He is one dream of a guide dog."

"You haven't seen anything," bragged Auntie Em. "You should have seen him on the plane and in the airport. This dog was born to be a guide dog. The only less than positive thing that happened was while I was talking with one of the hotel employees, I failed to notice that Venture in his delight at being there was happily wagging his tail. I'm afraid that big plant down there took quite a beating and didn't weather the experience too well—but we can hardly discipline the dog for being happy and wagging his tail, can we?"

There was general laughter about this incident, then conversation moved on to something else. I laid my head near Auntie Em and went to sleep. I would awaken if she needed anything.

The next few days were filled with meetings but we did do a little shopping. When Auntie Em told me to find the escalator, I did it as though I were used to doing such things every day although I had only done that twice in my life. She was very impressed with me and told me how very special I was. It made me feel good to hear her acknowledge the facts. Of course I was spectacular and that is why she took me, but it really was nice to hear her state the obvious.

Our trip back to the training center was uneventful, and I had lots of stories to tell the other dogs.

Of course, they couldn't get along without me for long and soon I was called for again. This time, we went to a TV station and I wasn't the only guest of honor. Auntie Em also brought along a little black Lab puppy.

His name was Endear. He really had things mixed up because he was under the impression he was the main attraction but I, of course, knew better. I knew this program was important, so I acted my most polished. When I was worked, I moved smoothly and professionally, taking care to perform each request with precision.

Endear was another matter. For one thing, I don't think he ever stopped wriggling. The nice man who was talking to Auntie Em held him. Endear chewed on his tie. When the man held him close to his face, Endear sucked on his ear. Then the little monster decided to demonstrate his vocal chords by barking at me.

They put him down on the floor while I was working. Of course I was perfect and when Auntie Em told me I was a good boy, I wagged my tail. Unhappy that the spotlight had shifted to me instead of him, Endear pounced on my tail. I tried to ignore him, but he wouldn't leave me alone. He tried to crawl under me and bite my tummy.

He barked at the TV camera. Then he tried to play with the nice man's shoe strings. Everyone laughed, but I thought he was disgusting. I lay poised and quiet, while this clown acted up instead of being quiet and listening to Auntie Em and to her explanation about the important things guide dogs are supposed to do.

The interview was just over, and again Endear grabbed my tail.

I had had enough. Snarling at the little brat, I snapped at him.

"Well," said Auntie Em to the nice man, "Venture has a lot of patience, but as you just saw, there are limits. Isn't it interesting that he waited until the show was over?"

I was glad to get back to the Guide Dog Foundation Training Center and associate with my more mature friends, but across from us I could see a pen full of puppies. From where I stood I could hear an unmistakable clear little puppy voice. It called at the top of its lungs to the other puppies, "I know what we are going to be when we grow up! I know I know I know!"

Endear's piping little voice flooded my mind with memories of my own puppyhood. So much had changed, yet it was amazing how much things were the same.

Six

Diana

It had been pretty dull the last few days in the kennel. We were, of course, still fed and groomed, but for two days the Trainer hadn't taken any of us out to work. Rumor had it that a class of blind students had come for dogs. We had been playing one of our delightful games in the run and saw some people with the Trainer. All of us barked at them; we were told to shut up.

I had heard Endear's piping little voice bragging that he and another puppy had seen these students, but otherwise we had heard nothing—that is, nothing until this morning. Then the word spread like wildfire that today guide dogs would be placed. No sooner had I heard this report than I was taken out of the run, given a bath, and brushed till my golden coat rivaled the sun.

"You are such a wonderful boy, Venture," said the young woman who had been one of my favorites in the kennel. "I want you to go out there and do us proud. Be happy, Venture, and always remember us and know that we love you."

Eight of us had been bathed and groomed and now waited in a special place for the Trainer. It wasn't every day a dog was placed and excitement ran high. Soon I would meet my person. What would that person be like? Once my person saw me would he realize he had finally found the pot of gold at the end of the rainbow and that all his troubles were going to melt away like lemon drops? I could hardly wait. Other dogs were taken first, but finally my turn came.

My first clue about my person was interesting. While we were in the kennel, we didn't wear the choke collar. That was put on when we were rounded up to work and then it was taken off once we returned to the kennel. Now I discovered that was to change. The Trainer slipped a new choke collar over my head and that is where I got my first clue. These collars had been given to the students along with harnesses, combs, brushes and leashes. As a result, my person had been handling the collar, and a delightful fragrance clung to the metal collar allowing me to determine my person was a lady. From the scent on the collar, I could tell that she was someone who was polished and thus would be able to appreciate my fine qualities. I had never thought that I might be given to a lady before. The idea was novel, but then I figured that Auntie Em was a lady and no one could do better than that. All of these thoughts raced through my mind as the Trainer and I took the short walk from the kennel to the dormitory.

"Well, Venture," said the Trainer, "time to strut your stuff. This person is going to be a tough customer because she has had a wonderful guide dog before, so if you try to fudge we'll hear about it. It is going to be tough. It always is when someone is getting a new dog as opposed to a first guide dog. But I have my money riding on you so don't let me down."

I responded by wagging my tail. Naturally, I could handle anything. I, Venture, was the darling of the kennel and the Trainer ought to know that. I couldn't help wondering about him. How quickly he could forget and I loved him so much. Oh well, I was about to meet my person and I figured to wow her.

We entered a room where a lady was waiting for us. She must have been cold because she was bundled up like a snow bunny. The Trainer asked her for the leash he had given her, and he snapped it onto my collar.

"Venture," he said, "this is Diana. Diana, this is Venture," and he handed her my leash.

Diana held out her hand to me. "Come to me, Venture, and let me get a look at you," she said. Her voice was soft and the gentle fingers that explored my body confirmed my guess that here was a person who appreciated the finer things of life.

"Goodness, Venture," she said, "you are a big dog and such a good boy too."

I wasn't sure what to do or how to act. My life and training were all calculated to bring me to this moment. But now that it had arrived, I didn't know what to do. It did seem, though, that I ought to do something. After all, she was nice, and she couldn't be all that bad, for she was telling me how beautiful I was. I bestowed a kiss on her hand. This seemed to thrill her and she gave me a hug and said that in time we would become the best of friends, what with me being so elegant and all. She made no special demands on me. She just stroked me and told me over and over how lovely I was. I had no objections to this so I lay down beside her and she began to massage my body with sure, even strokes. I liked this so I rolled onto my back so that she could rub my tummy.

"Venture," she said as she rubbed my tummy, "I don't know if I can protect you if you keep assuming that position. It is considered indecent to expose yourself like that so you better stop. Otherwise someone may call the police and they will put you in jail because you exposed yourself. I won't be able to visit you there or bring you treats or play with you or anything. They will just leave you there and forget all about you."

I responded by waving my paws and wriggling so that my back was scratched on the carpet. That done, I flopped on my side. Diana continued telling me how wonderful I was. I enjoyed this attention and responded by lazily wagging my tail. Actually, I thought it added dignity to the surroundings. It made a *thud thud thud* sound on the hardwood floor.

Diana immediately investigated. She reached out and took my tail in her hand and gently pulled it. I learned later that Diana had just read a novel where the people used short thick throwing clubs. She decided that my tail was my own personal club.

"What a wonderful club you have, Venture," she laughed. "It's so thick. It really is mighty."

I waved my mighty club much to her delight. I was pleased that she had the good taste to admire it. I hadn't realized it was a club, but in my delight I whacked her good on the head with it.

Diana laughed. "With that mighty club swinging around here, I can never be in danger," she said "But how about not hitting me in the head with the mighty thing? Otherwise I will just have to think of some mighty big thing to do to you. Why do you suppose they gave me such a mighty golden butt?"

I had no answer for that, but I got up and tried to grab my mighty club. First I whirled in one direction and then the other. The leash was a little confining, but since Diana thought me mighty, I had to demonstrate my abilities.

Diana appreciated my antics but encouraged me to sit beside her and let her pet me. I laid my paw on her knee.

"No, Venture," she said gently as she removed my paw from her knee. "You don't want to do that. Suppose I was wearing an evening dress and your paw was muddy? If you put it on the dress, I would be upset with you. If you don't get in the habit of putting your paws on me, then there will never be that problem."

She got down on the floor with me and put her arms about me.

"Venture," she said, "you are a butt. Granted that you are a very beautiful golden butt, but you are a butt and you are going to be my butt. I already love you and I hope that someday you will find it in your mighty heart to love me."

I had always dreamed of the day when I would meet my person, the special person I was so uniquely qualified to be with. At that time I just knew bells would ring, lights would flash, and there would be magic in the air. Diana was very nice to me, but there was no magic here. There was a lot more excitement in the kennel, but as she stroked me, I sensed an unvoiced longing or need of some kind. She was very kind and my heart went out to her. Maybe it wasn't the magic I had expected, but there was respect and love, and that isn't a bad way to start a relationship. I responded with a mighty *thud thud thud* of my club.

The Trainer came upon us together like this. "Venture is real special," he said, "and the two of you seem to be getting on well together."

"Venture has a problem," said Diana. "Do you have a knife handy? He is unraveling."

"How's that?" asked the Trainer.

"Well, look," said Diana as she pulled gently on my club.

The Trainer laughed and I gave her several good swats on the head with my mighty club. "See how he treats me," laughed Diana. "He is just a great big wonderful butt!"

"Well," replied the Trainer, "he learned early on that a male keeps you females in your place. See? He already knows that if you threaten him, he should use that club of his. He knows to go for your head. This dog is real special. You should be glad to have him."

"Oh yeah?" laughed Diana. "This here is an old butt nobody else wanted, so you gave him to me to save his life. Now you won't have to feel guilty about nobody else wanting anything to do with him. But I know the truth about him. I know that when you give us a dog you just tell us their name, sex and breed so that we will grow to love them for what we see in them, not what they may otherwise have going for them. But in Venture's case I have guessed the truth. I know that he is a worthless golden butt that you didn't have any use for so you gave him to me. But that's all right. I know I can come to love this worthless good-for-nothing golden butt."

More and more, I was coming to like Diana. I think she saw beyond what they told her. I think she realized how very special I really was and by calling me a butt, she was paying me a tribute, forging a bond of love that could never be equalled. I had no way to express these ideas, so I settled for waving my mighty club. I was beginning to think this might work out really well.

Diana, the Trainer, and I walked together down the hall. The Trainer helped us to find a seat and showed Diana the best method to tuck me underneath her seat. The other students joined us and we were all pretty calm while the Trainer gave a lecture. Then class was dismissed and all of us went to our rooms and the people got ready for dinner.

Diana's roommate was older than she and they had given her Beth, a very blonde little golden retriever. Beth was a good steady loyal girl. I think what was special about her was her ability to really care and to be a loving, tolerant friend. I was glad to see this fine dog paired with someone who obviously already loved her.

Diana talked to me a lot about doing strange things. I understood why she was cold. Her home was in California, a long way from here, where the climate is much warmer. As she talked with me, I put my paw on her knee again.

"No, Venture," said Diana. "When we get home, my work requires that I wear hose. Your toenails would rip them up.Maybe if I show you a pair of panty hose, you will get the idea."

She went to the dresser and brought back a pair of hose.

"See what I am talking about, Venture?" she asked.

I had no interest in the hose at all. They seemed dumb to me. I didn't understand the things Diana was talking about either but I did like to hear the sound of her voice. I ran my mighty club in appreciation of her efforts because it was obvious she was trying to include me in her life and I wanted that.

That night, the Trainer took me out so I could go to the bathroom. He took me out the next morning too. This was an important part of life. The training meant that the blind person would learn about all aspects of our care. Going to the bathroom ranks right up there at the top, so after breakfast, the students took us on leashes to the run provided for that purpose.

The leather leash was made to extend about six feet. Each of us was told to "get busy." Although I really didn't need to go very much, I knew what was wanted and asserted my leadership right away. Diana proclaimed how wonderful I was and encouraged me to try to do some more. I felt a little hesitant, but after a little encouragement I did my first two as a guide dog.

Diana and the Trainer were so pleased with me. You would think I had done something earth-shattering. I guess that was because some of the other dogs overcame their shyness to follow my lead, with the result that everyone thought they were very special.

From that point on, that business became a matter of routine, though Diana still praises me for obeying her wishes. I usually go out right after I have my breakfast and a drink of water. I go out again just before lunch, just after dinner, and just before bedtime.

The schedule varies when we are traveling. Diana generally keeps track of the time. If I have a need other than that, all I have to do is whimper and she figures it out. This is a frequently-asked question about guide dogs, but it is probably the simplest part of our lives.

Each day was packed full of activity. Everyone was up by six and I was fed and ready to go out by seven.

After breakfast we usually went out in the vans and worked until noon. Then it was back to the training center for a break and lunch for the students. The afternoons were usually devoted to going out and working. In the evenings we had lectures. In the lectures, students were taught how to care for us—how to clean our ears, what to do if we had bad breath, common problems, and how to solve them, and of course, obedience.

I will never forget the first time I did obedience with Diana. She extended the leash to full length and then gave the command to heel and sit. I did as directed. She checked to see if everything was as it should be and proceeded with the exercise. But the Trainer stopped her.

Diana stood confused. The Trainer said, "Venture, I don't know how you are going to bear this life with that woman but I can assure you that when you die you will go straight to heaven for being such a wonderful, devoted guide dog."

Diana was flustered. "He knows he is a wonderful butt. I tell him all the time," she said.

"I don't really care what you tell him all the time," explained the Trainer. "Praise is very important to these dogs. They are asked to be quiet and not do things that are natural for other dogs to do. What's their reward? It is impractical and not even a good idea to carry around food for them. They are better off staying on their diets. What is important to them is your love for them. Venture loves you, and it is out of that love that he would lay down his life for you. The least you can do is to show him that you return that love by telling him what a good boy he is. When you tell him that he is a good boy, put lots of feeling into it. *Mean* it. That isn't a lot to ask."

We went everywhere. To stores, shopping malls, the business sections of town—everywhere you might go.

When we were at the Training Center, we were kept on tie-down beside our person's bed. However, my tie-down was not secured properly, and several times I got loose. I am very agile and I eluded Diana as she tried to catch me in our bedroom. Once in the hall, I realized I had a wonderful opportunity to run, so I cantered off, trailing my tie-down behind me. Diana was trying to follow, but she just wasn't as fleet-footed as I was. I had a wonderful gallop down the hall and back. I was on my second run down the hall when the Trainer came at me yelling for me to get back to where I lived. I headed back toward Diana but again I slipped past her and started back up the hall. The Trainer lunged at me so I whirled toward Diana. By this time he had cut off my path of retreat so I stood before Diana, growling an invitation to play. She grabbed me and snapped on my leash.

"You old worthless butt," she laughed as she hugged me. "See, this just proves he isn't any good. But I love him anyway."

"Good," said the Trainer. "Don't scold him. He did come to you, even though he didn't do it on his own, so he would be confused if you scolded him."

The next day showed me that I had stronger feelings about Diana than I had realized. That morning, we had been out working when just out of the blue, Diana got a very severe headache that made her feel dizzy. She managed to take me out, then fell in a heap on the bed. I stood there not knowing what to do.

Her roommate called for the housekeeper, and they got Diana's coat off. After helping her to lie down, they covered her with a blanket and made sure that I was tied up.

I was very concerned. It was obvious to me that my lady did not feel well, and I felt more attention should be paid to her. I sat beside her and laid my head on hers. Maybe if I let my love flow to her, the peace and tranquility I radiated would make her well.

The Trainer laughed when he came to check on us. Diana said she felt tired. "Do you want me to make Venture leave you alone?" he asked.

"No," said Diana. "He is just concerned." She threw her arm around me and soon she was fast asleep. When she awoke, she was fine. But that incident showed me that my feelings for her had become very different. I know she called me her worthless golden butt. At first this had been a joke, but when I thought she might be really ill, I discovered that I wanted to be her golden butt if that was what she wanted me to be, and I would be willing to follow her to the ends of the earth. That was real magic.

There were other special things that happened between the students. When Diana was ill, everyone was concerned. When someone became discouraged, it was interesting how the others would rally around him and boost his morale.

Time flew by and all too soon the class was over and the students were arranging to return to their homes with their new guide dogs. For me, this would mean a trip across the United States to Southern California.

As Diana packed for the trip home, I felt some confusion. I was comfortable with her, but I didn't know anything about California—and the Trainer wouldn't be there to help us!

Seven

California, Here I Come!

It was very late when Diana finished her packing for our long trip to California. She then took me to the basement to groom me.

These times while I was being groomed had become special for both of us. At these times, Diana completely devoted herself to me, and as she brushed and combed my shining coat she talked to me about whatever was on her mind. Tonight, our trip was on her mind.

"Tomorrow, Venture, we will go to the airport and get on an airplane," she explained. "The airplane will be a little noisy, but it is very safe. It will actually go up in the air and you will feel it tilt, but you need not be afraid. I will be there, and I will take care of you. If you feel frightened, just turn to me. I came here on the airplane to get you and I know that it is safe."

I ran my mighty club. No one had explained to Diana that I had already experienced an airplane. She also had it mixed up about who was taking care of whom, but that was all right. I knew that as a guide dog, I was the one responsible to solve any problem. I just loved the way Diana made me feel that she was looking after me, though. In lots of ways she did take care of me. She fed me, she took me out, she played with me and kept me groomed. When we got into the school's vans, she always made sure that my mighty club was tucked under me so that it wouldn't get stepped on or caught in the door. I know that she had called California and had someone deliver the food I was used to eating, and when we were in the mall, she had bought me a ball. She had also bought other things for me from the school, such as a stainless steel bowl, just like the one I ate out of while I had been at the Guide Dog Foundation.

She had also gotten me a specially processed bone, and heart worm medication. I was presently on this medicine. Heart worms don't prey upon humans, but they can kill dogs. They get into our bloodstream when a mosquito bites us. The larvae travel to the heart where they grow like spaghetti and wrap around the heart, squeezing it to death. Where Diana lived, it wasn't a problem. However, she traveled a lot and thought it would be better to be safe than sorry.

The next morning the great adVenture began for both of us. We both ate hurriedly and then were driven to the airport.

This airport was busy like the one in Washington, D.C. Although I was excited, I remained calm and professional. The Trainer had to leave us because he had to get the other students there in time to catch their planes. Just before leaving, he reached down and gave me a quick hug. "Goodbye, Venture," he said. "Remember that your club is for keeping that woman in line if she tries something she shouldn't. Be a good boy and remember to do all the things I taught you. The two of you have a wonderful life together."

I ran my mighty club. The Trainer had lately been drawing away from me, only stepping in to correct me. I loved him and didn't understand this change in him, but I had Diana and she really loved me. I wondered why this brief return to his old attitude of caring about me.

We had to wait several hours for the airplane, which had been delayed. Finally it came and they invited us to board first.

We were given the bulkhead seat. There were three seats across, and since there weren't a lot of people traveling, they gave me a seat. I didn't use it, of course, but I did appreciate the extra leg room that was available because another person wasn't sitting there.

Sure enough, the plane soon took off and I felt the familiar tilt upward. Diana reached down to pet me and reassure me that everything was all right. I wondered if just maybe she felt a little bit nervous about everything that was happening. I wasn't sure what I should do if this were true, so I laid my head on her foot and waved my mighty club. Its measured *thud thud thud* certainly made things feel normal. Soon Diana was settled back drinking the inevitable cup of coffee. (Everybody laughed at her because she loved coffee so much. She said that when the clock struck twelve o'clock midnight she must surely turn into a coffee bean.)

The food smelled interesting, and Diana ate it, but I don't think she was really hungry. It was just something to do.

The flight attendant came by and admired me. "What a lovely dog," she said. "His fur looks soft and plushy, but I'm confused about whether it's all right to pet those kinds of dogs."

"Well," answered Diana, "different schools do it different ways but you never go wrong if you ask."

"Can your dog be petted?" asked the young woman "If so, are there times he mustn't be petted?"

"Yes, you may pet Venture," replied Diana. "Petting some people's dogs causes a problem for them because the dog becomes very excited and the blind master can lose control over him. However, Venture is very placid and I don't have a problem with your petting him. For us, the important rule is, please don't pet him when he is working."

"But I don't quite understand," said the flight attendant. "Isn't Venture always working? If he's not, then why do you have him with you?"

"I haven't heard it put quite that way," replied Diana. "I guess you are right. Venture is, in a sense, always available to work, but the cue to him that he is working is that he is wearing his harness. Dogs don't see things the way you and I do. To him the harness means he is working. Although he may be sleeping, I may rouse him at any time to do something for me. Right now he is just resting even though we are traveling. If I were on the subway, or a short bus ride, you can be sure he would be wearing his harness. But this is a long trip and there is no good reason why he can't relax. Since he's not working, you are very welcome to pet him."

The flight attendant reached down and stroked my shining coat. I licked her hand and ran my mighty club.

"He likes me," exclaimed the flight attendant.

"Of course! He likes people who are nice to him," laughed Diana. "Don't you like most of the people who are nice and admire you?"

As they talked, a piece of paper fluttered to the ground from the flight attendant's hand. I picked it up and began to chew it. It wasn't especially tasty, but it was something to do. Diana heard me and bent down to see what I had.

"Venture must have found this on the floor," said Diana to the flight attendant. "I'm afraid he got it kind of soggy, but it feels like money. I don't have any so it must belong to you."

"Oh my goodness, Diana!" said the startled flight attendant. "That is a hundred dollar bill. I must have dropped it when I leaned over to pet Venture. It is part of the money I have for the sale of drinks on the plane. If you hadn't found it and given it back to me, I would have had to make it up out of my salary. Thank you so very much for returning it to me."

"Well," laughed Diana, "it wouldn't have done much good in Venture's tummy, now would it?"

"What do you do?" asked the flight attendant. "Do you work?"

"Yes," said Diana. "I work for an organization. We have several projects going. My area of concern is advocacy. There are many people who are disabled and are entitled to services that are available for disabled people. I work with organizations such as the Social Security Administration, medical organizations, and housing organizations. Those are all areas that are of concern to me and they often present very serious problems to people. I often go to hearings, project meetings, seminars, and other such affairs."

"And will you take Venture with you to these meetings?" inquired the flight attendant. "Every once in a while my boyfriend and I go to formal banquets, and I've never seen a dog at such affairs."

"Well, sometimes our lives take interesting paths. Maybe someday you will see Venture and me at a banquet. Then you can tell the people that you know us, and you can educate them about guide dogs."

"Wouldn't that be exciting?" mused the flight attendant. "We are getting near our stop and because we are so late, you won't be on the ground for very long. The new crew that will be taking over from us is already waiting. So until I see you at that banquet, you and Venture have a wonderful life together."

"Thank you," said Diana. "You have a great weekend. Who knows, we may meet again. Sometimes life is stranger than fiction."

Since we were going to have a short layover, and I had no need to get off the plane, we relaxed right where we were. We were waiting for the trip to begin when an older gentleman approached us.

"Hey, Miss," he said to Diana. "How much do the airlines charge you to let the darg ride up here with the passengers?"

"The law is very clear about that, sir," replied Diana. "A guide dog is welcome to ride with its blind master and the other passengers at no additional cost."

"That ain't right!" responded the man, beginning to raise his voice. "It ain't at all right, and you and that cur are a'gonna git off this here plane right now!" He came toward us, shaking his fist at Diana.

"I don't understand what the problem is, sir," she replied.

"Here's the problem," yelled the man. "My daughter has a beautiful collie dog. They made her crate the darn thing and put it in the baggage compartment. She had to pay over a hundred dollars. I'm gittin' you off this plane if it's the last thing I do."

"Sir," said Diana sweetly, "do you by chance wear glasses?"

"If you weren't so dumb," yelled the man, "you'd know I do."

"Did the airline charge you extra to bring them aboard—or perhaps suggest they would need to be crated and put with baggage?" asked Diana.

"Obviously you're a mental patient and somebody feels sorry for you so they let you bring the cur on the airplane. But I'm takin' you off!" the man fumed.

"I don't think you understand," said Diana quietly. "I am a blind person and the dog is a guide dog. He is for me what your glasses are for you. Just as no one would interfere with your glasses, no one will bother with mine. The difference between us is that you wear yours on your face. Mine are at the end of a leash and have a cold nose."

"You little smarty britches!" yelled the man. "I am takin' you and the cur off the plane this very minute. I'll teach you a lesson you won't ever forget!" and he grabbed for Diana.

My training hadn't prepared me for a problem like this. A guide dog is never supposed to be aggressive, but how could I be expected to lie there and put up with this? I decided to warn him that he was getting out of line and I wouldn't take much more. I rose to my full height and issued a low growl. At the same time, other passengers pulled the man away from Diana.

"Don't you touch her!" said a male passenger. "Who cares if your daughter's dog was put with the baggage? I think that's too good a place for a slimeball like you to ride. If anybody's getting off the plane, buddy, it's you. Now go away and quit bothering the lady, although I personally would cheer if the dog tore you apart."

"You jes' listen to me," yelled the first man. "Little Miss Smarty Britches and the cur ain't a'goin' on this airplane. I got my rights and she ain't a'stayin' on the plane. I'll git the police to throw her off!"

"You go try that," said Diana. There was a hard coldness in her voice that frightened me. "You see if you can get us off this aircraft," she continued, "because if you do, then you won't be continuing your trip either. If the airline makes me get off the plane, I will do so, but the plane won't go anywhere. You see, what you would be asking them to do is against federal law, and if they comply with your request, a call to the FAA will suspend their carrier license. That will mean that you won't be going anywhere either. I don't think the airline would enjoy paying the fine they would be assessed, nor would they want all the bad publicity they would get."

"We'll see, Smarty Britches," he yelled as he left the airplane.

"Could that really happen?" asked the passenger who had pulled the angry man away from us. "I sure hope it doesn't, because I'm getting married and it's a very large wedding. I don't even want to think about what it would be like if I couldn't make it."

"Don't worry," laughed Diana. "In the first place, the airline will ignore him. Even if they didn't, though, it would take a little time for the things I talked about to happen. Trust me, they would happen, but probably not today. You would get where you need to go."

"If they took you off the plane, a lot of us would get off, too," he replied. "After all, they aren't the only airline that flies to Los Angeles!"

Just then an agent appeared.

"Excuse me," he said. "There has been an objection made about the dog."

"I can't understand why," answered Diana. "When we booked the flight, we advised you that I would be accompanied by a guide dog."

"She and the dog got on in New York," said a woman passenger. "That dog has been perfect, which is a lot better than you can say about some of the other people on this plane. Can't you find something better to do than pick on this blind woman? Or is this 'pick on the handicapped day'?"

"Ma'am," said the agent, "my business is with the lady with the dog, so if you would please keep out of it..."

"You don't understand," said another man. "We are all making it our business, and the fact is, you don't need to bother this woman."

"There is a real question," replied the agent, "whether or not this dog is really a guide dog. If she can prove it, I'll be on my way."

"The guide dog harness is in the overhead compartment," said Diana. "I am unable to reach it, but here is my guide dog ID card."

The agent looked at the card. "Do you have any other proof this is a guide dog?" he asked.

Diana showed him my guide dog tags.

"Anyone could get these," the agent said. "Have you any other proof?"

Diana had me expose myself. On the inside of one of my legs is tattooed "Guide Dog Foundation" and their telephone number. Inside the other leg was tattooed my own ID number, matching the number on the card.

"Well," said the agent. "It appears he's a guide dog. My next question is, can you prove that you're blind?"

"I wonder if I could speak with your supervisor," said Diana. "I would also like to know your name. I have proven beyond question that I have a guide dog, placed by a guide dog school. That is surely all the proof you need."

"I guess I'll just be getting along," said the agent as he hurried from the plane.

"That was disgusting," said the man who had befriended us. "Is there anything that we can do about it?"

"You can tell one of the flight attendants what you saw and how foolishly their representative behaved. I will complain to the airline and they will investigate the complaint. If a couple of people could tell one of the flight attendants what happened, the airline will question them. It will be as though I have you there as personal witnesses, but you won't have to disrupt your personal lives."

"I'd like to know what happens," said our friend. "Is there any way we can find out?"

"Sure," said Diana. "Give me your name and address and I'll be glad to let you know what I find out."

Soon the flight attendants announced that we were ready to go, and again we became airborne. The gentleman who had befriended us approached. "Would you mind if I sit here with you?" he asked. "The only other seat available is beside that slimeball that was bothering you. Looking at him turns my stomach, and rather than smash his face in, I thought I would see if I could sit with you."

Having him sit there certainly didn't cause a problem for us, so Diana agreed readily. However, the adVenture wasn't over. No sooner had he settled himself than a flight attendant appeared and asked to see my ID card. The gentleman beside us was outraged.

"Look lady," he said, "I think this woman and her dog have had all the hassling by this airline they need, and I for one have had enough. I travel a lot, and you can just bet I'll never use this crummy airline again."

"I apologize to everyone for this inconvenience. I think a dozen people have related the shameful happenings before we boarded and I can't even begin to express my embarrassment at the situation," explained the flight attendant. "I just want to see if her ID card gives enough information to help agents verify that the dog is a guide dog. If not, I can notify the guide dog school and perhaps the problem can be prevented from happening again."

Diana held out the card. Both the flight attendant and our gentleman friend gasped. On the card was a photograph of Diana and me. It plainly showed me wearing a guide dog harness. The card certified that I was a guide dog from the Guide Dog Foundation.

"I was told," said the flight attendant "that our agent checked the dog's tags and your card, and still wanted further proof that he was a guide dog."

"That is correct," said Diana. "He also wanted additional proof that I was blind."

"Our airline doesn't often treat people like that," said the flight attendant.

"They did today," said our friend, "and I think it is disgusting. I want to complain about this myself. Whom do I contact?"

"I will be glad to give you that information," said the flight attendant. "Several other passengers are going to do so, too, and I am going to file a complaint based on what you folks have told me. What I want you to do, Diana, is be sure to file one also. The agent was out of line to act as he did after he saw this card. To tell you the truth, I would find it hard to believe one of our employees had behaved that way—except that there were about a dozen witnesses who all tell the same story. You may have all the drinks you like, on us. Be sure you write that letter."

"I will write a letter," answered Diana, "because this just shouldn't happen. It did make the trip entertaining, but what if I had been a different kind of person? I might never use my dog again, and that would be tragic."

"Point that out to the airline," said the flight attendant. "Now what can I get you to drink?"

"A cup of coffee will be just great," said Diana, "and maybe you could get something for my friend here."

"Of course," she agreed. "What would you like, sir?"

"A sunrise would be just great—thank you, Diana."

After a light luncheon was served, the flight attendant returned.

"I know you must be getting tired of this subject," she said, "but the man who created this disturbance asked me to give you this twenty-dollar bill."

"Diana," said our friend, "you aren't going to take that, are you?"

"No," said Diana. Handing the money back to the flight attendant, she said: "Please tell the gentleman thank you, but guide dog Venture has everything that he could possibly need. However, if he'd like to make that donation to the Guide Dog Foundation, it would undoubtedly be very well received."

"Why didn't you take the money and give it to the school?" asked our friend. "That old scumbag probably won't give it to them."

"He would say the same about me if I accepted it," said Diana. "He wouldn't learn a lesson, and the other passengers would think I had been bought off for twenty dollars. If he does make a donation to the school, it will leave a positive impression in his mind."

"We'll never know," replied our new friend. "The flight is almost over—I can see Los Angeles out the window. Is someone meeting you at the airport?"

"Yes," said Diana. "A girlfriend of mine should be waiting for us. She will really enjoy hearing about this trip."

"Be sure and write that letter," said our friend.

"I will," said Diana. "Have a lovely wedding and a wonderful life, and my best to the bride."

Soon people were getting off the plane. We waited until everyone was off, then the flight attendant walked off with us. Diana's friend, Fritsey, was there to meet us.

The two women seemed happy to see each other and chattered together happily.

"Oh, Diana," gushed Fritsey. "Venture is so beautiful. He is just about the same color as Little Haze and he has that same sweet look on his face. When do you think I can pet him?"

"Venture is very calm," said Diana, "so I would normally say you could pet him when I take his harness off. But you're going to see him so often he will come to think of you as family. Let's give him a chance to adjust to his professional role before you start playing with him. You and I both know it's not going to stop with just petting him. You'll romp and play ball and have all kinds of fun together, so let's not start that until he's adjusted a little bit to his new home."

"Well, OK," pouted Fritsey. "But you will let me play with him sometime, won't you?"

"Of course," answered Diana. "Right now, I'm exhausted. Something very interesting—but not altogether pleasant—happened on the trip. I'll tell you about it on the way home. Right now, let's see if we can get the luggage. I think I told you that it was lost when I went to get Venture. It took them a week to find it. Thank goodness I wasn't wearing a suit, hose, and heels, and had some extra clothes in my carry-on."

I have since discovered that traveling with Diana usually means lost luggage. After waiting around for forty-five minutes, the airline agent agreed the luggage must have been put on another plane. He promised that just as soon as they could find it, they would deliver it to Diana's home. They did, too—a week later.

Since Fritsey hadn't eaten, we stopped at a restaurant on the way home. I was quite amazed as we got out of the car. When we had left New York that morning, it was cold—four degrees above zero, somebody said. Fritsey said that it had been eighty degrees in Los Angeles that day. As I walked across the parking lot, the ground felt warmer under my feet. The air was drier, and I could detect the delicate perfume of flowering shrubs. Certainly I had stepped into a whole new world.

I don't think Diana ate much, but the two women chatted for a long time. Diana related our adVenture on the airplane, and I was very much admired by everyone who saw me.

Diana was very tired, so after a while, Fritsey took us to Diana's apartment.

"Can't I just give that sweet thing a hug?" pleaded Fritsey.

"Let him settle a little first," suggested Diana. "This boy is a real love bug. Once you start to pet him, you will nevermore have peace. He will make it your calling in life to be a petting machine."

"Well, goodnight, you two. See you tomorrow," said Fritsey as she hurried to her car.

We had much more room in Diana's apartment than we did in her room at the school.

"I know you'd like to check out your new home," said Diana.

"But until you have adjusted to your new surroundings, they said to keep you on tie-down for the first month. What I'm going to do is feed you and take you out. Once you have taken care of yourself, I will allow you to be loose for a few minutes. I will be watching you, you old butt, so don't give me any trouble."

I was hungry and enjoyed my dinner. When Diana took me out, I took care of my business right away, although it was really a temptation to stay outside in this fairyland. The sun had set and the air was getting cool, but nothing like the cold back East.

Diana kept her word about letting me check things out. For about ten minutes, we wandered about the house together looking at things. I observed that a female dog had visited not too long ago. I found one of her toys and Diana said I could have it. I loved it. It is called a kong toy but Diana said the pet shop called it a tuffy. She explained to me that she had gotten it for Little Haze. Little Haze didn't come to visit often, but I would come to know her very well because her master worked very closely with mine. I didn't know it then, but Little Haze would become one of the most important influences in my life. Now, however, checking out my new home and playing with the tuffy were what was important and I threw myself wholeheartedly into it.

"All right, you mighty butt! Play time is over," said Diana. "I'm going to take a bubble bath. You may come into the bathroom with me if you like."

I ran my mighty club.

From where I was, I watched Diana pour her bath. The delightful fragrance I had first noticed on my collar floated strongly in the air.

Diana brought me into the bathroom and closed the door. After undressing, she stepped into the mass of bubbles.

"Boy, I sure missed a hot bath at the school," she said to me. "A shower is great when you are in a hurry, but it is hard to find a more pleasant way to relax than in a hot tub."

She had left the door to the tub enclosure open, so I stuck my golden head in to get a good look.

"Get out, you butt," laughed Diana. "This isn't for you."

I pulled my head back, but I was fascinated by the bubbles, so I put my paw in.

"No!" yelled Diana. "This is not for a big butt like you," and with that she pulled the tub enclosure closed.

I was very happy and ran my mighty club. Its mighty *thud thud thud* made a very loud noise as I ran it against the tub. Diana continued with her bath, but told me while she was bathing what a very good boy I was. This made me run my club some more.

Finally, Diana emerged, saying that she was very tired and wanted to go to bed. She put the tie-down by the bed and secured me there.

"Since this is all so new to you, Venture, and since you might feel a little strange, I will spend a little time on the floor with you," said Diana as she got a blanket and a pillow for herself.

She lay on the floor stroking me and talking to me, but as she talked her voice became slurred and soon the fingers that had been playing in my shining coat were still. The conversation was replaced by slow heavy breathing. Diana had fallen asleep.

I thought back over the day. How interesting life with Diana was. I was very lucky to have such a kind and loving master. She didn't have to spend the time on the floor with me. I would have been glad to serve her without the new toy and all the special attention she lavished on me. But I was more than glad to have it. I wondered idly if Banner had it this good. Well, Banner was pleased with his life, and I was delighted with mine.

As I snuggled against the sleeping Diana, I laid my head on the pillow next to hers and renewed that vow I had made a long time ago. I would be the very best guide dog I could be and I added that my ambition was to be the greatest golden butt ever, the envy of everyone who saw me.

Hanging Loose

A secure home life is very important to the stability and well-being of a guide dog. That is why Diana took an additional week off from work—to be with me, to orient me to my new surroundings, and to strengthen the working relationship between us. I was lucky that Diana realized how vital our relationship is, and, although sleeping on the floor with me was not at all necessary, it was very special to begin my first day at home as a pro, with my very own person on my level.

Diana didn't think that it was so great, though. You should have heard the moaning and groaning when she woke up.

"Venture, you big wonderful butt!" she said as she pulled herself off the floor. "The floor is a good place for a mighty butt like you, but an old woman like me needs to be on a bed. I can't believe how exhausted I must have been. Poor baby, you must have been tired, too. Also, all of this must be so strange to you."

I ran my mighty club in agreement. Experience at the school had taught me that Diana could become very busy, and when that happened, she didn't have much time to spend wondering what might be on my mind. I think I heard a saying once, "Make hay while the sun shines." To me, Diana's attention was as good as the sun, so I rolled over and let her rub my tummy.

After she had fed me, given me water, and taken me out, I was again allowed a few minutes of freedom. I enjoyed romping about and playing with the kong toy.

"I have been gone a long time, so I have some things to do," said Diana as she secured my tie-down to the dining room table. "You be a good boy and take care of things for me. After I finish these chores, we have some errands to run, and after that we will take a long walk. If you are very good, and do everything perfectly, then we will go to a special store where I will buy you a surprise—but I really don't expect you to be perfect the first day. If you are distracted in your work, or if you act up, then you will have to wait for your surprise. Being professional means being under full control. If I let you play and have too many toys all at once, it will interfere with that control. What I am trying to explain is that you have to grow into things. Maybe the tuffy is all you can handle right now, but soon you can have other things. Do you think you understand, Venture?"

I ran my mighty club. I didn't really know what she was talking about, but I did know that her attention was centering on me. I was happy. Perhaps this was really going to work out well. I liked her concern about me so I settled down contentedly and chewed on my bone.

Soon, the air was filled with the smell of brewing coffee. Diana's coffee smelled different than the coffee did at the school. That is because she prefers to grind fresh coffee beans. It smells wonderful. But I tasted it once, and I prefer other things. I think anyone who would like that stuff is weird.

Diana put a plate on the table and placed something called a Zinger on it. Now, that Zinger did not smell weird, so I moved over to get a better look. Just then, Diana's telephone rang and she stepped away to answer it. I looked at the Zinger. It seemed so interesting. I stood up and stretched my neck up to get a better look at it. Um, that Zinger sure smelled good! My tongue came out of my mouth, and that Zinger kind of came onto my tongue. I ate it hurriedly. It was good, but it sure didn't last long.

Suddenly, Diana was there prying open my mouth.

"Venture!" she said. "You are bad. I know you ate my Zinger, because it is gone and I can smell vanilla on your breath. Oh, but I guess I can't punish you for it because I didn't actually catch you stealing it! Watch it boy! I have been very good to you, but you will be punished for stealing from me."

I ran my mighty club. Diana brought the telephone over to the table beside me.

"I know that butt stole my Zinger," she said to her friend over the telephone. "Venture is such a doll. He is so sweet and charming about everything and he acts so innocent about his stealing. It really is hard to keep a straight face when scolding him. However, it isn't good for him to eat things like that and if he can get away with stealing that, he will go on to bigger and better things. Pretty soon, if I don't put a halt to it now, no one, including me, will want him around. So this kind of thing will have to stop. He got away with it this time, but he will try it again and next time, I will catch the little butt. I told him that if he is good I will get him a special surprise. He really has been a good boy, but I want to be sure that he is working OK before introducing him to more excitement."

After she finished with the telephone, Diana busied herself around the apartment. Then she changed her clothes and got my harness. My interest immediately perked up because I was going to have to work.

I was amazed as we walked down the sidewalk. The sun put forth caressing fingers, the pavement was warm beneath my feet, and the air was warm and dry. Again I noticed perfume from flowers, and wondered anew at this beautiful place Diana had brought me to. I had been happy at the Guide Dog Foundation. They had been very kind to me there, and all of my needs had been met. Now that I was in California, all my concerns about a strange place were disappearing. Certainly I had stepped into a fairyland, and my person was like a fairy godmother. No one since William seemed to worry about how I felt and what I wanted as much as Diana did.

The building Diana directed me to enter was called a bank. I was a little confused about what one did in such a place, but someone saw Diana and me and came over to us.

"Oh, Diana!" she exclaimed. "I see you have your guide dog.

He is just gorgeous. What was the weather like in New York? I saw on TV that they had a blizzard while you were there. I wondered how you were getting along."

"It was really cold," said Diana. "But what bothered me was the rain. It was so bone-chilling."

"This must be a big change for the dog," said the woman. "What is his name?"

"Venture," answered Diana. "I think it really fits him because he is very much into business and ventures, not to mention the adVentures that he seems to take in stride."

"I can tell by his eyes that he is a real heartbreaker," laughed the bank lady. "But I think he is unsure what he is supposed to do. I will help you." With that, she grabbed my harness and began to pull me after her.

"Excuse me," said Diana. "Venture does need help, but that is not the best way to do it."

"Why not?"

"First of all," said Diana, "although Venture doesn't know what he is supposed to do, it is me you are actually helping. Think of it like this. Venture is like my glasses. Granted, he is very charming and delightful, but still, he is like my glasses. Now, if you were going to help someone, you wouldn't grab their glasses, would you?"

"No, of course not," said our friend.

"So," said Diana, "though you may desire to help Venture, he's here for me, and I'm the one you should help. The best way to do that is to let me take your arm. That puts you a half step in front of me so I always know what to expect, even if it involves going up or down some steps."

"But I thought Venture was supposed to tell you if there were something you could fall over," said the lady.

"That's true unless someone else is helping me. When you are guiding me, he is no longer responsible. Did you notice that I am not holding his harness?"

"But I still don't understand," said our friend. "Why does Venture abandon his role as guide when I take your arm?"

"Because," explained Diana, "you have become the guide. I am now taking directions from you, so he just follows along. Two guides are definitely not better than one. Also remember, the reason you're helping me is that Venture wasn't sure what to do."

"He didn't look pleased when I touched his harness," admitted the lady. "Why was that?"

"To him," said Diana, "the harness is very private. It is the thing that links him with me. He would never bite you, or show any violence toward you for touching it, but you might expect the same reaction if you wanted to touch his feet. They are his personal private possession and he would doubtless be disturbed if you wanted to handle them."

As they talked, we joined a line, and soon it was our turn to be helped at the counter.

"Thank you for your help," said Diana to the lady. "Because you showed him about waiting in line, Venture will probably know what to do when we come in here next time. He probably will understand lines in other places now too. He is very smart, and catches on quickly."

"Thank you for explaining it to me," said the lady. "You explain things very well. If you need help again when you come in here, you know where I am."

After we finished at the bank, we went to the post office because Diana had letters to mail. "Later, Venture," she told me, "I will teach you what a mailbox is."

We had to go several other places. Then Diana took me to where we would catch the bus. It was there waiting for us as though it knew we were going to need it. We got on and Diana told the driver that we wanted to go to the mall. When the bus arrived there, we got off, and the adVenture of trying to find our way around the mall began.

Diana knew about the layout of the mall, so that made things easier. However, there was a post in the middle of the mall. I had my mind on getting across the mall, and I didn't really have my mind on guiding Diana like I should have. I didn't leave enough room for her to clear the pole, and she smashed right into it.

I was dismayed. Diana had been so nice to me and I didn't mean for her to get hurt.

Boy did she ever get mad at me. "Venture!" she said loudly. "You nasty, wicked dog! You are bad! Bad! Bad! Bad!" and she began striking the pole.

"You better not do that bad thing again, you evil, bad, wicked thing!" she stormed. "If you ever do that again, you bad dog, I won't keep you around! Bad! Bad! Bad!"

I was very upset that my person was so displeased with me. I licked my lips and hung my head in shame. This was just terrible. What could I do?

A woman came bustling up with a security guard.

"Look here!" she cried at the top of her lungs. "This woman is a being mean to this here poor blind dog. I demand that you arrest her this very minute!"

"Well, now just a minute, lady," answered the security guard. "Seems to me like you don't know everything there is to know about this situation. For instance, looks to me like the woman is blind and the dog can see just fine."

"I saw her hitting the pole with her hand a'scarin' that nice dog. Look at how upset he is and him bein' so beautiful and all."

"Unfortunately, his beauty has nothing to do with it," explained Diana. "Look at my face. If you want to be upset about something, let me tell you, it hurts a whole lot to run into that pole! Yes, this is a sweet, sensitive dog, but my safety is his responsibility. He wasn't paying attention. If I ignore this, next time it may be a flight of stairs. He has been trained to watch out for things like this, and if I don't enforce it when he does wrong, I basically untrain him. That's not the best thing for either of us."

"What right do you have to put such demands on that beautiful dog?" snarled the woman. "What are you going to do to him if he makes the same mistake again?"

"Wait a minute," said the security guard. "I don't see that she is doing anything wrong."

"Yes, she is," screamed the angry woman, "and your boss will fire you for not arresting her!"

"No, he won't," said the security guard, beginning to lose patience. "You're the one who is making a scene. It was the woman who got hurt, not the dog. Did she hit the dog for his error? No, she hit the post. The post can take a lot worse than that before it becomes my problem."

"You've got to arrest this unreasonable blind person," the woman raved.

"The only person who is going to be arrested is you, ma'am, if you don't stop causing a disturbance," said the security guard, putting aside all semblance of patience.

Diana turned me around and took me back to the entrance of the mall.

"Now, Venture, let's try this again. This time I expect you to be more careful."

As we passed the post, I made sure there was lots of room for Diana. She told me that I was a good boy, so I guessed she had forgiven me. She directed me to a restaurant. When the hostess appeared, Diana told me to "follow" and we were shown to our table.

Soon Fritsey joined us, and over luncheon, Diana told of our morning's adVenture.

"I will take you home," said Fritsey. "There is a lot of mail. Do you want to go by the pet store?"

"No," said Diana. "I think Venture needs a few days more before I get him new toys. I think it would be best just not to go there. Anyway, I am just dying to hear about all those sweepstakes I have won. What are there, about twenty of them?"

The two women left the restaurant, accompanied by me. Of course everyone watched them and there were murmurs of what a wonderful, beautiful dog I was.

They went back to Diana's apartment, where they worked on things they were interested in. They pretty much ignored me until just before Fritsey left. Then Diana took me out, and I was given a few minutes of freedom.

I grabbed the tuffy in my mouth and went over to Fritsey, where I growled an invitation to play.

"Oh, Venture, Diana says I can't, yet, but our day will come. I have already bought you a frisbee, and it's at home waiting for the day Diana will let us play together in the park."

I ran my mighty club, dropped the kong toy on her foot, and growled very loudly.

"Do you think it is a little early to give him the freedom you are giving him, as well as letting him play with the kong toy? Could that be causing problems for him?" asked Fritsey.

"I don't think so," said Diana. "I only let him loose for a few minutes, and that time is very closely supervised. I didn't plan for him to have the kong toy right away, but he found it himself, so I figured he may as well have it. I don't think he needs anything new yet, though."

"Well," said Fritsey as she picked up her purse and her car keys. "If we could get any of those sweepstakes, Venture could have all kinds of things. How many of them did we throw away?"

"Thirty-five!" said Diana. "I know all these things are junk. That's why I never enter any of them. You would think that when they don't get a response, they would take me off their mailing list."

"Well, they are really wasting their time when it comes to us," said Fritsey. "See you two later."

That evening Diana brushed and combed my shining coat.

"I think you're doing quite well, Venture," she said as she rubbed my fur. "I wish what happened in the mall hadn't happened. But it is normal for a guide dog who is new to make a few mistakes. On the whole you are doing well, and I know your Trainer would be proud of you."

I ran my mighty club.

That night, Diana went to sleep in her own bed, but I was comfortable with that. When she was at the school, that had always been the way it had been. During the night, Diana reached out and stroked me and murmured that I was a good boy. It had been nice to have her on the floor with me, but I could accept her not being there.

The next day was a lot like the day before, with some important differences. Diana took me out as usual, gave me water and food, and then proceeded to make coffee. If only it tasted like those fresh beans smell—but it doesn't, so that ended my interest in it.

Again, Diana put a plate on the table beside her coffee. I think she had a Zinger on it, although it didn't smell as strongly as it had yesterday. No sooner had Diana sat down than the phone rang and she went to answer it. I got up to have a better look at the Zinger. As before, I stretched out my neck, and the Zinger kind of came into my mouth. But this time it was different. It didn't have much taste and it kind of crackled as I chewed on it. Finally, I punctured the crackly stuff. Just as the good, full flavor of the Zinger was coming through, Diana swooped down upon me, pried open my mouth, and took away the Zinger.

She shouted, "Shame! Shame! Shame! You wicked, filthy, disgraceful, evil thief! Bad! Bad! Bad!" She administered a sharp snap on my collar.

"You bad dog!" she continued as she pushed away my toys, and put me in a corner. "After all that I have tried to do for you, the least you could do is try to be good, but oh, no. What I have done for you isn't enough. You have to steal from me. Bad! Bad! Bad! I don't know if I ever want to see you again. If you don't straighten up, I am going to send you back to the Guide Dog Foundation, and ask them to give me something better than a thief like you. Bad dog! Bad! Bad! Bad!"

I was ashamed. I never meant to make Diana so angry. I didn't mean any harm. I hadn't expected her to mind if I ate the Zinger. I lay very quietly. Not even my mighty club disturbed the silence.

Diana ignored me and went back to the telephone.

"Well, I got the little devil!" she said to her friend. "Remember yesterday, I told you he had stolen from me and that I was going to catch him. My plan worked perfectly. I put the Zinger on the plate, but this time I didn't unwrap it. When I heard the cellophane, I knew he had it. You couldn't have called at a better time if we had planned it. Now, he is tied over in the corner, and he is very quiet. He thinks I am real mad at him. I am going to let him continue to think that for a while. He is so very charming. I hate to set him up to hurt his feelings like that, but I know that if I don't, I may lose the opportunity to break that unfortunate habit."

After a while, Diana seemed to forget about the Zinger.

"Today, Venture," she said as she got my harness, "I am going to show you what a mailbox is."

I ran my mighty club in thanks. Again it seemed Diana loved me. I knew what a lot of things were. I understood "Find a phone," "Find a bus bench," and "To the elevator," but I had no idea what a mailbox was.

Diana harnessed me, and we walked around the corner. Diana dropped the harness handle and said softly, "Venture, find the mailbox. Mailbox, mailbox, mailbox." She began going toward the curb. Her hand encountered a big container.

"Good boy!" she said "Good mailbox, good boy. Isn't this a good mailbox?" she said as she patted the mailbox.

I got the idea and I was very happy. I jumped around waving my mighty club, while Diana continued to praise me and pat the mailbox.

"You mighty butt!" said Diana. "You are a very wonderful boy. Now what I wonder is, do you think you can remember what the mailbox is? We are going home now, but throughout the day, I will take you to the area of the mailbox and ask you to find the mailbox. After you show me you can do that, then we will look for a mailbox in a different place. Do you think you can handle that, you mighty butt, you?"

I waved my mighty club. Working with Diana was so much fun.

Several times that day we went to the corner and Diana told me to "Find the mailbox." I needed help the first time, but then I understood and took her to it when she asked me to.

"Now comes the acid test," said Diana as we walked for several blocks. After we had crossed the street, Diana said softly, "Venture, find a mailbox." She did not drop the harness handle nor did she try to find it. I didn't see a mailbox right away, but I spied one in the middle of the block. I hurried to it and placed my nose on it.

"Good boy!" exclaimed Diana. "You are wonderful! What a good mailbox!" and she patted the mailbox.

A little old lady came bustling up to us. She grabbed Diana's hand.

"Oh, Miss," she said. "That thing there is a mailbox. This here's your dog," and she placed Diana's hand on my head. Just as quickly as she had come, she was gone.

Diana petted me and laughed. "That lady thought I couldn't tell you from a mailbox!" she exclaimed. "Let's catch a bus and go to the pet store. I think you know what a mailbox is, and that we've created enough confusion for today. Remember I promised to get you a surprise? I have decided to get you a couple of things because you are such a wonderful boy."

I agreed with that, so I waved my mighty club.

We made an about-face, and soon we were at the bus stop. This time Diana asked that the bus driver let us off at a different place. She told everyone how wonderful I was, and that we were going to the pet store for a very special treat.

When we got off the bus, Diana directed me to cross the street, then turned left. We had gone up the street a little way when Diana began to say "Inside, Venture. INSIDE."

I discovered a door that led into a fascinating place. Little birds chirped. Kittens cried, and the air was full of interesting smells. Diana told me to find the "counter." With all those interesting sights and sounds, it was very hard, but I did what I was told, then sat quietly in front of her while she conducted her business.

"I have a very good boy here," said Diana to the man behind the counter, who seemed to know her. "I would like a very special latex squeak toy for him."

"Yes," said the man. "I got your message that you wanted me to keep my eyes open for something really special, and I think I have something unusual. Before I show it to you, I need to ask you a question. Have you given any thought to whether or not this is a safe toy for this valuable dog to play with? You know, it has a little squeaker in it and if the dog chews it out of the toy, it could catch in his throat and kill him. So before I show it to you, please tell me if I am worrying about nothing."

"That could be a real concern," agreed Diana, "and it might happen if I allow Venture to play with the toy unsupervised. You are correct. It is not like a bone, or the kong. This is a toy that has to be watched very carefully. It is something that he cannot play with alone. Whenever he has it, I must be there to make sure what you talked about doesn't happen. I will explain it to him in a way that he will understand, and yet will be fun for him."

"OK," said the clerk. "Just so you know what you are doing. As you know, there are two kinds of squeak toys. Latex is best. It is a fine, strong, durable rubber. Vinyl is different. It is not durable and it cracks. Although it is much cheaper, it will not last very long. I have something really cute for you—a green hedgehog. Let me show you."

Diana took the hedgehog into her hands. "This is perfect," she said. "A big toy, and it looks so interesting. I think Venture will like it. Do you want to look at it, boy?"

I waved my mighty club and reached up to take it.

"No, Venture," said Diana. "For now you only get to look at it. When we get home I will introduce it to you."

I watched as she gave the man money and then put my new toy into her purse. I nosed her bag, but Diana pushed me away, and together we left the interesting store. We caught the bus and went home. All the while, Diana held onto my new toy and never once even let me have a peep at it.

When we got home, I remembered that it was dinnertime, so I forgot about the toy for a while. After I had been out, Diana got her purse and took out the toy.

"Venture," she said, "This is your surprise. This is a very special toy, because it is different from the ball, the bone, and the kong. It is different because it has a little voice. So you must be very gentle. Say hello to Mr. Hedgehog."

I nosed the toy and Diana made it squeak. I was astonished.

Diana held out the hedgehog to me. "Here, Venture," she said. "You play with him, but remember that because he has a little voice, you must be gentle with him."

I took the hedgehog gingerly. It squeaked. I ran my mighty club with delight and batted the hedgehog with my mighty paws. He squeaked again.

"Bring him to me, Venture," said Diana. I did as she said and after making him squeak a few times, Diana tossed him in the air. I caught him and ran around the room making his voice go.

"Good boy," said Diana. "Bring him to me."

Diana threw him several times more. Then she said, "The hedgehog is tired now and your play time is over."

I made his voice go.

"Bring him here, Venture. He needs to go to bed now. Night night. Night night."

Diana washed him under running water, then put him on the table. She secured me to my tie-down across the room. This had been a wonderful experience and I was sad that the hedgehog was tired. I lay down with my bone and the kong.

"You have done very well," said Diana. "Tomorrow, we go to work. Vacation is over. I think you will enjoy the office, and the hedgehog will be here ready to play when we get home."

I had enjoyed myself very much, so I chewed contentedly on my bone and ran my mighty club. Its measured *thud thud thud* seemed to heighten the importance of tomorrow.

Billyum And
Little Haze

We got up quite a bit earlier than usual, and Diana bustled about getting ready to go to work. She took care of me, of course, but I didn't feel that her attention was centered on me. I understood that this was the way things had to be sometimes. That didn't mean that I had to like it.

When Diana finally sat down to drink her coffee, I decided to bring up her lack of attention to me. However, I knew there were certain things I mustn't do, such as get her Zinger. I bounced my kong about, then I spied my hedgehog. I wanted to play with that hedgehog but I knew better than to try to get it off the table. I couldn't reach it anyway because of the tie-down, so I growled my wishes to Diana.

"All right, you mighty butt," she said. "I will let you loose for a few minutes to play with your new toy. In fact, I will play with you, but then I have some things to talk with you about. Now remember, I want you to have fun playing with Mr. Hedgehog but his little voice makes him delicate, and you have to be gentle with him. Also you will have to be a good boy and work carefully, or Mr. Hedgehog will have to go away. Do you understand, Venture?"

I ran my mighty club.

Diana unsnapped my tie-down, and got Mr. Hedgehog. She made his voice run, then threw him into the air. The game was on. I kicked him around the room and ran his little voice. I brought him to Diana when she asked me to, and she played with me an extra long time.

"OK," she said at last. "Time for Mr. Hedgehog to go nighty-night. Night-night. Night-night!" and she rinsed him off under running water and put him back where he lived on the table.

"Venture, come," she said as she snapped on my tie-down. "I want to explain some things to you before we go to work."

Diana sat on the floor beside me. I put my head in her lap and ran my mighty club.

"I want you to know what it will be like when we go to work," she said. I exposed myself and she began to rub my tummy.

"Our business is very small," she began. "I work with disabled adults. Some of them are going to be afraid of you. I will keep you on tie-down for a while. Many of these people lack confidence. You and I are a team now, so I expect you to do your part. I don't know just what that is, but I know that you will know. I expect to see results, OK?

"The other thing that is important for you to understand is about my co-worker, Billyum. Billyum is an expert in computers and adaptive equipment. He also has an exceptional guide dog whom we call Little Haze.

"My family had this expression when we were growing up. If you did something that was good, then it was yum, or yumston. However, if you were bad, then you were yuck or yuckston. You already know about yuckston and yumston, because I have called you yuck and yum."

I remembered. In fact, I am always yumston except for those few times I displease Diana. At such times, Diana calls me yuckston. But considering everything, I am most yumston, and Diana is lucky to have someone like me. Now, I didn't argue with her, I just ran my mighty club—my yumston mighty club.

"Once he understood the principle of yuckston and yumston," continued Diana, "Bill decided that he would proclaim himself as yumston. I argued that this was not the way you do it. It is our acts that make us yumston, not we ourselves. Bill kept saying he was yumston and a lady friend of his said she believed that maybe he was right—after all, his name was Will-Yum. So, from that day forward, he has been Billyum. He even signs office memos that way.

"Of course, Little Haze is often called Hazeyum and when I do something he really likes, he calls me Diyum. I have to go get dressed for work now. Because it is my first day back, I will dress a little more casually so I can get down on the floor and say hello to Little Haze. You would do well to use her as a role model, Venture. I have seen a lot of guide dogs, but it would be hard to find one as good as she is. Little Haze is very special."

I ran my mighty club. Diana had said nothing about Little Haze being mighty, and we both knew that the best guide dog anywhere was right there at her feet. Maybe I was new, but I would be the role model soon enough.

Diana always carried on regular conversations with me. I did not always know exactly what she meant, but hearing the sound of her voice and knowing I was included in her thoughts and plans really made my life special. I know lots of folks don't do that with their guide dogs. Fortune had really smiled on me when Diana came into my life. I didn't always know what she needed from me, but I would always give her better than the best. No other guide dog would try quite as hard as me, and if I do say so myself, you would have to look long and hard to find my equal—with the possible exception of Little Haze.

Diana and I made our way to the bus. On the way, Diana asked me to show her a mailbox. This I did with no coaching from her. She was very pleased, and when I found the bus bench for her, she praised me effusively.

It took a little time to get to work. We had to change buses, but everything went smoothly. Soon Diana was telling me to go "Inside" an office building. We walked down a hallway and Diana unlocked an office. I looked around with interest. The female dog who had been in our apartment—the previous owner of my kong—had been here recently. In fact, I was pretty sure she had been here only a few minutes ago. However, Diana didn't care about the office. She snapped on my tie-down and went right to the telephone, where she talked for some time. Sometimes I think Diana would consider herself in a life-threatening situation if she didn't have a telephone and a cup of coffee.

Finally, though, I heard her make a call and say, "I'm ready to bring Venture in to meet you now. Are you braced for this experience?"

We walked across the hall to another office. Diana knocked, then went in.

At first, it looked to me like just another office. Then a rather dull mechanical voice said "Welcome to California, Venture, you mighty butt."

The little voice had come from Billyum's computer. He sat there laughing and said, "How did you like that, Di?" It seemed to me that I had seen Billyum somewhere before. Then something caught my eye that made me forget all about the computer and Billyum.

When I had lived with William, one of his mom's hobbies was collecting little sculptures. She used to brag to her friends about how extensive her collection was, and I suppose it was very valuable. When I was near, William was constantly reminded to keep me under control because Royal Dolton and Casada were very fragile, precious sculptures. One of them was quite large and beautiful.

What now caught my attention far exceeded the beauty and poise of any sculpture. There, sitting regally, was the most beautiful and delicate little dog I had ever seen. I guess that some folks would call her a big dog, but I wouldn't. She weighed fifty-three pounds, and if you compare that with my eighty pounds, that is a little dog.

She just sat there, like a treasured museum piece, except her wonderful eyes didn't miss a thing. I guess you could say I really lost my heart. How could anyone walk away from this glorious creation unmoved?

There was a small silence which was broken by the sculpture coming to life. As she bounded to me, her every move was pure poetry.

"Welcome, Venture," she said as she gave me a delicate kiss and wagged her lovely tail. "Goodness! You are mighty and you are beautiful, too. I hope that you are not upset about being called a 'butt.' I wonder why they gave Diana such a large dog. She is only five feet three-and-a-half and weighs all of 112 pounds. Billyum is six feet tall and weighs about 180 pounds, and I am only eighteen inches tall from the shoulder to the floor, which is the way they measure us. How tall are you?"

"Twenty-four inches," I said proudly. "And how did you know that I am called a 'butt'?"

"Oh, Billyum told me," laughed Little Haze. "I don't know why they give us such terrible nicknames. Mine is 'Sleaze,' or 'Slimer,' but when Billyum calls me those things, I know that he loves me."

"Get back over here, you Sleaze," said Billyum. "You don't need to hog the show. Let Billyum get a chance to see the Butt," and he held out his arms to me.

I went to Billyum. Something was sure familiar about him, but I just couldn't recall where I had seen him. I knew, though, that it was very important. When was it? I couldn't remember but I did enjoy the way his fingers played with my ears. I exposed myself so that he could rub my tummy.

He and Diana discussed business for a while. I guess the two of them worked together on a letter to the airline. Diana can type, but she worked on composing the letter, while Billyum put it on the word processor in the computer. It was interesting to see how they worked. Little Haze and I watched them as we got acquainted.

"Well," said Diana after quite a long time had gone by, "I think that takes care of that. I will address an envelope and Venture and I will mail this on the way home. How about lunch, Billyum?"

"It's in the refrigerator," said Billyum. "After we take the mutts out, and have some lunch, I thought I would take you and Venture to that new ice cream store. I heard that it had opened while you were gone. As you know, I don't give Little Haze ice cream often, but today, I will treat all of you to ice cream if you would like."

"That sounds yumston," said Diana. "I haven't let Venture have any yet, but he has been being a good boy and I can see no reason why he can't have some."

As we lay under the table, Little Haze asked, "Do you like ice cream, Venture?"

"I've never had any," I answered.

"Well," said Little Haze, "if you enjoy Zingers, you are going to love ice cream."

"How do you know about the Zingers?" I asked.

"Oh," laughed Little Haze, "you know about the telephone. Diana was talking to Billyum when she caught you."

"But I don't understand," I said. "Why is it all right to have ice cream, and wrong to have the Zinger?"

"We as guide dogs are here for the pleasure and well-being of our blind masters," replied Little Haze. "Doing what they want is part of our job. Now Zingers aren't really good for us and although they taste wonderful, they could make us very sick. I eat that same special kind of food you do. It is perfectly balanced to meet all of our needs, and it is good too. Sometimes though, your master may decide that on some special occasion such as your birthday, you may have a special treat. If she offers it to you, then of course you may accept and enjoy it. If however, you don't want it, then it would be all right if you refuse it."

"Forgive me if I seem dumb, Little Haze," I said, "but you just said that Zingers weren't good for us. If you're Ms. Guide Dog Extraordinaire, as you seem to be, how would you know what a Zinger tastes like?"

"I guess all of us have done little badnesses," confessed Little Haze. "When I had been home for just a few days, I helped myself to one on Billyum's plate. Talk about a reaction! Billyum got real mad at me. He gave me a very severe correction, and called me the most yuckston thing he had ever heard of. He wouldn't forgive me for a long time."

"Diana did the same things to me," I confided, not feeling so alone. If the perfect Little Haze could be guilty of an indiscretion, then I guessed that there might be hope that I could be considered Mr. Guide Dog Extraordinaire.

"I wonder, though, Little Haze," I said. "If a Zinger wouldn't be good for us, and ice cream tastes like a Zinger, what makes it OK?"

"I am certain that it isn't the best thing for us," answered Little Haze. "But what makes it different is that your master offers it to you. Ice cream is very yumston. It is my favorite treat although I usually just get it on my birthday. It probably isn't good for them either, but humans are often not careful about what would be best for them. For example, did you have people in your class that smoked?"

"Yes, we did," I said.

"Well, there you go," said Little Haze. "There is a lot of information to tell people that smoking is not good for them. People know they can suffer and die a very painful death from doing it, but does that make them stop? Oh, no! They just keep puffing away and very bad things happen to some of them."

"Is ice cream as bad for them as smoking?" I asked.

"I don't think so. You never know what's going to make them sick, though. I don't think they could eat our dog food, for instance, even though it is one of the more yumston things in the world. Ice cream is one of the things they call 'junk food'."

"Junk food? What in heaven's name is that?"

Little Haze smiled. "Since you haven't been a professional guide dog for very long, it is easy to understand that you don't know about a lot of things that have to do with humans. But you won't be Diana's teammate for long without learning a whole bunch. Junk foods are stuff like Zingers and candy and potato chips and things like that. The reason they are called 'junk foods' is that they don't really nourish the body. They just fill it up and usually they cause yuckston things to happen to the body."

"Well," I said, "maybe I should turn down the ice cream."

"You do that, Venture," said Little Haze. "I will be more than willing to eat yours for you."

After lunch, we went to the ice cream store. They had a big list of flavors and the young girl at the counter was reading them off to Billyum and Diana when the girl's boss yelled at her across the room.

"If people come in here that are too dumb to read, then they don't need anything here. Tell them to go to school. We don't have time to do their reading for them."

"But these people are blind," said the young girl.

"OK," said the lady and returned to what she had been doing.

Billyum and Diana sat at a little table and began to eat their ice cream.

"All right, Haze, you little Slimer," said Billyum to Little Haze. "Even though you are a worthless Sleaze, I am going to get you some ice cream."

"Excuse me," said a lady. "I wish to apologize to you if I insulted you when my girl was reading the menu to you. We get a lot of kids in here who either can't or won't read and I don't feel that my people's time should be taken up with them. I didn't see the dogs, so once again I would like to tell you that I am sorry. But don't you think it was a little much to call me a sleaze and a slimer?"

"I wasn't calling you a sleaze or a slimer," answered Billyum. "I was talking to this old sleaze here on the floor and telling her that although she isn't any good, I would get her some ice cream. If you consider yourself to be a sleaze, I guess that's your problem, but I will only buy ice cream for this old sleaze and that worthless butt over there on the floor."

"Please excuse me," said the woman, "But I could have sworn you said Haze or Hazel."

"I did," said Billyum. "The dog's name is Hazel, but I call her 'Little Haze'."

"That is my name," said the woman. "Some of my friends call me Haze, though I'm not sure the term 'little' would apply to me. I'm glad to know you weren't calling me a sleazer. Whenever you want ice cream here for yourselves or the guide dogs, it's on the house from now on—I'll let my girls know."

"Thank you very much," said Billyum, "but that isn't really necessary."

"I know," said the woman, "but I want to do it. I admire you and those dogs so much. What is the other one's name?"

"His name is Venture," said Diana. "He is a new guide dog and has never had ice cream. We only get it for them once or twice a year, but I get a cone once in a while. When that happens, I plan to let Venture have the bottom of it."

"Well, whatever you would like," said the woman. "What kind of ice cream would you like for the dogs today?"

"Vanilla," said Billyum.

"Coming right up," said the woman as she went to get the ice cream.

Billyum took the cone from the lady and extended it to Little Haze. I watched in amazement as Little Haze seemed to inhale the cone with one gulp.

Diana offered me a cone. I licked it daintily. It was very yumston, and I savored its goodness.

"If you don't want it, Venture," said Little Haze, "I know what to do with it."

I ignored her and continued eating my cone. I knew what to do with it, too, and soon that ice cream cone was history.

"Well, Billyum," said Diana, "Thank you for the ice cream. And thank you, too," she said to the owner of the store. "I guess we should go back to the salt mines."

"I don't know, Diyuck," said Billyum, "I wanted to see the butt, and get that letter off to the airlines, but I fear that you are looking and sounding yuckston."

"Yes," admitted Diana. "I am feeling yuckston. Probably all the changes of weather I've been experiencing have something to do with it."

"Well, I have to go back," said Billyum. "There are a couple of things I have to do. We have a new client and you are supposed to see him tomorrow, but with you getting yuckston, I will cancel it. Little Haze needs to see the vet and I bet you didn't get to take Venture. So why don't we go tomorrow? Also, if you get much more yuckston, I think you better go and see your doctor. Maybe he can give you something to get rid of the yuckston."

Diana's voice had been getting different, so I took her home. After letting me play with Mr. Hedgehog for a little while, she lay down. By the next morning it was very clear even to me that she was much worse. Her hands when they touched me felt odd, and her voice was totally gone. I was relieved when Billyum called and Diana croaked that she was very yuckston. I knew that it would only be a matter of time till help was on the way.

Ten

Vetting

When I heard Fritsey's knock at the door, you have no idea at all how glad I was to see her. There was just no question about it, Diana was extremely yuckston, and she needed to see the human vet.

Diana had called the human vet earlier, and they weren't going to be able to see us until that afternoon. Billyum had made arrangements for Little Haze and me to see our vet first.

As we got into the car, I was filled with joy to see Billyum and Little Haze waiting for us. Diana hugged Little Haze.

"What on earth is wrong with Di?" Little Haze asked me. "She is very yuckston, and when she pressed her face against me, it was burning up. It's a good thing we're going to the vet. Maybe he can fix her."

It was kind of a long ride to the vet's office. Fritsey and Billyum chatted away, but Diana remained quiet. I guess that was because she had lost her voice.

"Well," said Fritsey to Billyum, "we finally found something to shut Diana up."

"That's true," said Billyum. "Enjoy it while it lasts. When we got our insurance, I should have signed up with Allied Health Association. I didn't like the representative, and you know how health maintenance organizations tend to look at you—as a number, not a name."

"I have a doctor that I have seen for years," said Fritsey. "I've spent a lot of money at his office, so you would think they would notice me and not treat me like just another patient. They are nice but I have never in my life seen anything that can compare to the loving attention those folks at Allied pay to Diana. I've watched them. They seem to be very caring people, but the way they treat Diana is something special to behold. I can't fathom it. I know that she has had clients that they have made decisions against, and that Diana has appealed their decisions and many times gotten them reversed. I know that sometimes those decisions have cost them quite a bit of money. So you could well understand if they treated her a little coolly, but it doesn't happen that way. They really put themselves out for her. It is simply amazing."

"But you know why that is," explained Billyum laughing. "It's because I am so very yumston and my yumston flows out to her through Little Haze."

"You jerk," croaked Diana as she playfully swung her purse at Billyum.

"Ouch! You little yucker," exclaimed Billyum. "I'll tell you what I think we need to do about her. After we see the vet, I think we should just leave Diyucker somewhere. She is filled with yuck anyway, otherwise she would be talking a mile a minute, so I think we should just let her out somewhere, and I'll take the dog."

"But you already have Little Haze, Billyum," said Fritsey. "What would you do with two dogs?"

"Well, I have two sides," said Billyum, "and I think Venture is yumston. And besides, Venture and Little Haze would each have someone to play with. What do you think of Billyum's idea, Diyuck?"

Billyum covered his head to avoid the purse he knew would come hurtling at him. "Billyuck," hissed Diana.

"No," laughed Billyum. "It is you who are yuckston. You are so yuck that your voice won't even work so you can say those untrue things about Billyum."

"It would seem that you have a point there," agreed Fritsey.

"Do they always go on like this?" I asked Little Haze.

"All the time," she laughed. "And yet, if there is something serious to attend to, I think you would have to look very hard to find two people who will work as hard and be as effective."

"They seem so very close." I said, "Could anything ever come of it?"

"No," answered Little Haze. "Both of them see other people. They are just the dearest of friends, although Fritsey has certainly made very direct suggestions."

Fritsey's car turned in at the vet's and we all piled out.

It seemed to me as if we had entered a whole new world once we were inside the vet's office. It reminded me a little of when we went to the pet store, but it was different than that. There were strong smells of medicine and disinfectant—like the smells in the vet's office back at the Guide Dog Foundation.

Since Diana couldn't talk, Billyum carried on the business at hand with the receptionist. He explained that Little Haze was there for her semi-annual checkup. Venture, on the other hand, was a brand-new guide dog just home from the school and needed a get-acquainted visit.

Billyum explained that Diana had lost her voice and couldn't talk, so he was doing it for both of them. He gave them the necessary information to start a file on me, and we sat together to wait until the vet could see us.

When our names were called, Diana, Billyum, Little Haze and I went into the examining room. The man who met us was very charming. He clapped Billyum on the back as if he were a long-lost friend, and the adoration and respect he showed Little Haze had to be seen to be believed.

"How does Little Haze seem to be getting on?" asked the vet.

"She seems fine to me," said Billyum. "I weigh her every week, and her weight is holding steady. She seems to have a few allergies, though, so I have been giving her the pills you gave me. Plus I have been bathing her about every two weeks, like you recommended, even though it sounds like a lot to people who aren't familiar with Southern California."

"That's right," said the vet. "Our air is so smoggy, and what with the other problems we have, bathing the dog with a good medicated shampoo is necessary. I know there is always a question about giving the pills for the allergies. True, they can have some side effects, but on the whole, I feel the benefits outweigh the disadvantages. I know that these dogs work very hard, and Little Haze is my sweetheart. It is my feeling that it is in her best interest to be comfortable. There are a few in my profession who feel that these steroids may shorten the dog's life a little. Even if it does, which is still open to debate, it would be better to have the dog's life spent in as much comfort as possible. If she doesn't need the medication, then of course don't give it to her, but if she is scratching, you know what to do. Continue the bathing, whether she seems uncomfortable or not. Now, Little Haze, according to your records, it is time for a booster vaccination. I think your nails could use a trim too, so wait while I draw up the shot and retrieve my clippers."

Little Haze sat gracefully on the table and softly swished her lovely tail. The vet left us for a moment, and we could hear him talking to other animals as he passed them.

"I know the vet is talking to an animal," Billyum said to the assistant who had stayed with us. "What kind of animals are back there right now?"

"Two cats had surgery this morning but I think those two are still sleeping it off, so that would mean he is talking to just the birds and the turtles," she said. "Doctor always treats all the creatures, great or small, with kindness and respect. You never know how important it is. A soft word often soothes the savage beast. And now I have a question for you," said the assistant. "When you were talking to the vet, you said that you weigh Little Haze every week. How can you do that?"

"I have a talking scale," said Billyum. "Little Haze is small enough that I can get on the scale and hold her. But I think monitoring Venture's weight is going to be another story. For one thing, Venture is too heavy for even me to lift, so of course Diana will not be able to do it either."

"How does the scale work?" asked the assistant. "How accurate do you think it is?"

"It has a speech chip in it," explained Billyum. "I press a button to turn it on and it says, 'Please step on the scale.' So I do that with Little Haze in my arms. It will then tell me how much I weigh. Actually, it has a memory feature, and I use the memory. First I find out exactly what I weigh. Then I get on the scale with Little Haze. The memory will calculate how much I have gained, so I don't even have to stop and figure out that."

"That is very interesting," said the assistant. "How much does something like that cost?"

"Oh, about a hundred and twenty dollars," said Billyum.

"One hundred and twenty dollars for a scale?" asked the assistant. "That is just plain taking advantage of people."

"It seems a little like that sometimes," agreed Billyum. "However, if you stop and realize that this is not a mass-produced item that you can get in the supermarket, then I guess it makes sense. Also, it is a good scale. It is supposed to be accurate within a half a pound."

"Maybe," said the assistant. "But I paid $10 the other day for one, and I felt that I had paid much too much."

"I wish I could get one for $10," laughed Billyum.

"What else do you have that talks?" asked the assistant.

"I have a calculator, a clock, and a thermometer," said Billyum. "Diana has a talking wrist watch and a talking VCR—and, of course, for the business we have a talking computer."

"I just look at a computer and my tummy does flip-flops," said the assistant. "How can you use one? What does it say?"

"It says whatever is on the screen," Billyum explained. "The speech system consists of two parts: a speech card, which is a kind of printed circuit board that gets installed inside the computer, and screen-reading software that resides in the computer's memory."

"I can't understand anything about that," said the assistant. "Anyone who can operate a computer would have to be a lot smarter than me."

"Who would have to be smarter than you?" asked the vet.

"Anyone who could run a computer," said the assistant. "Bill was just telling me that they have a computer that talks."

"Well," said the vet as he gave Little Haze a shot, "I'll leave the running of a computer to you. I will stick to the simple things I know—like giving dogs shots and cleaning their ears."

"You make it sound too grand," laughed Billyum. "It isn't all that difficult to use a computer. I don't know why people are so intimidated by them. It must take a lot of knowledge and skill to be a vet, but kids in school can use a computer."

"That, I guess, is true," said the vet. "Right now, though, I need to know about this new dog. Diana, he must belong to you. Tell me about him.

"She really can't," explained Billyum. "His name is Venture and he is from the Guide Dog Foundation for the Blind, in New York. Unfortunately, Diana did not react so well to the extremes in climate between here and New York. She has a very bad cold, and has all but lost her voice. I will help her and tell you all about Venture. Venture is a male golden Lab. He is nineteen months old, and he and Diana have just completed their training a week ago."

"He looks a lot like Little Haze," said the vet. "Let's get him up here on the table and we will get acquainted."

"My!" he said as he lifted me onto the table. "What a handsome gentleman you are. Why, you are a sweetheart just like Little Haze. You even have the same sweet expression as hers on your face. The difference is that you are a much larger dog than Little Haze is. Why didn't they give Diana Little Haze, and give you this big brute, Bill?"

I ran my mighty club with pleasure at his attention. Diana stood there stroking my shining coat. Unlike the vet at the school, this man really was in awe of me. I exposed my belly, and wriggled my delight.

"The difference in the two dogs' sizes is rather comical," agreed Billyum. "Their personalities are also very different. Little Haze is like the bubbles in champagne, while Venture, although he has some bubbles, is really very placid and calm. I find him very interesting, Although he is so calm, he has a lot of energy and can work all day and still seem to hold up under it. You are right about his being a sweetheart. If I didn't have Little Haze, you can bet I would steal Venture for myself. He is very lovely."

"I see by his papers that he has been altered. In fact, he was less than a year old when that was done. That seems a pity. He is so charming, behaves so well, and is absolutely perfection to look at. I can't quite believe that they wouldn't want his line to continue."

"The Guide Dog Foundation has a very good supply of perfect dogs to carry on the line," explained Billyum. "The work of being a guide dog does not allow for having puppies and all the attendant problems."

"I can certainly understand that," laughed the vet. "But both these dogs are such beautiful and perfect creatures. Little Haze is a perfect vision of femininity. I will agree that she is so light and fragile looking—well, perhaps it would be better, if she were having pups, that she be a little bigger boned. But she looks like a petite little femme fatale while Venture's majesty and perfect noble bearing make him a very desirable male. If you look into either of their eyes— well, that is a very wondrous experience. I know that Little Haze also can't have pups because she has been spayed. Both of them are real treasures and I am very glad that you bring them to me for their medical treatment."

"When Diana came home with Venture she was told that they are the same color, but I have been told differently. What would you say?" asked Billyum.

"They are both a beautiful golden color," answered the vet, "But Little Haze is a lighter gold than Venture. Looks like you are just great, Venture. You remember to tell Diana that you want to come back and see me in six months. OK, big guy?"

I ran my mighty club. It was very obvious that this was a very smart man and it would be fine with me if we didn't wait six months before coming to see him again. I followed Billyum and Little Haze to Fritsey's car. It was becoming much more obvious that Diana was really ill, so Fritsey dropped Diana and me at the human vet's and took Billyum and Little Haze home.

Going to the vet had been wonderful, but if you can believe it, going to Allied Health Association was almost as good.

The moment we walked in the door, I realized that here was something very special. People who worked there gathered around us. The chatter was amazing and it all revolved around me.

Everyone was trying to outdo everyone else in their expressions of welcome and adoration of my beauty. Even the maintenance man came over to gaze at me and compliment Diana on how beautiful I was. What made all this so special was not just their admiration, but the atmosphere of love and caring we were shown. My heart bounded with joy, for I realized two things. These people were very smart people. They had to be to demonstrate such love, admiration, and caring about me. The other thing was that Diana was really yuckston, but these folks were human vets, so they ought to be able to make Diana well. I ran my mighty club in happy thanksgiving. It was truly wonderful to be a guide dog. Nothing on earth could possibly compare with it.

I escorted Diana to the stairs. I really had to pay attention to the little croaking commands she gave me. She sounded so very weird, but by now, if I paid attention, I could almost hear her thoughts, so in tune with one another had we become.

They soon took us into the vet's office and I discovered that many vets worked at this place. Their assistants, which they called nurses, all came out to see me and admire me. I watched with interest as they put something around Diana's arm and then it sounded as though they were pumping air into her.

"I will have to try to get your blood pressure again," explained the nurse to Diana. "I couldn't get a reading."

"Maybe the problem is that I am not alive and my body didn't realize it is supposed to cool off," croaked Diana.

"No, you are alive all right," laughed the nurse, "but you do have quite a fever. We will take care of you just as fast as we can so that you can go home and go to bed. By the way, the whole clinic is talking about what a beautiful dog you have there. When people talk, you figure things get exaggerated, but if anything, that dog is more beautiful than we had heard. Just wait a minute and the doctor will be right in."

Just then the door opened, and another lady entered the room. "Oh, he is just beautiful," she said. "What is his name?"

"His name is Venture," answered the nurse, "and he really is special. Looks like Diana got herself a real spectacular cold too. She is running a pretty high fever, so I think you will want to take a look-see. I couldn't get a reading on her blood pressure but I'll try again in a minute."

"I'll do it," answered the newcomer, who—I realized with a start—was the human vet.

After taking Diana's blood pressure again, the human vet examined her. Diana began to cough and the sound was ugly. The human vet looked in Diana's ears and mouth, just as my vet had done, and I wondered why it was she didn't just see my vet instead of coming over here. But my role was not to question her decisions on such matters, so I lay at her feet and waited to see what would happen.

"You have a very bad cold," said the vet. "I think pneumonia may have set into your lungs, but I can't be sure of that until you have some lab work done and I can see the results. So I am sending you to the lab and to X-ray. When they are through with you, come back and we'll see what to do from there."

One of the employees, a very charming lady, went to the lab with us. I watched as they drew blood from Diana and then I went with her to X-ray. When I was X-rayed, I was given a shot that made me sleepy, but they just had Diana undress and get in front of the machine. Again, I wondered why a dog was treated differently than a person, but since I had no objections to the way Diana treated me, I just let it go out of my mind and was there for her. Believe me when I tell you that she was very yuckston, and she needed me to be there for her. My training hadn't covered this problem, but I'm a very smart fellow and very resourceful, so I figured that somehow I would get her through it.

After what seemed an eternity, the human vet came in with all the reports.

"Well, my dear," she said, "you have a bad cold and it is going into your lungs. But with a few days of bed rest, and some of these little magic pills I'm going to give you, you should be as good as new. I have called them down to the pharmacy, as well as some cough syrup which I think will help you to be a little more comfortable." Then she looked again at me. My chief concern now was Diana, who needed all of the help this human vet was capable of giving, so I gave the human vet a sad, pleading look and put my nose on her leg.

The watching nurses ooh'ed and ah'ed over how precious my action was, but not the human vet. She understood my plea for help, and instantly a bond of love and compassion connected us. Bending over me, she caressed my silky ears and spoke softly to me so that only she and I heard.

"Diana seems very sick, Venture, but you don't need to be upset," she said gently. "The medicine I am giving her is a real wonder drug, and you will see an improvement almost immediately. Be patient with her. See that she drinks a lot of water and gets a lot of rest. I don't think she ought to go back to work for a few days either. I expect her to get better, but if there is a problem, I will be here."

I ran my mighty club.

The lady who had helped us before went to the pharmacy for Diana and, after collecting her medications, brought them to her and explained to her how to use them. Fritsey came just then and took us home.

After she had taken me out, Diana made herself some hot tea and changed into the soft wooly bunny-like sleeping things she had used in New York. She took her medicine and drank the hot tea, then covered herself with a heavy blanket and lay on the sofa. Soon she was fast asleep.

I watched her for a time and then I too went to sleep. When I awakened, Diana still slept, but I noticed that her breathing sounded a little better. She wasn't well, but she was better. I was grateful even though it was some time past my dinner time. I sat by my master and watched her sleep.

Finally, she did wake up, pulled on a heavy coat over her fuzzy sleeper, fed me and took me out. Then she fixed herself some soup and went to bed.

In the morning, she was greatly improved, although she still had trouble talking. Billyum called and although she couldn't talk, he could and did. He told her that she wasn't to come to work for the next week.

"This client that is coming in is going to be very troublesome," he said, "so you need to be well when you deal with that."

In a couple of days, Diana seemed more herself. She didn't have the use of her voice yet but still we went for walks. Diana listened to books that were on tape, and I faithfully took her to the mailbox to return them. The weather was getting warm again, so one day Diana and I went out on the patio. Diana lay on a chaise longue and enjoyed the sun. She allowed me to be loose and I played with the tuffy and rolled around enjoying the sun. Diana was getting her voice back and she called Billyum to tell him that next Monday she would be back.

That evening before bed, Diana and I played with Mr. Hedgehog. That night as I settled beside her bed, I was very thankful indeed that she was again the Diana I knew and loved.

The next day Diana took me to the bus stop. "You have been such a very good boy, Venture," she explained, "that I am going to get you another toy." I ran my mighty club with happiness. We again visited the pet store. This time Diana selected a ball of yarn made from latex. I was very pleased that Mr. Hedgehog had a friend, but most importantly, I was so very glad that Diana and I were slipping into a comfortable routine together. I was very happy with my life. Everywhere we went there were admiring looks and gracious compliments, but what mattered most to me was that I pleased Diana. I now knew beyond question that I was the perfect one for her. I had met my destiny; just as all real gold is true and can be relied upon, so I, too, the golden one, could be trusted. Our experiences were showing that to Diana. It was like reading a magic book—I couldn't help but wonder what would come next.

Eleven

Rabies

I was happy that sunny morning as I escorted Diana to the bus bench. The weather was pleasantly warm, and I was grateful that Diana was up and at 'em again. When we got to the office, I was delighted to see Little Haze and Billyum.

"I need to talk to you about this new client," said Billyum. "He is a little on the strange side, and he will most definitely be a handful. There is a new problem that has surfaced since I did his intake. Lee Randolph has taken quite an active interest in him although, of course, that in itself wouldn't make any difference in whether you took his case or not."

"Why is Lee interested in this person?" asked Diana. "There must be a pretty serious problem if the county's Adult Protective Services is interested. They are so overburdened that it must be serious indeed."

"That is true," said Billyum, "but you haven't seen this guy. I mean he is really something."

"Perhaps you could tell me something about him—like maybe his name," said Diana.

Billyum chuckled.

"Don't make me play twenty questions," said Diana. "Just tell me about him."

"Oh, I am willing to do that," said Billyum. "But the problem is where to begin."

"Try at the beginning," said Diana. "For example, I can't keep calling him 'the client.' What is his name?"

Billyum responded with peels of laughter.

"All right," said Diana. "Billyuck, I need information about this man and I cannot understand for the life of me why you are acting so yuckston!"

"No, Diyuck," laughed Billyum. "It is you who are yuckston. Oh, all right, it is the client who is yuckston, and after meeting him, I am glad you work with people like that and I work with computers and adaptive devices. They are a lot more pleasant and predictable.

"I will tell you about our client. I think I mentioned that he belongs to Rev. Shaw's church. I guess he has belonged for many years and has been a faithful member. He was employed as a private courier, but not just an ordinary one. The people he served were the stars in Hollywood and I think he made a great deal of money. I would further guess that perhaps he made large contributions to the church, and that may be how he and Rev. Shaw became such good friends.

"Anyway, some time ago, he started to feel really badly, so he visited his physician. They ran routine tests and the doctor said he would get back to him. He had put Rev. Shaw's name as a person to contact in an emergency, and when the doctor couldn't reach our client, he contacted Rev. Shaw. It seems the man needed to be hospitalized immediately. His blood work showed that he had a very serious problem with diabetes, and his blood sugar was dangerously high. When his employer learned of his problem, he fired our client on the spot. Now he has no income, his insurance has run out, and he is having a lot of physical problems that are making his life and everyone's around him miserable."

"Oh dear," said Diana, "sounds like a mess. What I don't understand is why Lee is interested, and why you find it so funny."

"What I have told you is really tragic," agreed Billyum. "That part isn't one bit funny. It's his name that's a hoot."

"And pray tell, what might that be?" asked Diana.

"Well, I guess that his name isn't so funny," said Billyum. "His name is Ray Butz. But it is his nickname that is so funny, although in all seriousness, it really makes me wonder about this guy."

"What's his nickname?" asked Diana.

"His nickname is Rabies," said Billyum. "He is very careful to point out that it is pronounced like the disease. He is very proud of being a human disease. It seems that when he was just a kid in high school, he had a crush on this girl. She was embarrassed because of his last name, so she suggested they call him Ray B. Of course the other kids picked up on that but they changed it to Rabies and added that he was a disease. I guess that this girl really meant a lot to him, and he still insists that is his true and rightful name, and he will refuse to answer unless he is called that."

"Yuckston!" said Diana. "How very odd that he would want to hold on to a nickname like that."

"To say nothing of the way that must effect him at least on a subconscious level," agreed Billyum. "I don't think that this is a problem caused by the diabetes either. I guess he got that unique name when he was only fifteen. He is sixty-two now and yet he clings to that revolting name like you wouldn't believe. Then putting into words that he is a human disease—I just do not understand. But that isn't the only thing that is yuckston about him. You have straight hair now, Diyum, but after you see him, it will be tightly curled. You see, Rabies has another problem. You know, with that disease, they foam at the mouth. This Rabies does not foam—he stinketh!!!"

"Poor man," sighed Diana. "Probably with the difficulties he has had, keeping himself clean and getting his clothing laundered must be a real problem."

"No," said Billyum, "that's not the trouble. There is a laundromat right near his house, and he told me that he washes his clothes every week. And he told me about his baths too. Don't laugh at me, Diana. He told me that he takes 'dry baths' so that he will not waste water. He thinks that he does enough of that by using the washing machines. He just doesn't use any on himself when he bathes."

"Just what the Sam Hill does he do?" queried Diana.

"He told me that he just gets in the tub or shower and rubs

himself real good all over with a cloth. He says he does it till he works up a real good sweat. He further says that a dry bath is good for you because it gets the blood to circulating, and, of course, it saves water."

"You can't be serious!" exclaimed Diana.

"Oh, but I am," answered Billyum. "I tell you, Diyum, he smells yuckston. You will really believe him when he brags that he is a disease. Even Little Haze tried to get away from him. Really, the smell is very offensive. I took the liberty to put a 'magic mushroom' in your office. You will wish I had put several in there before he leaves. I think he is going to be a very big problem."

"Another thing that is very distracting is that he cries about every little thing. For example, somebody in one of the other offices got an extra bean burrito. She stopped by to see if I would like it. You know I don't care for those bean things, but Rabies was here and he said that he would just love to have it, so she gave it to him. Rabies burst into tears. You know, I thought that perhaps this was a side effect of his physical problems, but now I don't think so. After crying for a while, he ate his food while he explained to me how macho it was for a man to show that he had feelings and cry in public. He then sought out the woman who had given him the food, and went into her office to tell her what a manly thing it was to show true feelings. According to him, gone are the days when only women can cry and then he started bawling again. I tell you, Diyum, he is a real problem."

"Sounds like it," answered Diana. "Before I see him, I better set up an appointment with Rev. Shaw."

"That is a very good idea," said Billyum. "There is another complication to his case. If you can overlook the stink, and that weird stuff about being a disease, and the bawling, he is really a very sweet man. He has a daughter who, when she learned about his problems, said everyone should just stand back and let him die. I guess that he has a tidy life insurance policy, with her as the beneficiary. This man is a human being. He has worked hard all his life. Now it seems that his health is broken, his medical insurance is cutting him off, what family he has is drawing away—his life must be one bitter trial and my heart goes out to this lonely person. Something really must be done for him."

"Something will be done for him," said Diana. "That is what I am doing here. But of course I need more facts and it will depend on how much Rabies himself will let me help him. Venture, come, we have a lot of work to do."

I ran my mighty club. It was sure good to see Diana coming back to herself.

Diana first called Rev. Shaw's office but he was not available. She chatted with his secretary about me and our trip to New York. When she finished her telephone conversation, Diana came over to me and stroked my shining coat.

"You know, you butt," said Diana as she played with my ears, "I was just talking to Caroline. She and I have been friends for a long time and she was her usual, charming self. However, just as soon as I said I needed to talk about Rabies she got real quiet and just said it was very necessary to attend to that problem at once and she had to go. That is not at all like Caroline."

I ran my mighty club. After all, with Diana in charge, what was there to worry about? She met all of my needs, so I was certain everybody else would be taken care of, too.

Diana left me and went back to work. I chewed thoughtfully on my bone as I watched her answer the phone, then move over to her typewriter. Billyum came in to say that he had to go out for a while. Little Haze and I exchanged happy looks.

"Is this something like what a normal work day is like?" I asked Little Haze.

"Just about anything around here is normal," answered Little Haze. "Often, you will find work creeping into your evening, too. It will take you to all kinds of interesting places. This Rabies person, though, is really something. I don't think that he feels well at all, and I hope that we can make him not so sad."

"I don't know, Little Haze," I answered, offering my bone to her but grabbing it again when she looked interested. "I understood that my job was to take care of Diana and meet her needs, but you make it sound as though I am supposed to get involved in helping Rabies. Is there something I have mixed up?"

"No, you are supposed to help Diana," replied Little Haze as she snatched the bone away from me. "But part of meeting Diana's needs is being her teammate. That means filling in when she needs you to do something she can't. You and I are very unique creatures, and sometimes our special abilities can get things done when our supposed human superiors can't."

"But Little Haze," I said, "There was nothing in my training that would prepare me to help Diana in the way you are suggesting."

"I know that," said Little Haze quietly. "Your training just gave you the barest essentials to serve your master. But between those golden ears, there is a wonderful brain. You have resources that the Guide Dog Foundation has no understanding of. Just because they don't understand them does not mean they aren't there. They say that necessity is the mother of invention, and that's as true for us as it is for people.

"We are like them in lots of ways. They need to be seen by vets just like we do, but these vets are specially trained to work on people. Humans can think, too, though not exactly the way we do.

"As you need to use your special resources, you will do so, perhaps without even realizing you are doing anything out of the ordinary. I also have a feeling—call it an inner knowingness—that it is your destiny to use these special resources to help many; that, at the end of your life, we will all stand amazed at the lives you have affected."

"I don't understand how I could do what you are suggesting," I said as I scratched my ear.

"That doesn't matter," said the beautiful Little Haze. "As I said, it is just a feeling that I have. If I am right, when the time comes, you will do it without realizing it. Right now, I am concerned about Rabies. What he needs is for someone to reach out to his heart and soul. Since you and he are both males, and since you are so sweet and compassionate, I hope you can touch him in the way he desperately needs."

"I have faith in Diana," I said.

"I do too," said Little Haze. "What I hope for is a team effort. I shied away from Rabies on one occasion but it still may be that we and our masters will succeed."

"Come on, you Sleaze," said Billyum to Little Haze. "I'll be back," he called to Diana as he slipped the harness on Little Haze. "I'll go by and check the mail."

"Have fun," said Diana as she hurried to answer the telephone.

Diana talked on the phone for quite a while. When she finished, she took me for a short walk and a nice cool drink of water. It was so pretty outside, I was sorry we couldn't stay there. But Diana said she had a lot of work to do so back we went to the office. It was pretty much the same boring routine for the rest of that day. I was not very happy about this. Up to now, I had always been a vital part of Diana's life, but suddenly, the things in the office seemed more important to her. So I was decidedly glad when Diana said that we would call it a day, and we caught the bus home.

After being neglected for other things, I was glad to have dinner, play with Mr. Hedgehog, and have my shining coat groomed. As Diana talked to me, I realized that my earlier fears about not being important to her were groundless. So I stretched out beside Diana and ran my mighty club.

When we got to the office the next day, Billyum was already there. As we came down the hall, I could hear his computer chattering away and it was with great joy that I said good morning to Little Haze.

"How are you progressing with Rabies' case?" asked Billyum.

"I am going to be seeing him this afternoon," said Diana. "Rev. Shaw's secretary, Caroline, called me back to explain that the reason she didn't want to say anything about Rabies was because he was right there. It seems that things are pretty much as you describe them, even the stink. However, I haven't been able to reach Lee yet. I just hope this man will let us help him."

"He really needs helping," replied Billyum. "But I am certain you can reach him. However, there is something else I need to tell you about. You got an answer to your letter from the airlines. You said it would be all right if I opened it so I did."

"What did they say other than we are sorry?" asked Diana.

"Oh they really did make a production about the fact that they were sorry, and the letter is signed by the president of the airline. You know, Diyum, you really attracted a lot of attention with that letter. I know I helped you write it, but I don't mind saying so, that letter was a work of art."

"Well," said Diana as she gathered some things together to work on in her office, "art or not, I just hope that it will keep the same thing from happening to someone else."

"I don't think they will ever make that mistake again," said Billyum.

"I hope not," said Diana, and she started to leave for her own office.

"That isn't all there was in the letter," smiled Billyum.

"No?" said Diana, stopping in the doorway.

"No," said Billyum. "They are going to do something nice for Diyum."

"What?" asked Diana.

"Something very nice for Diyum," repeated Billyum.

"But what is it, Billyum?" asked Diana, returning to his office and closing the door.

"Oh, I don't know if I should tell you now, Diyum. Maybe what you should do is go back to your office and get your work done, and I will try to decide if I should tell you, because I think you are going to really think that it is yumston. I wish somebody would do it for me."

"Do what, Billyum, please tell me?" pleaded Diana.

"Ummmmmm," said Billyum, savoring his secret. "Tell you what. After you see Rabies, you could take us for ice cream and maybe then, if you are real yumston, I could tell you."

"Billyuck!" hissed Diana. "Tell!"

"No," said Billyum with a smile in his voice. "I will not impart yumston to someone who calls me yuckston."

"Oh, all right, Billyum," conceded Diana. "You are, for purposes of telling me the yumston, very yumston."

"We see a lot of yuck in people's lives here in this office," answered Billyum, "and I guess that is why it is fun to tease you once in a while, but this is really a good yumston. The airline did wish to convey how unhappy they were to learn of the poor conduct of their agent and they would be pleased to give you a round trip ticket anywhere in the United States for two, good for the next year."

"Oh Billyum, that really is yumston," exclaimed Diana.

Just then the telephone rang and in a minute, Billyum said "It's Lee for you, Diyum." I knew another work day had begun.

After she had talked for a few minutes, Diana hung up the phone and turned to Billyum with a sigh. "Well," she said, "Another piece of the puzzle just fell into place. It seems that a couple of calls have come in about the substandard way Rabies is living. After visiting his home—she mentioned that the stench made her feel ill—something had to be done about him. When he told her that we were getting involved, she wanted to wait and see what we could do for him."

"What are you going to do?" asked Billyum.

"Meet with Rabies, and see how much help he is willing to accept," answered Diana. "From there, we'll have to play it by ear."

As Diana settled me, I felt happy. It had been nice to see Little Haze, and the good-natured give and take between Billyum and Diana made me feel comfortable. I knew whatever might be difficult, Diana would straighten it out, so I ran my mighty club. Its measured *thud thud thud* brought a quality of normal serenity to the office and I drifted off to sleep.

I awakened suddenly. Billyum had poked his head in to advise us that Rabies was on the way. Soon I could hear voices in the hallway. I wrinkled my nose because there was an unpleasant odor in the air. But it was not the smell of filth. I recognized that smell from the kennels when one of the dogs had a serious infection. It was obvious to me that the person coming to visit was not at all well. I was very curious and although I was very alert, I assumed my professional pose of utter relaxation.

Diana greeted her two guests graciously. Rev. Shaw admired me and then introduced Rabies. Rabies limped badly, and walked with a cane, but as I looked into his eyes, I knew that this was a good man who had serious problems, and who needed help. As we looked at one another, a bond formed that would last the rest of our lives.

Diana stepped outside the office with Rev. Shaw, and asked him to go see Billyum while she got acquainted with Rabies. Then she returned and asked Rabies to tell her all about himself. Rabies did so, and we pretty much learned from him what we already knew.

Then Diana said gently, "Rabies, what would you like for me to do to help you?"

Rabies began to cry. "I don't feel well, I don't have any money, I don't have a purpose in life," he sobbed. "I don't know what anyone can do to help me. But Rev. Shaw seems to think you can work miracles."

"Not quite," laughed Diana. "What I do think is that we need to get you to a doctor and get you some medical care."

"How are you going to do that since my insurance has run out?" asked Rabies.

"Oh, I will find a way," smiled Diana. "Excuse me for a moment."

Diana crossed the hall and I could hear her talking with Billyum. "I need your help," I heard her say. "I am going to fix lunch and bring it in here to you. Then I will invite Rabies to eat with you. He can have my lunch. Rev. Shaw and I need to talk a little turkey." Both men agreed. Soon lunch was ready and Rabies had hobbled across the hall to join Billyum. Diana and Rev. Shaw faced each other in the privacy of our office.

"Your friend has a serious problem," said Diana. "For one thing, he must get some medical care immediately, or Adult Protective Services will be telling us how he is going to live. I think I can help him, but it is going to take a little time. What I am wondering is, how much can I count on you?"

"You can count on me as much as you need to," said Rev. Shaw. "Rabies has been a faithful member for all the twenty years I have been at the church. But, while we are willing to help him, we have other indebtedness. I don't think that the Lord expects us to give and give and give to one person."

"I certainly wouldn't feel in a position to make a judgment about what the Lord does or doesn't expect," said Diana. "I can make no guess as to how much should be given. I would assume that would be a decision best made by the pastor. That is you. I further agree that it is not your responsibility to support this man forever. However, I remember I read a story in my Bible about a Good Samaritan who helped a complete stranger who had been pretty badly beaten up. Not only did he get this injured person whom he did not know to a place where he could be cared for, he also told the innkeeper to get this stranger anything he needed and to put the expense on his bill. You have just told me that Rabies has been a faithful member of the church for the last twenty years. Doesn't that kind of make him family? Isn't it easier sometimes to reach out to family as opposed to a complete stranger?"

"What do you want me to do, Diana?" asked the pastor. "Knowing you as I do, you have a plan."

"I have ideas," said Diana. "The first one is to get this man to a doctor. He needs medical attention. But first I will have to qualify him for that attention."

"What do you want me to do?" asked Rev. Shaw.

"Take us to the Medical Center," said Diana. "Then go on about your business, because this is going to take hours."

"I can take you right now," said Rev. Shaw. "But I will be tied up in a meeting, so I don't know if I can come and get you when you are through."

"Rabies lives on a bus route," said Diana. "I can get him home if you can help me to get him to the Medical Center."

Soon we were off to the Medical Center. It seemed that we were there for hours, but finally, we were able to get the bus back to the mall.

As we made our way through the mall, Rabies fell behind. Diana went back to see what was wrong.

"My foot hurts real bad," moaned Rabies. "I don't think I can make it home."

Diana slipped an arm around the trembling man. Her concern about him was immediately transmitted to me. How very thin he was, and how very unwell. Diana half carried, half dragged him along the mall. There was no way on earth he could follow my brisk stride, so I moved along very slowly so that he and Diana would be comfortable. At this point, Rabies was so tired, he ceased to know where he was going. Suddenly I realized that it was all up to me.

Ahead of us were some stairs. Next to them was a ramp. Diana and I always took the stairs, but it was clear to me that wouldn't do this time. I eased them over to the ramp.

As we began our ascent up the ramp, Diana spoke to me.

"You are a very good boy, Venture! Good Boy! Wonderful Boy! How on earth did you know that I had to have the ramp?"

I just looked lovingly at Diana and kept up the slow ascent. After all, I was just doing my job.

We finally got Rabies home. We retraced our steps but this time we did it at our normal speed, and I took Diana to the steps.

"How did you know, Venture, that I needed to take Rabies up the ramp?" Diana said again as we sailed to the bus bench.

That evening Diana was very tired. Even so, she spent a long time with me playing with Mr. Hedgehog. She also continued talking to me as she brushed my shining coat. Over and over again she praised me for being such a wonderful boy and wondered how I knew she needed to use the ramp instead of the stairs. Couldn't she understand that there was a special bond between us and I would do whatever it took to meet her needs? I suppose it didn't matter much if she understood. The bond was there; that is what mattered. I knew that Diana returned my love, so I did what I knew would soothe her tired nerves. I gently kissed her and ran my mighty club. Its measured *thud thud thud* relaxed her and let her know all was right with the world. Whatever problems there were, we would face and solve them together.

Twelve

Merry Christmas, Venture

Time passed quickly. One happy day followed another and soon it was Thanksgiving.

Many changes had occurred in my little world. No longer was I kept tied. Now Diana completely trusted me, and I had free run of her apartment. This was really nice because if I heard something in the night, I was free to go out to another room and check it out. Before, being tied meant I just had to lie there and see what would happen.

Changes were taking place at the office, too. These changes were truly little miracles, and they were good to behold.

Diana had many clients, but the one who stands out in my mind is Rabies. Once he knew someone cared about him, and he got some badly needed medical care, the changes in him were truly astonishing.

I really was proud that I was one of the reasons Rabies began to have faith in himself. The day Diana had brought him home was an important day. When he had become so disoriented, and I had come to the rescue, he knew he could trust Diana. But what a struggle it had been. Rabies had a serious infection in his foot and a lot of the bad smell was coming from that infection. Also he wasn't eating regularly and when he did eat, he didn't eat the right things. I really wondered how on earth Diana was going to fix this problem.

The answer came from Rev. Shaw. When Diana explained that Rabies needed help, Rev. Shaw produced a miracle. Her name was Claudia.

Claudia was a registered nurse. She was retired, but when she worked as a nurse, she had specialized in diabetes and its attendant problems. Her warm, caring personality was just what the doctor ordered. Since retiring, Claudia had become a widow and the experience had shattered her world. Rabies' need couldn't have come at a more opportune time. Claudia desperately needed to be needed, and Rabies certainly had a genuine need for her help. It took a while, but under her capable care the infection healed, Rabies' spirits lifted, and things began to be much better. Of course, Rabies would never be able to go back to his former job, but he was able to get back into life and that's a real milestone.

Rabies and I became special friends. Sometimes when he was feeling down, I would go lay my head on his knee, look into his face, and thereby place my confidence in him. Rabies really loved me, and he would go on for hours singing my praises.

One morning Little Haze told me she was getting quite bored with hearing how wonderful I was. "After all, Venture," she said, "females are pretty special, and without us you wouldn't be here. Besides, if our skills were put to the test, my smallness would win out. You know, you are not the only one who has the corner on being beautiful."

We had come in very early that morning, and only the building staff were there. There was a long hallway by our office—it looked about a thousand feet long. It was very quiet. "Bet you can't catch me!" she trilled, and with that, she dashed down the hall!

I stood amazed watching Little Haze skim down that hall. Her dainty feet didn't seem to touch the floor, and her every move was a study of poetic grace. Other people came to watch this enchanting vision. Then the maintenance man clapped his hands and said, "Why are you leavin' the spotlight to some female, Venture? Go boy, kitch her," and the race was on.

I hurled my mighty golden body after that will-o'-the-wisp. We were having a wonderful time when Mrs. Newcomb, the building superintendent, appeared, scowling.

"What are those dogs doing running loose in this office complex!" she snapped. "Get them under control this minute!"

"But Mrs. Newcomb," exclaimed Tom, the maintenance man. "It is so much fun to see them runnin' and besides nobody will be here that they could bother for another hour. The dogs aren't hurtin' nothin', and they sure are having themselves a good time."

"That has nothing to do with it, Tom," said Mrs. Newcomb sourly. "As the building superintendent, I have the responsibility to keep things orderly. You are paid to work here, not urge this kind of disruptive behavior. If you can't find something better than this to do, I will take the necessary steps to cut your hours. We don't have the money to pay you to loaf around here with the dogs," she added as she stomped off into her office.

We all went into Billyum's office and Tom closed the door.

"That old bag gets to me sometimes," he complained. "Truly it was wonderful to watch those dogs running, and with these hardwood floors, I won't forget the delightful sounds their running feet made. Besides, it'd do that ole woman good to begin the holiday seasons with an act of good will, and watchin' them dogs now was enough to gladden the most stony heart. But I reckon old Miss Newcomb don't have a heart."

"Yep," said Little Haze to me, "and all of you have forgotten that I won."

"You did not," I sniffed. "I got back first."

"And you started last," laughed Little Haze. "Face it, Venture, you are just an inferior male and you lost, you old butt! Have you given any thought about what you will give Diana for Christmas?"

"This will be my first Christmas as a guide dog," I answered. "What is expected and what would she want? I let her play with Mr. Hedgehog as much as I play with him."

"Diana always finds something for me to give Billyum," said Little Haze. "I am sure Billyum will do it for you. The things we give our masters are always little things that don't cost much. It is just a gesture anyway."

"It sounds like fun," I responded.

"It is," said Little Haze. "Diana always makes a big thing about it, and I think Billyum enjoys it. I think I gave Billyum little candy bars last year, and Diana bought him a case of peanut butter cups. He really liked that."

"Well, I am looking forward to it," I said.

"You will probably get a lot of gifts, too," laughed little Haze.

"Like what?" I asked.

"Oh, dog cookies and balls, and stuff like that," answered Little Haze.

"Come on you old butt," Diana called to me. "This place closes up early today because of Thanksgiving, so we've got to get working."

I went with Diana across the hall and chewed contentedly on my bone while Diana worked.

As they were leaving, Diana said to Billyum, "You know I ordered that laptop computer, and I was told it would be here right after Thanksgiving. I know you are going to work with me on using it. The people who raised Venture must be wondering about him and his new life. You told me I should think of a project that we could do on the computer. How about a letter to those people?"

"Good idea," said Billyum. "We'll get started on it just as soon as the computer gets here."

Thanksgiving Day was an interesting experience. Diana slept late but when she got up she had her usual coffee. Then she got all dressed up and we went to a big house. Billyum and Little Haze were there, so that was nice, but the wonderful smells of food would make you think you had died and gone to heaven. I noticed that Little Haze's nose was twitching and she laughed when she saw me looking at her.

"Venture," she smiled. "Thanksgiving really begins the Christmas season. This is a very big day, and the humans will eat a lot of special yumstons that have been prepared for this special holiday. It is the beginning of the Christmas season. It is most interesting to watch the way humans behave because they are different than they are the rest of the year."

"What do you mean?" I asked. "I know that it's cold outside, but won't it be cold after Christmas too?"

"Maybe colder," laughed Little Haze. "But there is something really wonderful about the Christmas season. Because it is a human custom to exchange gifts at Christmas, the malls will be swarming with shoppers—but those people who are often rude and thoughtless will, for a few weeks, be the kindest people you could meet. The air will be filled with special scents that you will notice only at Christmas time, and the food—well, it is one of the few times when I wish that, for just a few hours, I could be a human. They have the most delightful things you could imagine. It is my favorite time of year."

"Will we get anything special to eat at Christmas?" I asked.

"Yes," answered Little Haze, "and you will probably get some turkey today too. You know that lots of people eat turkey on Thanksgiving. That is why it is often called 'Turkey Day.'"

"What is the big deal about Thanksgiving?" I asked.

"Long ago," said Little Haze, "few people lived here. There were people who lived in another land across the water. These people were not very happy. They didn't have a good life and many of them were persecuted because of the way they worshipped God. These people came across the water, suffered terrible hardships and went through trials that today we can't even begin to understand. Many of the people became very sick and sometimes died because there wasn't any food for them to eat. They stuck with it, though, and eventually, they began to carve out a life for themselves in this great land. Most of these people were very religious. They set aside a time where they feasted on the good things they were now able to have, and they gave thanks to God for His bounty. It became a national holiday and most people eat turkey because that was what these early settlers— who became known as Pilgrims—served at their feast."

There was a cozy fire burning in the fireplace. I stretched out in front of it and let its warmth caress my body. The warmth felt good, and the food smelled divine. I did the only thing I could do to put the finishing touch on the atmosphere. I ran my mighty club. Its *thud thud thud* made the special surroundings elegant.

"You sure know a lot of things, Little Haze," I said, "but right now I feel sleepy. Wake me up if there is any of that turkey to be had."

The next day, Diana got her little computer. True, it was very cute, and I know it was valuable but you would think nothing else existed. Thank goodness for Little Haze. If it weren't for her, I would have died of boredom. All Billyum and Diana talked about was that little computer, and they spent hours working together on it. Fortunately, the computer was not all that strange to Diana. She had spent regular amounts of time working with Billyum's computer. Now she dug into the project she had set up—a letter to the people who raised me. I would like to have been more help to her. I watched, and sometimes placed my golden head on her knee. Diana did listen to me, and considering no one had ever told her anything about my time as a puppy, she did finally put a wonderful letter together. Here it is.

Dear Friends:

Little boys dream of growing up and doing important things like being firemen or garbage men. Little girls dream of being mommies, or becoming nurses. I have become a guide dog. Let me tell you about my life and about my person.

When I arrived at the Training Center at the Guide Dog Foundation, I really missed you but I soon made a whole lot of new friends. But as I am sure you remember, that wasn't at all difficult for me. The people who took care of us were very nice. True, it wasn't like being with you, but then it wasn't like languishing away in some forgotten prison either. The Trainer was a very nice man, but he always wanted his own way all the time. I did my very best because when I did what he wanted, he was really nice to me, and I heard him saying to the other people what a special dog I was.

Then the time came to be placed. I was very excited. My person is a lady. She lives in California. It is a long way from where you are, and the climate is very different from what I am used to. But you know, Diana is a lot like the Trainer. She always wants her own way too, but boy, is she worth pleasing! I turn myself inside out to make her happy, and she appreciates it. She has bought me lots of toys, bones, special dishes to eat out of, and she is always doing nice things for me.

She has taught me things that the Trainer didn't teach me. For example, she has explained to me that my beautiful golden tail is really a club. Often when she is on the floor with me, I hit her with it right in the head. The Trainer said that it was for keeping her in line.

At first Diana scared me because she used to say some awful things, like she was going to beat me or cut my club off. At first I was worried and I tried chasing it and hitting her with it. Many times, she would take it in her hand and say 'crunch' but then she said a miracle happened and it grew back. Very soon, I came to understand that this was a little game Diana and I played. Now I know that she will never hurt me. This is a way she has of telling me that she loves me.

Diana is a very active person. She works, and we get to do a lot of interesting things. Diana is not a regular person, so I don't have the regular life of a guide dog. Wherever we go, something is always happening and I can hardly wait sometimes to see what will happen next.

When we left the school, we came to California in an airplane. These things actually go up in the air, and they travel very fast. Have you ever ridden on one? When we came to California, there was a mean old man who didn't want me to ride the plane because I am a dog. His daughter had a dog that had to ride in a crate down with the baggage. He wanted us to be put off the plane, but Diana took care of me. People on the plane saw how beautiful I am, and they made the man leave us alone. The airline is giving us a ticket free and we can go anywhere we want to go in the United States, but I don't think Diana has decided where we will go yet. I know one thing. It is going to be interesting because anywhere we go, interesting things happen.

I think I told you that Diana works. When she was growing up, her folks used to say if something was good they would say it was yum or yumston. If it was bad, they would say it was 'yuck' or 'yuckston.' Of course, I am 'yumston.'

Diana has a friend who works with her. His name used to be Bill until he got to understand about yumston and yuckston. Then he proclaimed himself 'Billyum.' His girlfriend said that was so and anyway, his real name is Will Yum.

Billyum also has a very special guide dog. She is little and dainty, and brings a whole new and wonderful meaning to 'Yumston.' Her name is Hazel but often they just call her 'Little Haze.' I used to feel badly because Diana calls me a butt. She says I am very wonderful, but I am a butt. This started when the Trainer tried to tell her how special I was but she said that they needed to get rid of me and rather than see me starve, they gave me to her because I am a worthless butt. Well, if I am so worthless, then why does she need me so much? If I were to stop working sometime when we were out, she would truly be up the proverbial creek without a paddle. However, I have learned not to be offended because you see, I am very special and there is no other like me and I would rather be Diana's 'butt' than anything else on earth.

I get to do a lot of exciting things. I have been on TV, I have prevented Diana from falling and getting hurt and once a bus full of people saw me do it. I get to go to important places like meetings and court hearings, and fancy restaurants, and I do things some people just dream of doing.

Diana just got this really cute little computer.

It is called a laptop computer. It has a precious little voice that lives inside of it. The little voice tells Diana what is on the screen. Diana is writing this letter on the little computer and Billyum is helping her. Little Haze and I are taking care of things.

You know, I have been thinking, and I have a hope for some other puppy. I hope that he or she will belong to the Guide Dog Foundation and that the puppy will have a wonderful life like I have and if he is very lucky, maybe you will be there to help him grow up.

I have to go now.

Lots of love,
Venture

Little Haze wasn't kidding about the flurry of activity that came with the Christmas season. Diana does most of her shopping well before the holidays, but she told me that she still needed to get a few things. She said that working around all the people would be good for me and a lot of fun besides. She was right.

We again visited the pet store, where Diana bought another Mr. Hedgehog for me to give to Little Haze. I looked with longing at it as Diana put it in her purse. She also bought dog treats, and some other things.

Then we went to the mall. It was very crowded, but everyone seemed to be in a good mood. It seemed as though we must have visited every store in the mall. Diana was obviously getting tired, but she explained to me that she was looking for a very special gift.

We went into the new sporting goods store that had opened only a few weeks earlier. There she got a fancy Swiss knife that had all kinds of things on it like a can opener, a wrench, different kinds of screw drivers, and other interesting things.

"This is going to be for Billyum," she said to me. "Did you see that nice leather case they have for it? It comes with a little knife sharpener, so I thought you could give him that. The knife also has a ring on the end of it, and they have a little leather leash that you can snap on the knife and secure it to your belt. I thought it would be nice if Little Haze gave him that. What do you think, Venture?"

Whatever Diana wanted to do was fine with me so I ran my mighty club in approval.

After we returned home, Diana fed me, then lay down on the sofa. Soon she was fast asleep. On the floor was a large stack of presents Diana already had gotten. These were wrapped in pretty paper, waiting for the time they would be given away. I buried my nose into the pile. Something squeaked. "That must be a toy," I mused to myself. "Since Diana bought another Mr. Hedgehog, this must be for me."

I moved other packages with my nose. I could tell by the smells that some of them contained food. Another box smelled pleasing like the cultured scent that clung to Diana. Although it wasn't usually my favorite smell, something about that box seem to call out to me, and I simply had to open it.

I carried the box over to another corner of the room while Diana, poor tired thing, slept peacefully. I held the box between my paws and chewed on the corner of it for a while. It wasn't very special, but it was something to do. I got tired of the soggy paper after a while and used my claws to shred the paper. Diana slept on.

Once I had removed the paper, I was stopped by a different kind of plastic-like paper, but again I used my claws and it gave way. At times like this, I wouldn't have minded if my nails had been a little longer, but Diana has the vet keep them cut very short. Actually, I heard the vet say one time that he didn't need to do much with them because I did so much walking that I kept them worn down.

Anyway, once I ripped off the plastic-like paper, three little cakes fell out of the box. They were wrapped in a crackly kind of paper like the Zinger had been.

I removed the paper with some difficulty. Once the little cake was out of the package, I took a bite. It was yuckston, so I tried another. Diana stirred a little but went on sleeping.

The second cake was also yuckston, so I tried the last one. It had the same problem. "How could something smell so dainty and delightful and yet be so yuckston?" I wondered as I went back to chewing on the paper.

I heard Diana stirring, and then she called to me: "Where

are you, Venture, you old butt you?"

I ran to her and rolled on my back, running my mighty club.

Diana got down on the floor and hugged me. "I love you, Venture, you old b-butt!" she said as she rubbed my tummy and put her face in my golden coat.

"Venture," she said as she pulled away from me. "Your breath smells really weird, like you have had perfume in your mouth. What have you been up to while I was asleep?"

Her fingers pried open my mouth, but she didn't find anything.

"Venture," she said, "I know you have been into something that you shouldn't have and rest assured, I will learn what it is in time."

She started into the kitchen, and I went back to the paper I was chewing. Suddenly Diana was on top of me. She had heard the crackle of the paper. Boy was she mad. It seemed that the yuckston little cakes were specially perfumed soap. Diana said they were very expensive and now I had ruined them. She took me into the bedroom and tied me up.

I think she was really overreacting. True, the little cakes had an interesting smell, but they were very yuckston. Diana could still give them to whomever would want them although I can't imagine who would want to eat those yuckston things.

Diana was upset, though. She said they were very expensive soaps and that they made a bath delightful. Now, however, because I had unwrapped them and taken a bite out of each one, she couldn't give them as a gift. I really didn't mean to get Diana so upset. When I got the chance, I kissed her and tried to make it up to her.

She threw the paper and the little soaps away, and after while she untied me. Later on that evening, I knew I was forgiven when we played together with Mr. Hedgehog.

Everywhere we went I saw Christmas trees. Some were very tiny and sat on a desk. Others were very large and were covered with many shining lights and other interesting decorations. Once I snuck over and bumped a pretty ball with my nose. Everyone laughed but Diana made me leave the trees alone. Then she told everyone about my opening the Christmas present and eating the scented soaps. "You really haven't lived until you smell Venture's breath after he has eaten perfumed soap," she would say.

Always people would ask if the soap had made me sick, but of course it hadn't. Diana often said that if I had eaten more of it she was sure that it would have made me quite ill.

The Christmas season did really change the routine, though.

One day, Billyum and Little Haze and Diana and I went to a very fancy place for lunch. There we met Lee Randolph, the lady in Adult Protective Services. Lee was very charming. It was obvious that she knew Little Haze, and loved and respected her.

Lee exclaimed over my beauty, and we all had a wonderful time together.

"You know," said Lee, "I am totally amazed at the complete turn around I see in Rabies. By the time we get a case like his, it's pretty much a lost cause. I am going to start sending more of my problems to you."

"We were just very lucky with him," answered Billyum. "Rev. Shaw really saved the day when he produced that registered nurse, Claudia. She is a real godsend."

"I know," said Lee. "What I don't understand is how she got him to stop stinking. I know that a lot of that came from the infection in his foot. But still, how on earth did she make him stop taking those dry baths?"

"I guess she is just a very gifted nurse," said Diana. "I never saw anything quite like Rabies. I wish I could get him to give up that disgusting name."

"Well," laughed Lee, "you could always tell Santa that is your wish."

They went on to talk about many other things, and it was long after lunchtime that we left the restaurant.

Just before we left, Lee gave Billyum a Christmas present. "It isn't much," she said. "It's for Venture and Little Haze."

Billyum opened the package. It was full of little treats for us. Billyum thanked Lee, wished her a merry Christmas, and we were off.

"Rev. Shaw wants to have dinner sometime next week," said Billyum as we left the office.

Rabies and Claudia had been invited to dinner and everyone

seemed to be having a real good time when Rabies banged on a glass with his silverware.

"I have something to tell you," he said and then began to cry.

"Chin up," said Rev. Shaw to Rabies. "Now is not a time for tears. If you cry, Billyum and Diana won't be able to understand what you are telling them."

Rabies was near me so I laid my head on his foot and looked him straight in the eye. He gathered strength from my confidence in him. Turning to Diana he said, "I want to thank you for giving me back my life. I really felt it was all over till you and Billyum came along and showed me I was still worthwhile and that there still was a lot more for me to enjoy in life.

"Me and Claudia and Rev. Shaw have been talking it over and he has told me that you don't like me calling myself a disease. You know I have been called that for years but I have made a lot of changes in my life and I have decided I don't want to be called a disease any longer. The new year signals new beginnings, so from now on I don't want to be called Rabies anymore. From now on I am going to go by my initials, R.T. What do you think?"

Everyone at the table clapped and cheered R.T. I found R.T. looking expectantly at me, so of course I applauded him also—that is, I ran my mighty club.

"Well," said Diana to Billyum the next day in the office. "I almost can't believe the change in Rabies—I mean R.T."

"Yes," said Billyum. "It is really hard to believe that poor health can have such a strong influence on someone's life. You know when he first came here he was really in bad shape. What you did was wonderful, Diana, but I don't think R.T. would be the person he is today if it hadn't been for Claudia."

"I know," said Diana. "It is just unbelievable what can be done when someone feels better about himself and feels that he is worthwhile. But I agree with you, I don't think we can attribute all of it to just his health. R.T. has been alone for many, many years. I know that having Claudia in his life has contributed a whole lot to his new-found well-being."

"Yes," said Billyum. "It has worked out well for both of them.

Have you noticed that he doesn't cry nearly as much as he used to?"

"I noticed," said Diana. "The only thing that has me a little concerned is his daughter. Rev. Shaw told me she isn't one bit pleased about his relationship with Claudia."

"It really is too bad that children can't be glad for their parents' happiness," said Billyum.

"I agree," said Diana, "but the problem in this case is very sad. Rev. Shaw told me that when R.T.'s wife was alive, he was a very happy, healthy, hard-working husband and father. When she died, R.T.'s world really fell apart. His daughter knew about that disease thing, and she got very angry with him and started calling him that. In time, he started thinking that was what he was, and as the years passed and his loneliness increased and his health went down hill, more and more he got into that awful mind-set. It really is sad."

"Yes, but things are so much better for him now," said Billyum, "and what little I have seen of Claudia would lead me to believe she can handle this bratty daughter. I don't guess she takes any guff from anybody."

"Venture and I are planning to spend Christmas in San Francisco," said Diana. "Should we do our gift exchange now, or when we get back?"

"Little Haze and I are also going away for Christmas," said Billyum. "Nancy and I are flying to Las Vegas, so why don't we wait until afterwards when we won't be rushed, because I don't have all my shopping done. You can leave the old butt in my office for a few minutes so I can talk to him."

"OK," said Diana. "Little Haze, would you like to come to my office for a little visit?"

Little Haze jumped to her feet and Diana led her across the hall. I got up to follow, but Billyum closed the door and got down on the floor with me.

"We need to have a little talk, you old butt, about what you are going to give Diana for Christmas." I loved Billyum so I rolled onto my back and exposed my tummy.

In a short time, no more than five minutes, Diana returned with Little Haze. "Here is the Sleaze," she said. "May I have my old butt?"

Little Haze looked at me with a twinkle in her eye. "I am giving you something really nice for Christmas, Venture," she said. "You had better see to it that you do as well by me."

Since I knew that Christmas was a time for secrets, I said nothing. I just ran my mighty club.

Our trip to San Francisco was very pleasant. We took the train, and it was delightful. The Christmas holidays were most festive. I really enjoyed lying in the sunshine. The people we visited had a yard, and I had a lot of fun playing in it.

When we returned, we had a little Christmas celebration in the office. Diana gave Billyum a tin of special cookies and a big box of candy bars. I gave Little Haze the little Mr. Hedgehog, and Diana gave Billyum the Swiss Army knife. Little Haze and I gave him the things that went with it.

Billyum gave Diana some perfume and Little Haze gave her a package of fresh coffee beans. But the most special gift was to me from Little Haze. It was a ring. Not just an ordinary ring, but something very special. It was made of a special rubbery-like plastic and had ridges on it like a vacuum hose. I was beside myself with happiness. That ring, above everything else, became my most beloved toy, and it still plays an important part in my life today.

"Billyum," said Diana. "You might not consider this much of a gift, but if we could work it out, I would like for you to consider it."

"Consider what, Diyum," asked Billyum.

"You know that convention you want to go to in Georgia in a few months? Maybe I could arrange to visit my friends in Georgia while you are at the convention. You would have to pay your own hotel bill, but we could go on that free ticket from the airline."

"That is really yumston," exclaimed Billyum. "If it will work for you, it certainly will work for me. Diana, you are truly Yumston!!!"

I agreed and as I played with my ring, I ran my mighty club.

Let Me At 'Em
Friendly Skies

Time passed quickly; soon, Diana was packing for the trip to Georgia. We were only going to be away for a long weekend, so it wasn't necessary to take a lot of things. However, Diana did send our food on ahead so she could pick it up from her friends when they met us at the airport. They were going to take Billyum and Little Haze to their hotel, then for us it would be out to the farm. They had a pond that I had heard was excellent for swimming, and it promised to be a splendid trip. Since we left for the airport directly from work, Diana took her baggage into the office where Billyum was waiting for us with his.

"Have you ridden in an airplane much?" I asked Little Haze.

"Oh yes," she said. "I just love it. I never had a weird experience like you have had, though, with someone wanting to throw me off the plane."

"Be glad I had that experience," I laughed. "It's paying for our trip."

Billyum, Diana, Little Haze and I settled together in the bulkhead seats that had been assigned to us. The flight was quiet, although the stewardesses paid a lot of attention to me and Little Haze. Traveling with another dog meant I wasn't the main attraction, but she was so delightful that I really didn't mind.

However, it did get interesting when we had to change planes in Texas. The lady who helped us was so awestruck by me and Little Haze that she got really flustered. But we finally got on the plane.

Billyum first realized something was wrong when he heard the stewardess talking about departure to Boston.

"Ma'am," he called loudly, "we are on the wrong plane."

"No, no," said the stewardess, "you are on the right plane. The airline wouldn't make a mistake."

"Yes, they have," said Billyum. "I heard you just say that we are going to Boston."

"That's right," smiled the young woman. "So just fasten your seat belt and when we are airborne, I will bring you something to drink."

"No!" said Billyum. "You don't get it. Diana and I are going to Atlanta, and if we don't get on the right plane it is really going to be a mess."

"Goodness," laughed the stewardess. "Our people don't usually make errors like that. Do you think I could see your ticket?"

"Not only can you see it," replied Billyum, "you need to let us off this plane and see that we get to the correct one."

"Heavens!" exclaimed the Stewardess. "You're right. Wait just a minute while I talk with someone."

They held up the flight to let us off, but by then our plane was long gone. Billyum and Diana were quite upset until another woman from the airline told us she had found us a flight with a different airline that was leaving for Atlanta right away. She asked Diana who was picking us up and promised to call and tell them where and when we would be arriving.

The flight went smoothly, and Diana's friends were there to meet us. They said the airline had called just as they were leaving, and they hadn't had to wait long. But before we got into their car, we found out that Diana's luggage was lost.

"Mine probably would have been too," said Billyum, "if I hadn't carried it with on."

"What am I going to do?" moaned Diana. "I can't wear these

clothes all weekend, and besides, I have to wear a suit on the return trip. I have a court appearance to make on behalf of one of my clients. Oh, what shall I do?"

"Not to worry," laughed Diana's friend. "You and I are about the same size, so you can change into some things of mine. I'm sure that by the time you leave, the airline will have found your luggage. if they haven't, I have something appropriate you can wear on the return flight."

Little Haze and I didn't have much to say as we rode to Billyum's hotel.

"We'll give you a phone call, Billyum," said Diana's friend. "It would be nice if all of us could get together for dinner before you have to go back."

"If it weren't for this hearing Diana has," said Billyum, "I would take you up on your invitation to visit the farm. I really enjoy the South, and Diana has told me about all of your little animals. I would just love to come visit you. Maybe another time."

Georgia was certainly very different from New York and California. I had a wonderful time. We had left on a Thursday and didn't have to return until Monday. I spent hours playing in the pond and romping around on the grass and following Diana as she went horseback riding. Diana works very hard, and she needed this vacation very much. I just wished it could be longer. It would have been so much fun to play with Little Haze and show her once and for all who was better. I was really looking forward to seeing her and telling her all about the fun I was having.

"Oh, Little Haze!" I exclaimed when I saw her that weekend. "I am having the most wonderful time. This is a wonderful place. I have had just barrels of fun!"

"Like what?" asked Little Haze.

"Oh, everything!' I said. "Diana went horseback riding this morning. I ran along and chased squirrels. Then in the afternoon, after a picnic, Diana let me go in the pond. The water was a little too cold for her but it was fine for me. They threw tennis balls until I thought they would drop. I have had so much fun—"

"Hush up, Venture," commanded Little Haze. "You are downright mean. You know I would have loved to do the wonderful things you are talking about, but Billyum is here at this convention and needs me. You know very well that I have spent my time lying under a chair."

"But I have been having so much fun!" I exclaimed. "Don't you want to hear about it?"

"As a matter of fact, I don't!" retorted Little Haze. "It is hateful of you to brag about the good time I've been missing out on."

"Well," I said, "I was just trying to share it with you. You don't need to bite my head off."

"Tell you what, Venture," said Little Haze. "A time will come when I will swim with you in a pond. At that time, I will sink you, and then you will see once and for all that I am better."

I thought Little Haze was not acting very social but I was very tired, so I just went to sleep. After all, she was just a female. What can you expect?

Monday morning, Diana's luggage had still not arrived and she was very unhappy.

I had slipped outside and run down to the pond, where I took a long drink of water. Diana's friend saw me and came running towards me, so I splashed her a good one as I plunged into the water.

"Oh goodness gracious," cried the lady. "Venture has gone into the pond after drinking at least half of it."

"You old butt," said Diana. "I doubt you will be dry when we get to the airport, and for you there are no potties in the sky. However, for a change, we are in luck. We have a stopover in Texas, so I will have a chance to take you out. How does that sound, you old butt you?"

I ran my mighty wet club. It sounded as though Diana wasn't too displeased with me.

Actually, by the time we met Billyum and were ready to get on the plane, my coat was pretty dry. The ride was not very pleasant, though, because there was a bad storm. Billyum and Diana were uncomfortable but Little Haze and I assured them that everything would be all right. By the time we reached Texas, however, I had a pretty urgent need to let that pond water out. Diana explained that I needed to go out, and the gate agent called a skycap to help us. Since we only had a little time, they suggested that Diana not bother using my harness. The weather was awful outside, and Diana was glad to have the skycap's assistance. Since we had help, Diana left her purse, her computer and her harness with Billyum. Having gone outside the airport, we had to go back in through security. The man in charge of security had a bad mood to match the weather.

"You can't bring the dog in here," he said. "It's against airline regulations to bring a dog in here."

Over the public address system we could hear the final boarding call for our flight.

"Excuse me, sir," said Diana, "but this is a guide dog."

"Ummmm," said the agent. "Looks like a regular dog to me."

"No it isn't, said the skycap. "This lady just got off a plane that landed here. She should be on this flight that is leaving."

"If the dog were a guide dog," said the agent, "Then it would have a special harness, which yours definitely does not have."

"But he does have a harness," explained Diana. "It is on the plane that is leaving—along with my purse."

"I suggested that she not bother with the harness," said the skycap. "With the weather so bad I thought it would be quicker if I just took her out."

"That is a good story," chuckled the agent. "However, I'm too smart for your silly tricks."

"This really is a guide dog," said the skycap. "You are making a terrible mistake and it may cost you your job."

"Yeah? Well, you can tell it to the judge. The law says no dogs allowed, and I ain't letting nobody break the rules. My job depends on seein' people like you don't pull something over on us law-abidin' folks."

"Do you have a supervisor?" asked Diana.

"Yeah," drawled the agent.

"Could I speak with that person?"

"Soon as she gets back from lunch."

Diana turned to the skycap. "I am really in trouble and I need your help," she said. "I know that you make your living by assisting people. If you stay with me, I'm afraid you'll get in trouble. On the other hand, if you leave me, I may never be able to leave this airport. How can I prove this is a guide dog?"

"I don't think you will have a problem once you talk with the supervisor," said the skycap. "Don't worry on my account, though.

I'll stay with you till we get this worked out."

"Thank you," said Diana. "I am due in court this afternoon and there is going to be a real problem because I am not on that plane."

"I wouldn't believe this if I hadn't seen it happen with my own eyes. I am certain that the guy will lose his job over this,"said the skycap.

"I'm not interested in the guy losing his job so much as I need to be on that plane," said Diana.

"Well, said the skycap, "that plane has been gone for some time now."

"What am I going to do?" cried Diana. "My purse with money and credit cards plus Venture's harness are on that plane."

"I am sure that the young man you were with will take care of those things," smiled the skycap.

"I know that," said Diana. "The problem is when I leave here I will have absolutely no proof that this is a guide dog. That probably means I couldn't use a taxi or a bus even if I had the money."

"Come now," laughed the skycap. "Don't you want to live in Texas?"

"Well, not like this," said Diana glumly.

"I was trying to be funny," said the skycap. "Don't worry, this will get sorted out. I don't know how the hearing will work out, but trust me, next week you will be laughing about it. This is the kind of crazy thing that ought to be in a book. Have you had other interesting problems with the airlines?"

Diana told him about how we happened to come on this free trip.

The two of them talked together for about an hour while I slept. Finally, the supervisor appeared and we explained our problem.The supervisor went over to the agent, who said he had never seen the skycap before and so didn't know if he was on the level.

The supervisor then talked to agents at the gate and then went to her computer.

"This agent for security is new," she explained. "That is why he didn't recognize the skycap, who has worked here for some time. There is no excuse at all for what has happened. If he had a question, there is someone who relieves me for lunch, and he could have called her. We will get you back home, and we'll be replacing this agent as of right now."

"He was most unpleasant," said the skycap. "There is no question that this lady has been put through a lot of embarrassment. What I wonder about is, how will she manage when she reaches her destination? No money, no ID, no harness—I don't think she will be able to use any kind of public transportation."

"We will take care of that," said the agent. "We will charter a plane for her and arrange for ground transport when she arrives. Ma'am, we can get a message to your friend so he'll know what's going on. Whatever either of you need, we will try to provide."

"I wouldn't think you have to charter a plane," said Diana. "Other airlines are flying out there all the time. But do you think there would be any way someone could give me a letter about what happened? I had a court hearing today and because of this fiasco, I have missed it. I don't think a judge is going to believe this crazy story."

"We will take care of it," said the agent. "This is a most unusual situation. You may be right about using another airline, though. It probably means another two-hour wait, but I don't think we could get a plane ready any faster. Are you in a rush to get back?"

"The hearing was the only urgent reason I had to be back by a certain time," said Diana. "Now I guess that it doesn't really matter."

"I will work out everything," said the agent. "Now you," she said to the skycap, "take Diana over to our best restaurant and the two of you have lunch as our guests. We will, of course, compensate you for your lost time, as this is certainly our responsibility."

Diana and the skycap had a delightful lunch. "I am certain this is a whole lot better then anything Billyum is eating," laughed Diana. By the time we left, Diana had become friends with the skycap and they had agreed to exchange letters. I thought he was a very nice man. He had a family and lived on a ranch and as he talked about his kids, I thought it might be fun to play with them. But that never happened.

We were given first-class seating, much roomier than I was used to. I enjoyed the trip.

When the plane landed, we were met by a very nice man from the airline. "I am here to take you home," he explained as he handed Diana my harness and her purse.

"The airline got a message to your friend that we would be taking care of you," he said as he helped us into the car. "We even took care of your hearing."

"How on earth did you do that?" asked Diana.

"Your friend had your laptop computer," laughed the agent. "When you didn't return to the plane and they went on without you, your friend got the stewardess to let him use the computer on the airplane. He had all your records there and used the travel time to prepare for the hearing. I met him here at the airport and he explained about the hearing. He told me he was going to go in your place but he needed to go home immediately and change his clothes. I explained that because this was our fault, I would do everything to help him. I also explained that I would need your things. He gave me your purse and Venture's harness, but kept the computer as he was going to be needing it.

"I took him home, waited for him to change, then drove him to the hearing. The hearing went on for a little while but I waited for him and then took him home again. I think he was very pleased with the way things turned out. By then it was time to get you. Now I would guess that you would like to go home."

"Yes," said Diana tiredly. "I would appreciate that very much."

"Oh yes, there is a message I am supposed to give you," said the agent. "Your friend will see you in the office tomorrow. He had a headache, so he said he would be turning off his telephone. So you will have to wait until tomorrow to talk with him. Is there anything else I can do?"

"My luggage is lost," said Diana. "I would appreciate it very much if you could have someone look for it."

"Consider it done," said the agent. "You have a nice evening," he said as he dropped Diana off in front of her house.

Diana took me out, fed me, then collapsed on her bed. It had certainly been a very busy day.

The next morning she called Billyum.

"I am glad that you keep such good records, Diyum," said Billyum. "When the plane left without you, I was really upset. I had your purse and Venture's harness and I knew you were in a heap of trouble. I talked with the flight attendants, but they told me there was nothing they could do. I decided I'd better see what I could do about the hearing. I didn't have a lot of hope, but I figured I would try. I knew that even if I had an idea what to do, I probably couldn't get there in time. But I got into your files and found everything laid out clearly. It showed me pretty much what to do.

"Imagine my surprise when I was met by that nice man from the airline. He really was sorry about what was happening, and he wanted to help in any way he could. I figured that I could go to the hearing if he would drive me home, wait for me to change, and then drive me there. I never could have made it without his help. That was really a badness that happened, but I really must say that I think the airline did do their very best to remedy the situation. I did well at the hearing. The client was sure upset when you didn't show up, but I told him I had everything under control. Actually, I was very concerned, but for the sake of the client, I let him think I had it under control. I guess the judge thought I knew what I was doing too. I explained what was happening to you and that I was your associate standing in for you and that was accepted. I then went on to win the case. But I assure you that I would rather have you do it next time."

"I will be in the office this afternoon," said Diana. "I have a few things around here I need to catch up on."

Fritsey came over and we went through the mail. One letter was very interesting. It was from the mother of the little boy who had raised me. Diana was very pleased with this letter and said she would tell Billyum all about it.

That afternoon, we went to the office and I was overjoyed to see Little Haze.

"I see you got back all right," she said as she gnawed on her bone.

"I wasn't sure there for a little while," I said. "It looked like maybe we would be living in Texas. Thank goodness, we finally met some really helpful people at the airline and we got back all right." I went on to tell her about the adVenture.

"I got a very nice letter from the mother of the little boy who raised Venture," Diana said to Billyum. "Actually, he is not a little boy but a teenager who will be leaving for college in a few months. They were just thrilled to hear from us. The boy's name is William.

I guess that when they took Venture back to the school, he was afraid he would never hear about Venture again."

"I admire people who take those puppies into their homes and hearts," said Billyum. "It must take a lot of patience and dedication and it must be heartbreaking to have to give up the pup. I couldn't do it."

"Me neither," said Diana. "William's mother told of how when Venture was just eight weeks old, they used to carry him to church. However, he outgrew that stage in no time. I guess they tried to take him everywhere. They seem very pleased about hearing about his interesting life out here."

"Are you going to tell William about yesterday and your weird experience?" asked Billyum.

"Probably," said Diana, "But I am not going to make a big fuss to the airlines because, although they created a potentially bad problem, they solved it—and very graciously, too."

"Yes they did," replied Billyum. "I forgot to tell you just before you got in they called to say they had found your luggage and would bring it to you this evening."

Just then the phone rang and Billyum answered it.

"It's for you," he said.

Diana took the call. She was not on the phone very long, but when she hung up, she was smiling.

"That was the president of the airline," she said, "apologizing personally for what had happened during our trip. He wanted me to know that his staff had tried hard to rectify the problem and he hoped I hadn't been put out too much. As a gesture of goodwill, he asked me to accept round-trip tickets for two. I told him I appreciated the way we were treated once the mistake was found and that I was pleased to accept his generous gift. You know, Billyum, the skycap who was so kind to me told me that by next week I would be laughing about this, but I sure found that impossible to believe."

"Well," said Billyum, "I put your computer in your office. Let's both write thank-you letters to the airlines."

Diana agreed and I was lulled to sleep by the *click click click* of the computer keys as Diana typed her letter.

Fourteen

Revving It Up

Life moved along at its predictable or, should I say, unpredictable pace. Things were going well at the office and I was doing great. Life was pleasant and when Fritsey said she would like to take Diana and me to the county fair, it sounded exciting. But when I told Little Haze about it, her reaction was very different than I expected.

"When Roger, that nice young man, came by the other day, didn't he say he would like to take you two to the fair?" asked Little Haze.

"He surely did," I admitted. "As a matter of fact, I thought that Diana was looking forward to going with him. She told him it sounded like fun, but they hadn't made any definite plans. She mentioned the invitation to Fritsey, who got really upset, saying Diana only did things with her when she needed something done. Rather than have a brouhaha over it, Diana told Roger that she forgot she had already told her girlfriend they would go to the fair. So Roger isn't taking us."

"Fritsey worries me," said Little Haze.

"Why is that?" I asked.

"I've been watching her for a long time," replied Little Haze as she licked at her paw. "Fritsey is a very good and kind woman, and I like her a lot. I know that she is helpful to Diana, but haven't you noticed how smothering she can be?"

"She is a very dominating woman," I said. "But that is just her nature. She is really a good-hearted soul and I don't think she asks much in return."

"That is how it appears on the surface," said Little Haze. "But give it a little thought, Venture. Fritsey is old enough to be Diana's grandmother. I think it is wonderful that she wants to be friends with us. Certainly she has been very helpful to both Billyum and Diana. However, have you noticed how few friends of her own age she has? Have you observed how eagerly she runs off other people who want to be friends with or help Diana?"

"Well," I said as I chewed on a bone, "now that you bring it up, I remember she was very upset at the idea of Diana going out with Roger. He is a little older then she is and he is disabled. Fritsey said Diana spent enough time with flakes like him at work and that there was no call for her to spend her personal life with someone like that."

"I think," said Little Haze, continuing to lick her paw, "that sooner or later serious problems are going to develop and then we can all stand back and watch the sparks fly."

"Why do you say that?" I asked, laying down the bone.

"I have been watching the two of them for some time," said Little Haze. "I do not at all like what I see. Before Diana went to get you, she was seeing a young man once in a while. I am certain that it wasn't serious, but it was a pleasant happy friendship. The young man was very well off. I know that he made a gift to Diana of the ticket she used to go and get you. This was before the Guide Dog Foundation was able to provide free airfare, which they do now. I also know for a fact that while Diana was away Fritsey called this young man and explained that he needed to pull back from Diana. She told him that she, Fritsey, was able to help Diana and Diana is so busy with her work—well, Diana must not be made to suffer any emotional turmoil that this man's friendship was causing her."

"I'm sure Diana didn't appreciate that," I said.

"Not a bit," said Little Haze. "She was madder than a wet hen when she learned about it, but by then it was too late."

"Oh dear," I said. "That doesn't sound so good. Why do you think it is happening?"

"Oh," said Little Haze, "It is not unusual for someone to latch onto a handicapped person. The problem is, that person kind of tries to live and be what they couldn't through the person they are trying to help. Now Fritsey is a very good woman. The trouble is she is very lonely. If the truth were known, she sees Diana doing and being some of the things she dreams were happening to her. She has a need to control. Billyum and Diana do a lot of good and Fritsey feels she deserves a lot of the credit. Her help has been very important, but mark my words, Venture—something will happen that will change things."

"Like what?" I asked.

"One of these days, Diana will meet 'Mr. Right' and Fritsey may not be able to scare him off. Believe me, then the situation will change drastically."

"Who is 'Mr. Right'?" I asked. "I don't remember meeting him."

"That is because neither of you have probably met him yet, you old butt," laughed Little Haze. "'Mr. Right' is just what we would call the man who would be the perfect addition to Diana's life."

"Look here, you sleaze," I said as I glared at Little Haze. "I am a very capable male. Maybe I'm not so dainty and delicate as you, but all the same I meet all of Diana's needs. She doesn't need to meet any 'Mr. Right.' She has me."

Little Haze chuckled and gracefully wagged her lovely tail.

"Of course you are wonderful," she said. "All the same, since you are not a human, you don't bring the same things another human would bring to her life. When 'Mr. Right' comes along, you will understand."

"Well, I doubt that," I said. "But we'll see. When is this 'Mr. Right' supposed to come into the picture?"

"At the right time."

"When will that be," I asked "and why do you keep licking your paw? Does it taste good?"

"I have no idea when 'Mr. Right' will come," said Little Haze. "I had a wonderful experience this afternoon. For lunch, Billyum had a Polish sausage sandwich. As he was eating it, the Polish sausage fell out. I was just lying there but I was ready. That sausage never hit the floor. Boy, did it taste good! It makes my mouth water just thinking about it. I keep licking my paw and remembering. I don't think Billyum was real thrilled about it, but I hope it happens again real soon."

As Diana and I waited at the mall for Fritsey, a woman came over and started to pet me. Since I was wearing my harness, Diana explained to her that I was working and shouldn't be petted.

"Oh, I just love dogs," gushed the woman.

"He is very sweet," said Diana. "I'll give him a hug for you."

"But you can't do that," said the woman. "You just explained that while he has his harness on he is working and so can't be touched."

"It's OK for me," explained Diana. "I'm his master."

"It certainly is not!" exclaimed the woman indignantly. "If you say he can't be petted, that is fine, but you have to follow the same rules we do."

Diana smiled. "I don't think you understand. You see, Venture works for me and pats and praise and things like that are, for him, a kind of salary for helping me. Now, if he were your guide dog and working for you, then I couldn't pet him but you could."

"You young folks today have an answer for everything, don't you," muttered the woman as she stalked away.

"What was that all about?" asked Fritsey, coming up as the woman retreated.

"That lady thought it was unfair that she couldn't pet Venture but I could," said Diana. "Let's get out of here before something else happens."

The evening was balmy and just right for going out. I guess other people thought so, too, because when we got to the fair there were a lot of people there. Our first stop was a health exhibit where they were taking people's blood pressure.

"I'd like to get mine checked," said Fritsey. "Why don't you have yours checked too?"

Fritsey went first. As usual, it was very high.

"Your turn, Diana," she said as she got up from the chair.

Diana sat down and they tried to take her blood pressure. They couldn't get a reading.

"Don't worry about it," laughed Diana. "The problem is that I have died and nobody bothered to tell me, so I'm still walking around. Actually, my blood pressure is very low—even my doctor sometimes has trouble getting a reading. It really isn't worth worrying about. I feel fine."

"Well, if you are sure you are all right," said the young man who was doing the testing.

Fritsey and Diana walked by a lot of exhibits. It seemed pretty boring to me, but I went along with it. Then Fritsey said, "Oh, there are some gypsies over there. Let's go have them tell our fortune."

We walked over, but the man pointed to Diana and said "We no can do."

"Why?" asked Fritsey.

"We no can do," repeated the gypsy.

"Don't worry about it," said Diana. "I have heard they won't do blind people."

"Yes, but why?" asked Fritsey.

"I don't know," laughed Diana, "but who cares? Maybe it is because they can't read my reactions in my eyes so they don't know if the stuff they are making up is close to the truth. I have read interesting things about palmistry but I have no real interest in it. I think, all in all, it is more fun not knowing what the future holds. For me it is wonderful to wake up each morning wondering what the day has in store for me."

"I think it would have been fun," said Fritsey.

"Oh, forget it," said Diana. "I will read your palm and I don't even need to see it. I predict that in a little while, you will eat two hot dogs. You will have everything on them. Later on tonight they will talk back to you and you will ask yourself why on earth you ate them. That will be five dollars, please," Diana chuckled.

"Forget that," said Fritsey. "I'll just pay for the hot dogs."

Both of the women laughed. They were walking along towards the hot dog stand when Fritsey said, "What on earth is 'The Church of the Eternity?' I never heard of them. They have a big display. I can't imagine what they are doing at a fair."

"Oh, I know about them," said Diana, "and I think they should be right at home in a carnival. These people have a real racket going on. They sell ordinations to become a minister and you can buy all kinds of doctorate degrees from them. The reason I feel this is so sad is that people with less than lofty ideals buy these degrees. Then, saying that they are men of the cloth, they will involve themselves, let us say, with a woman who may have a little nest egg but who is having personal problems. Believing herself to be talking with a man of God, she will tell this guy who has bought this degree things that should only be discussed with a professional counselor. Often such people are financially taken advantage of and there is no counting the cost of the emotional havoc they leave in their wake. You know, people like me worked for years and practically sweated blood for honest degrees and it irks me that some teenager can buy one of these things, and the state recognizes it. I don't think you could get a license to practice psychology with the thing, but you would be recognized by the state as a religious entity. If I could do anything to expose what they are, I certainly would do so—but I doubt I will ever have an opportunity."

"I want to go see," said Fritsey.

"OK," said Diana. "We'll go with you."

We went over and looked at the exhibit. Diana's description was pretty correct. Fritsey was really surprised at the artwork used to make up the degrees. "They really are impressive," she said "and they sure do look real."

"Oh, they are," breathed a young man in a white robe. "My name is Brother Jonathan. Dr. Devaul is such a wonderful man. He has made all of this goodness possible and all that you see here, all this opportunity—this wonderful chance to be a blessing to your community, to truly be a channel of service to God and to your fellow man, is all made possible here. You know," he continued in a dreamy voice, "this magnificent dog is truly a wonderful gift from God. I love the beautiful dog so much, and great goodness comes from you, ma'am. It is such as you that God would choose."

"I am afraid I don't have any money," said Diana.

"Well, we can accept VISA, MasterCard, or American Express," said the young man in his ethereal voice.

"I didn't bring a credit card with me," smiled Diana.

"Oh, that is sad," whispered the young man. "However, you are blessed by God tonight. When I see someone I can recognize as a spiritual brother, I am authorized to ordain them free of charge. Later when you see the benefits, you can purchase another degree or two."

I knew Diana was snickering inside but she remained very calm as she answered the young man.

"Sir," she said, "I don't think that I am of ministerial quality. However, I have a friend who truly is. Would it be possible to have my friend ordained?"

"Certainly," said the young man. "Just have your friend here write his name and address on this piece of paper and I will take care of the rest."

"You expressed such disgust at these people, I am mystified by your actions," said Fritsey. "Are you going to get the ordination for Billyum?"

"Of course not," said Diana. "Remember how I told you I would like to have the chance to show the world what creeps these people are? Here is my opportunity. It will take some time, but I will make these folks look like what they are, and I think I will honor R.T. at the same time."

"I don't understand," said Fritsey. "What on earth do you plan to do?"

"Keep your voice down," cautioned Diana. "It is very necessary to my plan that they do not realize what I am doing. Now, do you have something to write with?"

"Yes," answered a puzzled Fritsey. "What is it that you want me to put down?"

"Well," said Diana, "we will give the whole thing away if we write down Venture. That is not a person's name. So we will use his initial. For the second initial we will use the letter A. Now Venture is a butt so we will honor R.T. by using his last name. So we have V.A. Butz. For the address, just put down the office. There is no reason why these folks should know where I live."

Fritsey giggled and wrote the information on the paper the man in the robe had given her. She then returned it to him and in a few minutes he presented us with a card. Diana thanked him graciously.

"Come on, Fritsey," she said. "I am dying of hunger," and the three of us hurried away from the exhibit.

"I don't believe what you just did," said Fritsey when we were safely away.

"Don't tell anyone about this just yet," said Diana. "You haven't seen anything yet. I will really make these people show their true colors."

"What are you going to do?" asked Fritsey.

"Just wait and see," laughed Diana. "They will have egg on their faces before this is over. You know, we tried three things tonight. The blood pressure test, that failed. The gypsies, that failed. And the third thing, the Church of the Eternity. That is our lucky charm."

"It is awfully funny," laughed Fritsey. "This sure has been an eventful evening."

The next morning, when Diana told Billyum about my new status, he laughed and laughed. Little Haze held her head high and looked down her pretty nose at me. "You may be a Rev," she said, "but you still don't have a wagging license."

"Whatever is a wagging license?" I asked.

"Well," said Little Haze, "You know how us dogs have to be licensed or else we are not legal. It is the same way about wagging. You wag a lot. Oh, I know you call it clubbing or running your mighty club, but it is wagging, and since you don't have a license to wag, it is illegal. What is more, you need a certificate of forgiveness so that even when you do get a license, your past illegal acts can be forgiven. I have such a license and I could give you one and absolve you of illegal wagging, but I won't."

"Where did you get your license?" I asked.

"From the Secret Order of the Growlery," answered Little Haze.

"How can I get one?" I asked.

"Well, Rev. Butz, that is for me to know and for you to find out," she sniffed as she nudged the bone out of my reach.

Over the next few weeks, the coming of the mailman became an occasion for a lot of laughter. The first letter was written by Diana to Dr. Peter Devaul. This letter was written as though I wrote it. It read:

Dear Reverend Doctor Devaul:

I wish to express my gratitude to you for the wonderful gift you have given me. Ever since I was little, I have had great respect for those who wear the collar. It means a lot to me to now be considered a minister.

My goal in life is to provide guidance. Not just OK guidance—ultra-special guidance, the kind that the person would say was truly heaven-sent.

My friends are awestruck now that I have attained this new plateau. I am really putting it to good use and already it is said that I have brought a whole new meaning to the gift of tongues.

Thank you again for this opportunity. Triple blessings upon your head, good friend.

Sincerely,
Rev. V.A. Butz
VAB/mm"

"Oh, he would die if he knew the truth about that letter," chuckled Billyum. "Tell me, though, who is 'mm' supposed to be?"

"His secretary," replied Diana.

"Who might that be?" asked Billyum.

"Mickey Mouse!" she laughed. "That is what this whole dog and pony show is about in my opinion, just Mickey Mouse stuff."

"Well," said Billyum, "if he ever finds out what this is all about, I seriously doubt you will make it on his '100 most admired women' list. But you just may make it on his most despised list."

"He is already on mine," said Diana. "I plan for him to learn all about what I am doing."

We expected an answer. However, we were surprised and disgusted at it when it came. Most of all I found Diana's anger interesting. The letter read:

"Dear Rev. Butz:

I received your letter this morning and I join you in your celebration of thanksgiving. It gladdens my heart when I hear that through my efforts I have been the channel through which goodness and multiple blessings flow. I am glad and rejoice with you now that you can lead your flock in a way they will see as more professional. Welcome, Rev. Butz, into the fraternity of the ministry.

I would not, however, be fulfilling my God-given mission if I do not make you aware of the inside track in this business. It is wonderful to help people, but never forget Rev. Butz, helping people is Big Business and that means big bucks. Big Business needs to be managed adroitly but never Fear. I have had many years of experience in this field and I know the tricks of the trade. I am gladly going to share them with you.

First of all, atmosphere is everything. If you want to turn a profit in this business, it is necessary to give the people what they want. I suggest that you begin with your dress.

Since money is often a problem when you are first getting started, I recommend simplicity. When you lead services, I highly recommend a pure white robe. Very simple, but of fine fabric. It is important to wear these vestments, let's say, for a baptism. We also have available a crocheted white fur scarf or it is available in fine lace. It is truly an awesome picture if you can imagine yourself standing before the flock in your vestments holding in your arms the precious babe you are going to baptize, wrapped in this splendid fur scarf. Your flock will love it.

As you have more money, you can buy different costumes so that you will be arrayed differently for different celebrations. Never forget the importance of the stained glass effect. People just eat it up and your flock will grow from just a few, to hundreds. The flock will feel that they can trust the shepherd who gives them ambience. Just think how wonderful it will be to be able to help hundreds of people.

Using the stained glass principle does seem to help the collection plate, too, on Sunday mornings and perceiving that lump in your wallet is a reassuring feeling believe me.

For your convenience, I have enclosed a catalogue that has a full line of vestments, and other articles that will add style and grace to your performance.

The other thing I would like to point out is that your influence would be heightened and you could have a much more profound impact on your community if you can add Ph.D. to your name. You will see that we offer a wide selection in the catalogue and of course we welcome all major credit cards here.

We are here to serve you so fill out the enclosed order form today.

Thank you for joining our family and we look forward to serving you.

Yours In loving Service,
Rev. Doctor Peter Devaul
Pastor
Church of the Eternity

Diana and Billyum practically rolled on the floor with laughter when they heard the letter read.

"Actually," said Diana, "This guy is quite an artist with words. Yet the whole idea makes me feel ill. This is really funny but it stops being funny if you stop and realize this con man is peddling this garbage. The door is being thrown wide open to the confidence man who is trying to gather up people's money without doing an honest day's work. It makes me very angry!"

"What are you going to do now?" said Billyum. "I don't think any of those robes he has are going to fit Venture."

"I am going to write him a letter and tell him just what a creep I think he is," said Diana. "I wonder how he is going to feel when he learns Rev. Butz is a dog."

"I wouldn't know," said Billyum. "I would enjoy seeing a copy of the letter you send him."

Diana vanished into her office. When she emerged, she had this letter.

> *"Dr. Peter Devaul*
> *Church of the Eternity*
> *Dear Dr. Devaul:*
>
> *I have always thought of myself as a decent person. Not always perfect, but not a confidence man either.*
>
> *A few weeks ago, a friend took me to the county fair where you were putting on a display. I am knowledgeable about your activities. I know that the state of California recognizes your claims as legitimate to ordain people to the ministry. I, however, do not. I have real problems with the idea of just any Tom, Dick, or Harry for ten dollars being ordained to the clergy.*
>
> *You know as well as I do that this is just opening up the door to confidence schemes to say nothing of how you degrade the idea of Ph.D. There are many people who work and sacrifice for years to get these degrees and it is such people who have made them respectable. I think it is distressing that some punk can, for a small fee, become in many people's eyes, a true man of God.*
>
> *For a long time, I have wished someone could do something to expose the danger I think you pose to the community. My golden opportunity came while we were at the fair. Brother Jonathan approached me and offered me an ordination. I explained that I didn't believe I was the type but I*

had a friend who would be just perfect. He asked me to write down my friend's name and address, and he issued a card right on the spot.

My friend's name is Venture, so I put down V. A. Butz and that is with whom you have been corresponding.

True, Venture does have a lot of respect for the collar. He has even more respect for his leash and the public has great respect for his harness. You see, Venture is a guide dog. He is certainly a very special guide dog, but the bottom line is he is still a dog. Yet your church has licensed him as a minister. What on earth are people going to think of such an organization?

I just could not believe the garbage you sent showing how to be commercially successful as a 'man of God.' I don't know just yet how I will be best able to expose this for what it is but I am sure I will have my chance.

One thing you can count on though. When I get my chance to expose the bad thing I believe you to be, I hope that I will be able to make a lot of noise and the public will be more aware to watch out for confidence men playing the role of ministers. I realize that you are not the total source for these disreputable people but you are a large one.

Sincerely,
Diana Dawne

P.S. You made reference in your letter that following the stained glass principle would make Venture's congregation more respectful of the shepherd. Please be advised that Venture is not a German Shepherd. He is a Golden Lab."

Almost in the next mail, Diana got this letter:

Dear Ms. Dawne:

When we made the offer of an ordination, we did so in good faith. It is not our policy or practice to ordain dogs no matter how wonderful they may be.

You obviously knew this and the subterfuge you used to conceal the fact that V.A. Butz is, in fact, a dog proves that you meant to deceive us. You should be prosecuted for your illegal offense, but we here at the Church of the Eternity want to extend compassion to you. So if you will just return the certificate of ordination we are prepared to forget the whole thing.

If, however, you wish to mount a crusade against us, then we will have no recourse but to take you to court. You need to think carefully about this as you seem to want to attack a right that is guaranteed to all Americans in the constitution of the United States—the right to freedom of religion.

Please advise us of your plans.

Yours in honorable service,
Dr. Peter Devaul
President of the
Church of the Eternity"

"What are you going to do?" asked Billyum. "This man is obviously angry with you."

"Oh," laughed Diana. "I have already composed my response. Do you want to hear it?"

"Sure," said Billyum.

Diana showed him the letter. It said:

Dear Dr. Devaul:

In answer to your letter I want you to know I plan to keep the ordination certificate and you should want me to keep it. After all, it is more blessed

> *to give than to receive so don't expect to receive.*
> *If you want to take legal action, then I guess*
> *that it is a-courtin' we will go.*
> *Sincerely,*
> *Diana Dawne*

"Ummm," said Billyum after he heard the letter. "I am not sure that you are handling this correctly, Diana."

"I am," laughed Diana. "If they take me to court, can you imagine the field day the press will have with this story? And besides, about all a judge can do is to tell me to give it back."

"Maybe so," said Billyum. "The thing is, though, that I think they are right about having the freedom of practicing religion in whatever way they want."

"Right," smiled Diana. "So I guess that people have the right to be led by the Butt as their spiritual counselor."

Billyum and Diana laughed together as Little Haze and I exchanged happy glances.

"You do have the ego to be a Rev," laughed Little Haze.

"I haven't exactly noticed you acting modest," I wagged. "I don't believe you mind at all when people admire your dainty silhouette or remark on your lovely color."

"Of course not," agreed Little Haze. "One of our qualifications to be a guide dog is that we be beautiful and so be a source of pride to our masters. Besides, this attitude of caring about ourselves is an integral part of being a good guide dog. If we have a lot of respect for ourselves, then of course we will share that respect with our masters. After all, they are an extension of ourselves."

Several weeks passed and Diana and I had to attend a hearing held by the PUC (Public Utility Commission) because the telephone company was trying to raise rates again.

"I am sure that my going will not stop them," explained Diana to Billyum. "But I wanted you to know why we will be in to work late. If I don't go and the rates are raised, then I will feel that I should have been there. It's kind of like voting. It doesn't seem to matter much but if you don't participate, you have no right to complain about the way things are done."

"I wish I had known about this sooner," said Billyum. "I would have liked to have go, but I have an appointment in the morning."

The hearing was pretty routine. Different people got up and said why they felt the telephone rates shouldn't be raised. Diana and I also got up and Diana spoke. There was a lot of applause when we sat down. Diana said she thought she had scored a couple points. I am pretty sure having such a beautiful escort didn't hurt her cause at all.

A couple of older women were watching us and admiring me. I heard one of them say I just had to be the most precious thing alive.

During the break, Diana had to go to the ladies' room, so of course I took her. The two older women who had been admiring me were also there and they watched us go into a little booth. One of them said to the other, "You know, that dog helping that girl has to be the most wonderful thing I've seen all day. I wanted to help her but I didn't know how."

"I know," answered her friend. "I wanted to help her also, but I didn't know how to ask the dog."

Diana smiled behind the closed door. "You old butt," she laughed as she played with my ears. "They think you are the one who is intelligent."

I ran my mighty club. Naturally, I am intelligent, but I knew what Diana meant. These women did not realize that the two of us made up the team. True, without me, Diana wouldn't be nearly so impressive, but without Diana I couldn't do much either. It took both of us. I would have liked to explain this to the women, but there was just no tactful way to do it even if they wanted to understand. So we just went back to the hearing. When it was over, Diana and I returned to the office. As we came down the hall we could hear Billyum laughing with someone I did not know. He and Little Haze greeted us enthusiastically.

"Well!" said the gentleman whom I had heard laughing with Billyum. "So this is the Reverend Butz. I just bet he is the prettiest minister there is, and I am sure he starred at the hearing this morning. Do you think you two were able to do anything about our high telephone bills?"

"I would like to think so," said Diana, "but I don't have a lot of hope. It's just that if we don't protest these things then I don't feel we have a right to complain if they happen. At least I know I tried. Who are you?"

"This is Larry Carlson," said Billyum. "He is the attorney for the Church of the Eternity. It seems that Dr. Devaul sent him down here to talk some sense into you, Diyum. I have been talking with him for quite a while and he is really a nice fellow. You have some of those vanilla coffee beans here at the office, don't you?"

"Sure I do," said Diana.

"Why don't you make us some of that special brew?" said Billyum. "I want to watch while Mr. Carlson here tries to talk some sense into you, although I have already warned him it is a losing proposition. Your brain, Diyum, is like a sieve and. . ." Billyum put up his hands to protect his head from the purse he knew Diana would swing at him.

While Diana made coffee, I made friends with Mr. Carlson. I could tell that he already held Little Haze in the highest esteem, but it was soon very clear he respected me too. When Diana returned with the pot of coffee, Mr. Carlson was sitting on a chair between me and Little Haze. Her head was on one knee, and mine was on the other. Diana seemed to relax a little when she saw what a cozy atmosphere we had created. Mr. Carlson exclaimed over the unusual coffee, and several pleasantries were exchanged before he got down to the purpose of his visit.

"When Dr. Devaul called me to complain that some woman had had a dog ordained as a minister, I thought it was very funny," explained Mr. Carlson as he sipped his coffee. "However, Dr. Devaul didn't think it was one bit funny and he demanded I get to his office immediately so that we could draw up papers for a lawsuit. I urged him not to be so hasty, and after reading your correspondence I suggested that it might be best if I pay you a visit before we consider any other action."

"I don't have the certificate here," explained Diana. "However, if I did, I am sorry but I would not give it to you. I feel that what this group represents is wrong in principle. That is why I got the certificate, and it would seem to me that if I gave it back to you I would be endorsing what I feel is not right."

"I have been talking with Bill," said the lawyer. "He showed me the correspondence from Dr. Devaul. Understand, there is nothing illegal in what he said to you, but after talking with Bill, I do have another perspective on this matter. All I plan to do is ask you to listen to me so that you can know where I am coming from.

"I am a lawyer and forgive me if I brag just a little bit but I am very good at what I do. I am paid a very handsome retainer by Dr. Devaul because of my expertise with the law and I was sent to talk to you and get you to surrender that certificate.

"When the Church of the Eternity was set up, the purpose was to help individuals who were sincere to get a credential that would be accepted by the community. You and I know that there are good people out there who want to start their own church, but they don't have a lot of education and if they are older people sometimes good horse sense can mean a lot. Of course, once we got that business started, it kind of followed that it would be a good idea to provide a line of church ware—robes, candles, etc. After all, people were going to be buying them so why shouldn't the Church of the Eternity take its fair share of profit. This practice is very legal, and makes good business sense.

"What disgusts me, and I acknowledge that Bill had to point it out to me, is the almost immoral way Dr. Devaul sells the church. I believe that you made a very good point. It is one thing to offer items used in a service for sale, it is quite another to do it as though running a confidence ring.

"My job is to represent Peter Devaul and the Church of the Eternity. Part of representing him is not losing. You and Reverend Butz are not good for business, and I am confident that should you take this into court, the consequences to you might be more severe than you think. A judge very well could rule that because you hid the fact that the candidate was a dog, and the Church of the Eternity does not certify dogs, you practiced fraud, and should be fined thousands of dollars.

"On the other hand, the judge might look at the facts on hand and after talking with you, he might very well decide we were harassing you. Either way, the press would have a field day and I think by the time you were through, you wouldn't have to pay the fine, but the Church of the Eternity would never recover.

"I have given this matter a lot of thought, and I would like to suggest a compromise. Keep the certificate. Let the Reverend here enjoy his honored status. Tell this crazy story to anyone who will listen—but kindly refrain from using our name. Make one up, or say it is some mail order church without naming us. That way I think we both win. You make your point about what is being done in the religious community, but we come away unscarred."

"I have nothing personally against Dr. Devaul except this racket he is running," said Diana, "but in the letter from Dr. Devaul I think that he said that influence could be greatly impounded within the community if he could add "Doctor" to his name, and I think we should add a few Ph.D.s."

"We could do that, and he could become the Right Reverend Doctor Butz," said Mr. Carlson.

As this conversation proceeded and I heard the wonderful title "The Right Reverend Doctor Butz," I stretched up so that the nice man could better scratch my ears.

Mr. Carlson laughed. "It appears that the good doctor here likes the idea. He is reaching upward to receive from my hand some of the honor these titles should provide. How many do you want?"

"I think," said Billyum, who had remained quiet up to this point, "that what we should do is give him twelve. He just adores Christmas and it would kind of go with the twelve days of Christmas."

"Consider it done," said Mr. Carlson.

I conferred my first blessing on this great man.

"I just wanted to make a point," said Diana.

"And you made that point quite profoundly clear," laughed Mr. Carlson. "Hopefully, better judgment will be exercised in the future. I do have to say this job has been very interesting."

"You have been most pleasant to work with," said Diana as she picked up the coffee things.

"Well," said Mr. Carlson, "I will be on my way. It was very nice to meet you and the Reverend here and this other sweetheart and of course I had a lot of fun talking with Bill. Thank you, Bill, for explaining to me those problems I was having with my own computer."

"Any time," smiled Billyum. "If you have any more questions please feel free to call me."

"I'll do that," he said as he picked up his briefcase.

"Now that is a really nice man," said Billyum after the lawyer had left. "He doesn't just seem to be interested in the law but in humanity as well." He changed the subject. "There isn't much going on here and I know you and Venture are leaving in a day or so for your trip to New York, so why don't you just go on home. I'm sure you have a million things to do before you go."

"That is so," agreed Diana as she gathered some things together. "I am looking forward to my trip."

That evening as she brushed my shining golden coat, Diana told me that again we were going to ride in an airplane. "I just hope we don't have any weird experiences this time," she added.

I didn't really care so long as I was with Diana. So I just stretched out and ran my mighty club. After all, what would be would be.

Fifteen

Banner

It has always been interesting to me to note the differences between seasons, and the differences even between the evenings and the early mornings. But this morning it was much earlier than our usual rising time. Fritsey didn't like it too much, either, and she said so when she came to take us to the airport.

"Why on earth, Diana, did you schedule this flight at such an ungodly hour? Even poor Venture looks sleepy. Why on earth are we leaving in the middle of the night?"

"So I won't be getting into New York in the middle of the night," said Diana. "It is going to be a bit difficult for the people who are meeting me to come pick me up, so it seemed simpler to make it easy on that end."

"It sure makes it bad on this end," complained Fritsey.

"Now Fritsey," sighed Diana, "I think we have been over this before. Originally I planned to take a limo to the airport, but you wouldn't hear of it. It would have been no trouble at all, and it will work out better for me to be met since I don't know the New York area all that well."

"I know all that," said Fritsey. "It's just that if I had gone with you it would have made it so easy. I could have rented a car and taken you and your friends wherever they wanted to go. After all, you do have that extra ticket."

"That is true," said Diana. "But as I explained before, my roommate didn't have a place for you to stay, so it would have been really difficult."

"Didn't you tell me that William, the little boy who raised Venture, is gone for the summer, so you aren't going to get to meet him?" asked Fritsey.

"Correct," said Diana. "William is away for the summer. I was very happy to get a telephone call from William's mother. She said that although William wasn't going to be there, others who knew Venture were, so they would like for us to visit them at their home. I will get to see where this old butt grew up and maybe learn a little more about what it was like for him. I did explain to Venture that we were going to the home where he grew up and although William wouldn't be there, many other people that he knows would. He did run his club, but then he does that any time you talk to him so it is very hard to tell if he understood any of what I told him. But I know one thing. I am certain he will remember those people when he sees them. Won't you, Venture?"

I ran my mighty club with joy. This trip was already yumston and I was going to enjoy every second of it.

All the way to the airport, Fritsey moaned about the fact that she wanted to go and all Diana really had to do was give her the ticket.

"The problem is," said Diana, "I can't invite you to other people's homes, and to put you up somewhere would run into a great deal of money. Otherwise, you would be welcome to come along."

"At least hand over the ticket," said Fritsey.

"Oh, I don't think that is necessary," laughed Diana.

"Yes it is," said Fritsey. "I am going to need it when we get to the airport so that I can get your luggage checked and get your seating taken care of and everything."

"OK," sighed Diana. "Here it is. Be sure you give it back to me before you leave the airplane. Under the terms of the ticket, if you went along with me, you would have to wait until I was ready to come home. I don't have a reservation until three weeks from tomorrow."

"Don't worry, Diana," said Fritsey. "I am not going along. I wish you had some friends who would have a place for me to stay, though, because when you visit the place where Venture grew up, I surely would like to be there."

"I know," said Diana. "Maybe sometime something can be worked out."

"The problem is that you have the ticket today," said Fritsey.

"True," said Diana. "I really would like to have seen it used but it just didn't work out."

I was happy when we reached the airport. The bustle and noise relieved some of the tension that was building over the trip and I was glad when we boarded the airplane. We got our usual bulkhead seats, but this time it was delightfully different. Because it was summertime, the plane was full so they needed the extra seat I usually got. However, what made this different was that our companions were children going to visit their grandparents. They were age seven and ten and were thrilled that they got to sit with the dog. I was pleased with them too. In the excitement, we hardly noticed that Fritsey had left. After we were airborne, the children got down on the floor with me. I just loved it, so I kissed them and ran my mighty club. They were thrilled with the loud *thud thud thud* it made, and their delight made me run it all the more. They hugged me and stroked my beautiful shining coat. To show them just how much I loved all this attention, I exposed my tummy.

"Lookie," squealed the little girl. "Venture is upside down!"

"How do you figure that?" asked Diana. "He is just on his back, isn't he?"

"Yes," said the little girl, "but that is upside down. When he is right side up, his paws are under him and we can just see his back."

I waved my mighty paws in the air and ran my club some more. There was just no question about it, these kids were completely blown away by my charm and beauty. They told Diana that they had been dreading the trip, but I, Venture, had turned it into a great event. Then Diana remembered the ticket.

The stewardess laughed when she saw how distressed Diana was. "Don't worry," she said. "The lady who came on the plane with you gave it to me and when we get to Texas, I will give it to you. I am responsible for these young people here, and you have to change planes. So I will be escorting all of you. I will help these young people find who is meeting them, and I will see that you are in the right area to catch your plane. I will give you your ticket at that time."

"That sounds fine," said Diana. "Could I have another cup of coffee, please?"

"Coming right up," said the stewardess.

The rest of the flight to Texas was pleasant. Our travel companions asked all kinds of questions about me and I continued to entertain them. All too soon we were ready to land and this enjoyable phase of the journey was over.

The stewardess escorted us from the plane and gave the children to their happy grandmother. As they left the airport, I could hear them talking excitedly about me. Diana asked the stewardess if she could use a telephone. When she was told she might use one of the airline's telephones, she thanked the young woman, who was going off duty but who was explaining Diana's needs for assistance to another agent.

After Diana completed her phone call, the agent asked to see her ticket. Diana explained that she thought the stewardess had it and probably had given it to him.

The agent looked through his papers but there was no ticket. He managed to get the stewardess on the telephone. She said that she had had Diana's ticket and thought that she had given it to him but if he didn't have it then it must have gotten mixed up with the children's tickets. If so, the ticket was gone; that family had been seen leaving the airport.

The agent called his supervisor. She determined that Diana should be on the flight and gave instructions for her to be put on the correct plane to New York, which was just leaving.

"Do you think there is going to be a problem with my luggage?" asked a distressed Diana. "The baggage checks are with the ticket."

"I am afraid there probably is going to be some confusion," said the agent. "Be sure that you call the airline, and don't let them forget that this has happened. We do want to get this straightened out for you."

"I do, too," said Diana, and we boarded the new plane together.

This time we had the seats to ourselves. However, I got a lot of attention from the passengers and the nice flight attendants, who all were aware that Diana had a problem. Even so, time sped by and before you knew it we were in New York. But who knew where the luggage was?

New York is a very different place from Southern California. I grew excited by its special hustle and bustle, its honking horns, its interesting smells, and the higher pace of living. Guide dog Beth was there to meet us with her person. Now Beth always did have a crush on me. When we were in training together, she always looked up to me and thought that I was just the greatest. Now she still looked up to me and listened rapturously as I told her story after story about the magic land of California and what my life was like there. She exclaimed over Rabies, Billyum, and Little Haze. She wanted to see the kong, the ring, and Mr. Hedgehog.

Being a guide dog had made a big change in Beth. She always was a good steady girl, but now the stature of being a guide dog gave her a queenly bearing which complemented her good looks. I had always liked her, but after watching her with her person and hearing her spellbinding stories, I respected her. Beth was not at all the mysterious femme fatale that Little Haze was. She was nevertheless very special. This quiet, lovely dog had come softly into her person's life and then ever so gently, opened doors for her person. These newly opened doors made both Beth and her person loved and respected in their community. They lived a simple life, but one that was very fulfilling for both of them. It wasn't the crazy hodgepodge that my life with Diana often was, but it was a good life and I had to admire Beth for her industry, love and loyalty.

The next two weeks were very special. There was a little forest near Beth's house, and Diana and I spent many hours in its cooling shadows. Sometimes we visited friends for quiet dinners. Other times we went to the beach. It was wonderful. The countryside was really restful, and the opportunity to relax did both of us a lot of good.

There also were a few trips into town so that Diana could get some new clothes, since hers were with the luggage that was lost. Probably more than anything, Diana was upset about losing her luggage and the things that were packed in it. Diana takes a lot of pride in the way she dresses. I'm sure no one has any idea how much time and trouble it is when she goes somewhere and is well dressed. She considers an outfit very carefully, and everything must go together perfectly—shoes, hose, purse, belt, and jewelry. Many of the things she felt she had to have to give an outfit that perfectly-finished touch that is her trademark were not available. Boy, you should have heard her squeak! It would take a mighty lot of oil to stop her squeaking, and one morning it was especially bad.

It was obvious something was about to happen that was very important to Diana. There were lots of clues as Diana put on her hose and heels. She doesn't do that unless she's going somewhere special, and it was obvious to me that she really planned to do this occasion in style.

I was sleeping soundly, but was awakened when I thought I heard a familiar step. I stretched, thinking I had dreamed it. But when the doorbell rang and our visitor came into the room, my club began frantically pounding the floor and I lifted my voice in soft, whimpering greetings. For there standing before me was William's mother.

After exchanging warm greetings with Diana, she turned her attention to me.

"Oh, Venture," she said as she hugged me. "You are much more beautiful than I remember and we are so very proud of you. You have turned out to be such an outstanding guide dog. When you were a puppy, we had no idea you would become such a wonderful addition to another human being's life. We knew you would be a blessing to someone, but we have heard about the marvelous things you and Diana are doing together and you have no idea how proud it makes us to realize we had a part in making these things happen."

The women went on talking. Their praise flowed over me like honey. I listened for a while then lay quietly beside Diana and gently slipped in and out of sleep.

"I hope you will be up to meeting some of Venture's friends," said William's mother. "You know we are very active in our church, and being involved with the church was an important part of Venture's growing up. When it was learned that you and Venture would be visiting us, we decided to give you two a good, friendly church welcome. After you have gotten acquainted with us, we will be having a potluck. We hope you will talk to us as a group and share some of the experiences you and Venture have had together. We will also have a very special surprise for Venture. We were told by the folks at the Guide Dog Foundation that you have a beautiful singing voice, Diana. Reverend Stone, our pastor, hopes that you will sing for us."

Diana is many things, but shy she is not, so I knew before the day had started that it would be a roaring success. How could she not be successful? After all, she had me, and that guaranteed a stunning happening.

During the ride to the Church, the two women chatted together happily about when I was a puppy and about my life with Diana in California. Of course, Diana told William's mother all about Billyum and little Haze. After all, they were a very important part of my life.

When we got to the church, I think everyone I had ever known was there and there were a lot of people I didn't know. They all treated Diana and me like visiting royalty. I was hugged and kissed and I knew that although this was said to be happening for Diana, it was gratifying to know I was the real reason.

Things hadn't changed, though. When that yumston food came out, people were very careful to see that I didn't get a bite. Now there are a few times—not many, but a few—when being a guide dog does have its downside, and missing all that yumston food is certainly yuckston. I wouldn't give up being a guide dog, though, for anything.

After everyone had eaten, Diana and I were formally introduced amidst cheering and applause.

Diana began by thanking these people for the wonderful welcome and for the great interest they had in us. She told them that she knew it was because of them I had developed into the beautiful, useful tool that I am. She went on to explain how I had brought a whole new meaning to her life, and for that she was very grateful. She explained that my influence extended far beyond the good I do for her.

Knee-high to a daisy.

…Daisies at my knees!

Sweet nothings.

Eyes on a leash.

I'll watch your step.

Good mail box!

Rin Tin Tin, eat your heart out!

The brush that binds.

*Billyum —
it's a love
thing.*

Yumston!

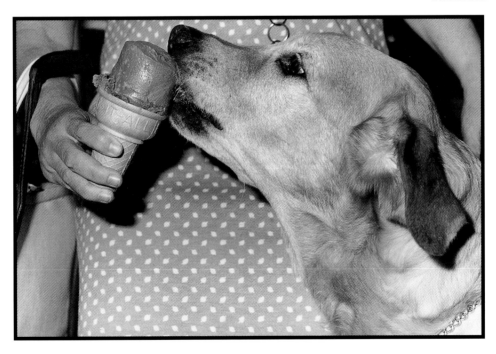

Magnificent obsession!

Semi-annual checkup with Dr. Bruce Levine — whether he needs it or not!

Please don't pet him — he's working.

*"Mr. Hedgehog, bring
me some toys…"*

I have a coat and tie.
Now I've got a tail!

Who deserves 12
Ph.D.s more than
me?

Eighty pounds of love.

This guy could be <u>the</u> catch of the day!

Match-maker.

We three docs ...

When I said "heal,"
I meant Diana!
(Diana's human vet,
Dr. Eugene Louis.)

Diana's BNS
upstages me
again.

Retrievers can shepherd.

Bless the beast and the children.

Kickin' back.

Stealing a kiss.

One in a Billyum.

I love you, Venture.

*Who is the
fairest of the
mall?*

Joy ride.

FOUR EYES.

He's got a cold nose, a warm heart, and eyes for two. But without you, he won't be able to help the visually impaired realize their independent, mobile, productive lives. So please contribute generously to the Guide Dog Foundation for the Blind. You'll be giving someone the gift of vision. And someone else a home.

GUIDE DOG FOUNDATION FOR THE BLIND

Call 1-800-548-4337, or write us at 371 East Jericho Turnpike, Smithtown, New York 11787-2976

She then went on to tell these people about Billyum and Little Haze. She told the story of Rabies and how I had made such a difference in his life. It is true, of course, that it was Diana's knowledge and skill that had brought about the needed changes in his life, but if it hadn't been for me and my special ways, Diana said she didn't even want to think about what that poor man's life would be like today. I saw a lot of people get out their tissues when she told the story and it made me very proud to be her guide dog.

Diana has a sweet strong voice. As she sang, it floated over the quiet group there.

When Diana sat down, Reverend Stone addressed the people.

"Ladies and gentlemen," he said as his deep bass voice rang through the quiet crowd of people. "I have always been a fan of Venture's. That day when I first saw him, I was captivated by those beautiful eyes. I see time has not dimmed their beauty. In fact, Venture has demonstrated that his beauty comes from inside his heart. He sets a worthy example to us. Most of us never reach the heights we are capable of. What we have seen here tonight should inspire each of us to try harder to fulfill the plans for our lives God would have us follow.

"However, there was someone very important to Venture and without his help, Venture probably wouldn't be the wonderful creature he is today. All of you know William. I know better than most the dedication that boy showed as he worked with that puppy. I also know how blessed he was to have Venture in his life. Not only did Venture grow from this experience, so did William. When it came time to say good-bye to Venture, I think it just about broke William's heart. He grew from this experience. William has been away visiting his grandparents—something that is very important to him. However, when he learned that Venture was coming, he had to be here. Remember, Diana, you were told there would be a special surprise for Venture. Well, he walked in while you were singing. Come, William, and meet the team you and your family made possible."

All the people cheered, and the applause was deafening.

Up to now I had been acting the perfect guide dog. True, I had been happy to see my old friends, and I had done a lot of swinging my mighty club. But when I saw my beloved William, I forgot about being the poised and polished guide dog that I am. William and I ran to each other. My cries of gladness filled the air and my club went back and forth so fast you would have thought it would come off, but it didn't. William took me in to his arms just like he did when I was little.

"Venture," he said softly as he pressed his face into my shining coat. "You are beautiful and I am so proud of you and what you have accomplished. And what a nice person Diana is. You know, when I had to give you back to the Guide Dog Foundation I was worried that the blind person who got you wouldn't appreciate the fact that you are a dog who loves to play and have fun. I prayed for you, and God gave you even better than I dared dream of. Diana, Mom says you will be staying a couple days. Will it be all right if I play soccer with Venture?"

"Sure," said Diana. "I live in an apartment and don't have a place for Venture to play ball as I know he would like. I hope he hasn't forgotten how to play. Anyway, I know it will be a real treat for him."

I never forget about playing ball. The next day was like a dream come true. William and I played ball until we both were about to drop. Some of the people who were at the church social came by to see us and wish us well. It was all so very exciting, but vacations always have to end. The next day, we piled in the car for the trip to the Guide Dog Foundation.

Usually the trainers like to visit the students in their own environments and see how the team is working together. However, since we hadn't had any special problems and we were so far away, they just let us do our thing. Now that we were in New York, Diana had asked if we could come by. So we would be staying for a couple days at the school. While we were there, Diana and I would go to a Lions Club meeting and I would do what I do best—show them what a good guide dog can do.

I've never been able to understand the Trainer. When he saw me, he acted like I was his long-lost brother. I tell you I just don't get it. When we were in class he had started acting like he didn't care any more. Now he was being so sweet. I was glad for his approval because he was the first person I had really learned to respect and who in return had respected me. I put aside pettiness and gave myself up to basking in the sunshine of his admiration and love.

We went out with the class and I showed the other dogs how a perfect guide dog performs. All of my moves were fluid and Diana and I moved together with that artless grace that is so typical of me. I made it look as though we were one unit, which, of course, we are.

Often sighted volunteers come to the school and do things for the students. It is just about the only way the students can get away from the school to pick up little things they might need. The training staff is very good about getting things like toothpaste and razors. But if the person needs something like a new pair of shoes, he or she needs to be present. At such times the volunteers are very necessary. Students are not allowed to take their new guide dogs away from the school without a trainer being there. If you think about it, this makes perfect sense because a blind person is not yet proficient in using his new guide dog. Today a volunteer group had arrived who wanted to take students to the beach. Diana had requested that I be given a bath, so she was encouraged to accompany the group of students and volunteers to the beach. They could use the time for bathing me. I was taken to the kennel. The girl who was going to bathe me was busy, so they put me in a cage with another dog.

I stood amazed. There is only one other dog that is just about as good-looking as me, but whereas my beauty is golden, his is shining black. I bounded forward toward my old friend. So much had happened in my life that I wanted to tell him about. Besides, when I had last seen him, he really had done a lot of bragging and now it was my turn.

"Banner," I said joyfully. "It is so wonderful to see you."

Banner gave his tail a few token wags but it was obvious that his heart just wasn't in it. As my eyes met Banner's I felt a shudder go through me. One of Banner's most appealing traits was his beautiful expressive brown eyes. Now those eyes looked at me with such pain and despair, it made me ache inside. It brought to mind the bad state

Rabies was in and all my instincts told me something needed to be done right away to reach this very troubled creature. I wished Little Haze were here to handle this difficult situation. But she wasn't, and I was. So I stepped forward, eager to do what I could for my beloved friend.

"What is wrong?" I asked, gently settling down beside the dark beautiful one.

"Nothing you can do anything about," said Banner despondently. "Talk is all over the kennel that you are really it—Mr. Perfect with a capital 'P.' I'm very happy your life is going so well, Venture, but it might be a good idea if you keep in mind that all good things come to an end."

"I have already learned that, Banner," I said. "What has happened to cause you to lose your eternal optimism?"

"It's my person," said Banner. "He died a few days ago."

"Oh, Banner," I said, as understanding dawned. "I just got here a little while ago and I've only been in the kennels a few minutes so I hadn't heard. How did it happen?"

"Scott had diabetes," explained Banner. "He hadn't been well at all and when he fainted at school, he was taken away to the hospital where they said he died. Venture, I might as well have died too. We had such a wonderful life together. We did so many things as a team and I felt I helped him to be a part of life. But I guess I didn't do good enough. I just know that if I had really been a good guide dog like you are, then Scott wouldn't have died. I am a magnificent failure. Here I am only three years old and I'm all washed up—a disgrace to guide dogs. I'm so frightened, Venture, because I just know that some terrible punishment is going to be given to me for allowing Scott to die. I deserve whatever comes my way and I would gladly undergo anything if it would bring Scott back—which I know it won't. Well, I don't want to go on living without Scott. Will this be my punishment, Venture—to live on, knowing I killed Scott? I just don't think I can handle that."

I took a deep breath. Banner was really hurting and I didn't think I had the ability to help him. However, I was the only thing at hand. I knew that Banner was feeling a lot of grief but he didn't understand things. I was going to have to try to explain the facts to him. No one should carry the burden of guilt he was carrying.

"Banner," I said as I extended one of my golden paws over his black one. "You may or may not know that my person is a lady. Her name is Diana. She works with people who have special problems, and as her teammate, I work with them too. I have picked up a lot of knowledge about different kinds of situations and I know quite a lot about diabetes.

"As I'm sure you know, diabetes is a disease that attacks the body's ability to make insulin. Insulin controls the way the body uses the food it is sent, especially sugar. When a person has diabetes and it is very bad, that person has to take injections of insulin because the body is unable to make what it requires. Scott was one of those people—I overheard the trainers talking about it. Without that medicine he would have died a long time ago. However, Scott lost his vision as a side effect of the insulin.

"After he became blind, his world fell apart. But then he came to the Guide Dog Foundation and got this wonderful guide dog, Banner. Banner completely changed his life. Because of you, Banner, Scott felt he was a human being again. He threw himself into life and got back his life—a life he thought was gone forever. Naturally, everything was not the way it used to be, but because of you, Banner, Scott got back into life.

"Of course it is awful that he died but I think that was expected. The point I'm trying to make is that this young man had a disease that would have cheated him out of the things he wanted from life, but thanks to you, his life was very rich. You brought him friends and experiences and pleasures he could have known in no other way but through you. I know this doesn't stop the pain of loss, but it is a very precious thing to be able to contribute that to a person's life. Not all dogs have done what you have done. I know that you hurt very badly, but don't you think it is worth your personal pain to have made such a difference in a human's life? And just think—you had fun to boot. What is important for you to realize is that you didn't kill Scott. The disease did."

"Then you don't think I will be punished?" asked Banner. "This pain is awful. What will I do with the rest of my life? Scott was my life and I just don't know now."

"Humans take pictures," I said carefully. "Their pictures are reproductions of what they see. You have pictures in your heart. Pictures and memories of your life with Scott. Perhaps you will never forget him. He may always be like a lingering fragrance in your heart. But life goes on. Yesterday's dinner isn't enough. You need another dinner today. You also need another interest in your life. You are a young, strong, beautiful guide dog, and the Foundation will give you to another person. This may not be a thrilling experience for you. But be honest—it wasn't thrilling when you were placed with Scott. Most of us only have the chance to be of service to one person and we are considered good if our service is adequate. But you, Banner, were a real blessing in Scott's life and I'll be surprised if you aren't the same for someone else. Why, that person is probably hoping and praying for a miracle and you will be that miracle. It's going to be a while before you are ready for another person. I am not sure of the complete process but it won't be as long as when you were in training. I'm very sure that it is going to work out fine, though."

"Funny," sighed Banner. "I lived with Scott all this time and of course I knew he had diabetes, but I didn't realize it was a disease that would someday take his life. How come you knew that, Venture? Is your person a diabetic?"

"No," I smiled. "Diana is healthy, thank goodness, but she works with people who have special problems. Those special problems often involve other medical conditions so we have to know all about things like that. I am an important part of the team that solves these problems and as you can see, I carry my weight."

"What is your life like?" asked Banner. "I often wondered about you and wondered what had become of you."

"Well," I said, settling down to a topic I felt very comfortable discussing, "you were right when you told me that my wildest dreams couldn't match the reality of being a guide dog. The Trainer seemed pleased with my work and when I learned that we would soon be leaving for Diana's home in California, I can't say I was thrilled. But she was very nice to me and spent a lot of time petting me and making me a part of her life. I missed the kennels and the wonderful games we played. Diana really tried hard to make me comfortable, and as time went on I came to love and care for her. At first I was not really thrilled about the idea of always having to be with her. However, from the time we got to the airport and I was truly on my own with Diana, my life began its fairy tale-like quality. Life with Diana is never dull. It is a delight just to stay home with her and listen to books recorded either on records or tapes. I think I heard Diana explaining to someone that these books are made available through the Library of Congress. She reads a lot, often while brushing my shining coat. I am truly blessed to have her in my life, but she is just as lucky to have me. With me at her side, there is nothing she can't do.

"I am sure, Banner, you were that kind of an influence in Scott's life. I heard Auntie Em telling people how you had helped Scott to get back into life. I know you believe that your person and your life with him was much more important than mine could ever be with Diana, and for you that is true. That is the secret of how we are the best we can be. If you don't feel you are most beautiful and that your person is the best person in the world, then how can you make it a reality?"

"That makes sense, Venture," said Banner. "Indeed you make it sound as though your life is a fairy tale come true. My life with Scott was also wonderful. But you know, listening to you makes me realize that I want to get involved with life. Tell me more about your life. Your work sounds interesting, but what do you and your person do for fun? Don't you miss the wonderful games we used to play?"

I told Banner about the special people and things in my life. Of course, the story included Billyum and the dainty femme fatale, Little Haze. I told about the many things we did together and how Little Haze had explained to me about my special abilities. Banner listened enthralled as I told him about the really important things—Mr. Hedgehog, the kong, the ring, and the other really profound parts of my life.

"But Venture," said Banner, whose eyes had begun to glow as he listened to my stories. "Are you sure all these things are really true?"

Banner was back to being his old self, I thought. I felt relief rushing over me. Banner had been really down but somehow, I had been able to reach out to him in his time of need. It gave me a good warm feeling deep inside like the feelings I get when I help Diana.

"Oh gosh," said the Trainer as he walked by our cage. "We forgot all about Venture's bath and now it's getting too late for it."

"Well," came another voice, "Venture really didn't need a bath anyway, but look at Banner. I haven't seen him so perky since we got him back here. I think it probably was a good thing we put those two dogs together. Wonder what might have happened between them."

"Beats me," said the Trainer, "but they are about the same age and have been in the kennel together before. You know we like to see old friends. I don't have any idea if they remember each other. If they do, I'll bet they have enjoyed their little visit. Come on, Venture," he said, snapping on my leash. "Visiting hours are over and you have to go back to work for Diana. She's not going to be real happy that you didn't get a bath. You and she will be just fine, and tomorrow the two of you will accompany me to the Lions Club meeting."

I ran my mighty club in understanding.

As you would expect, I was a hit at the meeting. Everyone who saw me was wowed by my beauty and devotion to Diana. All too soon our visit was over and we were again waiting in the airport for our plane. I remembered my first time in that airport. Then I had been concerned and worried that I might not do the right things. I laughed to myself. How silly it had been to worry. Not only had I done very well, I set an example for others. As we got on the plane, I accepted the looks of admiration that were cast my way.

The flight was uneventful. I guess Diana had had to hassle the airline to get a ticket home because they still hadn't located her ticket or the lost luggage. The flight was pretty routine but I was glad when we arrived in Los Angeles and saw Fritsey waiting for us.

Fritsey, however, was not so pleased to see us when she learned that we had seen William.

"If I had known that little boy was going to be there, wild horses couldn't have kept me from going to New York with you!" she exclaimed. "Diana, you told me he wasn't going to be there!"

"I didn't know he was going to be there," said Diana. "I was told that he was away visiting his grandparents, and it came as a real surprise when he came to that party. Venture was certainly thrilled to see him and I think William was just as thrilled to see Venture. It was a very touching scene and I'm sorry that you could not be there to see it. But I assure you, Fritsey, there was no intention to keep you from seeing the reunion between Venture and the little boy who raised him. Besides, I have a major problem with the airline to sort out. They lost my luggage again, and this time they couldn't find it. Maybe it's better that you didn't go anywhere with me because every time I go somewhere I lose my luggage. I lost some really valuable things and it really makes me mad."

"Well, what's done is done," said Fritsey. "I know you didn't keep me away on purpose. But I have come to love Venture and it would have meant a lot to me if I could have met the little boy and his family who were so important to Venture. I just bet he did a lot of club swinging."

"That he did," said Diana, "and they took a lot of pictures which they said they would send us."

"I'm glad you both had such a good time," said Fritsey. "Maybe next time I can go too. Maybe the airlines will give you another ticket."

"If we can work it out, it would be fun if you went along," laughed Diana. "But let's not count on the airline giving us another ticket."

"Well," said Fritsey, "we can always hope."

As we drove home, I felt the tension that had been building up between the two women evaporating and I was glad.

When we went into the office, it was just wonderful to see Billyum and Little Haze. While Diana and Billyum talked about our trip and things that were going on at the office, Little Haze and I were filling each other in about the time we had been apart. Now there is just no denying that Banner is a truly wonderful dog. He even compares favorably to me. But when it is all said and done, I know in my heart that the dearest and most beautiful is the dainty, delicate, precious Little Haze. I will always adore her and she is the best female dog ever!

It took about two weeks, but finally the airlines contacted Diana. They had finally located her missing ticket and once they had the checks, they were able to locate her luggage. Of course they were very sorry about the problem and offered—you guessed it—free tickets for two, which Diana gratefully accepted.

I was very happy. My life was perfect. Our work was going well, delightful things kept happening and I couldn't imagine anything better could happen. Yet, no matter how good things are, they still seem to get better.

Would You Be
Mr. Right?

Something wonderful was about to happen and I was very happy. Billyum and Little Haze were coming for dinner. Diana and I saw Billyum and Little Haze at work each day, and we had gone over to their house a couple of times. Diana is a wonderful cook, and many times she had fixed special things and taken them in to work, but this was the first time Billyum and Little Haze had come to visit us at our house. We were busy getting ready for them. Diana bustled about in the kitchen making yumstons. She had a special recipe for spaghetti, and the air was filled with the wonderful smells as she cooked the sauce.

Although she explained that it really didn't go with spaghetti, Diana told me that one of Billyum's favorite desserts was a French silk chocolate pie. They are a lot of trouble to make but no effort was spared to ensure that Billyum would enjoy himself. Something special was even going to be given to me and Little Haze. Billyum and Little Haze would only be here for just a few short hours and Fritsey would be by to take him home. Boy, was the red carpet going to be rolled out! As we prepared for the dinner party, none of us could know that things would happen that evening that would change the entire course of our lives.

As I've mentioned, Diana was very busy, but the morning of the big day found us totally prepared. Diana and I made one last trip to the store to get something Diana felt we just had to have. As we waited at the light, an older woman came up to us.

"Oh my dear," she gushed. "I have been watching you and the dog for several days, and I finally decided that I would come out and say hello and ask some questions. I just wanted you to know that that has to be the most beautiful dog I have ever seen. It really touches my heart to see that wonderful creature."

"Thank you for noticing how pretty Venture is," smiled Diana. "I really enjoy him very much."

"I was just wondering about a few things," said the woman. "Have you been blind all your life?"

"Yes," said Diana.

"Why are you blind?" asked the woman.

"Well," said Diana, "I was a normal baby born prematurely, and very tiny. The doctor had me placed in an incubator to save my life. They didn't know, as they do now, that too much oxygen can damage a baby's optic nerves. All they knew was that oxygen is important to life, so they made sure I got plenty. It blinded me."

"That's enough to make a person bitter," the woman tried to sympathize.

"I'm not bitter," said Diana. "I find life to be a precious gift."

"You can't tell me you are happy to be blind?" asked the woman.

I fidgeted beside Diana. We had better things to do than talk with this woman, but I saw her lay a detaining hand on Diana's shoulder and I knew we were in for it. That was Diana's problem, but I saw no point in just standing there tiring myself, so I lay down and waited patiently for the conversation to end.

"Oh," said Diana cheerfully, "I am sure there are more terrible things in life than being blind. Maybe it's worse to be able to see all the terrible things that are around. But since I have had no experience with seeing, I would just be speculating about that."

"Well," said the woman. "If I were in your place I couldn't stand it. I would commit suicide. I don't see how you go so blithely through life knowing you are a total reject—a real lemon among normal folks."

There was a long pause. This woman had gone too far. Knowing Diana, I was sure that her reply—when it came—would be as smooth and polished as the woman's remark was crude and insulting.

I heard Diana draw in her breath.

"Ma'am," she said sweetly, "I don't think you at all understand."

"What is there to understand?" hissed the woman. "You are just a lemon in life."

"Oh," crooned Diana. "Believe me, that has many advantages. Probably you haven't been paying attention to your TV. Otherwise you would know that lemon oil is a wonderful additive to furniture polish. If you ask Procter & Gamble, they'll tell you that lemon-fresh Joy washes dishes right down to the shine. If you took a survey, you would find that lemon pie is one of America's favorites. But what is most important of all is that some of us lemons are so much fun to squeeze. Get up, Venture! Forward!" and we cruised back the way we had come.

We went another way to the store. Diana was laughing all the way home and when she called Billyum on the phone and told him about it, he laughed too. What no one has ever been able to explain is where some people get such nerve—or maybe I should say, such cowardice.

"I have everything ready," said Diana to Billyum. "However, I have been so busy that I haven't had the chance to get my laundry done. There is a laundromat right by the bus stop where you will be getting off, so why don't you meet me there and we will proceed to my house. By the time you get there the wash should be finished and you can help me haul it home."

"OK," said Billyum. "See you there."

Diana put her laundry bag, soap, and other things into her cart. She also took along a tape recorder with headphones. Diana always seems to be doing something, and while the clothes were washing and drying, she often used the time to catch up on her reading. Once she got the wash started, she put on her headphones and sort of went into her own private little world.

I was a little keyed up, what with the upcoming party and the chance for a nice long visit with Little Haze. Diana had taken off my harness and I began to look around a little. I didn't really leave Diana. I just looked outside to see what there was to see. After all, Diana didn't care. I never strayed from her, so she didn't even notice that I was looking outside. I wasn't hurting anything.

A gentleman came out of the office next to the laundromat and saw me standing there. He stopped to look at me and admire my beauty.

"You are a gorgeous dog," he said, extending his hand to me. I kissed his hand and ran my mighty club. As I looked into his eyes I couldn't help thinking that here was someone very special and we should take the trouble to get to know him.

"Do you belong to someone," asked the nice man, "or are you lost?"

I ran my mighty club.

"You are such a pretty dog," said the man. "Where is your owner? I think I should look around and make sure you are all right."

He came inside the laundromat. Diana was snuggled in a chair listening to her book so she didn't hear the nice man come in.

"This dog looks like he might be valuable," said the nice man. "Do you know anything about him?"

Since Diana couldn't hear him, she made no response, so the nice man just figured she didn't know anything about me.

He went back to the office he had come from, but the woman there was new and so knew nothing about me. Neither did the woman in the dress shop next to them. Had the nice man gone into the liquor store, the owner would have explained things to him, but that didn't happen. Instead the man came back to me and, taking my leash in his hand, said, "Come with me, nice doggie. I will take you home with me and we'll see if we can't find your people."

I gave him one of my most trusting looks and ran my mighty club. As we walked away from Diana, I kept looking back at her but this man had little intimate experience with a dog and he just didn't notice.

He opened the back door to his car and invited me to get in. He was a very nice man and although I really didn't want to go with him without Diana, I got in and we drove away to his home.

When we got there, he tied me up outside while he went inside to do a few things. I am not used to being left outside so I lifted up my voice in protest. The nice man stroked me but was unsure what to do. He went back inside and I again protested being outside.

The nice man was really concerned about my discomfort but he felt that a dog should stay outside. So he left me crying for about ten minutes.

When he came out, he brought a magnifying glass so that he could read my tags. The first one showed that I had had a rabies shot. The man seemed very pleased about this.

"Someone cares about you, pretty doggie," he said. "You are obviously very well taken care of and if no one cared for you, they wouldn't bother to see that you get your shots. Just hold on. We will find out who your owner is and you will be back with him in just a little while."

The next tag had him confused. It said "Guide Dog Foun." The nice man began to be a little upset.

"Why do you have a tag like this?" he asked as he stroked my golden shining coat.

I gave him one of my most appealing looks and ran my mighty club. Then I exposed myself.

The nice man saw my tattoos at once. He wrote down the telephone number he saw, then went into the house, taking me with him. I immediately went under a table and relaxed. I knew it was just a matter of time now until I got back with Diana.

The nice man called the telephone number and explained to the woman who answered how he had seen me and for my protection had taken me to his home until he could find my owner.

"Look on the dog's other leg," said the woman. "I am pretty sure that the dog you have is a guide dog. If you can give me his personal ID number, I can tell you who the dog belongs to."

The nice man called me from under the table. "Here, pretty doggie," he said. "Come out. Come out."

It took a little time for him to get me to lie on my back again, but finally I did and he got my personal ID number.

"Just a minute while I put this in the computer," said the woman. "Oh yes. You have a guide dog there. His name is Venture. He belongs to a lady, Diana, who lives in Southern California. We will contact her and tell her that you have her guide dog. If you will look on Venture's collar, you will find a tag with her name and address and telephone number."

"Oh dear," said the man. "That woman must be beside herself. I found the dog in a laundromat and there was a woman there who did not answer when I asked if she knew anything about the dog. I had no idea he was a guide dog. I will find her and return her dog to her right away. Is there anything I need to do for the dog until I can return him? Does he need anything to eat or anything special?"

"No," said the woman. "He may want a drink of water, and he may need to go outside to go to the bathroom, but otherwise he is just fine. He is a very well trained dog and should cause you no problems. He is accustomed to being in the house, and he has perfect house manners. Just keep him with you."

"If the woman who owns the dog calls you," said the man, "please tell her I'll be returning her dog just as soon as I can find her."

"That is fine," said the woman. "Thank you for calling and I am glad this story will have a happy ending."

The nice man got Diana's name and telephone number off my collar, and called, but Diana wasn't there. So he left a message on her answering machine.

"Well, fella," he said, "I guess we'll just have to wait until Diana calls us."

Meanwhile, back at the laundromat, Diana was still reading her book when Billyum and Little Haze arrived. When Diana couldn't find me, Little Haze told me later, Diana totally freaked out. Billyum had the presence of mind to call the police. When they came, they asked around in the other stores and were told that a gentleman had inquired about the dog's owner. He believed the dog was lost and had been seen putting the dog in his car.

"Well," said the policeman, "I really think the best thing you can do is take your laundry and go home. If the man is trying to return the dog, he's probably trying to get hold of you right now since you said your name and telephone number are on an ID tag."

The policeman helped Diana get together her clothes and followed her, Billyum, and Little Haze to her apartment.

Sure enough, when she checked the answering machine, there was a message from the man who had me. Diana called him at once, and the man said he would be at her home in about ten minutes. I happily followed the nice man as he took me to his car. I knew everything was going to be fine.

Once Diana knew I was all right, and that the man was on the way to return me, Little Haze told me her attitude completely changed. She went into the kitchen and prepared another salad. "Since this man is kind enough to bring Venture back," she said, "the least we can do is offer him dinner. Goodness knows we have tons of food—certainly enough for another guest."

When the doorbell rang, Diana flew to the door and I bounded into her arms.

"You are the woman I saw in the laundromat," said the nice man. "I had no idea this was your guide dog and I want to sincerely apologize to you for taking him."

"What is important," said Diana, "is that I have him back. Thank you for being concerned, and thank you for returning him. What is your name?"

"My name is John," said the nice man.

"This is my friend and business associate, Billyum," explained Diana, "and this is his guide dog, Hazel."

"I am very glad to know you, Billyum," said John. "I am sorry that it had to be under such strange circumstances."

"We are very glad to have Venture back," said Billyum. "As you can imagine, our guide dogs are very important to us. Why don't you take a load off your feet and have a drink with us?"

"Oh," said John, "I couldn't possibly do that. I'm sure you have seen enough of me and I just hope that I haven't spoiled your evening."

"Of course not," said Diana. "Please sit down and join us in a toast to Venture's return."

"Well," said John, "if you have a cup of tea handy, maybe I

could stay for a minute. Besides, I would like to ask a question."

"Tea coming right up," said Diana. "What's your question?"

"I was wondering," said John. "I have heard about guide dogs a lot. What is the difference between a guide dog and a seeing eye dog?"

"Oh," laughed Billyum, "that's easy. I think Diana may have some Jell-o in the Frigidaire. Do you have a camera—and if so, is it a Kodak?"

"It's a Polaroid," said John.

"Seeing Eye is a particular school, and the dogs from that school are Seeing Eye Dogs, just like Jell-o is a trade name for gelatin. Kodak and Frigidaire are other trademarks we use generically. Actually, all dogs that are trained as guides can be called 'dog guides'. However, many of the schools have the name 'guide dog' in them, so that's the term we use."

The conversation went on pleasantly. Then something very special happened. It is one of the most important things in my life. A new game was started. Little Haze was sitting there ever so smugly with my ring in her mouth. I couldn't allow that to continue, so I went to take it away. It was the very first time I got "rung." Little Haze kept a firm grip on the ring and the two of us pulled and pulled and pulled and growled and growled and growled.

"It certainly looks like those dogs are having a good time," said John. "Let me see that ring, Venture boy," and suddenly he was ringing me.

By this time, John had had a couple of cups of tea and everyone seemed so relaxed and pleasant that Diana invited him to stay for dinner.

"Oh, I couldn't possibly impose on you like that," said John. "I think I did enough taking Venture."

"Perhaps you have a better offer?" smiled Diana.

"No," said John. "I have no one waiting at home."

"Then it's settled," said Billyum. "You're staying."

"Are you really sure you want me to do that?" asked John. "Perhaps you have not noticed, but I am black and some folks feel mighty uncomfortable about that."

"The lettuce in the salad is green," said Diana. "I don't think anyone really cares so long as it is fresh."

"Mmmm," said John, "that food really does smell awfully good, so if you are sure you have enough—well, I will just take you up on your offer."

During dinner, the conversation was lively. Diana told her lemon story. Was it just that morning? Everyone laughed, of course. Billyum, however, had really had a disgusting thing happen on the bus on the way to Diana's. A German woman with a very heavy accent was asking him all kinds of personal questions, like how would he know what to do with a woman and how would he handle the responsibility of fatherhood should he actually be able to make a baby. As she got off the bus, she threw over her shoulder her parting insult.

"You poor ting be better off when you're dead."

"What on earth did you say to her?" asked Diana.

"She yelled that as she was getting off the bus," said Billyum, "so there wasn't much I could say. But to tell you the truth, I was in a state of shock. What on earth do you say to someone who has said something that is so obviously stupid?"

"That's terrible," said John. "What a disgustingly rude thing to say."

Just then the telephone rang and Diana went to answer it. It was Fritsey. She was calling to say that she had gotten tied up and that she wouldn't be able to take Billyum home as promised.

"Oh no!" wailed Billyum. "What am I going to do?"

"Well," said Diana. "I know you won't like the idea, but my sofa makes up into a really comfortable bed."

"But I have things that I need to do at home, Diyum," said Billyum.

"The buses aren't running," said Diana, rather matter-of-factly. "You do have a choice, though. You can sleep on my sofa or on the street. Take your pick."

"But, Diyum," said Billyum, "the vet has Little Haze on a special diet and you won't have it for her in the morning. When I agreed to come, Fritsey promised that she would take me home. I wouldn't have come otherwise."

"Where exactly do you live, Billyum?" asked John.

Billyum told him.

"Since I have pretty well messed up your evening and still enjoyed a wonderful meal, the least I can do is take you and Little Haze home, Billyum," said John.

"Maybe," said Diana. "But we still have dessert. I hope you don't plan to walk out right now."

"Of course not," laughed John. "Just take your time. You need not rush on my account."

The conversation and laughter flowed on, but I had had a busy day so I snuggled close to Diana and fell asleep. I awakened quite a while later as Little Haze, Billyum, and John prepared to go. As always, the silk pie was a real hit and Diana had made an extra one, plus there was some left of the first one. She packed it in little containers and gave some to Billyum and some to John.

"This is really nice of you, Diana," he said. "I hope you and Billyum will allow me to return the favor."

"That sounds like fun," said Diana as she hugged Little Haze. "Bye, Billyum," she said. "You were starting to become Billyuck, and thanks to John I don't have to put up with you."

"Well, Little Di," said Billyum, "if you weren't yuckston from time to time, you wouldn't call Billyum yuckston."

John laughed. He had already become acquainted with yuckston and yumston.

After Billyum, John and Little Haze left and the dishes were rinsed, Diana lay down exhausted.

"I ought to beat the tar out of you, Venture," she said as she stroked my beautiful shining coat. "However, you're safe. I'm just too tired."

I ran my mighty club with happiness. It was good to be home but I had never planned to leave it. Still, I couldn't help feeling we had met someone very important that evening. The next day, Billyum said much the same thing.

"You know Diyum," he said, "I think fate conspired to allow us to meet someone very special last night."

"Are you talking about John?" asked Diana. "I thought he was very nice."

"He feels very badly about taking Venture," Billyum went on.

"I don't see that he needs to," said Diana. "After all, he believed that the dog was lost and he was just trying to get him back home so that he wouldn't get hurt."

"That's what I told him," said Billyum. "But he wants to do something for us. I think he will arrange to take us somewhere if that would be agreeable. I think, Diana, that although he is a very nice man, his interests parallel yours more than they do mine. For example, he loves classical music, which you know I don't care for."

"Well," said Diana, "we'll just have to see."

"It seems to me," added Billyum, "that Fritsey is becoming quite undependable. I think you need to make a point of having several other sighted friends who would be willing to do things for you. John might just be such a person."

"Maybe," said Diana, "but Billyum, he is quite a bit older than me, don't you think?"

"So?" laughed Billyum. "Fritsey is a lot older than you are, too, but I don't see that getting in the way of your friendship."

"Billyum," said Diana, a little exasperated, "Fritsey is a woman. The relationship I might develop with John could be quite different."

"Oh for heaven's sakes, Diyuck," answered Billyum. "I am not suggesting that you marry the man, although, who knows, you might be quite happy. What I am saying is that you need to let this man into your life. Rabies is a lot older than you, but he thinks of you as a friend. If you hadn't worked out the friendship thing, he might never have let you help him. Now, I don't think John needs your help, but I think you are just being stupid if you turn away from his offer of friendship."

"I'm not turning away, Billyuck," answered Diana. "I will certainly give friendship a chance. All I'm saying is that I'm not so sure it will be the flourishing thing you expect."

Little Haze and I listened to the conversation with interest.

"What do you think about this, Venture?" asked Little Haze. "After all, you would have a better idea than anyone since you spent so much time with him."

"That man is a very nice man," I said. "I would like to see a lot more of him."

"I guess we will have to wait and see what time has in store," concluded Little Haze sagely.

Seventeen

Volt

We were very busy. I enjoyed the new game of ringing. Diana played with me and life went on at its usual pace. Diana and I had to go out to file some papers but when we came back, Billyum had a message for her. John had called and wanted to take us fishing. Billyum had said he would go and he was pretty sure that Diana would come too. Also, Little Haze and I were to be special guests.

"Have you ever gone fishing, Little Haze?" I asked.

"No, I haven't," said Little Haze. "Fish live in the water, so that means we will have to go to a place where there is water. I wonder if we will have a chance to go swimming?"

"I don't know about you," I said, "but if there is water, then I'm going swimming. You can do what you like."

"If we go to a place where there is water, the true reason has to be so we can swim. I just love the water, Venture."

It was a very pretty day for fishing. Diana had called John and she was going to bring her famous tuna salad. She also bustled about in the kitchen preparing other little yumstons because, as she said, it was very nice of John to take them, and she wanted to be sure that she did her part. Anyway, I was filled with happiness when John's car stopped outside our apartment and I was invited to get into the car with Billyum and Little Haze.

When we got to the park, all the goodies were unloaded. John showed Diana and Billyum how to set up a fishing line. I thought it was boring, myself, but Billyum and Diana seemed to be having a good time.

"Now, Billyum," said John. "Give me your hand so you can see, I mean, feel how we bait the hook."

"Yes," said Billyum. "I'd like to see how it's done."

"After I have shown Billyum," continued John, "then you can come over here, Diana, and see, I mean, feel how it's done."

Little Haze and I winked at each other. Both of us had heard this problem come up before and I was always amused how easily it was handled.

"John," said Diana in a normal voice, "both Billyum and I want to see it."

"You mean you want to feel it, don't you? Neither of you have any vision do you?" asked John.

"No," said Diana, "But we see things because that's the way the world does things."

"I know," said John, "and I must ask you to forgive me for forgetting that you can't see. I made a mistake. I should have said 'feel it' but you know that I'm so used to saying 'see it' that it just slipped out. You and Billyum seem like such normal people, I forgot."

Diana laughed. "We want you to forget, John," she said. "You see, we live in a world where it is normal to see. It is not normal for people to feel things. Because we want to be a part of normal life, we try to use the terms that you would use. So if you say 'see' and 'look' the way you do with others, you will feel more comfortable and it won't be a constant reminder that we are different from other people. Because deep down where it counts, we are just like you. True, we are different in some of the ways we do things. Most people don't use dogs or canes to get around. That is just something we are forced to do differently. But whenever we can, we try to do things the same way everybody else does them."

"Judging by dinner the other night and some of the things Billyum has told me, I would say you are a lot more accomplished than many so-called normal people," said John.

After that, things went smoothly for everyone. When lunch was served, everyone seemed happy except me and Little Haze. While they were eating, they caught two fish. Billyum and Diana were excited.

After lunch, Billyum asked John if he thought anyone would object if Little Haze and I swam in the pond. John was concerned because no dogs were supposed to be there. Then he decided that since we were there, we could swim. If anything was said about it, we would deal with it then.

Billyum, Diana, and John took turns throwing a tennis ball Billyum had brought for us. We swam and swam and swam until we wore those people out. Suddenly the day had stopped being boring, although I must admit that with Little Haze there, it was really nice anyway.

When we finished swimming, the question came up about what to do with the fish. Diana was a little uncertain how to cook them, so John cleaned them and we went over to Diana's house and John cooked those suckers. The wonderful smells just about drove me and Little Haze crazy, but somehow we survived. Later on that evening, John took Billyum and Little Haze home.

John, Billyum, and Diana often went places together but as Billyum had expected, John and Diana had a little more in common and frequently they could be found together. John, of course, was the perfect gentleman, but I was there as a chaperon just in case. I usually sat between them if they weren't in the car. I was always available for petting and made a fuss if I didn't get the attention I deserved.

Fritsey, however, did not like this friendship one little bit. She talked to Diana, explaining that it wasn't proper for a young woman like her to be seen in the company of that black man. Diana said she felt Fritsey was being a little silly about the situation and this made Fritsey angry. She then called Billyum, who told her rather plainly he thought she was way off base.

"But Billyum," wailed Fritsey. "Maybe they are just friends now. All serious relationships begin innocently enough. I'm afraid that if this isn't nipped in the bud something just terrible could happen. Diana listens to you and I think she would consider what you would have to say. Diana has been a good friend to you, Billyum. Now it's time you show a little appreciation for her kindness by stopping this crazy situation she has gotten herself into."

Billyum came straight to the point and didn't mince words.

"Fritsey," he said, "I believe you are meddling in something that does not concern you. John and Diana are just friends. True, he is a lot older than she is, but then I think you are a little older than she is also. As for his color, I'm afraid I don't see what that has to do with anything. John is a warm and loving person. Right now, he and Diana, Venture, Little Haze and myself are just very good friends. Should that change, and should Diana discover that she could find a good life with him, then you are seriously in error to interfere. I would suggest that you get to know this good man before you go around blowing off hot air about him."

"What a way for you to talk to me!" sniffed Fritsey. "I think you owe me something for all the times I've carted you and Little Haze around. I don't see how you have the nerve to talk to me this way."

"Most of the times you have taken me and Little Haze somewhere," answered Billyum "you offered. Any time I have asked you, I have always given you money to do it. I have never had any illusions about this. You have always been Diana's friend and I know you have helped me because she asked you to. Now you want to call your favors in but it doesn't work that way. I can't in good conscience say anything against John, but I do have to ask you something. John is a good human being and if he would make Diana happy, would you cheat her out of that chance?"

"Well," said Fritsey, "if you can work it out, I will spend some time with you, Diana and John, but I'm telling you, Billyum, John could never be happy with Diana. A black person should get together with a black person. Why, if he gets involved with Diana, she'll be treated like scum. But, of course, she'd deserve it, going where she doesn't belong."

"I think we need to end this conversation, Fritsey," said Billyum. "It isn't getting us anywhere and frankly, I don't enjoy listening to this racial garbage," and with that he hung up the phone.

It was just about that time that Billyum gave John his true name. Diana used to call John on the telephone but she always had to look up his telephone number. For some reason she really has trouble remembering numbers and on this particular day she was complaining to Billyum that she couldn't remember his number. Billyum thought about it for a while, than told her that his number spells "VOLTPOT" on the telephone dial. After that Diana never had trouble remembering his telephone number. She disliked calling him John anyway, and little by little she began to call him Volt. When Billyum found out she was calling him Volt, Volt became his true name and he is called that to this day by those who truly know him.

Volt's son, Paul, has a beautiful boat. It is actually a sea-going vessel, 37 feet long, lined with teak, and fully self-contained. Paul takes very good care of it.

The first time Volt took Diana and me to see the boat and we were introduced to Paul, I am certain he had his doubts about me. Although he never actually said I couldn't come on board, I knew in my heart he was hesitant. If the truth be known, I'm sure he had his doubts about Diana too. However, Paul, like his father, is a gentle soul. While he may have had his reservations, he watched and waited. I wish more people in this world were like Paul. Although he knew nothing at all about a guide dog, or for that matter a blind person, Diana was his father's friend and, therefore, so was I.

Paul is an engineer, and they are not known for being stupid. Paul was not only sweet and gentle, but very, very smart. Even today, he might not admit that he loves me, but I know he is one of my biggest fans. Many times he has done real special things for me, and action does speak louder than words.

Of course, he had been around dogs—plain old dogs and dogs people tried to humanize. Once Paul understood I wasn't that kind, we became very special friends.

When Billyum and Little Haze were invited to go with us for a boat ride, both of them were very excited.

"I've never been on a boat before," said Little Haze. "What is it like?"

I explained to her all about the boat and about Paul. Hazel listened with interest.

"Oh," I said, "the ocean is very wonderful. It smells like nothing else. The boat is a little like a floating castle. It is very safe, although it is sometimes very rocky. Paul knows what to do and you are always safe. You are just going to love Paul, Little Haze. When you ride on the boat I think you will say it is one of the really wonderful things you have done."

The day we went on the boat was very important to me. When we got to the marina and Hazel approached the boat, it felt strange to her and she became a little frightened. Paul lifted the beautiful dog in his arms and gently stroked her and talked to her.

Paul is a very big man, and Little Haze was like a delicate and precious sculpture that has suddenly come to life. It was an experience to watch this beautiful, frightened little dog become calm and at peace with our new friend. This is a picture in my mind that will never fade. Little Haze looked up with her wonderful brown eyes so filled with trust that even if I had just seen this man, I would have known he was good.

Paul set the dainty Little Haze on the deck of the boat. He and Volt helped me to board. There was a large gap between the piling on the pier and the boat and it was hard for even me not to slip and fall. But with the men assisting me, I joined Little Haze on the deck.

Paul invited us all inside the cabin of the boat where there was delicious coffee waiting. Diana had also brought some yumstons and Little Haze and I lay quietly together while the people ate the yumstons. The boat rocked gently and both Little Haze and I felt very secure.

Volt and Paul went outside to make the boat ready for the trip. Volt brought us out on the deck. All of us were excited when we heard the engine come to life. We moved out of the marina.

It was very obvious that Little Haze was enjoying this outing. Usually when we went somewhere, our place was to lie quietly, awaiting our masters' wishes. On the boat it was different. The air was crisp and fresh. Birds circled about, and here and there over the whitecaps I could see the silver flash as a fish slipped in and out of a wave. This was really thrilling and I was alert to everything around me just as Little Haze was. I don't think Billyum was nearly such a good sailor, though. He sat on the deck looking greener and greener. Paul told him it would be better if he stood at the rail and he barely got him there in time. Poor Billyum was so sick he was sure he was going to die but Paul just laughed and told him that he would feel better in a few minutes. Volt and Diana weren't doing much better and it was true that the ride was very choppy. I knew, though, that everything was fine because Paul knew what he was doing.

As they got out into deeper water, things seemed to become calmer and soon Billyum and Diana were enjoying themselves.

Volt helped Billyum to throw out a line and almost immediately, Billyum felt a tug. He really got excited and before you knew it, he had forgotten how very sick he had been.

All morning the people fished and each time a line was thrown out Little Haze and I whined with excitement. With all that water out there it was downright mean for those folks to be having so much fun while we were tied to the rail unable to get at that lovely water.

"You dogs sure want to go swimming in all that water don't you?" asked Volt.

"See!" I said to Little Haze. "He knows we want to swim but he's being a meanie and not letting us."

"I wish we could let you swim," continued Volt. "We would let you do so if it were safe, but it's not. Out here in the ocean, a shark could get you and there would be no way we could rescue you."

"Do you think he is right about the sharks?" I asked Little Haze.

"I really don't know," said Little Haze. "I have heard that there might be some danger. But I think if Volt and Paul had really loved us the way they should, then they would have found a way for us to be safe. They are going to have to think up something very special before we can consider granting them forgiveness."

The people enjoyed themselves and, if the truth be known, so did we. We were offered drinks of cold water. We were played with when the fish weren't biting. It would have been perfect if they had let us go swimming. But when you are a guide dog, there is a lot that isn't fair.

As evening approached, Paul fired up the barbecue and soon the most wonderful smells floated over the water. Diana had brought things that were cold and those humans settled down to a feast fit for kings. Like usual, they gave nary a thought to us faithful workers.

Once they were stuffed, Billyum and John and Diana lay resting on the deck. We could hear Paul running a little machine of some kind and soon he appeared with two pie plates heaped with popcorn.

"I was talking with a friend of mine who owns a boat here," said

Paul. "He is a vet. I asked him if I could fix something that would be all right for the dogs to have. He said that probably it would be all right if I made the dogs some popcorn in an air popper. It has no salt or butter in it. Diana, you said you often fix it for Venture. Would you like to give the dogs this popcorn?"

Diana and Billyum often give us popcorn so we were very happy when each of us was given a heaping plate.

"I think," said Little Haze as she munched her popcorn, "we have to forgive them for not making it possible for us to swim."

"Paul is forgiven. I don't see that Volt, Diana or Billyum did a solitary thing," I sniffed.

Paul said we could head for home now because the tide would allow us to get back in the marina. Billyum and Diana, Little Haze and I went into the cabin because it was becoming very cool. The return trip was smooth and pleasant, and soon we were being helped onto the dock.

Billyum and Diana thanked Paul for a wonderful day and we piled into Volt's car and drove to our house.

"I'm going to take you home now, Billyum," said Volt.

"Before you do," said Billyum, "there is something I think we need to talk about. Diana is having a very serious problem. I don't know that you can do anything about it but I thought that maybe the three of us could talk it over and we could all decide."

"What kind of a problem is that?" asked Volt.

"The problem is Diana's friend, Fritsey," said Billyum. "She is very concerned about your friendship with Diana. Normally I would say, 'so what.' Whatever attitude she chooses to take is her problem. I still kind of feel that way. The problem is that this woman is a close friend of Diana's. She has spent many hours helping both of us and in many ways we treat her like family. A few days ago she called me and tried to get me to see how unreasonable this relationship is that is developing between you and Diana. I told her I wouldn't try to interfere between you two, but if she would like the opportunity to get to know you, I would be happy to talk with the two of you. Maybe we should see if we could do something that would involve her with us. I wonder if her opinion would change."

"Is she an older person?" asked Volt.

"Yes," said Billyum.

"A lifetime of prejudice is seldom erased in a few evenings," said Volt. "But we can give it a try."

"Yes," Billyum agreed. "Then at least we won't blame ourselves if she pulls away. A fishing trip might be a good icebreaker—Fritsey has said she enjoys fishing, and I know how she loves to eat."

The fishing trip was scheduled for my birthday. Fritsey said she would bring a frisbee. Diana put together the most exciting dinner four people—or even ten—could ask for. Little Haze made a sly comment about the abundance of food as we reached the park: "You know, if those people don't want to have leftovers, they ought to leave some of that food where we can get to it. We could make certain it would all be eaten."

"I know," I said, licking my lips. "You and I will each get a small piece of my birthday cake while the rest of them pig out. You would think that on this, my special day, they would watch me eat the cake."

"You are not much better than they are, Venture," scolded Little Haze.

"Well, I don't see that you have ever been over-generous with me," I said, chewing on some grass. "In fact, I have serious doubts that you would be so dainty and delicate if you weren't prevented from eating everything in sight. Little Haze, you are a regular pig."

"Watch it, Venture," laughed Little Haze. "I'll get you for that ungentlemanly remark."

I just ran my mighty club. No little twit of a female was going to get the best of me.

Little Haze and I exchanged glances as Fritsey began our outing complaining about all kinds of things. She didn't like it because the day was warm.

"It's always warm at this time of year," said Diana. "You know that, Fritsey. It was you who was wondering if the weather was going to be warm enough for it to be safe for the dogs to go swimming. Remember?"

"Well, that is a real concern," said Fritsey, "but I didn't mean you had to pick a day that would be so hot I could collapse of heat stroke."

"I don't believe it's that hot," said Billyum. "Did you bring some bread to feed the ducks?"

"I don't keep bread after it has gotten stale," said Fritsey. "So I went to the day old bakery and got ten loaves of their bread so I would have something to feed them."

Fritsey walked to the edge of the pond. She tore up bread and threw it out to the waiting ducks.

"We'll just see who is faster," said Little Haze as she hurled herself into the water.

"The dogs are getting the food I have brought for the ducks!" wailed Fritsey.

"We'll fix that," said Volt. "Just hold up some bread."

As Fritsey held up the bread, Little Haze and I came rushing over, our coats streaming water, our tails going full force.

"Got both of you!" laughed Volt, as he grabbed our collars and Billyum and Diana snapped on our leashes. We whined excitedly but it didn't do any good.

"Quiet, Venture," said Diana. "You're just being a butt when you want to get the ducks' bread, you mighty old butt you."

I ran my mighty wet club.

"What did you call, Venture?" asked Volt.

"Ever since I have known Venture," explained Diana, "I have called him an old butt."

"What an awful name to call such a noble animal," said Volt. "You should be calling him something very unique that would represent the fine creature that he is."

"He's a butt," said Diana. "I agree that he's a great big wonderful butt. Still, the bottom line is that he's a butt and he knows it."

I ran my mighty golden club.

"See?" said Diana. "He knows he's a butt and he accepts it, don't you Venture, you old butt you?"

I washed her face lovingly.

"I don't think you should call him a butt," insisted Volt. "A beautiful noble creature like him should be called 'the Brother'."

"I think you're right," said Fritsey. "I have felt that calling Venture a butt is demeaning, but 'the Brother'—now that's classy."

Diana smiled. Maybe Volt was getting somewhere with Fritsey.

The people spent the morning fishing.

"This is not as much fun as the boat, is it, Venture?" asked Little Haze.

"No," I agreed. "However, I think Diana is hoping that this trip will help Fritsey to become more positive about Volt and I wouldn't do anything to cause a problem. If it would help, I'd even give up swimming."

"You know that wouldn't help anything, Venture," said Little Haze.

"Do you think Fritsey will ever come around?" I asked.

"For Diana's sake I hope she does," said Little Haze. "You heard what Volt said, though. Fritsey is not a young woman. I consider it most unrealistic to expect her to change a whole lifetime of values in a few short hours even if those values aren't correct."

"Oh dear, Little Haze," I said. "I fear that Diana may have some sad days ahead."

"Maybe," said Little Haze. "That doesn't mean we have to let it spoil today. I know for a fact that Billyum has the tennis ball in his pocket, and you know what that means!"

As the people sat down to the wonderful food that was supposedly for my birthday, Volt noticed two young boys fishing. He heard them talking and gathered that this day of fishing was a special treat for them, but that they were having personal problems. One of them said to the other, "I know a half sandwich isn't much but if you eat it slowly and drink a lot of water you'll be all right. This is all the food I could find for us. Maybe we'll catch something and we can share it with the others for supper."

Volt came over to Diana and told her what he had heard. "We have more food here than we could ever eat," he said. "Would it be all right to fix plates for these young boys?"

"Sure," said Diana. "Just be sure to tell the boys that this is Venture's birthday party."

Volt explained the situation to Fritsey. Fritsey, who up to this time hadn't seemed very happy, now began to smile. One thing Fritsey loved to do was fill up a person's plate and then watch them stuff themselves. Now she happily went about that task, causing Volt to smile and wonder aloud if the paper plate would stand up under the weight of all the food Fritsey had piled on it.

"Look," smiled Fritsey. "These are just young growing boys and you know all teenagers have a hollow leg."

"I've heard that," said Volt. "Besides, we sure have enough food, don't we?"

Diana smiled. Maybe things were going to be all right with Fritsey after all.

When the people were finished eating, Volt brought out my birthday cake. It was a wonderful chocolate creation. Little Haze and I really could have done without the singing of "Happy Birthday," but they did it. Even our new friends came over to join in.

"Don't get too big a head, Venture," said Little Haze. "I'm sure all they really want is a piece of that wonderful cake."

"I don't have any illusions about their motives, Little Haze," I said. "Or yours either."

Volt had brought out a package of little party hats, and Little Haze and I wore our hats while eating our stingy little pieces of the yumston cake.

After the cake was eaten and the food was cleared away, Fritsey got out the frisbee. Little Haze and I had a wonderful time playing with it, but it was a flimsy one and soon we tore it up.

"I thought that might happen," laughed Billyum. "So I brought what never fails." He reached into his pocket and pulled out the beloved tennis ball. I thought Little Haze was going to go crazy as she jumped up and down. She had certainly forgotten all about being dignified. Her joy was contagious; soon both of us were cavorting in the water with the ball. I am always graceful; when I am in the water, I float like a gracious boat. Little Haze was very, making up in enthusiasm what she lacked in size.

Billyum had just thrown the ball out and I had retrieved it. That Billyum really has a good pitching arm! Little Haze was swimming in circles, not bothering to go after the ball. As I swam toward the shore, she plunged forward and leaped on top of me, forcing my head underwater.

"Remember that nasty comment you made about me?" squeaked the excited dog. "Consider this your payback!" And she began to wrestle with me.

I knew it was just fun and besides, there was no way Little Haze could have sunk me. I let the ball go and she pounced on it. But that was not what Fritsey thought as she watched us from the bank.

"Little Haze is trying to kill Venture," she hissed. "Somebody put a stop to it right now!"

"Don't worry about it, Fritsey," said Volt calmly. "I have seen them play together like that often and they're fine. Both of them are very skillful swimmers and they are in no danger at all."

"Venture is a very valuable dog," said Fritsey. "But I see you don't recognize that! However, if you depended on Venture as your eyes, you might have some realization how important he is."

"The dogs are in no danger," repeated Volt. "They are just enjoying themselves."

"The dogs are in danger," screamed Fritsey, "and it's all your fault. You're pushing yourself into the lives of these poor blind people and then taking advantage of good white people. It makes me sick."

Billyum and Diana softly called us over and put on our leashes.

"The party is over," said Billyum to Little Haze. "Volt, when you can get packed up, would you take us home?"

"He sure will," snapped Fritsey, "and I'll take Venture and Diana home. Diana, we have to have a talk. I guess I have stayed out of this long enough. I'll take you and Venture home, and then I'm going to wake you up to the true facts of life. If you won't save yourself, then I'll have to!"

She grabbed Diana's arm and began to propel her toward the car. I had never seen Fritsey so angry in my life.

"I think you should go on," said Volt to a protesting Diana. "I'll pack up everything here and call you later."

As Diana, Fritsey, and I rode home together they didn't say anything to each other, but the air was tense with emotion. When they got to Diana's house, Diana broke the silence by asking Fritsey if she would like something cold to drink.

"I have some wonderful mint iced tea," said Diana. "Volt showed me a special way to make it that really gives you the feeling you are drinking something exotic."

"I don't want a thing Volt has had a hand in!" snapped Fritsey.

"All right," said Diana, "but I'm going to have a glass and if you change your mind, just speak up."

Diana went to a cupboard where she kept her fancy glasses and took out a beautiful crystal wine glass. She put ice in it, then poured the tea over the ice. The ice cubes made a pretty sound as they clinked against the glass. I moved over to Diana because I knew she would give me a yumston ice cube.

"Well, Diana," sniffed Fritsey. "Hanging around with that—that *colored* guy is starting to make you act real uppity. The Diana I have always known and loved drank her iced tea in one of those big plastic glasses, but now that you've started associating with that trash, your old plastic iced tea glasses aren't good enough for you! Now you have to sip your iced tea out of a crystal goblet because that man suggested it. Diana, this has got to stop! You're going to ruin your life! You're not going to have any friends! Pretty soon no one is going to want to have anything to do with you because you are associating with the wrong kind of people. Sure, Billyum will still be your friend, because he doesn't know any better. Pretty soon you and he are going to wind up in the same boat—no one will want anything to do with you because of the company you keep! Wake up to reality, Diana, before it's too late!"

The apartment fell silent as Diana gathered her thoughts.

"Fritsey," she said calmly after a minute or so, "don't you think that you are over-reacting? I didn't get the idea of drinking the iced tea out of the crystal goblet from Volt. We went to this fancy restaurant on the pier and they served it that way. It is so special this way, and those glasses should be used for something other than collecting dust. Your comments about Volt are simply unfair. He's as nice a man as I have met—much nicer than most. He is kind and sensitive and good. I don't see how you can call a man like that trash. And so far as my other friends are concerned, you seem to be the only one who objects. I know that we don't like everyone that we meet, but Fritsey, you have never given this man a chance. You don't even know him, yet you really get into it when you start telling me what a bad person he is. That just doesn't seem fair. How can you dislike someone so intensely when you hardly know him, Fritsey?"

"Diana," said Fritsey, "perhaps I haven't been a real friend to you. It is my fault for allowing this unacceptable situation to continue.

Come sit down over here and let's have a good talk. I know that you appreciate the nice things Volt has done for you but Diana, you don't know the truth about people like him. When God created man he made each to mate with his own kind. Venture is most special, but he's still an animal. In the same way, Volt may appear to be a nice cultured man, but he simply isn't your kind!"

"Maybe you're right about one thing," Diana said quietly. "Perhaps you and I are not his kind because we lack his goodness."

"Diana!" Fritsey said sharply. "Colored people sometimes adopt the nice customs of the better white people but that is just a ploy to worm their way into our society. It is God's plan that whites be with whites and that blacks be with blacks. You are a beautiful white girl, Diana, and this black man is using you to score one against us, his white betters. Mark my word, Diana, he will make your life miserable. Should you get involved with him, very bad things will happen to you. I know you may feel that I am being overly harsh. He took us all in by making those classy remarks about Venture being 'the Brother,' but Diana, if you get involved with him, he just couldn't help himself. He and his family would just have to degrade you. That's the nature of darkies. You would lose all your good white friends. Once that happened you would be astonished to see how mean those blacks would be to you. They couldn't help themselves because by nature they want to hurt us white people. It would just be a matter of time before they broke your heart and hurt your devoted companion Venture too. You cannot expect any of us to remain your friends if you continue pursuing people that aren't acceptable."

Diana had been sitting with the crystal goblet in her hand. I had been waiting patiently for ice cubes but Diana had been so intent on listening to Fritsey she forgot about my needs. Now I heard a sharp little click as she set the goblet down hard.

"Fritsey," she said, her voice straining under her attempt to speak with quiet control. "I have never been to those racist rallies, and I can't believe the garbage I have heard coming out of your mouth. If you want to talk about other human beings that way, it's your right—but not around here! Constructive criticism is one thing, but when you spread these hateful vicious lies, you really lower yourself as a human being."

"You look here!" yelled Fritsey. "I'm just telling the facts about those animals. Apes in the jungle are better than them!"

"I think you'd better leave," said Diana quietly.

"I don't want to be around a person like you," yelled Fritsey. "I thought you were a nice person, but I guess I was wrong. You don't deserve the company of good white folks!"

Diana closed the door on the last words. I was upset and frightened. I had never seen anyone behave like that. I went to Diana and put my head on her leg. Diana sat on the floor stroking my shining coat.

"This woman has really behaved in a very disgusting way," said Diana as she wiped away tears. "I have read about things like Fritsey expressed, but I can't believe a sane person could express such hate and stupidity." Diana lay on the floor close to me until we heard a soft knock. I became much happier. It was Volt and I knew he would bring some calm to the situation.

Diana told him how Fritsey had behaved.

"Well," said Volt as he scratched my ears, "I told you when we first met that some people would react to me like that. Time and again I have warned you that a friendship with me might have its difficulties."

"But Volt," said Diana, "that was not just an unconcerned person talking. It was a rabid hate-monger posing as my friend. If I hadn't heard it with my own ears, I wouldn't believe it."

"Attitudes like that have been around all my life and I've had to live with them as best I can," said Volt. "If you want to share my life, I'm afraid that will go with it."

Diana and Volt were sitting together on the sofa and I lay at their feet with my head touching both of them. Diana and Volt talked together till very late. I slept peacefully because where love reigns there can be no discord.

Eighteen

Why?

Little Haze had this remarkable gift of understanding other points of view. For all her dainty ways, she was always firmly grounded in reality. Talking things over with her made me feel very focused. Right now, with all that was going on in my life, I really needed that.

"Venture," said Little Haze, "wonderful things are happening in your life. I've heard that Volt has given Diana a very beautiful diamond. I guess that means the three of you will be getting married soon. Let me be the first to congratulate you on such a spectacular match. Billyum says that Volt is most yumston, and I couldn't agree more."

"I loved Volt from the very first time I laid eyes on him," I said, "and he really did a yumston thing making me 'the Brother,' now didn't he? I just bet you wish you were being accorded such honors. Even though you're a female, I love you anyway and want only yumstons for you."

"Look, 'Brother'," said Little Haze, "you might keep in mind that you still don't have a wagging license."

"I guess that's not all that's wrong with me," I sighed. "A whole lot of things seem to be happening all at once. Fritsey has come unglued and I don't understand why. I also don't understand why Volt gave Diana a diamond ring. I have heard people tell her how beautiful it is, but it seems to me that food would have been a better gift. Do you know what is so special about a diamond, Hazel?"

"People consider the diamond to be the symbol of love," replied Little Haze.

"Volt is very wonderful," I said. "Still, it seems to me that a diamond is pretty useless. Where's my gift? If not for me, they would never have met. When they were dating, it was me, the beautiful golden one, who provided elegance and style in a chaperon. You would think that would mean something to those two—but, oh no! All they think about is themselves and not the fact that this is going to be a tri-marriage—Diana and her two V-boys."

"That should not disturb you at all," laughed Little Haze. "You and I know that without us our blind masters would be, shall we say, seriously out of luck—but they cooperate better if we let them go on believing they are the superior species."

"I always heard that love would smooth out the rough spots in life," I said, "yet to me life still seems rough! rough! rough!"

"Quit yapping," said Little Haze. "How on earth can you say that?"

"Fritsey was by yesterday! She was so angry with Volt and Diana you wouldn't believe it. She yelled and cussed till I thought she was going to have a stroke. She said she would try to have me taken away from Diana and she hoped Diana would soon die—and she went on to describe the horrors of hell, where Diana and Volt would both go because of the way they are corrupting society. She yelled that she never wanted to see or talk to us again because Diana should have known better than to marry a nigger. Volt is so yumston, Little Haze. Why does Fritsey hate him so much and why did she call him that? Could she be jealous and wish she were a nig—"

"Hush, Venture," said Little Haze. "Don't use that 'n' word."

"Why not?" I asked. "Fritsey used it. She said Volt was a nig—"

"I told you not to say that word, Venture, and I mean it," snapped Little Haze.

"Why are you getting so upset?" I asked.

"Don't ever say that 'n' word again if you want to be around me. It's very crude and crass. You wouldn't want to be considered common and low like people who use the 'f' word."

"You know I have better breeding than to use the 'f' word, Little Haze. How can you suggest such a disgusting thing?"

"If a thing smells like trash and talks like trash, odds are it is trash," said Little Haze calmly. "And it is trash when you say the 'n' word."

"I am very well groomed," I contended. "Just tell me what this is all about."

"I'll do my best to explain," said Little Haze. "I do have to admit, though, that it is a strange story." She rubbed her ear thoughtfully. "Many thousands of years ago people lived in a faraway country called Africa," she said. "This country's climate was very warm. For generations the heat and blowing sand beat down upon these people. They didn't mind. Like all of us, they loved their homeland. As years went by, nature began to help these people to adapt to their surroundings by turning the color of their skin to a dark hue. This made them more comfortable in the terrific heat. Nature also gave them very kinky, coarse hair which tended to keep heat away from the head. Their noses developed in a flared-out way so that breathing when the sands were blowing was easier."

"None of that sounds undesirable," I said, still puzzled. "We Labradors have developed in special ways too. Our bodies can handle very cold temperatures and we can swim in icy water without problems. Our coats have developed so that they can handle the water yet keep us dry. Humans admire our special qualities. Why can't they admire each other's?"

"A lot of humans just aren't very smart," Little Haze said bluntly. "They have to think they are better than others even when it isn't true—*especially* when it isn't."

"The collie down the street doesn't look a bit like you or me, but I still treat him like a dog."

"If you go around expecting humans to be as enlightened as we are, you're in for some very upsetting moments," said Little Haze. "That's why I am explaining all this. Now, people in colder climates like Europe developed light skin and smaller nostrils to protect against the cold, and that became their standard of beauty. When the

Europeans set out in ships to conquer the world, they found people who looked different wherever they went—just as you encounter different-looking dogs when you go out for a walk."

"Did they sniff each other?"

"There you go again, expecting them to be civilized. No, they did something called 'converting' them, and something else called 'enslaving' them, but..."

"But they never made friends?" I asked, incredulous.

"Some did, but often others—the ones with the guns—betrayed the trust that had been established."

"You're pulling my tail again," I scoffed. "Nobody would act that way."

"What about Fritsey?"

"Hmm. I see your point."

"Anyway, Europe was getting very crowded and for that and other reasons, many of the people from there came to the new place— America. You know how it is. Some people are like Fritsey and have a lot of money. Others don't. The people who had lots of money wanted to set themselves up as fancy gentlemen. They built very fine houses and grew big fields of things like cotton. But they had a problem. They had such big houses and so many things, they needed help in taking care of them. But they didn't want to pay for that help. So an awful thing happened.

"In Europe, there is a country called France. Some of the people from there got interested in a large part of Africa. Since they thought they had discovered it, they gave it a name. They called it Nigeria, which means 'black river,' and they called the people who lived there 'Nigerians,' which was later shortened to 'Nigers.'

"Like I said, the people in America who had these big estates needed people to do the work. Someone discovered that the 'Nigers,' or people from that part of the world, did well in that climate—and boy could they work! So traders would go to the villages and steal the people, then bring them to America in ships. They were treated very cruelly—worse than cattle. They were beaten, kicked and abused.

"Around that time, the name 'Niger' got corrupted. In the English language there is a word 'niggardly.' It means small-minded and stupid. The Niger was having a lot of trouble adjusting to the strange language and different customs in this new land—especially the whippings and beatings. The honorable word 'Niger' was corrupted to 'nigger' and came to mean something considered less than human. That's why it is a crude and nasty word that cultured folks don't use."

"But Little Haze," I said, "you said they thought of black people like cattle. Yet I have heard you say that humans all come from one family."

"They do. Recently I have heard some things that suggest that all human culture may have its roots in Africa."

"Well," I said, "if that is so, isn't it very evil to call black people 'cattle?'"

"Yes," said Little Haze. "It is very wrong and it is very shameful. The good people recognized this and fought an awful war to free the slaves."

"Then everything is fine now."

"I wish," Little Haze said sadly.

"Why? Is something else wrong? Volt isn't a slave and no one beats him, I'm certain of it. And if anyone tried, I'd put a stop to it right now."

"It would be against the law to beat him, and they have police to make sure things like that don't happen," Little Haze replied. "But they can say awful things to stop people from being friends."

"I noticed something else," I said. "I know Fritsey said some terrible things but down in my heart, I don't believe they were motivated by race. I think she said those awful things because she is mad that Diana is spending her time with someone besides herself. She really couldn't find much to criticize about Volt, so she repeated the same old things over and over and over again. You know how upset she has always gotten when Diana spent time with other people. But I'm worried because she said all our friends will desert us and Volt's family will be mean to Diana."

"You have gone with Volt and Diana many places," answered the wise Little Haze. "Have you seen any of these things happen?"

"Well, no," I said. "People for the most part have been very accepting of us. Sometimes I have felt disapproval from a few people but they usually leave us alone. What does worry me is that not all of Volt's children are real warm to us. Could they be a source of trouble later on?"

"I doubt it," said Little Haze. "If you feel that they are snubbing you, just don't worry about it. Remember that it is perfectly natural to like some folks more than others. Their mother has been dead for many years, and there is no way Diana could take her place. Then too, having a dog in the marriage might make them uneasy.

"I have always believed that people will be your friend when they have the maturity needed to accept you. If they aren't ready, don't force the issue. They'll come around—or perhaps, like Fritsey, they won't."

"Well, Little Haze," I said, as I bit down on the ball. "Come to think about it, that light color of yours is very inferior to my beautiful deep gold. Obviously I am much better than you."

Little Haze gracefully wagged her lovely tail.

"Huh," she sniffed. "Remember when we were in the water. If memory serves me, it was the 'superior one' who got sunk, and had to let go of the ball to save himself."

I just looked at her and ran my mighty club, my fine darker golden club.

"Venture," said Little Haze softly, "can I ask a favor of you?"

"Sure," I said. "You females always need us males to do things for you. What is it that you need?"

"Lately," said Little Haze quietly, "I haven't been feeling too good. At first it was a bad day now and then but recently I have been having a whole lot of bad days. I know that your life is very full and you are very busy now, what with getting married and everything. I know that you won't see Billyum as often as you used to. But if something should happen to me, promise me you'll keep an eye on Billyum."

I whirled around and looked at the delicate Little Haze. She was as lovely as ever, but her eyes looked sad.

"Little Haze," I said, "you are going to be around forever!"

"No," said Little Haze gently. "No one lives forever! Not even you, Venture!"

"But Little Haze," I said. "We all love you and need you."

"Each of us has a time to serve and then we go on," said Little Haze. "I didn't mean to alarm you, but I have been thinking we should talk about this."

"Does Billyum know you don't feel well?" I asked, drawing closer to my friend.

"Yes," answered Little Haze. "He has taken me to the vet often and they are always running tests, but they can't find out what is wrong. Hopefully it will pass. But I would feel better if I could go to sleep at night knowing that, if something happens to me, you will keep an eye on Billyum. I know your main job is Diana and Volt but I also know what a big heart you have. So please give me your word you will look out for Billyum."

"Of course I will do anything I can for Billyum," I said. "But you will be here a long time, and who could take care of Billyum better than you?"

"I'm planning to be around," laughed Little Haze. "But thanks for giving me your word, you old butt!"

A day that had begun with blue skies had suddenly turned very bleak. Our talk had made me start to feel happy again, but now the idea that something might be wrong with Little Haze settled in my heart like a heavy stone.

Nineteen

Tri-Marriage

The next few weeks were filled with hustle and bustle. Diana and I were very busy, what with closing the office and getting ready for our wedding trip to Atlantic City. I had heard that was one nice place to be. I was very excited. Diana had gone shopping for a beautiful dress and there were so many places to go and people to see. This getting married took lots of legwork, and once again I proved myself indispensable.

Even with all the excitement, my thoughts never strayed far from Little Haze and her disturbing request that I look after Billyum if something happened to her.

A friend of Volt's drove us to the airport. He was a black man and was very nice to Diana and to me. In all of our time together, I have yet to see any of the dire things happen that Fritsey predicted. I know now just how foolish it was to even be alarmed by such idle chatter. But I didn't know that then, and although she never said so, I think there was a little sadness within Diana because of the way Fritsey had chosen to act. Hate has no place in our lives. Both Diana and Volt have said that life is too short to bother with things like that. There are a very few people who aren't mature enough to appreciate us and when we meet such people, we understand they haven't grown up yet and we just go on our way. There are plenty of people who already love us and we have a large circle of friends.

I thought that maybe when someone else was with us, people might not be so interested in me as they were when I was alone with Diana. That, however, was not at all the case. Volt's sweet nature seemed to attract more people, not discourage them. This resulted in my being treated like real royalty, which is only appropriate. I may not be the reason there is a sun, but I am the reason it shines so brightly! I gained even more respect for Volt because I could hear the pride in his voice when he talked about me and Diana.

When we got to Atlantic City, it was so busy and exciting! People were rushing all over the place and it was a thrill to be part of everything. When we got to our hotel, I strutted in as if I owned the place. There was some kind of machine called a "wheel of fortune" and it gave out a trumpet call of welcome as my golden feet were placed upon the luxurious carpeting.

"You ought to see Venture," smiled Volt to Diana. "The way he's acting you would think all of the fanfare is for him instead of the person who just won the game."

Of course I knew all the fanfare was for me—everyone should realize that. But even, I who know a lot about everything, could not begin to imagine how yumston things would become once the three of us were married. It kind of works out like this: Diana is for working, Volt is for playing, and both Diana and Volt are for loving and having fun!

On the way to the airport Diana and Volt had had their first disagreement. The subject had been Diana's wedding dress. Diana, knowing how the airlines lose her luggage, wanted to take the dress as a carry on. Volt thought it would be safe with the luggage, and Volt won. Volt must have some power over the airlines because when we arrived, everything was there just like it should be. Diana began the task of getting ready for the wedding. Her dress was very exquisite and it made a pretty rustling sound as she walked around. Although people said it was lovely it was I who got most of the comments. But I give credit where credit is due—Diana has kept my beautiful coat up by daily combing and brushing and by providing me with the best food money can buy.

I assumed a pose of dignity and watched Volt and Diana promise to love, honor and cherish one another. Then the priest turned to Volt.

"John," he said, "it was my great pleasure to come here today. Diana and Venture and I have been friends for a long time and I am very proud and honored that you chose me to celebrate this sacred ceremony with you and to rejoice with you in your happiness. I know this situation is just a little different than a regular marriage. Although Venture is just a dog, you will have a different relationship than most men have with their dogs. His position in your lives is a very interesting one. In lots of ways, he's childlike, but in other ways, he shows the wisdom of a sage. So, John, before I can pronounce you and Diana man and wife, I must ask you if you understand fully the honored position Venture will now share as a part of your lives."

"Yes," said Volt. "And I promise to at all times remember his very necessary service to Diana. I will always love him and respect him."

The priest then bent to stroke my golden head. I kissed his hand and looked directly into his eyes.

"Venture," he said solemnly, "a very big change is happening in your life today. Many dogs live with married people but your honored position makes your situation very different from other dogs. Starting today, Volt is a very important part of Diana's life and so will be important to you. Will you love him, trust him, respect him and allow him to take his honored place beside Diana so long as you shall live?"

I ran my mighty club. I thought its *thud thud thud* brought a real dignity to the occasion most other couples don't have.

The priest smiled down upon me. "We accept the wagging of your tail as your 'I will,' Venture. So by the powers vested in me, I pronounce you husband and wife—and since Venture is so important to this union, I pronounce it a tri-marriage. Volt, you may now kiss your bride."

Volt correctly understood his responsibility. As he kissed Diana, I moved close, and Volt scratched my velvety golden ears. Those around us applauded. The three of us looked very handsome standing together.

The celebration lasted well into the wee hours of the morning and all of us were tired as we made our way to the spacious wedding suite. Diana made certain I was comfortable. She gave me my ring and my bone, but then she stopped paying attention to me and started making a fuss over Volt. They were forgetting to include me, so I growled a soft invitation to play. They ignored me. I picked up my beloved ring and thrust it between them, growling my invitation loudly. Volt scratched my ears and told me I was a very fine fellow and that he would love to play with me, maybe tomorrow.

Diana completely ignored me. I didn't like the way I was being treated one little bit, so I barked loudly. If Volt had time to play, he needed to be reminded of his promise to include me.

However, it was Diana who reacted. She told me rather sharply to shut up. I didn't much like the tone of her voice so I lifted up my mighty voice in a series of loud yaps. That got her full attention but not the results I wanted.

"All right, Venture!" she said crossly. "I told you to be quiet! Since you choose not to be good, we'll have to do what we did back at the Guide Dog Foundation," and from her suitcase she took the tie-down and very firmly she snapped it into my collar and around a table leg.

"Something you are going to have to learn, Venture," she said as she pushed me into a sitting position, "is to respect our privacy. Up to now, you have had all of my attention, but you see that is changing and you are going to have to respect Volt's feelings as well as your own."

It was really disgusting. Diana and Volt seemed utterly wrapped up in one another and I knew by the harsh, quick, snappy way Diana had tied me up she would brook no comment, so I lay down and pondered my fate. What was I going to do? My life seemed completely ruined. Just a few hours ago Volt and Diana had made a solemn promise that they would love me and honor me and include me in everything. How quickly they had forgotten their vow! They certainly weren't including me now and it was up to me to figure a way out of this mess. I wished Little Haze were available to advise me.

With a surge of sadness I recalled our conversation about her not feeling well. I faced the reality that I, and I alone, would have to make the relationship work. Everyone's happiness was at stake. I lay there and thought about my problem for what seemed hours when I noticed the familiar quiet, even breathing from Diana that told me she had fallen asleep.

I became aware that Volt was looking at me. I looked back at him, letting him see all the sadness I felt. Volt responded to my sad look and got out of bed and came over to stand beside me.

"Are you feeling left out, big fella?" he asked as he bent over to play with one of my velvety golden ears. "I'm sure you don't even begin to understand all the changes that are taking place in your life but I will do my best to make things pleasant for all of us. You do understand that, don't you, Venture?"

I gave him a very soulful look as I slowly but steadily ran my mighty club.

"Are you unhappy that Diana tied you up?" he asked as he bent to stroke my beautiful shining coat.

I ran my club with more enthusiasm.

"Tell you what, fella," said Volt. "I feel badly that you have to be tied up and if I were you I'd feel resentful. Tell you what I'm gonna do. I will untie you. But you are going to have to be quiet or Diana will wake up and be down both our throats. If I let you loose, will you be quiet?"

I ran my club with happiness and Volt reached down and unsnapped my tie-down. I got up and shook myself then I went over and lay down by Volt's side of the bed. He talked to me for a few minutes, then he got back in bed with Diana. He let his arm crook over the side and I laid my head within the circle of his arm and fell blissfully asleep.

After a while Volt took his arm away because, he explained, "my arm is going to sleep from your heavy head." I ran my club knowingly. It was going to take time, but already the bond was growing very strong. Even today, Volt probably thinks he and Diana run the show, and I prefer it that way. After all, without them there wouldn't be a show to run. Diana plus us V-boys equal a family. All three of us spent the next few days learning just how wonderful being a family was.

But all vacations must come to an end, and all too soon it was time for us to go to the airport and ride the plane back home. This time it was like usual—all the luggage was lost. In time we got it back, but Volt had never had it lost before and he was very unhappy until finally it was returned to us. I just ran my club with understanding each time I heard his voice raised in distress over it. I knew that in time he would get used to it and come to understand that this is just a normal part of travel.

When we got home we had to take up the serious business of moving and setting up housekeeping. Volt felt I needed a yard to play in and that meant a house. But that was a dream we had to wait quite a while for.

I have this problem with Volt and Diana. Although I think I am loved, and Volt often spends time and money on me, he seems to spend an inordinate amount of time and attention on Diana. A couple times, Volt actually closed the bedroom door so I wouldn't bother them. So I decided to teach Diana and Volt a lesson they would remember for a while.

When I was shut out I went in search of something I could get into. The perfect thing was sitting right there in the kitchen. It was the trash—and not just regular trash people throw in their wastebaskets! This was garbage from the kitchen with messy things in it like coffee grounds and potato peelings and banana peels. You get the picture!

I first upset the can, and then I carefully strewed this mess all over the carpet. Diana and Volt really helped me in my endeavor by giving me lots of time to do a really thorough job. Volt opened the door with a grin on his face that would put to shame the look of a cat that got away with all the cream. My surprise was waiting for him and I watched with joy as Volt came into the living room and beheld my handiwork.

He, however, lacked a real appreciation for my creativity. After he had expressed his displeasure at my act he called Diana and I knew my plan had backfired.

"You bad dog," snarled Diana crossly. "From now on we are going to have to start tying you up," she said as she administered several hard yanks on my choke chain. "Tell Venture that he is a bad dog, Volt," instructed Diana.

"Bad! Bad! Bad dog, Venture," said Volt, sounding very displeased. But, you see, I could get one over on Volt that I couldn't on Diana, because as Volt scolded me he looked at me. He told Diana later that although I had my sorry mask on, I was giving him a look that said "You know you deserved this for not paying more attention to me." At the time they were most unhappy with me but it was something I often heard them talk and laugh about. So you see, some good may have come from this evil deed. They don't always tie me up, but you can be sure they pay attention to where I am and what I am doing.

In time we did get our new home and both Billyum and Little Haze came over to spend the first day there. Several things were going to happen before we moved in. The telephone had to be installed and Volt was arranging for new carpets and drapes and some other things which were needed.

Before these things all began to be done, Little Haze and I had time to check out everything. Volt had taken the screens off the windows in the dining room and the window was wide open. I looked out. It was only a few inches from the sill to the flower bed below. I slid out easily.

"Come on, Little Haze," I called. "Just look at that lovely grass— and see down the street those little children playing ball. Come on! Let's show them how it's done."

"I can show them best," trilled Little Haze, as she seemed to float past me.

"Hazel!" called the stern, firm voice of Billyum. "Get your tail back in here."

Without a word or question, Little Haze changed direction. Quicker than it takes to tell, she was sailing back in through the window with me at her heels.

"I don't believe it," said Volt as he came running into the room. "Those dogs went in and out of that window as though it were a door. I never thought they'd do that! We will close that window right now and cut off their escape route."

"Well," said Little Haze, "it was fun while it lasted. But I was afraid Billyum would put a stop to it. They don't like it when we run off, especially in a strange neighborhood."

"This is a strange neighborhood to you, Little Haze, but it's going to be my home. So I plan to get to know it," I countered.

"If you sneak out, Diana and Volt will be very upset," said Little Haze. "Besides, that is a very busy street out there and I think it would be unsafe for you to wander out there on your own. Believe me, Venture, Diana will give you lots of opportunities to get to know your neighborhood. Let's go lie out in the yard. It is such a pretty sunny day and there's something I've been wanting to ask you about."

"OK, Little Haze," I said. The idea of lying out there in the sun and having a heart-to-heart with Little Haze was most appealing.

As we settled ourselves, I began to understand just how nice a yard was going to be. The sun was very warm. Although the grass was also warm, a gentle coolness came up from the ground and caressed my belly. Little Haze acted as though she were in heaven as she sprawled her delicate form in my yard. I was so pleased to be sharing this experience with her. For a while we just lay there enjoying the outdoors; then Little Haze turned to me.

"We haven't had much of a chance to have a heart-to-heart since you got married, Venture. Tell me, what is life like with Volt as a part of your household? Also, I have been wondering about some of the things we talked about before your marriage. I seem to recall that you were very worried about Volt's being of another race and all those dire things Fritsey predicted. It's very obvious you, Diana, and Volt are very happy together.

"Well," I said, "it has been a most interesting experience. Most of the problems I have had to deal with have been problems of their not paying the correct attention to me that I'm entitled to. There have been a few racial problems, though, but they are very different from the kinds of things Fritsey talked about."

"You have always wanted to be the center of everything that happens. When it was just you and Diana, I know you had it pretty good. When Volt came into the picture, though, I know Diana grew to love him very much. But that didn't stop her love for you. I'm certain she still treasures you very highly, even though you are a butt. It is very obvious that Volt loves you. I heard him say one of the reasons they got the house was for you. That represents a lot of love, Venture. Tell me, what kind of racial problems did you mean a second ago?"

"To begin with," I said, "Volt had told us there would be some people who wouldn't like him because he's black. This has proven to be true. We are always treated with great courtesy when we are in a public place but when we are with a smaller group of people, I can feel the disapproval that comes from many persons. We have found a solution to this problem. If people are uncomfortable with us, there are so many people in this world that are comfortable with us, we just don't worry about them. We move on to become friends with people who will accept us. But you know, what is funny, Little Haze, sometimes the people who are uncomfortable about us see us on a regular basis. We don't bother them, of course, but they have become so used to seeing us together, often they will come to us and indicate they want to be our friends, too. Volt says that it's a question of seeing us together so often, it just becomes acceptable.

"Another thing that is most interesting is that white people aren't always the ones to disapprove. Diana and Volt have visited black churches and in every case the people are often afraid of me, refuse to let me in, or treat Diana with unveiled hostility.

"There was also another problem. You know that Diana was raised in the South and certain ideas about black people were really impressed upon her. When a person has held certain beliefs for many years, they don't just go away."

"This does not make a whole lot of sense to me, Venture," said Little Haze. "You and I have talked about this in depth before you got married. I thought that Diana really loved Volt and he has certainly proved himself worthy of that love. I thought this color thing had been put to rest. I feel physical pain to think that of all people Diana might harbor evil thoughts in her heart."

"Diana does not harbor evil in her heart now," I said, "and I don't believe she ever did. What I am saying, though, is I do believe that in her heart, Diana did feel conflict—a conflict from the beliefs she was raised with, and a conflict with reality now. I didn't know how to fix it, so I wished in my heart for a miracle. When it came, I didn't exactly realize this was an important key to solving our problems.

"At first I thought it was just another thing that was happening in my life. Volt got a telephone call from a woman he had worked with and she invited us over for the Fourth of July. It is a little ways to her house, and I remember that Diana was not thrilled to be going. But Volt really wanted to go, so we went. The minute I laid eyes on her, I knew she was special. But I don't think that even I understood what a valuable influence she was going to be in our lives."

"What was she like?" asked Little Haze.

"Well," I said thoughtfully as I scratched my ear, "I think the best way to describe her would be to say she is very classy yet down to earth. Her feet are firmly planted on the ground and she doesn't have much illusion about nothin'. I would call her a very refined and respectable black woman. Her home is filled with African art pieces. She's dignified but unaffected. If you take the trouble to know her, you discover a heart of gold.

"As I have said, Diana did not feel comfortable with many black people, but soon she became involved in a stimulating conversation with a very educated professor and only later realized he was black. There were more gatherings at this lady's house, and little by little we began to have discussions with others in the group. As time passed, we became part of the group and before you know it, Diana began to really care about the individuals in it. Things finally fell into place for her. It's like she came to know in her heart what she already knew in her head. People are just people—just like all us dogs are just dogs."

"There has never been a question in my mind about Diana accepting Volt," said Little Haze, "so why would there be a problem accepting his friends?"

"You know, when Volt told Diana that he was black she promptly forgot. You have to remember, Little Haze, Volt is a professional person—on a par with Diana. His speech doesn't make you think about his color, and besides, he's so kind that you just have to love him for himself. Diana didn't instantly embrace all black people. It took the miracle lady to make their culture real to her. Now if she could just do that for the people who raised me. Diana felt so close to those people, but when we got married, Diana sent a wedding photo to them and hasn't heard from them since."

"You aren't suggesting those good people hold it against Volt that he is black, are you?" asked Little Haze.

"I have heard Volt and Diana talk about it," I said. "You know, there are those who can accept a black person—until he marries a white person."

"Can you think of anything that can be done to reach these people?" asked Little Haze. "After all, they are the ones who are losing by not getting to know Volt."

"That is true," I said, "but in this life we all make choices and they have not made a good one in failing to get to know Volt. But it is their choice to make. All we can do is to hope someday they will get another golden opportunity. Maybe then they will be ready for it.

"Now, Diana and Volt have joined a local church that is quite large. You would expect a church to be most tolerant. However, that is not the way it is. Although this church is very advanced in giving special consideration to the disabled, Diana was at first not accepted there."

"Was this a black church?" asked Little Haze.

"No," I said, "it was a large church with maybe one or two black families. But let me tell you about it because that story is also very special. Like I said, it is a big church. When we first went there, we did so because Volt had heard the pastor on the radio and thought he was special. The first time we went there, they refused to seat us because of me. When they saw Diana was going to be troublesome about it, they let us in for a trial period. It has been a while and the subject has never been brought up again. At first the people were just a little standoffish but I solved that problem. There were people who just had to meet me. Before you knew it, we had more friends than you could shake a stick at. We joined a Sunday school class and the teacher of that class was a very smart man. He realized how special I am, and soon I had won the hearts of all that attended. In time the teacher had to leave and of course you know who replaced him."

"Yes," said Little Haze, "I know Volt did, but that still didn't solve Diana's problems, did it?"

"Not right away, but they did get solved. There were two reasons. One is because of the sweet person Volt is. The other is because members of that wonderful class made it their business to help. When you go with us tomorrow, you will experience their love too. It's unforgettable."

The next day was Sunday, and Billyum and Little Haze got to experience first-hand what I had told her about the love. After Diana sang in the choir, she and I went to the Sunday school classroom to join Billyum and Little Haze. All those folks were paying court to my beautiful friend. There was no room for jealousy because, like water, the love simply moved to cover me and Diana the way it was over Billyum and Little Haze. Afterwards, Little Haze told me that if she hadn't seen it, she couldn't have believed it.

I smiled to myself. It just one of our little daily miracles.

A few weeks later, Diana and I again took a plane back east to attend a conference. On our way home, we had a layover and Diana took me outside so I could relieve myself. On the way back to the plane, I spotted a telephone and for some reason I cannot explain, I pulled Diana over to it. She thought my actions odd, but she called home to see if anything were happening. She got the answering machine. Disinterestedly, she decided to check for messages. The one she heard sent chills into both of our hearts and took the joy out of the day.

Volt was at the vet's office with Billyum and wouldn't be able to meet us at the airport. Little Haze was seriously ill. He told Diana to take a limo home and he would meet us there. He also said we should pray for Billyum and Little Haze because they didn't think Little Haze would live much longer. To say Billyum was heartbroken would be to put it very mildly.

The plane seemed to take forever to get to California. We got a skycap to find a limo for us, and Volt met us at home.

"If you want to see Little Haze one last time," said Volt, "I think we'd better get over to Billyum's house."

"I would like to see Little Haze," said Diana "and I want to offer what comfort I can to Billyum."

When we arrived, I was shocked at the sight of Little Haze. She was always delicate, but now she was very thin, and it was hard for her to breathe.

She did not get up as we came in but there was no mistaking the welcome as she wagged her lovely tail.

"Venture, you old butt," she exclaimed softly, "I was afraid you wouldn't get here in time."

"What do you mean I wouldn't get here in time, Little Haze, you old sleaze?" I countered. "You are just under the weather! You are going to be just fine!"

"No, Venture," said Little Haze. "My life is drawing to a close. It must be this way because everything has a starting point, and everything must end. I am about to complete this phase of it."

"Don't say such things, Little Haze," I said.

"Venture, an important part of life is accepting reality. That is what I am doing and you must do so too. There are a couple things I need to explain to you. First, I want to pass on to you my wagging license, and the power to grant wagging licenses and to forgive all past wagging offenses. The other thing I need to do is again request that you look out for Billyum."

Billyum, Diana, and Volt talked together, and as their attention was drawn away from us, Little Haze and I went through the ceremony that made me a member of the Secret Order of the Growlery.

As we left, my heart was very heavy because I knew I had seen Little Haze for the last time.

Twenty

To Everything
There Is a Season

Mornings were always special times for me and Volt. Volt rises early and we go together and check out what has been going on in the neighborhood. Both of us love the stillness and freshness of the early morning, and it's an opportunity to get to know each other better. By now the bond between Volt and me was very strong. We had learned to respect each other's ways and in the process of developing this respect, I had managed to wrap Volt firmly about my club. Volt and Diana have very different personalities, and quality time with him is important to our marriage.

Sometimes Diana would be up doing things, but other times we would return home to find her sleeping. Then I would help Volt get a pot of coffee ready for her. She liked that, but one day she decided to question Volt, impugn my character, and call my value into question.

"Volt," she said, "why do you insist on saying that Venture helps you make the coffee? Anyone hearing you talk like that would get the idea that this dog is a really super dog, but you and I know he doesn't do a thing to help."

"Yes he does," said Volt loyally. "Venture sees to it that your coffee is made and is perfect for you."

"He does not," sniffed Diana. "You are trying to impart human qualities to that old dog that he doesn't have. The dog is just a butt. He doesn't do a darn thing and you are wrong to pretend that he does."

"No, I don't do any pretending," said Volt with finality. "Venture here sees that everything is perfect for you. You should be showing him a little more consideration instead of calling him a butt."

"Look, Volt," said Diana with exasperation. "Face reality. Just how does the dog manage to make the coffee?"

"Oh, he does," laughed Volt.

"He does not," snapped Diana. "Volt, how can this butt help make coffee? Explain it!"

"Well," said Volt in his slow, gentle voice, "I know that Venture is responsible for the coffee. It's like this. Once there was a man who retired. There was a construction crew working just a little ways from his home and the man enjoyed watching the men work. So every day he would take a lunch and go and sit on a hill that overlooked the construction site where he could see everything that the men did. The job took many months and the man was there faithfully every day to watch. When the job was finished he went down and told the men how much he had enjoyed watching them work and how he respected the quality they had put into the job."

"'Gee!' said one of the workers, 'and all this time we thought that you were hired by the company to be our supervisor!' You see, in this case Venture is the supervisor. Let me assure you he follows every move I make. Nothing slips by him. He is a very good supervisor, so you see it really is he who is responsible for the coffee—he provides quality control." At that they had both laughed.

One morning we returned from our reconnoitering to find Diana sitting by the telephone crying.

"What's wrong?" asked Volt as he hurried to put his arms about the sobbing woman.

"Billyum just called," sobbed Diana. "Little Haze died last night."

"Oh dear," sighed Volt as he sat down beside Diana. "Billyum must be shattered. But the vet didn't hold out a whole lot of hope for her. I'm glad the doctor who takes care of these dogs is such a caring man. He did everything in his power to save her. He even put Little Haze on some very costly medicine to try to save her life. I'm so sorry that it didn't save her."

"I didn't know about the special medicine," said Diana. "None of us have much money so if it was expensive, how did Billyum pay for it?"

"You probably don't know about it because you were away when the problem came up," explained Volt. "There was no way Billyum could afford it and he was just going crazy with grief. I didn't feel that I could get it for him so I went to one of the doctors I do business with and explained the situation. It was he who provided the medicine. He lives near Billyum and often has seen the two of them together, so he was glad to lend a hand. He'll be very sad to learn things didn't work out. Better give me the telephone and I'll call Billyum and see if there is anything we can do to help."

Volt spoke quietly on the phone for a little while, then he turned to Diana.

"The vet sent his ambulance over to pick up Little Haze's body," said Volt. "I think we should have breakfast and then we'll go over to Billyum's house and see if there is anything we can do."

"I don't feel hungry," said Diana.

"Well, have a cup of coffee with me and then we'll go," said Volt. "Maybe it would help him to talk about Little Haze and see Venture."

"It must just be awful for him," sighed Diana. "Everything around him must be like a sharp knife because his whole house was centered around Little Haze."

"Let's go see what the situation is for him," said Volt. "I don't think he should be alone right now. I know that he is really upset and needs to talk. Let's let him talk and then take it from there."

Soon we were in the car and it wasn't long before we were knocking on Billyum's door. It was almost a frightening experience to me—the house was so silent. When he came to the door, Billyum seemed gaunt and tired. As he told us to come in, his voice sounded hollow and drained and my heart went out to him, so I lay close to him, letting my head rest affectionately on his foot.

"I'm so glad you could come," said Billyum. "You can't imagine how awful this day is. I got up this morning to take Little Haze out, and she wouldn't move."

Volt put an arm about Billyum's shoulders and everyone just sat quietly grieving.

"The vet came with the ambulance," explained Billyum, "because he said he wanted to see exactly what had last happened with her. He said that even in death, Little Haze was a most beautiful creature, and that I had been given a great blessing by the two of us being able to share one another's lives." Volt, Billyum, and Diana hugged each other. Then Billyum said, "Volt, there is just something I need to talk about."

"Go ahead," said Volt. "That's what we're here for."

"Well," gulped Billyum, "I know that you are a Christian minister and I respect that, but I'm having a real hard time right now with some Christian teachings."

"What teachings?" asked Volt gently.

"In my studies of the Bible," said Billyum, "I've learned that there are wonderful rewards for those who are good. However, my pastor is adamant that although Hazel was a wonderful creature given to me by our Father in Heaven, dogs do not have souls and no salvation is possible for them. When I have heard him present the gospel, he makes quite a point that no animal can be saved. I am really troubled about this, because Little Haze gave all she had to help me. It seems callous and unloving for a creator who supposedly loves all His creatures to just throw all her love and faithfulness aside and give it no future consideration. To be honest with you, Volt, it makes me feel very angry and it makes me wonder about such a God."

"Well," said Volt quietly, "I think I understand how you might feel. For many years I might have spoken as your pastor did. Knowing Little Haze and Venture as I do, however, I have had to rethink this question. I will be happy to share my ideas with you, but you must remember something, Billyum—I am speculating. I believe that it is wrong to argue with things God has made specific statements about, such as 'Thou shalt not steal'. It would be wrong for me to try to justify a bank robbery. If there are special circumstances, God is the judge of that, not me. But where we are not given guidelines, I don't feel it is wrong to raise possible theories."

"Do you feel there is hope for a future for Little Haze?" asked Billyum eagerly.

"Well, some Bible scholars are redefining what a soul is," said Volt. "There are many who believe that the soul is the part of us that thinks. If you think about it, what part of you can I point to and say that is Billyum? It isn't something you can touch. I believe, and many Bible scholars believe, that the soul is the conscious part of you that thinks and feels and is your personality. That is your soul and it survives your body."

"Maybe my pastor doesn't understand how to define a soul," said Billyum. "Perhaps after I explain what you just told me he will have a different viewpoint about animals."

"I wouldn't count on that, Billyum," said Volt. "You see, he may not be very interested because the Bible is not very concerned about it."

"I don't see why not," exclaimed Billyum. "It seems very important to me."

"Of course it's important to you," said Volt, "and for Venture and Little Haze too, but it may not be important to a Bible scholar."

"I don't see why not," repeated Billyum. "If a Bible student understood the great service dogs like Hazel and Venture perform, don't you think they would have a different perspective about how important this question is?"

"If you study the Bible very carefully," said Volt, "it is my understanding anyway that salvation isn't available to these souls."

"You knew Little Haze well," said Billyum with passion. "You live with Venture, and he is a very sweet dog. No one can leave his presence and find his life untouched. Knowing these things, how can you see a God as loving and caring if He would allow a wonderful being like Little Haze to be lost?"

"But Billyum," said Volt tenderly, "man needs to be saved from his sins. I don't think Little Haze, or Venture, or other wonderful, faithful little creatures need to be saved from anything. The way I see it, they are pure and innocent. I believe that God's love is so great that were they lost, He would find a way to save them. But since that isn't necessary, I don't think you need to have any concern about it. Look at it like this. If you were to describe God, and then you were to describe yourself, how would you liken the two of you?"

"I don't even know how to answer that," said Billyum.

"My point exactly," said Volt. "The Bible says man cannot understand the thoughts of God, so high are they. And just as there is difference between you and God, there is a vast difference between you and Little Haze. I am not trying to belittle her but it is a fact that her brain is different from yours, so the way she would approach things would have to be vastly different. Let us not forget, however, that when Jesus was on earth, he valued faithfulness and the act of looking out for details. Remember, he said: 'You have been faithful over a few things, I will make you a ruler over many things. Enter into the joy of your Lord.' I am very certain the great God I serve loves Little Haze and appreciates what she did with her limited abilities to make your life worthwhile. I don't know what it is exactly that will happen, but somehow her unselfishness will be rewarded and I know that she will be rewarded and far above your wildest dreams for her. I believe the Bible is a guide for man and because we have resisted the will of God, we need a Savior. Venture and Little Haze, on the other hand, have never had the intent to resist God, so that is why I believe a lot of time hasn't been given to that subject except to be told of Our Father's loving care even for the sparrows.

"Another point to remember is the story of Balaam. He was riding on his little donkey to curse the children of Israel even though he knew he should not do that. The angel of the Lord came to block his way. Balaam couldn't see the angel but the donkey could. The Bible says that God had to open the eyes of Balaam so that he could see the angel. I would gather from that verse that the little donkey was able to see the angel without special help. We know that Little Haze and Venture have gifts we don't have. Their hearing is extremely sensitive and beyond our range. I believe that they can see things we can't also and that is why the little donkey saw the angel.

"Also, there is the verse that says 'inasmuch as you have done it unto one of the least of these, my brethren, you have done it unto me.' Many animal rights people have taken that verse to mean that the way we treat animals is like treating Jesus that way too."

" I don't really know about that. Volt," said Billyum. "If that were true, I couldn't eat meat or go fishing."

"Some believe that, Billyum," said Volt. "I'm not saying I do. Diana and I go fishing, though we don't eat meat for our own reasons. The Bible is clear that mankind has dominion over the beasts of the field and the fowl of the air."

"Volt used to have another job before he went into business for himself," said Diana. "When he left, they had a goodbye party for him. At the party, part of the table decorations were a couple of bowls containing goldfish. After the party, Volt took them home. I was not thrilled that he had them because he had no idea how they should be cared for. But he learned what they needed and he changed their water regularly and gave them food, and they lived for a long time. What I wonder about is, here were those little creatures who were not valued very much. Yet Volt fed them and did the very best that he knew how to do by them and he did it with cheerfulness. Could that be the same as doing it unto one of the least of them? Surely those little goldfish didn't rate very high on the scale but if I understand correctly, God even cares about those little fish."

"Do you think that the fish went to heaven?" asked Billyum.

"I have no idea at all where the fish went to," laughed Diana, "but there are a couple of points I would like to make. Those fish didn't amount to much. Yet Volt cared for them with cheerfulness and did what he could for them and somewhere I think that his attitude counts. The other thing is that I am absolutely certain that those fish wouldn't have the intelligence to appreciate what Venture or Little Haze could appreciate. What I am suggesting is that again, we see a division between Little Haze and Venture and the fish—they are completely a different type of creature but they may have their own parallel and they could have their own unique value just as Little Haze and Venture are different from us but they may have their own value. Maybe they are a-swimmin' in a big goldfish pond in the sky. I don't know, but I am certain that they are being looked out for. Of course you can carry this to extremes where you don't want to kill bugs because they are the least and I am sure that doesn't apply, but it is interesting to think about."

Just then we heard the musical chimes of Volt's pager. Diana and Billyum continued to talk while Volt spoke softly on the telephone.

I moved closer to Billyum and he slipped down on the floor and buried his head in my golden shining coat. My heart ached for him as I felt his tears, and my heart was wrenched by the terrible need and longing I felt coming from him. A part of me stood apart and remembered that feeling of longing. I had felt that same need before, and it had been a very important part of my life. Then, with a little shock, it all fell into place for me.

Suddenly I was a puppy again and Auntie Em was going to take me and some other pups over to see some blind students. I wasn't all that thrilled about seeing these blind people but if it meant being with Auntie Em, just about anything was worth it.

Then a young man took me in his arms and held me against his cheek. "What a special Puppins," he murmured. "You're such a good boy, I wish I could take you home with me." As he held me close, I felt his love and his desperate need to be accepted. My heart went out to this stranger. I felt myself answering his need with an overpowering feeling of love and compassion. I longed to tell him that I loved him, but his fingers were stroking my fluffy coat, so I laid my head on his shoulder and went to sleep. When someone said, "Time for this sleepyhead to go," I snuggled closer till the young man said, "I have to give you back, Puppins."

Now I remembered all those times Billyum had seemed so familiar but I just couldn't place him, and I knew. In this great time of need, I reached out to him as I had wanted to when I was that little pup in his arms. I wondered if Little Haze had known of our meeting and how much it had affected my life. Probably she did. She seemed to know all that was important. Perhaps she had understood that it was Billyum's chance meeting with a future guide dog that had helped him to be so open to her. Now when I saw Billyum, I saw him differently because it had been he who had taught me to trust and care and love and so be successful.

"Billyum," said Volt as he replaced the phone, "I am going to have to make some business calls. You have been through a great deal, and I know we can't take away the pain, but I wonder if you would like to come home with us for a while. You would be welcome to come with me on my business calls, or you can stay at home and relax with Diana and Venture. I know that we cannot bring back Little Haze, but I also realize that everywhere you turn here you can't help but be reminded of her. So please come back home with us."

"Are you sure I wouldn't be too much trouble and complicate your already busy life, Volt?" asked Billyum.

"Indeed not," said Volt. "We would enjoy having you stay with us for a little while, and being able to play with Venture might help take the raw edge off the way you are feeling. I understand, of course, that Venture is Diana's guide dog, so he must first take care of her needs, but that old boy has a heart big enough for just about the whole wide world."

"That is very kind of you," said Billyum. "It will take me a little while to get my things together but I would just love the chance to stay with you V-boys and Diana for a while."

Soon Billyum was ready, and we were on the way back to my house.

Billyum stayed with us for about two weeks. Of course I had to take care of Diana, but I spent every spare minute with Billyum, keeping the promise I had made to Little Haze. Billyum and Volt had more long talks about the Bible and where Little Haze might be, and little by little I felt Billyum finding some peace in these discussions.

"You know," said Volt to Diana, "I am not trying to make this a picnic occasion because I understand that there is real reason for Billyum to feel loss and to grieve. But I want to be positive about this also. I want him to celebrate the joy and beauty of Hazel's life and not just experience missing her and loneliness and sadness."

Everyone we met tried to help. Even Paul invited us out on the boat. I think Billyum felt a little pain remembering Little Haze's presence with us before, but I stayed close to him and I think he enjoyed the day.

The Sunday school class was very loving to Billyum also. People dropped by to be with Billyum and to show him through their actions that they cared. Even total strangers reached out in love to Billyum and his special need.

It was the last evening that Billyum would be staying with us. The next day he would be returning home. Several people had just kind of gotten together and they had had a most wonderful barbecue. I tell you that when Volt fires up that grill, everyone talks about how yumston it is. As usual, they didn't give me a scrap. After everyone had eaten, they sprawled around on lawn chairs and I lay on the soft, cool grass and looked at the wonderful full moon. My thoughts returned to the many acts of kindness I had seen over the last two weeks. Deep inside me, as I felt the pain of missing Little Haze, I also had a very strong wish. If only Little Haze could know how dearly she had been loved, and if only she could know about how people had reached out to Billyum, I thought she would feel a great measure of contentment.

Suddenly, a hush fell over everything. In the deep stillness that followed, a cloud floated over the shining moon, covering it from view. The air actually seemed to take on a life of its own. As it pulsated with that life, a strange exotic fragrance almost overpowered me. For just a moment, everything was frozen in that special moment and then everything was like it had always been.

I looked around at the people. They didn't seem to notice anything, but continued their lively conversation. I sighed. I guess this moment was for me alone and I rejoiced because in my heart of hearts, I knew Little Haze knew and was glad.

Things Seem
To Be Yuckston

Billyum! What on earth happened to the side of your face!" exclaimed Volt. "You are all bloody! We better get the blood stains out of your shirt before they set and we can never get them out. I thought you would be all right here with Diana and Venture, but by the looks of you, I ought to take you to the hospital!"

"I don't think that would be a good idea at all," said Diana. "Billyum got those wounds at the hospital."

"What do you mean, he got the wounds at the hospital?" asked Volt. "They help people at the hospital, not hurt them. Come into the bathroom, Billyum, so I can give you first aid."

"Remember my friend who is in the hospital at AHA, Allied Health Association?" asked Billyum. "Well, you know she has called so often while I was here to try and comfort me over the loss of Little Haze that Diana and I thought we would take the bus over to the AHA Hospital and say hello. However, things didn't go very well."

"What happened?" asked Volt. "Did you run into a tree?"

"No," said Billyum. "I ran into a security guard who couldn't speak English. He said no dogs and was unable to understand that Venture was a guide dog with special rights and privileges."

"Are you saying, Billyum, that the security guard did this to you and wouldn't allow a guide dog in the hospital?" asked Volt.

"That is pretty much what happened," said Billyum. "I told him this was a guide dog and we were going to enter, and as you can see by my face, he gave me a pretty good wallop."

"Slow down here, Billyum," said Volt, unbelieving. "Are you telling me that an employee of a hospital hit you when you tried to enter because you were with a guide dog?"

"Um-hm," said Billyum. "That is about the long and short of it."

"But where were you, Diana?"

"Well," said Diana, "When I saw there was going to be trouble, I ran with Venture to find a business so that we could call the police."

"And did you?" asked Volt.

"No," said Diana. "When we started to leave, the security guard heard me yell to Billyum that I was going for the police. I guess he was afraid of that so he radioed for help."

"Right," said Volt. "The security guard was scared of the police but just as long as it was two defenseless blind people, he felt he was in control of the situation. This is absolutely disgusting and I plan to make some noise about it. How did you leave the situation?"

"Oh, the guard got someone who could speak English," said Billyum, "and he escorted us into the hospital and apologized for the misunderstanding."

"The misunderstanding!" said Volt. "That seems to me a very understated way of explaining what happened. Why didn't they treat your injury since you were at the hospital, Billyum?"

"Oh, I think they felt that they did," said Billyum. "They wiped some of the blood away with a Kleenex, but they explained that they couldn't do more because I am not covered by their Plan."

"That is disgusting," said Volt. "I will call and make a complaint about that, because that is something I find to be very offensive."

AHA maintains a complaint line and Volt called and got a recording that they would return his call in three business days if he left a message. Although Volt left a message, his call was never returned.

"I really regret that your visit must end in such an unpleasant way," said Volt as we all got into the car to take Billyum home.

"There aren't often problems about guide dogs anymore," said Billyum. "But when they do happen they are usually very interesting. I am most surprised at AHA. Diana goes there all the time and really gets first-rate care. Sometimes I have thought I made a mistake not to join up with them, but now I'm not so sure."

"We do have to remember," said Diana, "that I don't usually go to that Center."

"That is really no excuse," said Billyum. "The law applies to all medical centers and they should have training to advise everyone of the rights of guide dogs. When you see someone breaking the law with such abandon as these people were doing, it makes you wonder what other laws they are breaking."

"I hope you don't have too much pain with your face," said Volt. "That guy really gave you some kind of special slap and we shall have to follow up on this problem."

I missed Billyum, but Diana talked with him on the phone often. She reported that although Billyum was experiencing the loss of Little Haze a lot more at home by himself, she felt he was managing.

"I know it is difficult," said Volt when she brought it up to him, "but it is an unfortunate reality of life that Billyum must come to terms with. If you think another visit is what he needs, of course he's welcome, but ultimately this is a problem that Billyum must work out for himself no matter how painful it is to do so."

Volt was very upset about the way we had been treated at AHA. He called a number of times, but no one would return his telephone calls.

"Well," said Volt to Diana one evening, "this is a matter I feel should be pursued but if there are no further incidents, I would guess that there isn't much we can do. The problem is that no one else actually saw the security guard strike Billyum. He could and probably would claim that Billyum already had an injury on his face. Their refusal to treat him after the incident really baffles me, but I guess I don't understand everything. You know, Diana, you have been getting cards and messages on the answering machine that they want you to come in for an exam."

"It's no big deal," said Diana. "They like for women to have special breast examinations, especially when there is a record of high risk as there is in my family. But I suspect that it is really busy work and something that they do to show they really care about the patient."

"Maybe so," said Volt. "But even so, I think you should let them do their little busy work. That way if you should have a problem, you have given them a chance to do something about it."

"OK," said Diana. "I'll go next week."

The next week found us at our regular AHA vet's office and I was pleased to see our favorite lady vet. She and Diana chatted happily and then it was time for Diana's exam.

The vet was not pleased with the results of the exam.

"You need to go for a special test," she explained to Diana. "This test is called a mammogram. It is painless and every woman should have it after she is thirty-five, at least every two years. I feel some things here that I don't like and that test will make it very clear to us what we are dealing with."

Then the vet reached down to stroke my beautiful shining coat.

"It is very important that Diana get this test," she said softly. "I am counting on you to help me. If the test turns out as I fear, then Diana will need all the love and support you can give her."

I ran my mighty club in agreement. I would do the best that could be done.

The test was scheduled right away and it only took a little while. They were very nice in the lab, but when Diana pointed out that they should be glad they were testing her instead of me because I had eight nipples, everyone including the doctor was down on the floor to check it out. I was in ecstasy having them handling me like that.

However, it wasn't good news for Diana. The nice lady vet called her and said that she must see a surgeon right away.

An appointment was made for her with this doctor right away and I could tell that Diana was scared, so I laid my beautiful head on her knee and tried to comfort her. Volt also tried to reassure her, but I knew she was very nervous.

When I took one look at the vet they call a surgeon, I knew that everything was going to be all right. True, there might be troubles, but this man was like me: kind, compassionate and capable. I knew that he would chase the yuckstons away from Diana. I ran my club at him although I knew that Diana was still uneasy and did not yet realize what I knew about this doctor. So I ran my club quietly and in a dignified way. The man noticed this about me and I could see his approval of me skyrocket.

He ordered more tests for Diana, and when they came back, he explained to Diana that she was going to have to enter the hospital for a major operation. He said there would be no problem with my visiting——in fact, she could keep me in the hospital if she wished.

About this time, I needed to go for my regular exam and Diana had been noticing a little growth on my chest, so she pointed it out to my vet.

"Well, now!" exclaimed the vet. "I have always known that Venture is a special dog, but this beats all!"

"What is it?" asked Diana.

"Well," said the vet. "Venture has an extra nipple. He has nine instead of the usual eight. His ninth nipple is ingrown. It happens sometimes. Anne Boleyn, they say, had an extra one too and it probably made her more exciting."

"No, I don't think so," said Diana. "Her husband cut her head off, so that doesn't sound very exciting to me. Maybe he thought doing that would square the equation."

The vet groaned at Diana's comment.

"You'd best watch out, Venture," he said. I looked at everyone lovingly and ran my mighty club. Volt immediately bestowed another honor on me because of my special status. He declared me Royal Master of the Ninth. Diana maintained, however, that although I might now have nine little nipples, I was still a butt. Sometimes there is nothing you can do with some people.

Diana has had many medical procedures, so I was not terribly concerned until the evening before she was to go into the hospital. Billyum came over. This must be something very special if Billyum was here. I was happy to see him but I became concerned.

"I expect you will be kind of out of it when you have your surgery. I know Volt has Venture and his friends at the church," said Billyum to Diana. "But I really felt that I wanted to be here for Volt. You know how he stood by me when I lost Little Haze. Actually both of you did. But Volt is likely to be hurting, and maybe I can lend a hand with the old butt. I will be happy to keep him combed and brushed for you so that he will remain beautiful."

The next afternoon, Diana entered the hospital. As usual, everyone paid court to me, so I felt a little better. However, that feeling was made less when the wonderful doctor came in to talk with them. He explained that according to the tests, both breasts had cancer in them and so would have to be removed. Diana expressed concern that she wouldn't be able to do the things she likes to do. But the nice doctor explained he would do the best that he could and also he would arrange for lots of physical therapy. He said that after the radiation they could consider a reconstruction which would make her as good-looking to the average person as she was now. I sensed real fear in Diana and I drew close to let her know we were there.

The next morning while Diana was in surgery, Billyum, Volt and I waited in the waiting room. Lots of people who know Diana and me came by. The nice lady vet came by. The charming champagne lady (Diana calls her that because of her bubbly personality) and many, many others who were there to see the doctor came to see me. All of this attention caused me to relax and I rolled on my back and exposed my many nipples. Even some of the people came from X-ray to see me and check out the great wonder I presented to their view. I was certain all of this attention meant that Billyum and Volt and maybe even Diana were overreacting to her situation. Diana really is a pretty balanced person, but from time to time she is in need of my help, and obviously this was such a time. She really ought to have been ashamed of herself, though, getting Billyum and Volt all upset like they had been.

The surgeon came down finally and said the operation was over and he felt that it was a success. He told Billyum and Volt that Diana was very weak, but that considering the way she is, he expected her to rebound quickly.

I thought this meant that Diana was fine so it came as a terrible shock to find her lying so very still. She seemed very far away and suddenly my heart filled with dread. The surgeon had said that she was going to be fine but if this was his idea of fine it spelled disaster. When Diana tried to speak, her voice was completely gone and she made a horrible rasping sound that sent chills down my back. Volt gave her ice chips and Billyum gave some to me. I ate them but their coldness seemed to be everywhere.

The surgeon came by to see how Diana was doing, and told Billyum and Volt that she was doing as well as could be expected.

"Diana won't yet feel like eating," he said, "but I ordered food to be sent to you. You must keep yourselves strong for her because she will need your strength and encouragement."

I looked up at him and allowed all the terrible despair and fear that was in my heart to be seen by him. Diana was so out of it, I really feared that any minute she might leave us to join Little Haze.

The vet bent down and stroked me with a gentle but firm hand. Through his touch he communicated confidence and caring both about me and Diana, so I very slowly ran my mighty club.

"Venture appears most upset," he said to Billyum and Volt. "Do you think it would be best for him if he stays the night here? I can organize a group to take care of his needs if you think that would help. By morning, I think Diana will be much more alert and that should make him feel better. Right now he is very distressed. We want to help him as well as Diana. Also, maybe having him here would make Diana more comfortable."

"That is very kind of you, Doctor," said Volt. "However, most of the time Diana seems to be drifting in and out of sleep. I don't think she would even realize that Venture was here or at home. I think we should leave soon and let Diana get her rest. I think Venture will be more himself in his regular surroundings and no one needs to be bothered. After all, we will be back tomorrow."

"You will be happy to see Diana awake and more alert, won't you, fellow," asked the doctor as he looked directly into my eyes.

I ran my club hopefully. She sure didn't look like she was going to be alert to me.

But the next morning when we arrived, sure enough, Diana was awake and able to speak in a slightly more normal voice. She told not to become alarmed. It was going to take some time, but with a lot of help from me and Volt, she thought she could make it. I was as pleased as punch that she was getting better. I strutted around the hospital when Volt would go for something, and Diana got lots of care because of my drawing it to her.

Diana slowly but steadily improved. When she was ready to come home, Billyum stayed with us for a couple of days, but then went home.

"When you are ready, Diana," he said, "I think you ought to become more familiar with computer bulletin boards. There are many people out there that I think you would enjoy interacting with, knowing how busy you like to keep yourself. I'm going to give you a membership to one of the world's largest computer information services. Also I want to link you up with Willie Wilson and BlinkTalk."

"Whatever is BlinkTalk?" asked Diana.

"To correctly understand BlinkTalk," answered Billyum, "you almost need to experience it. It was started by a young man, William Wilson, who early on understood how very important computer technology could be for blind people. It is an echo that is carried by FIDONET and any local board can pick it up off the backbone."

"You are going a bit fast for me," said Diana. "What is FIDONET, what is an echo, and what on earth is the backbone?"

"FIDONET is an association where a group of bulletin board operators agree to take conferences or echoes which are then distributed all over the country. It is expensive to do, but usually someone who has an interest in computers likes to carry this information. The different conferences are often called echoes because they are echoed across the country. However, since you have one of the faster modems, I am going to urge you to call Willie's Board, BlinkLink, in Pittsburgh, Pennsylvania. With the fast modem, it will only take a few minutes and I think you could manage a few minutes a week. The telephone number for BlinkLink is (412) 766-0732. Willie gets a lot of software that works well with speech. More and more today, the software is becoming graphical in nature instead of text-based, and that makes it hard for the speech synthesizer to handle. But Willie has probably the largest collection of speech-friendly shareware programs and files in the country.

"The idea of shareware is that you get it, you try it out and if it meets your needs, you register it with the person or company who wrote it. If not, you erase it and just go on with no obligations. So far as what the backbone is, well, when you feel a little stronger, why don't you write a private message to Willie and ask him to explain it to you? It will be a reason for you to get to know this interesting man, and he will be happy to answer your questions."

"Why do you think so?" asked Diana.

"Oh, I don't know," laughed Billyum. "I don't think they call him 'Wonderful Willie' for nothing. However, to return to the idea of the different conferences or echoes, they are on different subjects— cooking, automobiles, or just about any subject you could possibly have an interest in."

"It sounds most interesting," said Diana. "I will write to Mr. Wilson and ask him to explain what the backbone is."

Twenty-Two

Finding Peace
In War

Our lives took on a different rhythm as I undertook the great responsibility of getting Diana to her radiation appointments and her physical therapy. Sometimes, of course, Volt gave a hand; but when he wasn't available, AHA sent their van for her. At first it was very difficult but finally the worst of it was behind us.

When Diana felt well enough, she spent many hours with the computer. She exchanged messages with Willie and reported back to Billyum that she and had gotten a message of welcome and the answer to her question.

One day she was talking with Billyum on the phone and he was telling her about a new computer service he had heard of. It is a program for computer users. During the day, they charge quite a bit of money for using their data lines, but in the evening those lines are quiet, so for a fee that is less than the phone company would charge, they allow computer users to use them from six in the evening until seven in the morning.

"It sounds like something I would be interested in," said Billyum.

"Well," said Diana, "I have their 800 number. Let's call and hear their sales spiel."

The young man Billyum and Diana spoke with was a very pleasant person and Billyum decided to sign up. However, some documents were needed. Diana offered to fax them for him since Volt and Diana had a fax machine because of Volt's business.

There was some kind of a mix-up over the fax, and Diana had occasion to talk with the young man several times. He seemed like a nice person and finally they got the problem solved. In their last conversation, Diana thought that he sounded kind of sad and she asked if everything was all right.

"I hope so," said the young man. "I am a reservist and with this problem we are having in the Persian Gulf, I have to leave next week. Frankly, I am not exactly looking forward to it."

It was the enchanting Christmas Season, and all were touched by that miracle that happens every year. Yet as Diana attended celebrations and parties, she was nagged by the uncertainty of the young man who was being sent away to a possible war.

When the air war began, she stopped thinking and acted. She telephoned the company and asked if they might have an address. The young man she spoke with was eager to help her and got the information for her.

Diana and Volt sometimes used to leave the door open so I could wander in and out when the weather was nice. That day was one of those lovely days. As she hung up the phone from getting the address, I came running in and threw myself down at her feet happily and rolled on my back making soft little sounds.

Of course, Diana—being quite "with it"—immediately understood what I was trying to say.

"Venture," she said, "do you want to be the one who writes the letters to the soldier?"

I ran my club happily.

"That is probably a wonderful idea," said Diana. "I doubt that he will get many letters from other such special correspondents, and you, Venture, can say things I never would. Maybe you can make him feel supported and loved and help chase away some of the fear."

I wrote my first letter that very day. The soldier knew about me from Diana but I reintroduced myself to him and told him about my early growing up. I explained that I didn't want to lay too much on him at once, but that I would write again the following month. I also explained that I was going to ask several human friends to write him, and added that we all loved him and were praying for his safety.

Diana had joined a cancer support group and that night at the meeting, she told the people about our new project. Every one of them sent a letter or a card and many asked friends to help, so the young man got tons of mail.

Each month I wrote a letter of encouragement to our soldier friend. I realized that although America is strong, still he must be having some fears. So I tried to put love and hope and confidence in my letters. Had Diana been writing the letters, she might not have been able to be so supportive as I, a guide dog, could be. I described our daily life for him, including the important fact that I am a Rev. I mean, being golden and with my special background—how on earth could he not feel very special? Besides all this, I am a V-boy. It boggles the mind doesn't it? This young man had his own personal chaplain! One of my most important tools is the giving of love and I could express love and caring for the soldier very openly without anyone feeling awkward about it.

Then there was the night we heard that a Scud missile had made it through and hurt many people. I was worried and when Diana, who regularly talked with a person at the telephone communications company, found out our friend had been among those injured, I was very concerned. His injury was not life-threatening, but he was among the first of the troops to be returned to the United States. I was glad that he was back in this country. I wrote him a brief note. It said:

> *Dear Friend,*
> *I am so very distressed to learn that you were one of those injured in Teheran but I am very glad that you are getting to come back home.*
> *I am very glad that this war business is over for you and that you are safe. If you aren't with your family now, you will soon be.*
> *There is something very important that I need*

*to tell you. It is an important little hint that not
everyone knows. I'll bet you didn't know that you
have a tail. But you do. I want to explain to you
how you can keep your tail very beautiful and in
the process have a very successful life.*

Triple blessings upon your head!
With Love,
Your Brother,
Guide Dog Venture
The Right Rev. Doctor Butz"

A few weeks later I got a letter. It said:

Dear Venture (Right Rev. Doctor Butz),

*I want to thank you for your wonderful letters.
Not only were they inspiring, but I am certain I am
the only person who received mail from a guide
dog. To think that I had my own Reverend giving
me spiritual advice—well, let me tell you that all
my friends were very impressed. Also I want to thank
your many friends for their lovely cards and letters.
They meant a lot to me.*

*I am very curious about what you said about
my tail. I didn't know I or anyone else had a tail.
Could you please explain to me why it is important
that I have one and how and why I should keep it
beautiful?*

Love,
R. L."

I sent him this letter of explanation.

Dear R. L.

*I understand why you might feel a little
confusion being told that you have a tail. Of course,
everyone knows that I have a tail—it's expected—*

but you humans aren't always aware of your tails. But if you do not keep them beautiful, I assure you that, although others may not realize that it's your tail that is messed up, they will realize something about you isn't as it should be.

'But,' I can hear you say, 'Doctor Butz, if I don't know where my tail is, how can I be expected to take care of it?'

That is a good question and the answer is very important. You see, different people have tails in different places and I don't know exactly where yours is. But let me tell you a story which will point out your tail to you. Once you know where it is, the information I give you will help you know how to keep your tail beautiful.

Once upon a time I went to visit some people who were raising a little guide dog puppy. Her name was Liberty and she was the most exquisitely beautiful little ball of fur I had seen in some time, except for one thing. She had the most woebegone, droopy, yuckston-looking tail you ever did see. I mean her tail was a terrible disgrace. To make matters worse, she spent all her time chasing it and when she grabbed at it she would pull at what hair remained on it. It was making me dizzy just to watch her spinning around. So finally I asked what she wanted to accomplish running in circles like that, because it certainly did not seem too smart.

'Well, Venture,' she said very seriously, 'I have heard that true happiness dwells in my tail. I just want to be happy and so I am trying to catch my tail. I am sure that if I can capture happiness, then all of my life will be wonderful!'

'Oh, Liberty,' I smiled, 'you have heard correctly, happiness does dwell within your tail but happiness is a very strange thing, the more you

consciously pursue it the more elusive it will be. Now we know that happiness dwells in your tail but tell me truthfully: you have been chasing it a good deal, yet have you found happiness?'

'No,' sighed Liberty, 'but it isn't for lack of trying.'

'I know you are trying,' I said flatly. 'You are about the most trying thing I have seen today. That constant chasing of your tail is not at all dignified, and it is very tiresome to watch. Besides that, it certainly does not make you look smart. If you want to be a guide dog like me, believe me, people are going to have to believe you are intelligent. But that behavior of yours surely does not suggest that!

'Let me let you in on a little secret, Liberty. The more you chase your tail, the more happiness will elude you and your tail will be offensive to all who see it.'

'Maybe you could be right. You seem happy, Venture,' said little Liberty. 'No one can see you and have any question that you are very, very smart. You don't chase after your tail. But you have said that happiness dwells in our tails. Do tell, then— what is the secret to finding happiness?'

'It is very simple,' I said. 'The more anyone tries to chase happiness, the harder it is to find. But if you will be the best that you can be, if you will let your tail alone, a wonderful thing will happen—happiness will follow you like a glorious cloud and all will marvel at how good fortune follows you. So you see, that is the secret to keeping a most beautiful tail.

'Actually, though, it really isn't a miracle at all. When you apply yourself to what it is that you do best, success generally is the result. It has been my experience that hard work will do it every time.

Most people and puppies, I think, would rather chase after Santa Claus but you and I know, Liberty, that Santa Claus only exists as we ourselves imagine that he does.'

'Do people have tails?' asked Liberty.

'Yes,' I said. 'They are not so obvious as our tails. But the same principle works for them. The more they chase happiness the more it will elude them. The formula is the same for puppies and for people. Be the very best person or puppy that you can be and happiness will follow in your wake. We can tell where a human's tail is if he chases happiness because we just have to look at what he is chasing.'

I saw Liberty a few weeks ago. She has a beautiful tail, and you know what? She is very happy and she is a delight to everyone around her and very smart too.

I have enjoyed being your friend. When I began writing to you, your life was undergoing some very big changes. You needed me to be a special friend to you and rev you up when you were feeling low. Oh, don't bother to deny that there were times when you felt scared and worried. That is natural, and that is why I came into your life to help you with this very special problem, just as I daily help Diana with the special problems she has.

Now, however, your life is returning to normal and while we will probably always have a special bond, it is time for you to go on with your private life. You no longer need my special assistance. But it has been wonderful being your friend, and should you find that you have a special need that I can help with, you know how to get hold of me.

Also, remember the little story I told you about Liberty and happiness. It is a trick that will work every time. So have a wonderful life, and take very good care of your tail. Remember that the secret to success is keeping it beautiful!

We have these lovely friends. One of them is a special little Princess. As a young girl she developed a neurological disorder and she is extremely handicapped. She is in a coma and Diana, Volt and I visit her regularly. I call her a little Princess because she is the daughter of a King. If you ever get to feeling sorry for yourself, there are always those with bigger problems than we have, so please say a little prayer for the little Princess.

Triple blessings upon your head, my child, and go in peace into a wonderfully happy life.

With love,
Your Brother,
Guide Dog Venture
The Right Rev. Doctor Butz"

Life was going very well for us. Diana was almost through with her therapy and soon she would have the reconstructive surgery that would make her feel more normal. I was glad about this because her balance was very bad and the doctor had said that she would feel much more secure. I have learned throughout my lifetime you can't have too much security.

The night before she was to go in the hospital, the story of Morris Frank was on TV. His story is very interesting. Buddy, the first guide dog, was a female German Shepherd trained by the Seeing Eye—the first guide dog school in the United States.

When we went to the hospital, Diana took me outside since I had a need to go. Because of Diana's physical problems we had to move very slowly and of course, as I have already explained, Diana had a serious problem with her balance. As I escorted her back inside and we went toward the admitting office, a woman came rushing up to us and grabbed Diana, just about knocking her over.

"Oh my dear!" she gushed. "I am a social worker here at the

hospital. You are in extreme danger but I will help you!"

"I'm glad that you are here," said Diana, "but I am unaware of any danger except that you nearly knocked me down, and the way you are holding onto me is very painful. Please let go."

"Oh yes," said the social worker, "you are in extreme danger but I am going to help you!"

"I think you could begin helping me by letting go of me," said Diana, beginning to be upset. "I fail to see any danger, but I am feeling considerable pain from your squeezing me!"

The woman let go of Diana but stood by her protectively. I looked about us. There was no cause for alarm at all that I could see.

"Oh dear, you poor little thing," said the social worker. "It is your dog."

"There's nothing wrong with Venture," said Diana loyally.

"Yes, there is," said the social worker. "Last night I watched about the Seeing Eye dogs on TV and, honey, you have the wrong kind of dog!"

Diana laughed softly. "You don't understand," she said gently. "At first when dogs were trained as guides, all the schools used German Shepherds. However, Labs and Golden Retrievers are almost replacing German Shepherds because of their even temperament and non-threatening ways."

"I was only trying to help," said the social worker. "They never said anything about using other breeds in the story."

"I watched that program," laughed Diana. "I guess they felt it was the story of a special dog and so it wasn't necessary to explain that to the viewers. But thank you for your concern."

"What was that all about?" asked Volt, spotting Diana and the woman talking.

"Oh, just another person who thought all guide dogs should be German Shepherds," said Diana. "Are they ready for me yet?"

"No, not yet," said Volt. "It seems that they are waiting for orders from the doctor."

"Those will be along soon," said Diana. "Once I go to my room, why don't you and Venture make it an early evening?"

"I think we will do that," said Volt. "I spoke with your therapist while you were outside. She says that after you have healed from the reconstructive surgery, she will want to give you hydrotherapy. But she feels that you are doing very well and will be able to continue with a pretty normal life, apart from never being able to lift much more than ten pounds."

"The trouble is," said Diana, "that everything weighs more than ten pounds. You know I can't even use my laptop computer anymore as a portable unit."

"Diana," said Volt, "you're like the man who complained that he had no shoes until he met a man who had no feet."

"Don't give me any grief," snapped Diana. "You've got to realize this is quite a problem for me."

"Yes, it is a problem," said Volt, "but it is a problem that can be solved. I see the nurse is ready for you, so I am going to let you go with her. I'll see you tomorrow."

I left in Volt's company and we returned early the next morning. Volt seemed worried, but less so than after her previous surgery.

Again we waited in the waiting area and people flocked over to see me. I, of course, did the expected thing and exposed my tummy. People were overwhelmed and thrilled by such a wonderful sight. Once Diana was returned to her room, we immediately went there.

I was not very pleased to see Diana so very quiet again, but she was much better than the other time and her throat was not so messed up. When Volt and I left her, she seemed much better.

The doctor said that was, of course, because she was revved up by me. I was encouraged because I knew she was on the mend!

Yumston Is
Spelled BNS

Diana's recovery from the surgery was very slow, but each day found her better and stronger. She began to check into BlinkTalk and CompuServe regularly and before long she had many new friendships going and she often was on many of the bulletin boards.

As her strength began to return she developed an interest in using WordPerfect. At first she worked with tutorial tapes and learned quite a bit from them, but Volt encouraged her to go to a program operated by the school district. At first her strength only allowed for a once-a-week visit, but as time passed we began to take more and more long walks together. Soon she was back to using the bus. In fact, things became very much the way they used to be except that Diana could only lift ten pounds.

Even that wasn't a sure thing. If she went for a walk and had to carry something, two pounds could be uncomfortable. Once in a while she would give something a push to get it out of the way, and it might weigh more than ten pounds but that didn't seem to bother her.

Many people had taken an interest in me. They found some of the stories that Diana told about our experiences very interesting and they encouraged her to write a book telling of our experiences together.

I, of course, know that I am very wonderful and the things that happen to me are indeed thrilling. But despite the fact that I am so special, I also understand that the lives of all guide dogs are special. If others don't have the crazy things happen that we do, it probably has to do with the way those people choose to live life.

Diana began the project and I couldn't help but remember the words of a very great man who said, "Your work is your love made visible."

Boy, can I relate to that! That is what my life is all about. As she continued to work on the project, I felt this was the way that it should be. The same great man had said something to the effect that if you work with love, your work binds you to yourself, to one another, and to God.

It was wonderful to observe the good things that work and its effect of binding things together were doing. I really felt that life was taking on a whole new dimension. There were new problems, though. Diana could not use her laptop computer as a portable because it was too heavy. We really began to have a serious problem with time. Whenever you wanted to find Diana, she was either working with the computer, sitting at a bus stop wasting time, or riding the bus also wasting time. We truly meet some wonderful people on the bus, and some that are not so wonderful. I kind of doubted that the book would ever get finished.

One evening when we came breezing, in we had company. Volt introduced the young man to us. His name was Dean Martineau. Without sounding disloyal to either Volt or Billyum, I must say this young man radiated good things.

"I am glad to meet you," said Diana. "What is it that you do and how do you happen to be paying us a visit?"

Dean smiled. "I operate a company called Top Dot Enterprises," he said.

"I take it that you market Braille or adaptive devices?" asked Diana.

"Yes," said Dean. "We offer Optical Character Readers, Braille embossers, screen reading programs, and speech cards. Plus, I have made tutorials for many of these products and other programs such as WordPerfect, and other services blind persons might have an interest in. My company even offers transcription services and some Braille printing for those who don't want to invest in a Braille printer."

"How did you meet up with Volt?" asked Diana.

"He heard that I market the BNS, that is, the 'Braille and Speak,' and he contacted me because he thought it might be an answer to a need that you have. He has explained to me that you cannot carry much."

"It is very nice of you to be willing to show me this little 'Braille and Speak' machine," said Diana. "However, I am not the least bit interested. I understand that they sound really bad and they are so complicated that it practically takes an engineer to operate one of them. If you want to edit a file that you are working in you have to go through all kinds of contortions and let me tell you something, Dean, this girl ain't going to do it!"

"My," said Volt coming in from the other room. "I had no idea that you felt so strongly about this little machine. However, I have invited Dean to stay with us for a little while, so I would appreciate it if you would make sure he has towels and things like that. In the meantime I will show him his room."

Dean and Volt went into the guest room. I could see Volt was upset, but Dean seemed very calm and not at all disturbed at Diana's pointed disinterest in his equipment.

Diana was in the kitchen working on the salad for supper when Volt came up beside her.

"Diana," he said, "I felt that you were very rude to Dean."

"I am not interested in his BS," said Diana. "I have been told all about them and they are nothing but garbage and we don't need to spend money for garbage."

"Have you ever seen one?" asked Volt. "Also, I think it is called a BNS."

"Well, no," admitted Diana. "But I have been told all about them. If you had talked with Billyum you would not be pursuing this because he would explain to you that the BNS is not an MS-DOS machine and not IBM-compatible."

"I did discuss it with Billyum," said Volt. "He told me that this tiny little machine can hold up to 150 pages and that it can be uploaded to the computer or you can buy an optional disk drive accessory for it. If you do that you can use high density disks and the drive only weighs a couple of pounds, so you should be able to carry around a lot of disks. He did say that he himself might not want one since he can handle a heavy computer. But you have different needs than he does. I just wonder if this might do what you are looking for. I also contacted Wonderful Willie and he thought it was the best thing since sliced bread—and I know how highly you think of Wonderful Willie's ideas."

"Well," said Diana acidly, "Wonderful Willie goofed this time!"

"I would really appreciate it," said Volt quietly, "since you admit that you have never seen the device, if you would at least ask Dean to show it to you. I understand that they weigh less than a pound. What can be the harm of looking? You might just be surprised to see that this is the solution to many problems for you."

"I'll look at it," said Diana tartly. "But next time, it might be a good idea to consult me before you pull a harebrained stunt like this. I think I am in a much better position to understand what I need."

"Look, Diana," said Volt, "I have found this little device that may make your life easier. You admit that you have never seen it and yet you reject the idea out of hand without even being willing to look at the thing. I don't think you are at all fair to me and I know you are not being fair to Dean."

"All right," snapped Diana. "I have already listed many good reasons why it isn't for me, but cool your heels. I will look at it. I am certain we won't want to buy it, but I will look at it. Does that satisfy you?"

"That's all I am asking," said Volt, trying hard to be patient. "No one says you have to buy it or use it, but for pity's sake, try being a little pleasant about it!"

Diana left Volt to finish up in the kitchen and ran into Dean in the hallway.

"I was wondering," said Dean, "if there might be a telephone jack that I could use."

"If you would like to use a phone," smiled Diana, "we have

them all over the place."

"Well, that isn't exactly what I want to do," explained Dean. "I really enjoy using a modem and I thought if a telephone jack were available, I might get on one of the computer services this evening and chew the rag with some friends, if, of course, that would be all right."

"Oh well, if that is what you want to do," laughed Diana, "you are very welcome to use my computer and modem which are all set up."

"I have gotten used to using the BNS with my modem," said Dean. "I would really rather do that if you wouldn't mind. I don't think I know the speech package that you have, and for my needs the BNS is really perfect."

"I didn't know you could use a modem with a BNS," said Diana with real interest.

"I suspect there are many things you don't know about the BNS," laughed Dean. "For example, did you know that you can write a letter? The BNS has some simple word processing built into it, and if you are going to school or doing something where you need to give someone a hard copy of what you have written, it is possible to do that using a little printer that I have which is about the size of a roll of foil. It is very quiet but produces pretty good quality print and runs on rechargeable batteries."

"There is a phone jack in your room," said Diana. "There is also a table in there that you can use that no one will disturb. So you can spread everything out and leave it connected. I didn't know you could do all those things you talked about with the BNS. I have only heard and read little things about it. Would you show me yours and let me see how difficult it is to connect up to different peripherals?"

"Sure," said Dean. "Maybe there is a table out here that I could use to kind of get you acquainted with the machine."

Dean and Diana settled at the dining room table because Volt had said they would eat outside. I watched as Dean handed Diana a tiny little machine all wrapped up in leather. I mean it was very small. It was about eight inches long and maybe four inches wide and an inch thick.

"Gosh!" exclaimed Diana. "No wonder it doesn't sound very

good—it must have a very tiny speaker."

"It doesn't sound the best from that small speaker," agreed Dean, "but it sounds pretty good if you attach a big speaker to it." He produced a larger speaker which he hooked up to the BNS, and then opened the case and turned it on. A voice very much like the voice in Diana's computer said "Braille and Speak ready, help is open."

"What does it mean," asked Diana, "that help is open?"

"The BNS—that is what we call the Braille and Speak—is made by Blazie Engineering," explained Dean. "They put a help file in ROM. You know what ROM is—read-only memory. It is impossible to write in the help file or erase it because it is permanent information in a memory chip that can't be altered. Because there is nothing in the BNS yet, it is the only file. So when the BNS is turned on it says that whatever file you are working on is open. That means that if we make a file called Diana, and we turn the machine off, when we turn it on again it will say Diana is open."

"That is very interesting," said Diana. "I am surprised that with a bigger speaker it sounds as good as my computer."

"That should not surprise you at all," said Dean. "Think about it. When you got your computer, didn't you immediately plug in a bigger speaker?"

"Yes," said Diana.

"Why did you do that?" asked Dean.

"Well, said Diana, "you could hardly hear the little speaker in the card."

"If you are using the BNS to take notes someplace," said Dean, "you will probably want to use a little earphone. Even then, if you have a good earphone, you may not sacrifice much quality. In fact, you may gain quality. But the beauty of the BNS is that it is so portable. Once you get used to it, you come to appreciate that quality so much that the sound becomes secondary. If you are like me, you often ride the bus. Before I got the BNS I used to waste much valuable time waiting for the bus. Then when the bus came, if it was a long trip I wasted more valuable time on the ride. With the BNS in my life, I have time when I get to where I need to go to enjoy myself because I can do everything on the BNS and then simply upload to the computer. Then I sometimes spend a little time editing my files, but usually, I can edit them all right on the bus or while waiting for the bus."

"The BNS has a lot of advantages," Dean went on. "It has a clock built in so there is no real need for a watch. What's more, it keeps very good time. But I think the feature I really enjoy is the countdown timer."

"The what?"

"Countdown timer," said Dean. "Let's say that I had an appointment. Let us say further that it is a very hot day. So I want to stay inside where it is cool for as long as I can. Let us also suppose that I have tons of paperwork to do by a deadline. I consult the bus schedule and learn that I have forty-five minutes to wait. I know right where the bus stop is, so it will only take five minutes at the most to get to the bus stop. I set the countdown timer for forty minutes and then I begin working on my documents. I am told when time is up, and I simply go to the bus stop where I catch my bus and then continue on with my work. Sometimes if I know the ride will be long, I again set the timer so that I will know in advance to prepare to get off the bus—you know, put the earphones away and gather together whatever other belongings I have with me."

"What kind of battery life can you expect out of a charge?" asked Diana.

"Oh, about eight or ten hours," said Dean.

"That is really good!" exclaimed Diana. "The most I could hope for from my laptop was four hours. Let me assure you that does not work out very well on the bus."

"I know," laughed Dean. "Before the BNS was available I think I must have tried everything, and a laptop on your lap on the bus does not cut it. But we are only scratching the surface of all the practical things that this little thing can do for you."

"What else can it do?" asked Diana.

"It has a calculator built into the firmware," said Dean, "so you can manage your checkbook completely without assistance if you keep good records. It also has a smart calendar that can do many fun things. For example, you can put in your appointments and on the day of that appointment the BNS will say that there is a calendar alert. This can be very, very helpful. It is able to figure out when a certain date occurred such as the Fourth of July in 1776 and it can help you know what the date will be, let's say, in fifty days. It can also tell you what consecutive number a day falls on within a given year."

"I find what you are telling me very interesting," said Diana. "I really thought that the BNS was just a very expensive toy, but you make it sound extremely practical."

"The BNS has never been a toy," explained Dean, "but it has come a very long way from what it used to be. Now it is possible to download binary files to this model, which is the 640. There is now a spell checker available for the 640 and other programs also."

"I can't begin to understand how this thing can do everything that you say that it can, though, Dean," said Diana. "Look at the tiny thing. It really only has seven keys. You are talking about a very powerful instrument here. How on earth can you begin to do these things with only seven keys?"

"This should come as no surprise to you, Diana," said Dean. "I understand that you are a very expert Braille user and you know that Braille only uses six dots. But with those six dots it is possible to do just about anything—music, arithmetic signs—anything you want. The same principle applies to the BNS. The commands are so logical that within a few days they will become second nature to you. This little thing is the reason I was able to get through law school."

"You went to law school?" asked Diana. "Are you going to become a lawyer?"

"Oh, I am already a lawyer," smiled Dean, "and I expect that the BNS will be a mainstay to me in that also."

"The law seems to be a profession that many blind people are attracted to," said Diana. "I know that many law schools across the country provide counseling and help to disabled people. In our area, Loyola University has such a program."

"They have a very good reputation," said Dean. "Doesn't Western Law officially administer that program?"

"Yes, they do," said Diana, "and I have had occasion to talk with the director of the program. My gosh, but she is something else. She is very professional, but at the same time she has retained the attributes of femininity. I was amazed at the combination she presented of brains and humanity. In our conversation, I learned that she is a professor at Loyola. Now they have a reputation for having good people, but Dean, this woman is absolutely wonderful. I can't help but feel that this woman has made a sacrifice to be there. I would be astounded if she couldn't make a ton of money working on her own as a lawyer."

"Gosh," said Dean, "I certainly would hope that someday someone would pay me such a high tribute as you have paid her. You may be very right that she could do well for herself on her own, but you can just bet that she isn't going to bed hungry at night for working there. I have heard that there are some truly wonderful attorneys who donate their services, and of course that is not a small thing either. In fact, I'll bet some of them are almost as wonderful as your lady lawyer."

"That very well could be so," answered Diana. "On occasion I—"

"Dinner is ready, you two," called Volt. "Can you stop playing with the BNS long enough to eat?"

Dean relaxed with Diana and Volt. "I just cannot get over how peaceful it is here, and yet we are so close to everything," commented Dean. "Do you have a problem with your weight, Diana? If you folks eat this kind of good food all the time, you must have."

"I really have to watch it," confessed Diana. "I work out on a treadmill a lot. That is the only safe way for me to run and I do try to limit the amount of yumstons that this guy puts out. He really is a wonderful cook, isn't he?"

"He most certainly is," said Dean. "Any time you want a job, Volt, you are welcome to come to my house. We couldn't pay much, but boy would you be appreciated! I wonder if maybe that fountain doesn't have something to do with how tranquil it feels around here."

"Oh, I think the fountain helps," said Diana, "but it is my V-boys who give the atmosphere to this place. They turn a house into a home."

After dinner, Dean and Diana again sat together at the table with the BNS.

"How did the BNS come to be?" she asked. "I can't help but wonder if there is a story here, because to develop such a complicated machine for the blind, which would be a very small market, seems quite an endeavor."

"Oh, the story of the growth of the BNS is special," said Dean. "What is special about it is that the developer had a desire to help a group of people he felt needed help, rather than a grand marketing plan or a wish to get rich quick."

"Tell me about it," said Diana, sitting forward on her chair.

"You know that the BNS is made by a company called Blazie Engineering. Dean Blazie is its creator. But it took a long time before it came to be," explained Dean. "You have to understand that Dean Blazie is just about the nicest man you could meet. He is an electronic wizard, an amateur radio operator—a ham—and early on realized how important this technology would be for us. Although they have very different skills, I think you would discover that this man had very forward vision as does our friend William Wilson—or, as we often call him, Wonderful Willie. When Dean was in high school, he formed a friendship with a young blind man and he worked for that man on weekends making available his wonderful electronic skills.

"This continued through college, and afterwards they set up a company called Maryland Computer Services."

"I know about that company!" exclaimed Diana. "They made one of the first talking computers, but they were dreadfully expensive—and I think you could only run their special software which would work with speech."

"Yes," said Dean. "First, though, Dean's friend explained that he needed a way to store and retrieve phone numbers and so there was this big computer made and that was all it did. It recorded phone numbers and spoke back with a speech board. The computer you've heard about came later. But even Dean knew that it was not the real answer.

"He and his friend sold Maryland Computer Services and Dean began working on a note taker, which really is what the BNS is. As I have said before, this guy has a good heart and he wanted to make speech available to the blind for under one thousand dollars. That is what he did with the classic Braille and Speak. He had wanted to do it for five hundred dollars but he just could not manage that. Had there been a large market such as there is for some of the talking watches, he maybe could do it. Even so, the BNS is a bargain. Most speech packages cost around a thousand dollars and then you need to buy the computer and the programs to run them. The 640 BNS, which is the ultimate, is $1295.00 and you get everything you need to start right away."

"Another special thing about the BNS is the service that's offered," continued Dean. "Some of the vendors for adaptive equipment are, let's say, poor at best. Many of them have their product made in other countries, so arranging to have them repaired can be quite a problem. There is one that has quite a reputation of treating customers in a less than kind way. They have actually been known to refuse service and claim that the individual is not worthy to own one of their products. But that hardly is the way it is with Blazie Engineering. I think everyone charges something for a service contract, but for the BNS it is $99.00 a year. And there is never any arguing about whether the machine is working right—it simply is exchanged for another one. Also, each year when the machine is updated, updates are free to those with service contracts. I don't believe anyone else offers anything like that."

"No, I don't believe they do," said Diana.

"Tell you what, Diana," yawned Dean. "It is getting late. I want to show you how this little machine works because I think it will enrich your life just as it has done for many others. But if I want to get on the modem, I think I better do that now and we can start out fresh in the morning."

"Sounds good to me," said Diana. "I am tired and I want to get the most out of what you want to show me. So I will leave you to the modem, while I head for the hay."

As they had been talking, Volt and I had been cleaning up after dinner and we went upstairs to go beddy-bye. However, since we had a guest who also now fell under the need for my watchful care, I lay on the landing.

Dean's door was open and I could hear the little voice of the BNS babbling away. I sighed.

The next morning after breakfast Diana explained to Dean that she would very much like to work with him with the BNS but first she would like to go for a run on her treadmill. Dean came along with her to her computer room where she keeps the treadmill. While Diana ran, Dean played with the computer.

"What kind of speech do you have in the computer, Diana?" he asked her as she ran.

Without even sounding winded, Diana answered that the speech was a product called an Accent and it was made by Aicom.

"Did you notice that the BNS sounds very similar to the this?" he asked.

"I sure did," replied Diana. "But not exactly the same."

"Do you know why that is?" asked Dean, with a trace of a smile in his voice.

"Because they are all mechanical?"

"No, Diana," said Dean "That is not the reason."

"What is it then?" asked Diana, her feet pounding away.

"They sound the same," said Dean, "because they contain the same speech chip. But they sound different because different companies program different rules of speech into the chip so that it talks differently. What you are doing sounds fun. Can I try when you are through?"

"Sure," said Diana as she stopped the machine. "Have you ever been on a treadmill before?"

"No," said Dean. "This will be a whole new experience for me."

Diana often works on an incline but she flattened the treadmill out for Dean since running uphill—or walking uphill, for that matter—can be very difficult for someone who is not used to it. Diana has a very good treadmill. It has a protect key which is fastened to your belt, which, if pulled out, will stop the machine.

Diana explained to Dean how he should stand on the rails until the belt began to move, and she tried to encourage him to start slowly. But Dean wanted to turn up the speed and do what Diana had done. In a couple of minutes he had stopped the machine and was gasping for breath.

I think Diana made him feel worse by laughing at him as she hurried to bring a towel for him to wipe off his sweating face.

"I don't understand," panted Dean. "Here I am in good health, yet you ran and it seemed effortless to you. However, I was only on the thing for a couple minutes and it almost hurts me to breathe.

Diana laughed. "You may know a lot about the law and computers and the BNS," she smiled, "but I have found it very necessary to learn about exercise and even a gentle walk is something you must build up to. Of course, running takes longer but a good rule of thumb is that you should be able to exercise, including running, regularly and be able to talk comfortably. If you are having to breathe hard you are not doing quite as well as you think you are."

"What about sweating?" said Dean. "Right now I am sweating like a pig."

"Well," laughed Diana, "sweating seems to go with exercise. Why don't you go downstairs and take a shower! That will make you feel much better. Then we can go outside since it is such a lovely day and you can let me in on all the secrets of the BNS."

Dean seemed pleased with this idea and I walked downstairs with him and snooped around in his room making sure things were all right. I checked the trash but he hadn't thrown away anything interesting. I do think he was happy with us, though, because I could hear him singing in the shower. Apparently he had survived Diana's disinterest in the BNS very well.

Dean and Diana sat together at the table, each holding a BNS.

"Probably," said Dean, "we should begin with learning about the clock. It can be a twelve-hour clock or a twenty-four-hour one, whichever you would like. After that we will learn about the stopwatch and the countdown timer, since I think they are very important. Next I will show you how to set the calendar and how to use the smart calendar features. Then we will kind of take it from there. Does that sound like a plan to you?"

"Since I don't know a thing about the BNS and you are the expert, I would leave it to you to chart the waters, Dean," laughed Diana. "However, I don't want you feeling too arrogant. Do not forget what an expert is."

"Yeah, well, what is your definition?" queried Dean, suspecting the mischief he heard in Diana's voice.

"I have heard from good sources," said Diana, "when I was in school, I learned that an 'x' is an unknown mathematical equation. However, a spurt is just a drip under pressure."

"I see," smiled Dean. "I will keep that significant point in mind.

Now will you turn on your Braille and Speak, please?"

I lay in the sunshine keeping a watchful eye on the busy Dean and Diana. They seemed utterly engrossed in the tiny machines they were working with and I wondered even if it were all logical, how on earth could anyone hold all the information in their minds that Dean was showing Diana. But after several hours of work, Diana demonstrated where her priorities were.

"Dean," she said, "I think we need a break. I have some of the most special coffee you have ever tasted. Of course if you would like a soft drink, I can bring you that."

"I have heard stories about your wonderful coffee," said Dean, "but I don't like coffee. However, as I think you already know from working with computers, we want to be very sure that food or liquids are kept away from the BNS. Tell me something, though, Diana. You seem to know about things relating to health. I know there is sugar in a Coke, but is it enough to be overly worried about?"

"Depends on your point of view, I guess," said Diana. "In the average Coke, there are nine teaspoons of sugar."

"Oh dear," said Dean, "I guess we would do better to use diet drinks."

"Not really," said Diana. "The problem with diet drinks is that instead of sugar, you take in a whole lot of salt and that isn't very good for you either."

"That may be," laughed Dean, "but you know, that mint tea you served last night should be fine because that has no yuckstons in it and it is sweetened with fruit juice. So how about a nice glass of that?"

"I have some of that wonderful vanilla-nut brew that seems to make lawyers do what I want," laughed Diana. "I am going to make some for myself even if it might not be that good for me."

"You will have to drink the wonderful brew," said Dean. "I would rather have the tea."

Diana brought Dean his tea, ice cubes clinking in the crystal glass, and while he relaxed with it, I lay next to him where the sun could caress me. I really liked him. Some people put out what it is they want you to think they are. Dean was just himself and his honesty and willingness to help other people made him rank up there in my book. I didn't get the feeling that he was trying to sell Diana the BNS, just that he was showing her how useful it could be in her life. From time to time I bestowed kisses on Dean's hand when he would rub me or scratch my ears.

"You know," remarked Dean, "I don't like coffee and I don't want any of your brew but I do admit that it has a wonderful smell."

"You should try a little," laughed Diana. "It makes lawyers—."

"Forget it, Diana, we are working with the BNS, not practicing law," smiled Dean. "Last night you were concerned about understanding all of the commands. How do you feel about them now?"

"It seems very logical like you said," said Diana, "but I need you to spend some more time with me on these things."

Dean spent a good part of the day working with Diana. They did take breaks, though, and the following day they did pretty much the same. The day after that Diana went away for her word processing class but Dean was not left alone because Billyum came over to see him and the BNS. They told us about the conversation later, and it went something like this:

"I did not realize that Diana and the Butt would not be here," said Billyum to Dean. "I sure would like some of that wonderful brew Diana makes up and she must have made it this morning, but I don't know where she keeps things."

"Oh, she told me to tell you that there is a full pot of good brew on the counter and cups there also," laughed Dean. "Come and let me show you the BNS."

Billyum looked at the little device and commented that it looked efficient. "However," he said, "I don't believe the BNS is a real computer and I personally would want a real computer."

"In a way, you are right," said Dean. "The BNS is really considered a note-taker. It has many word processing features built into the firmware, and using the 640 you can download zipped files, which are data-compressed files. However, you cannot run WordPerfect on it as it has its own special word processor built in. It does word processing functions such as center, bold, cut and paste, although sometimes it does take a little more figuring. It really is best to upload it to your favorite word processor and do major things there. For Diana, I think it is a bridge. I certainly found it helpful when going to law school."

"My Braille skills are good," said Billyum, "but I really prefer a regular keyboard."

"Blazie has something for you, then, Billyum," said Dean. "It is called the TNS, the Type and Speak. It is like the Braille and Speak but it has a QWERTY keyboard."

About then, Diana and I rushed in. I was filled with delight to see Billyum, but Diana was so excited over her own adventure that she barely noticed him.

"Dean!" she exclaimed. "On the bus home, I used the BNS with the little earphone and I actually got quite a bit of work done on my book. I thought I would upload it to the disk drive and import it into my word processor. For me that is the acid test."

"Well!" said Dean, trying not to sound smug. "Remember just a couple of nights ago you told me that you knew all about the BNS and that it's really just garbage?"

"I did say that," admitted Diana. "But I also have learned a lot from you that I didn't know about it. Now if you folks will excuse me I want to see if my project is a success."

"Now look at her," said Billyum as Diana went away to work on her project. "She seems very pleased with herself."

"And of course, she will be successful with her project. You should have heard her a couple of nights ago," laughed Dean. Why, she was ready to throw me out of here and wasn't willing to take a second look at the BNS."

"When Volt spoke to me about it," confided Billyum, "I really thought it might be what she needed. Although notebooks are coming down in price, I wondered if that tiny little BNS with the Braille keyboard just might be her entrance back to life. Of course, you and I know she is still very vital, but being unable to lift things, or do some of the other things she used to take for granted, has been a real strain on her and Volt."

"Volt is really a nice man, isn't he?" remarked Dean.

"You couldn't ask for better," said Billyum. "Throughout the time I have known him, he has very helpful to me. More importantly, he provides something very stable in Diana's life that she very much needs. You can't help but notice that he simply adores her and will do anything that he can to help her. I don't think it is always an easy job."

"If it weren't for him," said Dean, "Diana would never have even looked at the BNS."

"If not for him, she wouldn't have many of the things that make her life comfortable," Billyum agreed. "He really looked into this BNS question. He even called Wonderful Willie about it."

"We all know what Willie thinks of the BNS," said Dean. "I really think that man provides a very important service to blind persons."

"I am not so involved with BlinkTalk," said Billyum, "but I guess all of us call Willie's board for his wonderful files. Have you ever met him?"

"No," said Dean, "but I have this picture of a large, handsome man."

"I think of him as Willie Wonka," said Billyum, "the guy in the chocolate factory. But instead of chocolates, Willie has sacks and sacks of disks with wonderful files on them. Speaking of special, Venture is very special also."

"I have never seen a guide dog quite like Venture," said Dean. "He and Volt are a real complement to Diana, aren't they?"

"They make this house most special," said Billyum. "Volt and Venture. Diana calls them her V-boys and I have to wish there were more V-boys in the world. I am wondering, though—if she gets the BNS, what will she do if she has trouble with it? I know very little about it, and Diana is not long on patience with things."

"I don't expect that to be a problem," said Dean. "The BNS has a help file that covers the commands which I have taught her. There are lots of BNS users on BlinkTalk and there are people there like me who will solve anything you can think of. She also can call Blazie Engineering. They have a full-time tech support person who is very patient and a really nice person. Considering all that, she won't have any trouble. Anyway, I know she knows all of the basic things plus some things that are quite advanced."

Just then Diana came running downstairs. "Dean! Billyum!" she exclaimed. "The work I did on the BNS uploaded perfectly into my word processor."

"What did I tell you?" laughed Dean. "It really makes you very productive when you can use your time so efficiently. However, I'm concerned—the equipment you already have represents a substantial outlay of money. Are you sure that you want to spend good money for garbage? Don't you think maybe you should hand over that BNS and the other things that go with it?"

"OK, Dean," sighed Diana. "I guess I deserved that comment, but I don't feel that you need to rub it in."

"You're sure, now?" asked Dean. "I just showed you that BNS and how it worked. Don't you think you should give it back now? Of course," he continued with a smile in his voice, "it would be good for me if you want to keep it but as you have so often pointed out, I am a lawyer and I feel responsible for being sure that you completely understand what you are doing."

"Look, Dean," said Diana. "You are not getting my BNS back so you are just going to have to live without it. Anyway, I happen to know that the V-boys have already paid for it, and you don't mess with the V-boys if you know what's good for you!"

"I think the lady has decided," laughed Billyum, "and when she decides, the V-boys always support her decision. I also think it is a wonderful idea. Congratulations, Diana. I know this will work out well for you."

"Well," said Volt, who had quietly come into the room, "I think she has decided and we better get moving if I am going to get you to the airport on time."

On the drive to and from the airport, Diana was busy with the BNS. It looked like Volt had brought another good thing into Diana's life.

That evening, Diana hooked up the modem as Dean had shown her, and the dull little voice droned on and on. I sighed. I had seen this coming from the moment I heard Dean working with the modem, so I added a normal sound to our surroundings: I ran my mighty club.

Twenty-Four

And The Beat Goes On

Remember the nursery rhyme that says, "everywhere that Mary went, the lamb was sure to go"? That is kind of the way it was with the BNS—wherever we went, the BNS came along. Now that she had the BNS, anytime she felt a little tired and thought she should lie down, Diana did so, always curled up with the little babbler. I think Volt drew the line one night when she came to bed bringing the BNS. I mean, really! There is a time to stop computering and I think the gentle Volt was able to make her understand. But still, the BNS was almost as much in attendance as I was. Diana continued her quality time with me, so I guess it was all right.

Billyum had come to visit again, bringing a little earphone that hangs on the ear by a little hook. I understand that it is not the greatest sound system in the world but Diana was really happy about it. It would allow her to work with an earphone which is, of course, required when she is out in public. With the one earphone on one ear, it allowed her to keep track of things around her.

Proof positive that things were getting back on track was when Diana took a plane and attended some function in Chicago taking me, of course—me and the BNS—but leaving the gentle Volt behind, confident that the two of us would get along just fine. But as usual the trip was not without incident.

We had a layover in Denver. Diana felt there was no real need to take me out since we hadn't been on the plane that long. The pilot came to meet the distinguished passenger on the plane and he very much wanted to do something for me so he kept asking Diana to allow him to take me out. Diana never lets me go with a stranger, and I don't think it will ever happen again, but "this once" Diana decided it would be most tactful to let him take me out. She suggested that I be led on my leash but wear my harness until such time as we were out on the tarmac. Then he could remove my harness and I would relieve myself and he could bring me back.

He really was a very nice man and all went well. The only thing was that before we took off, an awful lot of people seemed to have a change in plans and the plane left almost empty for the rest of the trip. That was fine with me, though, because the lovely flight attendants had lots of time to play with me. All too soon, we were at the terminal collecting our bags, which for once weren't lost. Then we learned why so many people had changed their plans. It seemed that the airline had gotten a lot of complaints from passengers. They felt that giving jobs to the handicapped was all well and good but to hire a blind man to fly a plane was a little more than they could accept.

"Venture, you old butt," said Diana as she brushed my beautiful shining coat later that evening. "When that nice pilot took you out they believed that he was blind. I guess you may have cost that airline some money, as I think they would probably have to make arrangements for all those people who did not go on to Chicago even thought they had tickets. I think it is very funny—but I guess the airline doesn't."

I just ran my mighty club. It certainly felt good to see things returning to normal. Our trip home, though, went without a hitch. Nothing normal about that!

A couple things happened when we got home that certainly were interesting, but which showed things were status quo. We got a call from a man who had the wrong number, but since this man was a salesperson, he decided to try to sell his product to Diana. Obviously he didn't realize what and whom he was dealing with.

This gentleman was selling cars and he was trying to get Diana to consider buying one. He described the wonderful new car and even offered to bring it by so that Diana could have a test drive.

Of course the poor man had no idea who he was talking to and Diana took full advantage of his situation. She explained that she might actually be nervous driving such a fine car as the man described, but he assured her he would be right there beside her helping her. Diana sweetly asked the man what his first name was and he told her it was Jim.

"Jim," she said sounding very tender, "are you ready to go to heaven, or to hell?"

Jim was flustered and asked her why she would ask a question like that because he was sure she couldn't be that bad a driver.

"No," purred Diana, "it is much worse than that."

"Oh, I'm sure it isn't that bad," responded the happy salesman. "I have solved some very difficult problems and I am confident I can fix yours."

"Well," said Diana, "good doctors have wanted to take a look and they agree they can't do anything."

"Doctors?" said Jim. "Why would doctors feel your buying a car would be of concern?"

"It seems that the law is not as open-minded as you are, Jim," said Diana. "You know discrimination is still practiced a lot. You see they don't like to give a totally blind person a driver's license. They aren't as open-minded as you are."

"Are you really blind?" asked Jim.

"As a bat," laughed Diana.

"Are you sure?" asked Jim. "Because you sound very normal to me."

"I am normal," said Diana. "The only problem of real interest is that my eyes don't work. But you see that doesn't show well on the phone."

"I guess I have really been had!" said Jim. "You really had me going there."

"Probably next time," smiled the naughty Diana, "it would be a good idea if you worked a little more at qualifying the buyer."

"That's good advice," said Jim. "You probably illustrated that better than anyone could have explained it."

"I have to admit that it was fun," said Diana. "Now I probably should let you go and talk to some real customers."

Diana smiled as she went about her chores. When she told people about the call, they all laughed at her and thought the incident was funny.

As I have commented before, the flow of our lives is always interesting and ever-changing. On one occasion, we were invited to a Christian rock concert and a reception afterwards. Many little children flocked around me, but one little boy seemed to have a special interest in me. Diana could not understand what he wanted to know about until I stood up and he took her hand and put it under my tummy. Then it became very clear what he was looking at and what he wanted to know about.

I thought Diana acted with real sensitivity when she asked if he knew how God had created little girls and little boys. The little boy understood that. Diana explained that God had made little girl dogs and little boy dogs too, and what he was looking at was the sign that I was a little boy dog. However, this little boy had just learned about circumcision and he wanted to know if I was circumcised. The little boy couldn't have been much more than five or six and his parents were very embarrassed about his question, but Diana hushed everyone and said we were all going to learn something very important. She then asked the little boy if he knew about Abraham and the children of Israel. He did and was pleased to explain to Diana about them.

Diana explained to the little boy that the way she understood it, God gave circumcision as a sign between men and Himself. However, when Jesus came, we were circumcised in our hearts and that is what counted. She asked the little boy to look into Venture's eyes and tell her if he thought he could see shining out of them a good heart. The little boy thought that in fact I had a very good heart.

"When I got Venture," explained Diana, "I could see what you see, that he has a very good heart and you know, I just was so excited about seeing him, why, I plumb forgot to ask." As the people went away, you could hear them talking about what a sweet moment that had been and how wonderful and sweet was the faith of a little child.

Christmas,
Crosstalk
And The Princess

If you can believe it, our life became even busier. With the BNS in our lives, it seemed that Diana was always very involved with something or other. Her activity with the cancer support group increased. This group that Diana ran was very large. To keep it intimate, Diana split it into smaller groups and she and I and Volt would travel between the groups.

One particular evening, Rachel came to our meeting and asked to watch. Now this woman was sad. Coming from her I felt such tension and sadness that my heart immediately went out to her. She had just been told that day that she had cancer of the breast but I understood that she was more ill than she knew. I knew this because illness sometimes causes infection to run throughout the body and I immediately became aware of this situation through my sense of smell. Diana, however, did not understand this as she lacks my special abilities to sense such things. But she did notice that a bond was forming between me and Rachel.

I knew Rachel needed comfort and I knew that while she was somewhat aloof I could reach her. So I went into action.

In these groups I was never required to wear my harness, as my participation was seen as positive by Diana. Now I moved over to Rachel and officially gave her what Diana likes to call my 'gift of bestowal.' I sat beside her, placing my head in her lap. As she reached to touch my golden head, I placed dainty kisses upon her hand and I looked into her eyes and poured my love and blessing into her.

Everyone commented. It was said that I was bestowing and so this gift of bestowal was acknowledged. Diana did realize Rachel had a serious problem and after the meeting, she made it a point to talk privately with Rachel to assure her there is life after such a problem. We talked together for a while, and then I escorted Diana and Volt to their car. Since Rachel was parked alongside of us, I escorted her also.

As we approached the car, there was a little irregularity in the cement, which is pretty common. The roots of trees often do this but Rachel, not noticing, tripped and fell. She was unable to rise, and her leg was at a different angle. An ambulance was called at once and we followed her to the hospital. Not only was Rachel's leg broken, the cancer they discovered had gone into the bones and was pretty well throughout her body.

Diana and I visited her each day, traveling by bus. Each time I saw her, I would bestow blessings on her, and she commented to Diana that somehow she felt that through me, her life had been blessed. She did not live very long after that accident, but I had made a difference in her life, and now my bestowals were sought by everyone. Actually bestowing became somewhat difficult because everyone wanted to be the object of my blessings. I loved all this attention, but having everyone want your attention all at once can get very stressful.

Volt had a business trip in Atlanta, and he suggested we come along. We love Atlanta, and I was delighted to again be on that wonderful airplane having everyone pay court to me.

The last night we were there, Volt took Diana and me to this very fancy restaurant. Diana was wearing an evening dress. Looking at her, she was the picture of health. The attention the maitre d' paid us was extremely unusual, though. They were beside us every other minute!

"I guess this is because of Venture," said Volt—even he noticed the difference.

The place was very wonderful. The carpet was beautiful and lush; there was a fountain whose lovely music certainly enhanced the atmosphere. The china and crystal and silver were beautiful, and the smells were heavenly. After the very excellent meal, the head waiter approached Diana.

"Madam," he said, "we pride ourselves on the fine coffee we serve here. May I offer you a cup?"

"Oh yes!" exclaimed Diana. "I just adore special coffee and that would be just perfect."

A beautiful cup was placed before Diana. The waiter and another man came and stood beside her. "I want to see how you like the coffee, Miss," said the man who had joined us.

Diana lifted the cup to her lips. Suddenly, in the silence that had fallen, it sounded like a rock crashed into the saucer. Diana had slammed the cup down, although it was only a sharp click.

"Oh, Miss, is the coffee not to your liking?" crooned the man.

"I have seen commercials," said Diana, "where the fine coffee of a fine establishment was secretly replaced with Folgers instant crystals. I suggest that has been done to you and that this is just that instant garbage. Get it out of here and if you have it, bring me some good coffee!"

There was an awkward silence. Then the strange man spoke. "Miss," he said sounding shocked. "I represent the Folgers company and in fact what you were served is Folgers instant coffee. We believe it is the finest—!"

"Save that story for your commercials," said Diana. "Does this place have some decent coffee or shall I go elsewhere for that?"

"Oh, Miss," said the maitre d', "we are, of course, very sorry to offend, but many people really don't feel the way you do."

"Do you have any decent coffee or not?" repeated Diana, sounding like she would not take much more of this nonsense.

"I will get you a cup of our own coffee," said the maitre d'.

"Since you have been put upon, there will be, of course, no charge for the meal!"

"Right!" said Diana. "And get these crystals out of here."

"Well," remarked Volt, "I think that commercial won't run!"

I just sighed. Anyone who messed with Diana's coffee was in serious trouble.

We returned home with no real further incident except that the bags were lost again. But they found them in about a week.

Meantime, Diana was spending a lot of time online. She became very interested in the Internet. The Internet has many kinds of people out there, and before long, Diana was browsing Web Pages and joining the IRC (Interactive Relay Chat.) There is a lot of garbage there, but there are some good places too.

A good friend of Diana's, Dr. Don Coco, had formed a channel on the IRC called Blinkchat. It was a place where many gathered to discuss technology and other advances for blind people. Many of those who visited had a Christian orientation, and Diana and a friend of hers felt that maybe they would like to form another channel and register it.

Diana had a number of discussions with Billyum and in fact it was Billyum who registered Crosstalk and got for it the x bot.

Having heard Diana explain this many, many times, I have become an authority on bots, as I am on so many other things. A bot is just a program that assists with channel management, which appears if you join the channel as a user. When you join, in the list of users that are displayed on the screen you will see 'x'.

One day, a friend of Diana's named Alice paid us a visit. She began asking all kinds of questions about the channel.

"The whole idea of the channel really puts me off," Alice said to Diana. "Computers generally put me off."

"They are just things," said Diana. "The only difficult part is getting there; once you're there, it is clear sailing. I have a friend who has made it easier than one-two-three. He puts together a computer system that is all loaded for the Internet so you just literally plug and play. Just think of the channel as a pleasant room where friends meet. I imagine it as a room with comfy sofas or chairs or cushions on the floor and a wonderful fireplace. There is, of course, an elevated dais where the channel saint sits."

"What or who is the channel saint?" asked the astonished Alice.

"That is st_tech", explained Diana. "He is the patron saint of technology."

"But Diana," said Alice, "many people believe the saints to be sacred. Don't you think this st_tech person would offend some of us?"

"Techy would never offend anyone! He is very devoted to the Salvation Army, and they are not known for hurting people," said Diana. "Little kids could even write to him, like they used to write St. Nick in the old days. However, the organization that made him a saint is disgusting, which is exactly why he does it. You know about Venture and all his degrees. Well, another group has a site on the World Wide Web. They will ordain anyone for free. After they ordain you, if you have 15 people ordained then they will make you a saint. They also sell doctorate degrees. The best way to discredit them is to make fun of them the way Saint Tech does, just as do I with Dr. Butz.

"We have a person called prof who is one of the ops. An op is involved with channel management. In real life the prof is a social worker. He has another personality, though, who is called forp. 'Forp' is 'prof' turned around. The forp is a most beautiful bird, but he is clumsy and bumps into things. He got himself ordained by st_tech! He also just loves to do crazy things. When he learned about the Folgers Crystals story, a tradition was born: with great pomp and ceremony, he makes instant coffee on channel and adds garlic to it. He has been ordered to stop, but he does it anyway. Diana actually banned him for Folgers' sake, but an op can use the bot to get back in."

"How does a ban work?" asked Alice. "I know what it means to ban someone, but how does that work on a channel?"

"If you think of the channel as a room," said Diana, "it is like closing the door and locking it to that user."

"Tell me about some of the other people," said Alice.

"Bill is, of course, Billyum," said Diana. "You already know him. He is the channel manager; st_tech is the assistant manager; and Diana is the senior administrator. There are others there, of course, and it is always changing, but there is a stable core group. There is Ariy, a very wonderful young man. He has a little vision but still needs a lot of special equipment to access the screen of the computer. He is very personable and charming, and most of all is going to be a great catch for some employer. I just hope some corporation won't be so foolish as to let him get away. The same is true of Montcalm, another wonderful young man."

"Are all the regulars on the channel blind people?" asked Alice.

"Not at all," said Diana. "Of course the forp isn't normal, but he can see. Jenni isn't normal either. I call her a bot because she gives time like a bot would."

I sighed. I know none of them are normal, and they have a lot of fun, but they have also been a big help to people who were having a hard time. And I know that I have reached out to people who are not Christians but who love to have fun. Diana is gonna get it for calling Jenni a bot though. Probably she will hit her with her Louisville Slugger.

They are crazy. For example, st_tech is always extending his ring for people to kiss. I heard the computer telling Diana what his saint's ring looks like one day. It has a band of 24 karats which weighs 24 pounds and it has a 12 karat diamond guarded by all manner of precious stones.

Of course Hon, a world-class boxer, is there. Two most unusual women, Lynn and Carrie, are there as well. They are in their 70's and instead of finding the rocking chair they have found the computer. We have people who are teen-agers, and it is wonderful to watch these people all interact together as equals. The channel even has its very own real live rocket scientist. James' works for NASA. Diana says he is typical of a government employee, too—if he throws a snowball at you, he always misses the mark! I know though that James' is a good rocket scientist.

Another of the important people on channel is Linda_M. This lady has got to be one of the most delightful people you could wish to know. She is loving, caring and just a wonderful human being. She also has projects in which she has a personal interest which could make a book all in themselves.

It really became very strange after the OJ verdict came down. Of course Crosstalk, being made up of different people, had different perspectives, but it was Linda_M who started the real fun on the channel. She told a story of how Diana went to biker bars and how she was hanging out in one when the verdict was read. She became upset, threw peanuts at the TV, toppled twenty-five bikes, hotwired another one, and got away.

Another adventure she had was to hotwire Gacman's classic old car and completely total it because she forgot that you should open the garage door first.

There is also a report Linda_M gave that Diana made a tatoo design of OJ in the middle of a bullseye and tried to sell it to the body piercing shop "Needles and Pins." When they would not take it, she spray-painted it on the building, hotwired a red roadster, and got away. They call her the Midnight Rider as she hotwires a hog and rides about at midnight without lights. Of course, she is always getting banned and every night we hear more of her adventures.

One of the things that Bill and Diana asked is that people who are ops write a profile about themselves. Just a bit of biographical material so the others could know something about them. Diana (who hasn't written one herself) told the other ops they better comply or she would make up things about them. Linda_M decided to turn the tables on Diana, writing this:

> *Well Diana, you know how you are always telling the ops that if they don't write their profiles you're going to have to make one up about them? We were pondering this one night and realized that you haven't written yours! I think you have left yourself wide open for this one, because we have decided to write some for you! Here they are:*
>
> *Lynn's profile of Diana:*
>
> *"How can any of us have been so lucky to have a friend with the STRENGTH to throw pretzels hard enough to break the TV at the Biker's bar,*

have enough DARING to hotwire red roadsters, enough CHARM to run for Miss America, enough NERVE to run the hog over Linda's web pages, the FORESIGHT to know that a tattoo of OJ in the middle of a target could be a bestseller . . . and the AUDACITY to call her best friend a "dog" . . . who has a friend who can make you feel good even when you don't find the right words when you've lost them . . . know what to say to troubled people, never complain, and have the motto "others come first"? Lucky we are to be able to call her friend.

My profile, by Diana Dawne, otherwise known as the Midnight Rider [actually written by the forp]:

Many years ago I was born at dawn. The sun rose and peeked upon my cute little hog-like self. For years thereafter, the sun ran around and around wondering why?

Anyway, I grew up, or up I grew and found I had this strange and wonderful craving for coffee. As a tyke, I would look for those jars way up in Mom's cupboard and poke my dainty pinky into those crystals. The aroma was so mesmerizing, and now the memories of those wonderful beginnings bring tears to my eyes.

Well, I grew up to find myself venturing into experiences that shall forever be the foundation of my innocent and peaceful life. You see, I found that if you put this wire here and that wire there, a wonderful moment and roar would ring through the air. Exhilaratingly I could dash into the nite, with no light, and tear off on the runway of funway. The sirens and the lights would blare, seeking the wonderous one of the night.

I learned that I could elude them though because I had the faith of the venturous ones. You see, one day as I raced throughout the valleys and dales, I met this bird who called himself the forp. Oh, a beautiful bird was he.

Anyway, I was tired and had no more energy to ride on toward the setting sun and had set my hog down beside this old tree. As I drifted off into the land of nod, this wonderful creature of the winds settled upon my shoulder. Softly he whispered into my ear, "Thou shalt be the queen of the nite."

When I awoke, I felt refreshed and found beside my side this crystal cup with a liquid sending an aroma into the heavens that enchanted me. I drank from the cup and lo and behold, I became one with the Folger's spirits.

I jumped on my hog and from then to now I proclaim the wonders of crystals. Each night I wire hotly the engines of time and race off wildly, bringing out the lights, so blue and true, and proclaim the magic of forp's crystals.

Well, to tell the truth, I am a true believer in the magic of the subtle and ingenious combination of the crystals and garlic. Of this I must say now to all of you, ride with me the midnite of venturous wonders and let me share with you the world of the forp.

The next one came from Linda_M. She writes:

I came of age in the 60s when so much was happening all at once. So much so that society took little notice to all my accomplishments. Yes, I have a Ph.D., and I have many talents, but of those talents, some are hidden. I am the Midnight Rider. I spread the message of justice to Southern California, and now that I am banned from practically every county in Southern Cal, I may have to move on. You see, I am an expert at hotwiring any hog I happen upon, which allows me to make those necessary switches when the heat is on my tail. I won't give up till I raze them there prisons to the ground! Yes, I sail through the desert wind, no helmet of course, singing "California Dreamin'" (John Phillips made a big mistake hiring Michelle instead of me!) and I forget all my troubles while the wind whips through my hair and stings my face.

So they won't let me in Sacramento anymore . . . big deal! I still have my hog and my dog, and all my brothers and sisters on Crosstalk to stand by me, and bail me out if necessary. Of course, I'm banned from the LA County Jail, so I guess I won't have that problem.

My life is a continuing saga, so a complete profile is impossible! I will never stop moving above and beyond all space and reason.

So let's hear it for all the Midnight riders out there, for in the shadow of God they sleep . . . and in the arms of the Holy Spirit they shall rest.

I watched Diana's reactions as the computer read each of the profiles to her. Diana commented to me as she heard Lynn's profile that it was very precious, just what she would expect from this wonderful sweet lady. Diana moaned and groaned over the forp's profile. I knew he was in for it—I suspect he realized this when he wrote it. She laughed over what Linda said.

Diana worked on my book and finally she was finished with it. She interviewed several people about publishing it but finally she found a person she was comfortable with and the process for getting it ready was begun.

"I am going to get Venture his own account," Diana told the forp, "so he can receive personal mail."

"Well," said the forp, "knowing you, once Venture becomes a star, I'm sure another book will be forthcoming."

"Yes," said Diana, "I think you can expect that just as sure as there is cold weather with snow. I also think I should mention Crosstalk. Venture has a powerful story and I know many people will want to get involved, and the Internet offers a way that won't cost anything for them to take part in. Also, forp, since you have set up the Crosstalk list server, people can take part even if they only have e-mail accounts. People will enjoy actually talking to Dr_butz in person, too."

People often fail to realize that this wacky channel is something I, Venture, the golden one, can take part in. I hear everything that is said, through the speech synthesizer on Diana's computer. This allows me the chance to be a real part of everything. Diana's feelings are transmitted to me and I am very much involved. I have a strong presence on the channel and I bring a lot of class to it.

In fact, I am even a channel operator. You can tell if the people are ops because they have an @ sign in front of their name.

The x bot was just not doing well enough for them, so they got another bot which is called y. This is a real cool bot and it does lots of things, though it is not really complete yet.

When they first put it up, the name 'y' was not available, so Diana disloyally named it 'u'. It runs under my protection too, and takes up a whole lot of room in my home directory, so it should have been called 'v'.

Christmas was approaching. I wrote a special holiday message to the forp:

> *O Forp! There are just things which you do not understand, but I, being a pro, will try to help you to understand. There is a great difference between those of us who serve, and those who are humans such as Diana and Bill and the other channel dwellers. We of course are just as good as they, but our role is very different and we are here to serve their needs and wishes. Forp, I have heard the Midnight Rider tell you over and over and over again not to bring the crystals into the channel as that is not pleasing to her. I think you perhaps should consider obeying. I am sending you something to enjoy inside the channel which I know*

*will not cause offense. I am sending you crystals
and garlic so that you may enjoy what you like in
private, but I would consider carefully bringing
them into the channel. People aren't like us.
Someday I shall be channel manager and at that
time, we can rethink those rules. However right
now, I would suggest that you go with the flow and
do not upset the Midnight Rider. Right now bad
things are being done to me also by the channel
manager and they have created another great
offense against me. Can you believe it, they were
going to call the bot 'y' but that is not possible, so
they have chosen to call it 'u'? Well, you know it
should have been called 'v' after me! How dare
that bot be put above me? There are some changes
that need to happen around there, and you and I
are the ones who will make it happen. Let us make
a pact to work together against those who would
not give us the honor we deserve!*

*May the holidays be very special for you and
may the coming year be filled with joy. Triple
blessings upon your head O forp!*

Love,
Your Brother,
THE RIGHT REVEREND DOCTOR BUTZ
Guide dog Venture

"When Bill saw that letter," explained Diana, "he responded that
if Venture chose to take that attitude, then he Billyum would be licked!"

Actually, like I said, they got the name "y" for the bot and I have
to admit Billyum has been yumston about things for me. The Crosstalk
channel we are on is on the undernet. There are several networks on
the Internet for interactive relay chat. Undernet, where we are, has
registered channels and so does dalnet—Billyum has made me the
channel manager on dalnet. Sometimes the bot y will make special
remarks about me when he senses that I am online. Also, "channel
dweller" is an affectionate way to refer to a guest to the channel or

even a regular. This delightful expression was something one of our administrators came up with.

That evening, I lay supervising Diana. In the evenings she often goes on Crosstalk, although sometimes she can be found there at odd times of the day. She and Wesley, another of the administrators, were taking the poor forp to task. I lay back and dreamed about my being famous. Perhaps they would make special Venture cookies in my honor. Of course, I would need to taste-test them before I could put my golden seal of approval on them.

Oh, by the way: if you would like to write to me, address your email to venture@yumston.com. St_tech has the neat computers I told Alice about. If you need info for that, I will see that you get it. Prof has an excellent course on using the Internet. If you get it through email, it is free. If you would like details about it, I will forward your questions to him. If you need directions on how to get to Crosstalk, you just let me know and we will work this out together. If you would like to be put on the Crosstalk list server, or if anything else is on your mind, just tell me.

Dreams are truly the stuff life is made of, but reality sometimes intrudes, as it did now. They sometimes sing to each other, and now I heard the droning of the little voice as it sang:

> *O where O where is the great channel saint*
> *O where O where is the great channel saint*
> *Away down yonder in the pawpaw patch*
> *You'll find the channel saint!*

All this talk about saints made my thoughts turn to Christmas once again. It had been decided that this year we would create a special Christmas event for my friend, the little Princess.

It took a lot of work, but we arranged for a special room for her party, and many of our special friends gathered around her bed to sing Christmas songs and give gifts.

Many people ask if I have a special relationship with the Princess. The answer is that the relationship between a reverend such as myself and the person is private and privileged. Diana knows about it, because she can be trusted to keep my confidence. Sometimes I choose people to extend special parts of myself to and some accept, like this young woman, while others don't. That is their choice, and I keep that confidential too.

A mob of people turned out for the Princess' celebration and gathered about her bed. Almost everyone we knew seemed to be there: Billyum; the Princess's mother and father; doctors and medical people who were close to Diana; Volt's friends, including the lovely black lady who had affected out lives in such a positive way; and even some of Diana's online friends. If you think people don't care about what goes on in the lives of others, this scene would gladden your heart.

After songs had been sung, stories had been told, and everyone introduced themselves, we waited to see what was next. Volt and Billyum had left the room. Soon we could hear the jingling of bells, and everyone began to sing "Jingle Bells" as Santa Claus arrived, escorted by Volt. He was hauling a very large sack of yumstons. From the way he kept saying "ho ho ho!" I knew that Santa was really Billyum. But, of course, I kept quiet.

Diana, who had moved over next to the Princess, bent over her and stroked her hair. "Little Princess," she said, "there are presents here for you also. Each of us has a gift for you and we will take turns standing where I am now so that the person who is giving you the gift can open it for you since you can't use your hands." The Princess smiled.

Santa bent over the little Princess.

"Little Princess," he said, "Christmas is magic and because it is magic, my elves have worked for you so that you will have presents to give your friends."

The Princess smiled wider.

One by one the gifts were opened and it was obvious that the little Princess was happy. Then it was Diana's turn. She had a very large box from her and me. The room fell silent while the box slowly and ceremoniously was unwrapped. When Diana lifted the lid, everyone gasped and the Princess looked at the gift, her face aglow. She bestowed a smile upon us of pure joy.

Epilogue

Suddenly there was a hiss and screech that made the old man sit up in confusion. Gone were the laughing people. Gone were the happy faces. Gone was the loving influence that pervaded everything including the smiling little Princess. Instead the old man saw Diana putting her BNS in her purse and he watched with dismay as he saw her and Venture join the queue of people who were going to get on the noisy bus. He watched with a sad, despairing feeling as they waited and those ahead of them boarded the bus. It was Diana and Venture's turn to get on the bus. The old man watched them climb the stairs but then just for a second, Venture looked back at him and he and the old man made eye contact. The old man could have sworn that in that minute, Venture winked at him. Then he and Diana disappeared into the bus and it moved on, screeching and groaning as though it didn't want to take them away.

The old man just sat there with a collage of memories flooding his mind. He thought of the little pup so proud and sure of himself and yet unsure of the life he would be called to live as a guide dog.

He remembered the young Venture who was so sure and full of confidence and Diana who treated the young Venture with such love and how the two of them had made their lives together like a beautiful song.

He thought about Billyum and the precious Little Haze who despite her fragile appearance understood truly the principles of life and who had what it takes to tough it out and yet still make life appear to be a beautiful poem.

He thought of the gentle Volt and how the two V-boys had made Diana's life so rich.

He almost got a lump in his throat when he thought about the loss of Little Haze and the way people and the V-boys had tried to keep up Billyum's spirits.

He thought of the health difficulties Diana had experienced and again he felt strong admiration for those wonderful V-boys and the way that Diana had resolved the problems.

He thought about the Princess resting peacefully in the love of friends and family. Just to think about it made him feel a happy glow inside his heart. He realized with a start that he felt himself very much a part of Venture and his family and such wonderful goodness should be shared and who better to share it with than his little grandson. Lillian was willing for him to visit, but of course if he visited, he would have to acknowledge Brad and he suddenly found himself gritting his teeth just at the idea.

Then a very strange thing happened. In his mind, he heard the melodic voice of Little Haze and it said softly:

"Sometimes people really take their little prejudices to heart and these ideas they hold are far worse than any prison bars. If you allow hate to grow in your heart, it will choke out all opportunities for joy and happiness. Hate and joy cannot live together side by side. Usually hate will kill anything and everything around it and if you allow it in your heart, you are to be pitied above all men. If you can only remember one thing in your life let it be this: Never let hate take root in your heart for anything or anyone. If it does, you will have a fatal disease that in the end will kill you. So either wrench it out or prepare to die as a miserable lonely wretch who probably deserves that state. After all, hate is a completely useless emotion and it can only hurt you. Had the person kept this evil out of his life, he probably wouldn't have had a problem in the first place."

"Oh but Little Haze," thought the old man, "you don't understand how different it is about accepting and loving Brad."

His thoughts were answered by silence, which made the old man feel very uneasy. It was as though nothing at all in his mind made his attitudes acceptable.

The old man sighed. "Maybe I should kind of give it a try and at least see if the years and being a papa has made any difference," he said to himself as he got up and went in search of a phone booth to call Lillian.

Wouldn't you know it, Brad answered on the first ring and the old man identified himself tersely and asked to speak with his daughter. He was told to hang on. He then heard Brad call to Lillian and tell her her father was on the phone.

Lillian was very surprised to hear from him but when she learned that he wanted to come for a visit she became very excited and happy and soon plans were being made for his trip.

"Lillian," said the old man, "please tell Brad that my name is Vince and I am a V-boy.

"What is a V-boy?" asked Lillian.

"I will tell you all about it sometime," said Vince.

"Well, we haven't heard from you for years!" said Lillian. "What on earth happened to make you want to be a part of our family?"

"I don't even know where to begin," said Vince. "All I can say right now is that something truly incredible did happen that has changed my whole outlook on life. I have had some very interesting and very novel experiences, but of one thing I am certain. What happened to me was a wonderful gift and after this experience I will never be the same. Great men might have very sophisticated ways of explaining it, but I don't."

"What happened?" asked Lillian, sounding puzzled.

"I will tell you about it maybe someday," said Vince, "but right now all I am prepared to say is that it is very special and very private and it was most certainly not a dream!"

TO ORDER YOUR COPIES OF

VENTURE'S STORY
LIFE & TIMES OF A GUIDE DOG

MAIL a copy of the coupon below with your check or money order to:

BookCrafters
P. O. Box 459
Chelsea, Michigan 48118

FAX the coupon below with credit card information to:

1-313-475-1395

E-MAIL the information below to:

distorders@mibookcraft.com

OR CALL 1-800-879-4214

and order by credit card.

Please send _____ copy(ies) of *Venture's Story, Life & Times of a Guide Dog* by Diana Dawne to the following address:

Name: _____

Address: _____

City_____State:_____Zip:_____

Phone number _____

Method of payment:	Soft cover	$19.95
Check: ❏	Shipping, per book	
Credit card: ❏VISA ❏MasterCard	4th Class	3.00
❏Am.Express ❏Discover	(allow 3-4 weeks)	
Card number: _____	Priority mail	4.00
Signature of card holder:	Sales tax,	
_____	8.25% (CA)	_____
Exp. date: _____/_____	Total Enclosed	_____